THE DEAD
OF SUMMER

Strange Tales of May Eve and Midsummer

THE DEAD OF SUMMER

Strange Tales of May Eve and Midsummer

Edited by

JOHNNY MAINS

Softer than moonlight the gossamer strands
Woven of dew by elfen hands
'MIDSUMMER', W. A. WALKER (1899)

THE BRITISH LIBRARY

This collection first published in 2025 by
The British Library
96 Euston Road
London NW1 2DB
bl.uk

Selection, introduction and notes © 2025 Johnny Mains
Volume copyright © 2025 The British Library Board

For product safety information, please visit
shop.bl.uk/pages/british-library-publishing,
or the Publishing pages on bl.uk.

"The Looking Glass" © 1923 Walter de la Mare, reprinted with permission of The Literary Trustees of Walter de la Mare and the Society of Authors as their Representative.
"The Black Stone" © 1931 Robert E. Howard, reprinted courtesy of Robert E. Howard Properties International LLC.
"May Day Eve" © 1947 The Estate of Nick Joaquin.
"The Sale of Midsummer" © 1970 Joan Aiken, reproduced by permission of A. M. Heath & Co. Ltd., Authors' Agents.
"Night on Roughtor" © 1973 The Estate of Donald R. Rawe.
"Where Phantoms Stir" © 1976 The Estate of Mary Williams.
"Foxgloves" © 1995 Susan Price, reproduced by permission of A. M. Heath & Co. Ltd., Authors' Agents.
"The Midsummer Emissary" © 1996 Minagawa Hiroko, reproduced by permission of Hayakawa Publishing Corporation. Translation © 2012 Ginny Tapley Takemori, reproduced by permission of the translator.
"Heaven and Earth" from *Midsummer Eve* © 2020 Jenn Ashworth, published by Black Shuck Books, reproduced by kind permission of David Higham Associates.

Every effort has been made to trace copyright holders and to obtain their permission for the use of copyright material. The publisher apologises for any errors or omissions and would be pleased to be notified of any corrections to be incorporated in reprints or future editions.

Cataloguing in Publication Data
A catalogue record for this publication is available from the British Library

ISBN 978 0 7123 5528 5
eISBN 978 0 7123 6898 8

Frontispiece illustration: "La Danse du Sabbat", illustration by Émile Bayard in Paul Christian, *Histoire de la Magie* (Paris, 1870).

Cover design by Mauricio Villamayor with illustration by Mag Ruhig.
Original interior ornaments by Mag Ruhig.
Text design and typesetting by Tetragon, London.
Printed in Scotland by Bell & Bain, Ltd.

CONTENTS

Introduction	vii
A Note from the Publisher	xiii

The First of May; or Wallburga's Night
    Caroline Pichler (translated by R. P. Gillies)   1

The Suitable Surroundings
    Ambrose Bierce   43

A Midsummer Night's Marriage
    J. Meade Falkner   55

The Looking-Glass
    Walter de la Mare   83

Midsummer at Stonehenge
    F. Britten Austin   97

The Black Stone
    Robert E. Howard   125

The Withered Heart
    G. G. Pendarves   147

May Day Eve
    Nick Joaquin   175

The Sale of Midsummer
    Joan Aiken   189

Night on Roughtor
    Donald R. Rawe   201

Where Phantoms Stir
    Mary Williams   221

Foxgloves
   Susan Price   237

The Midsummer Emissary
   Minagawa Hiroko (translated by Ginny Tapley Takemori)   255

Heaven on Earth
   Jenn Ashworth   281

Acknowledgements   302

INTRODUCTION
The Weird Is Icumen In

Over the hills the round moon rolls!
She reaches a white and summoning hand
And taps on the silver beech-tree boles,
And strange doors open at her command

"MIDSUMMER", LEAH BODINE DRAKE (1948)

The Christmas ghosts are in deep slumber. We have passed the Apple Wassail in January, and have reflected on Imbolc, the moment between Winter Solstice and Spring Equinox. The days are getting lighter, and we spot the first signs of spring that slowly take us to the Spring Equinox. When Beltane (or May Day) arrives, the sun yawns and stretches, its ascendance marks the halfway point between the Spring Equinox and Summer Solstice. Then in June, when Europe's part of the earth is at its peak worship of the sun, we will celebrate the Summer Solstice ("midsumor" in Old English) on either the 21st or 22nd of June (between 2025 and 2050 it will fall on the 20th nine times and the 21st seventeen times), the longest day of the year. And the magic of Stonehenge, where the sun aligns completely with that Stone Age megalith, will be broadcast and shared across the world. The Christian holiday Lammas is marked on the first day of August, when the first fruits of the harvest are picked. Lammastide falls at the halfway point between the Summer Solstice and Autumn Equinox. In September we will celebrate the harvest and prepare for the Autumn Equinox and beyond, when the nights grow shorter and the things that hide in the shadows come out to play…

Looking at our European neighbours we see the traditions of Walpurgis Night, an abbreviation of Sankt-Walpurgisnacht, celebrated on the night of the 30th of April and into the first day of May. The night is celebrated in honour of Saint Walpurga (*c.*710–777 or 779), who was born in ancient Devon and died in France. She was said to protect those who prayed to her from epidemics, the threat of witchcraft and the magic arts. In northern Europe the 24th of June was the date of the Summer Solstice, also known as Saint John's Eve (one of the very few feast days marking a saint's birth), Midsommar in Sweden (for lovers of the film *Midsommar* (2019), directed by Ari Aster, I see you! But why didn't they take GPS telephones?) and Jaanipäev in Estonia. In Greece the locals hike to the peak of Mt. Olympus (all 9,573 ft of it), a solstice tradition that's held fast for 2,500 years. On this night bonfires were lit to repel witches and evil spirits. In Japan, they celebrate Midsummer Ox Day (どようのうしのひ), when it is customary to eat eel, said to ward off the summer heat. There is also another fascinating summer festival, the Buddhist custom of Obon (お盆) or Bon (盆) (celebrated on the 15th day of the 7th lunar month. In Tokyo it is celebrated as early as 15 July), when people visit their ancestral graves to clean them, and the spirits visit the household altars.

Britain is a graveyard of ancient festivals that were hijacked by the church. The celebrations, if we can call them that, are now based on commercial interests, the old ways have been left to die. Where bonfires were lit almost all-year round to celebrate our pagan ways and reflect our worship of the sun, as *a nation* we now only gather round a bonfire based on the Observance of 5th November Act 1605, which turned into Guy Fawkes Day. In *The Golden Bough*, from 1890, the Scottish anthropologist James George Frazer posits Guy Fawkes Day as "the recrudescence of old customs in modern shapes".

INTRODUCTION

Midsummer, although not one of the Celtic "quarter days", was a time of great importance to us—those that built Stonehenge knew it, early sculptors of the land knew it, and nineteenth-century antiquarians decoding Julius Caesar's writing about druids who sacrificed humans inside giant wicker men* believed that the custom may have come from the associations of bonfires at Midsummer. In the countryside, where most of the ancient customs were born, it is said that on Midsummer Eve the spirits of the living leave their bodies and wander freely. So it was best to stay awake for as long as you could. An old superstition stated that if you kept watch while at a church and fell asleep you would be dead within the year.

In Orkney and Shetland they danced round their bonfires throughout Midsummer night—up there, darkness never truly descends and there is a weird light, one I was simultaneously truly privileged and utterly freaked out to experience while reading ghost stories at the haunted Skaill House in Orkney, next to the neolithic Skara Brae, Midsummer 2024.

Time passes, customs drift like lost ghosts. They surely faltered with Victorian advancement, whose interests lay more with conquering the world and less on traditions and silly superstitions, although it took a while for people to forget the ways of their grandparents. In Doris Jones-Baker's *The Folklore of Hertfordshire* (1977) she records that Midsummer bonfires were once lit across the Chilterns and elderly people living in Bishop Stortford in 1904 could "just remember" when the bonfires were lit annually.

We must still remember that the sun can be cruel during these months; it may not show her face and can be obscured by clouds. And as Sgt Howie says to Lord Summerisle in the moments before his death in *The Wicker Man* (dir. Robin Hardy, 1973), "Your crops failed because your strains failed [...] if the crops fail Summerisle, next year your people will kill you." Howie had a point; the sun gods have no control over the jet stream which brings cold and wet weather down from the arctic. Crops can be damaged;

---

* Book VI of his *Commentary on the Gallic War*.

INTRODUCTION

trees can bear no fruit. And on the flipside of this, with global warming, the sun can *burn*. 2018, 2022 and 2024 saw England's hottest summers, with the fourth hottest back in 1976, the year I was born.

This anthology attempts to bring together those ancient markers and customs and the shadows they cast upon us. The fruits I have picked for this book are bountiful, and I hope that as you feast on them you find them to your taste. I present from as far back as 1823 to 2020, different views of a constant presence in our lives, and perhaps one that we've always taken for granted because it's always there. From Caroline Pichler's "The First of May, or Wallburga's Night" with its rich, meaty language to J. Meade Falkner's "A Midsummer Marriage", which is all at once a supernatural story and a story laden with religious zealotry. F. Britten Austin's "Midsummer at Stonehenge" was a deeply considered choice; as with Neil M. Gunn's "The Moor", a story I used in *Scotland the Strange* (2023), it's not a genre piece, but for me it's about the mood and the place and the time and the language in which it's written. It's fantastic and fantastical. It's a real treat to be able to use a story by Joan Aiken. I've been a fan of hers since I read "Jugged Hare" in the very first volume of *The Pan Book of Horror Stories* (1959). It's also a pleasure to use authors who I feel will be new to my readers, such as Donald R. Rawe, a Cornish writer who really does immerse me with his language. He's a proper storyteller and I love how assured his writing is. It's a shame he only wrote one collection of supernatural stories, but I hope that "Night on Roughtor" begins a retrospective of his complete body of work. I'm over the moon to use another story by the fabulous Mary Williams, who I last featured in *Halloweird* (2024, British Library).

I'm really struck by how this is a themed anthology, yet the stories feel different and reach me in a deeply visceral way. Look, I'm no sun-worshipper. I don't tan, I *burn* and have to cover my skin and wear a hat every time the sun comes out. Maybe it's those stories with sacrifice in them that tickle some ancestral eldritch itch that we all possess!

Nick Groom says in his dedication of his 2013 book, *The Seasons: An Elegy for the Passing of the Year*, that it is published "in the hope that the

INTRODUCTION

English seasons do not become history". I'd like to widen this out a little, and dedicate my book to all who find it, in the hope that our folklore does not become history. I write this introduction not long after the "Sunset Fire" in Los Angeles which claimed lives and countless buildings with their own history along with people's belongings, family histories and memories. Also destroyed was the property and contents of the Theosophical Society, an occult movement co-founded by Madame Helena Blavatsky. It is a devastating blow and a reminder of how fragile the present is—and how easy it is to lose our memories and knowledge of the past.

An anecdote on which to end things. In 1943, The Great Beast, aka Aleister Crowley, diabolist, went to see *Brighton Rock* during its stage run at the Garrick Theatre in the West End. The play starred Richard Attenborough and Dulcie Gray. Gray's performance so moved him that he sent her his privately printed poetry called *The Fun of the Fair*. Mistaking her for a sixteen-year-old girl (she was twenty-eight, he was sixty-eight) he wrote on the back:

> "If you should go to Brighton Rock
> Prepare yourself for a shock
> It isn't she's playing Baddeley
> But in this world things turns madly:-
> A young thing stole the show away
> Her dulcet name is Dulcie Gray.
> —Aleister Crowley, with sincere homage and every good wish."

Thanking him for his letter she received another, proposing that Dulcie "be sacrificed as a virgin" at dawn in a Midsummer rite at Stonehenge. Asking her agent for advice, the outcome was she sent Crowley a letter back saying that she absolutely couldn't, she didn't like getting up early. The Beast never replied. Dulcie wasn't sacrificed and would go on to become one of the country's most gruesome authors (under her own

INTRODUCTION

name and that of the notorious "Alex White", writing for *The Pan Book of Horror Stories*) and acting as the sweetly irascible "Kate Harvey" in *Howard's Way*.*

Now, it's time to take this book outside, find a place where the glare of the sun won't hit your page and blind you, and let the bliss begin. You may notice, as the sun climbs and climbs in the sky, that everything around you may become *heightened*. Shadows will warp and stretch. Strange things will happen. The birds will fall still. Insects will burrow and hide in the soil. Then, terrifyingly, there may be strange subterranean chanting as the doors from another time are opened and ancient sun-worshippers come for their new sacrifice. You, dear reader, are the chosen one, to be ripped from your reality, and gutted like a fish at Stonehenge. Once those doors have closed, all that will be left is this book, dropped next to your bottle of sun-warmed water, waiting for its next willing worshipper.

JOHNNY MAINS, 2025

---

* Dulcie Gray, *Looking Forward, Looking Back* (Hodder & Stoughton, 1991).

A NOTE FROM THE PUBLISHER

The original short stories reprinted in the British Library classic fiction series were written and published in a period ranging across the nineteenth and twentieth centuries. There are many elements of these stories which continue to entertain modern readers; however, in some cases there are also uses of language, instances of stereotyping and some attitudes expressed by narrators or characters which may not be endorsed by the publishing standards of today. We acknowledge therefore that some elements in the stories selected for reprinting may continue to make uncomfortable reading for some of our audience. With this series British Library Publishing aims to offer a new readership a chance to read some of the rare material of the British Library's collections in an affordable format, to enjoy their merits and to look back into the worlds of the past two centuries as portrayed by their writers. It is not possible to separate these stories from the history of their writing and as such the following stories are presented as they were originally published with one edit to the text and minor edits made for consistency of style and sense. We welcome feedback from our readers, which can be sent to the following address:

> British Library Publishing
> The British Library
> 96 Euston Road
> London, NW1 2DB
> United Kingdom

"Grand old woods, ye will live and grow
When we have finished our tale of woe;
Ye will speak on in your eloquence,
When death has silenced our feeble sense."

"SUMMER WOODS", MARIANNE FARNINGHAM (1869)

THE FIRST OF MAY;
OR
WALLBURGA'S NIGHT

Caroline Pichler

Translated by R. P. Gillies

First published as "Die Wallpurgisnacht" in Sämmtliche Werke von Caroline Pichler (1823). First published in English as "The First of May; or Wallburga's Night" by "Anon" in German Stories, edited by R. P. (Robert Pearse) Gillies (William Blackwood, 1826).

Caroline (or Karoline) Pichler (1769–1843) was an author who grew up in a middle-class Viennese civil servant family that was favoured by the imperial court and whose house was one of the most important meeting places in the liberal literary scene. She was introduced to the arts as a small child; the poet Lorenz Leopold Haschka taught her literature and languages and both Mozart and Haydn gave piano and singing lessons, as a result of which she was considered for a while to be one of the best pianists in Vienna. Her first poem was published in 1782 and a prose poem, "Parables", was published in 1800, inspired by the paintings and poetry of Salomon Geßner, John Milton and Friedrich Gottlieb Klopstock. More early works were published anonymously, but her best known work, the epistolary novel *Agathocles* (three parts, 1808), was written as a religious rebuttal of Edward Gibbons' *The History and Decline and Fall of the Roman Empire* (1776–1789). This was followed by *The Siege of Vienna* (1924) and *The Swedes in Prague* (1827), two books which became the most borrowed from the public libraries in the Habsburg Monarchy. Caroline committed suicide in 1843, an act attributed to the loneliness she suffered after her husband's death and escape from the illness she was struck with.

"The First of May; or Wallburga's Night" is reprinted here for the first time since it was originally translated in 1826. Comparing the English text with the German original, I note that there are some changes (the most notable is that "Else" has been changed to "Alice"), but the spirit of the piece shines through. It's incredible to see that this two-hundred-year-old story is still as evocative and as uncanny as the day it was written, and I am immensely proud to be the first to present it to a new audience of readers.

CHAPTER I.

IT happened on a very beautiful evening of the year 163–, that a young lover and his mistress, by name Rudolf and Alice, were seated together on the banks of the Lake Constance in Switzerland. The sun had long since vanished behind the mountains, only the rugged pinnacles of the opposite shore on the south still shone with a roseate splendour. Twilight shades had settled dimly in the valleys, where wreaths of white vapour collected, and were slowly mounting towards the pine-tree forests above. Meanwhile, it was delightful to see how the stars, shining out one by one, and the red light from these lofty cliffs, were mirrored in the water; and, as it happened to be Sunday evening, no rounds of rural labour interrupted the quiet mood of contemplation. Only the light beating of the lake waves on the shore, the voice of a blackbird, or the call of a lone shepherdess from the Alps, broke the solemn stillness.

Rudolf and Alice were faithfully and ardently attached to each other. Many a severe trial had they already undergone;—they were long separated, and had encountered painful scenes of contention among relations,—but those evils were now past; their hearts heaved with mutual affection, and with gratitude to the Giver of all Good, for, on this Sunday, they had been regularly betrothed in the chapel of the Benedictin convent, and their wedding was appointed to take place early in the following month.

Rudolf's father had been a rich scythe-smith, well known by the name of Master Christoph, whose comfortable abode, with its workshop, foundry, and farm-buildings, lay in the neighbouring forest, where the machinery required for his art was driven by the rapid and thundering currents of the Giessbach. Rudolf was an only son, and his father earnestly wished that he should be a clergyman, in which case, he might, in due time, become a person of no little consequence in Switzerland, where, in those days, the presumptuous conduct of the freemen, as they called themselves, rendered the counsel of pious well-educated monks very desirable in promoting general tranquillity. Thus, in imagination, Master Christoph already beheld his son invested with gold chain and cross in the chamber of the Austrian representatives, or even at the Emperor's court; delighting himself so much with these anticipated honours, that, on this account, he willingly renounced the hopes he should otherwise have entertained of seeing his old age cheered by a circle of blooming grandchildren, for whom his property would have supplied ample means of support. Rudolf, however, had unobserved, and in silence, formed plans very different from those of his father. Even from earliest youth his inmost heart had beat with indescribable emotions, when bands of soldiers happened to stop on their march, and obtain refreshment at the farm-house. Then, if they perchance talked of their services under the banners of the great Wallenstein, and of the ferocious depreciations of the Swedish marauders, his eyes gleamed, and his blood circulated with new fervour through every vein. He watched with the greatest anxiety every expression on the lips of the speaker,—and afterwards, in his play hours, the battles, of which he had thus caught the description, were represented with the aid of his young comrades, over whom he had unawares gained a kind of supremacy. Of this disposition, so obviously betrayed, his father was determined not to take any notice. Rudolf was established for his education at the Benedictin convent, though, instead of profiting by the opportunities afforded him there, he only looked on it as a very miserable prison. But time brings changes; and when, after these boyish impressions, he stept into the years of adolescence, his feelings were more fully developed, and it was proved how utterly unsuited he was to the life and duties of a priest. It happened that he was chosen to play a principal part at a very grand procession on Corpus Christi-day. He was the handsomest and among the oldest of the scholars, so that he was chosen to carry the largest banner, and stand at the rustic altar, reared, according to Swiss fashion, on the banks of the lake. After the priest had read the Gospel of the day, there stepped forward from the procession six maidens clothed in white, with garlands in their hair, and baskets of flowers in their hands. They sang a choral hymn to the blessed Virgin, and then strewed their variegated wreaths on the altar. One of these girls, by far the handsomest of the party, happened to steal a glance at Rudolf from her innocent blue eyes, that shone under her coronet of narcissus flowers, when, as if struck by a magician's wand, he became lost to all besides that passed around him, and almost let the banner drop out of his arms. She also seemed equally confused, and after stretching out her hand, drew it back, and remained motionless like a statue, blushing with her eyes fixed on the ground, till, on a signal from one of her companions, she hastily threw her gifts before the altar, and retired to gain her former place in the procession.

From that moment, never did the cherished image of this beautiful stranger fade from Rudolf's remembrance; and in spite of school-tasks and discipline, he contrived, in a few days, to find out her name and place of residence; nay, more, he determined that he would see her and speak with her, though this could happen but seldom, and not without risk of discovery. Her father was very poor, and lived at a remote cottage of the mountains,— where he contrived to maintain his household by his own hard labour, and the produce of a small field. By circuitous and unfrequented paths through the forest, where he was sure that no one would meet him, he contrived to make his way thither, and it was easy to read in Alice's looks, when he first surprised her by coming, at the risk of his neck, down the rocks behind her father's cottage, that she had not forgotten the tall graceful standard-bearer of the Corpus Christi procession.

From that day onwards, the two young people were in the habit of meeting as often as their mutual plans of secrecy would permit, and if the slightest inclination towards a monastic life had ever existed in Rudolf's mind, of course it must now have been completely overcome. Accordingly, he took the first opportunity of declaring to his father that he never would become a priest, though, of course, he was on his guard not to mention the greatest obstacle that stood in his way; but watchful suspicion, aided by chance, had already discovered what the young man imagined to be securely veiled from all the world. His father fell into a violent rage, and threatened him with lasting resentment, even with his malediction, if he dared to cherish a single thought in favour of the contemptible goatherd's daughter, or offered another word against the cherished plans which had been laid for his future life. Not only should he now attend the school as before, but, according to an agreement that Master Christoph had already made with the Abbot, Rudolf should be received as a novice into the monastery; he should live there night and day, and be treated altogether like a younger member of the fraternity.

As it might have been expected by any one who was not, like Master Christoph, led astray by his own imperious temper, the consequence of all this was, that Rudolf disappeared that same evening and was nowhere to be found. The scythe-maker, indeed, tried to comfort himself by insisting that his son could not have travelled to any great distance, and that he would soon return again, when he found himself in want of money; but although inquiries were made at every house in the neighbourhood, not a single trace of the runaway could be obtained. After some time it was proved, however, that, in the neighbouring town, there had been a recruiting party, who had, by large bribes, endeavoured to gain soldiers for the army of the Arch-duke Leopold Wilhelm, as the danger from the inroad of the Swedes into the heart of Austria grew every day more urgent, and their generals, Banner and Torstensohn, were marching through and ravaging Bohemia. At this intelligence, the recollection of Rudolf's love of a military life fell, like an insupportable weight, on his father's heart. Indeed, about three weeks later, all doubts and surmises were at an end, for Master Christoph spoke at the market town with a travelling artisan, who gave a frightful account of the cruelties committed by the Swedes, bringing, at the same time, Rudolf's last greeting to his friends, and entreaties for his father's forgiveness and benediction. This man had already seen the lost youth, mounted on a fine horse, among the Pappenheim Cuirassiers, in the square at Linz, where the general mustered his troops, and dwelt with particular satisfaction on the appearance of his young and promising recruits.

Now, then, Master Christoph's fine schemes and cherished hopes were completely dispersed. Hitherto, the notion that his son had only concealed himself for a time, in order that, by this artifice, he might forward his own views, had kept up the old man's courage and usual severity; but the misfortune which he had long dreaded had fallen upon him, and not only was it fruitless to talk of the advantages to be derived from ecclesiastical dignity, but he could not even calculate on his son's life, who might fall in the very first engagement. Most willingly would he now have resigned every ambitious hope, if he could have once more possessed his son; but in vain did he send letters through the Benedictin Abbot to the general; for the regiment had already marched away to Bohemia, and in such disastrous times, there would be no chance that any man would obtain leave of absence.

Three years had, in this manner, passed away. Travelling artisans and merchants who attended the annual fairs, sometimes brought intelligence and letters from the now distant army. Notwithstanding Rudolf's dislike to the Benedictin convent, he had not altogether failed to profit by the instructions afforded in the school there; and being a ready penman, he sent many written tokens to Alice and his father, both that he continued in good health and spirits, and that his affectionate remembrance of them was unchangeable. Painful, indeed, as the separation had been to Alice, she would rather that her beloved Rudolf should be stationed among the Pappenheim cuirassiers than with the Capuchin monks, for, of his fidelity she never entertained the slightest doubt, but was convinced that, if only his life were preserved, he would return to her as constant as ever. At length news came that the youth had in such manner distinguished himself, as to be promoted to the rank of cavalry sergeant, and Master Christoph began to be comforted with the reflection, that, in those days, soldiers even of the humblest origin might rise at last even to fame and fortune, so that his anger quite subsided. Finally it happened, that, after the contracts of peace were signed and sealed at Osnabrugh, the old man fell dangerously ill; and consequently a letter was written to his son, who could now easily obtain furlough, or, if he wished for it, his final dismission. Rudolf hastened directly to attend the sick-bed of his once more loving and reconciled father, who lived only so long that there was time for mutual explanations, leaving to the young soldier, with his parental blessing, the whole of a property, which in Switzerland was looked upon as very considerable.

Henceforward Rudolf gave up all thoughts of returning to his military companions; for he had already seen enough of the world, and could retire from it with honour. Nor had Alice been deceived in her confident anticipations; for he had no wish but that of leading her directly to the altar, and of sharing with her the fortune which had thus devolved on him. Meanwhile, however, the return of the young soldier, who was at once handsome, rich, and distinguished for his gallant conduct in the wars, excited great attention in the neighbourhood. On the following Sunday, when he stood at the fountain in the market-place, waiting for the opening of the church doors, and dressed in his gay hussar uniform, with his red sash, honorary medal, large boots, and above all, the stately helmet with red feathers waving over his shoulders, the eyes of every woman, whether old or young, were of course turned towards this dazzling visitor. All of them remarked how well his military attire became his elegant form, which, indeed, was such as a statuary might have chosen for a model; while those who had been acquainted with him before, observed how much he had improved within the last few years, though, in despite of his warlike appearance, his fine eyes beamed with as much kindness and affability, as if he had never been absent from among them. There were not wanting also wise people, who calculated how much ready money his father had amassed, and estimated the worth of his farm and iron-foundry; so that, from that moment Rudolf became an object of the most flattering attentions from every family where there were unmarried daughters,—but all this passed over without leaving a single trace on his faithful heart.

Nor would such wise plans and speculations have led to any consequences; but there was one young damsel named Gertrude, daughter of the Baron's land-steward, on whom, unfortunately, his appearance that Sunday morning had left an impression far too deep to be effaced; nor did it seem reasonable to doubt that she, who was beyond comparison the richest and genteelest girl in the village, would succeed in winning the affections of this distinguished youth. Of course her father joined in these anticipations, and no method was neglected that seemed likely to promote such a result. Rudolf was frequently invited to the steward's house; the most brilliant prospects were held out to him for his future life, which, with the help of such a father-in-law, who was a person of no small consequence in the country, might doubtless have been realized. At last a more direct mode of proceeding was adopted; an absolute proposal of marriage was made on the part of the girl's friends; and, not without the most violent displeasure, she found out that the heart which had appeared so cold and insensible, had long since cherished an ardent and unalterable affection for the poor and almost unknown daughter of a cottager on the mountains. Thus enraged, but not utterly discouraged, they made every possible attempt by stratagem, especially by spreading abroad the blackest calumnies, to alienate his affections, so that Alice was tormented beyond measure.

Henceforward Rudolf heard from all quarters the most wicked insinuations against the character and conduct of his intended bride; and her father was intimidated by downright threats and defiance. The youth, however, pursued the even tenor of his way; he was vexed only because Alice had been thus disquieted; and at last having, in spite of the steward's menaces, received her father's consent, he saw himself at the very goal and summit of his wishes.

Now, then, they were met, as we have already said, on the banks of the lake; they sat under a thicket of elder trees newly covered with the rich verdure of spring; and their attention was quite absorbed in one of those delightful dialogues of which the charm is only known to true and affectionate lovers.

Twilight, meanwhile, gave place to the fast gathering night—the glow-worms began to twinkle amid the darkness, and over a high cliff, covered with fir-trees, that rises out of the lake, gleamed the slender solitary crescent of the new moon. The time had passed away unobserved; but now the owls began to shriek, and the night-hawks burst, flapping their wings, from the covert. Alice started often at these noises; even the rustling of a green frog or lizard among the grass made her tremble, and she clung closer and more ardently to her bridegroom for protection. He laughed at her childish fears, and tried to encourage her, but in vain, for she became every moment more timid. A hundred stories that she had heard of supernatural beings who, at certain hours, acquire unconditional supremacy, crowded at once on her mind, and, even under the quieting influence of Rudolf's presence, she was quite unable to conquer her inward agitation. Even the young man's attention was at last raised; for, while Alice was in this paroxysm of terror, he actually heard light steps through the darkness as of some one approaching them. He lifted the almost fainting girl in his arms, and walked forward to meet this intruder. "Who is there," cried he, "who wanders here at such an hour?" The moonlight, though very faint, was yet such that he could well distinguish a female form wrapped in a mantle, that came along the steep path leading from the mountain, and now, instead of answering him, only uttered a strange hollow cry, passed by the lovers, and went on rapidly, taking the road towards the village.

Alice was so frightened that, for a long time, she was unable to speak; for, according to her creed, the mysterious figure could have been no other than that of a witch, who was returning from some of her abominable orgies on the hill-top, where there stands a circle of large stones, and the ground is blighted by the unhallowed feet that dance at midnight, so that the grass cannot grow there. She believed, too, that Rudolf, by his question, must have disturbed the sorceress in her incantations, by which means he had stirred up implacable malice against himself, and must suffer, consequently, for all his life to come. In vain did the youth try to argue her out of these notions, and insisted that, by the moonlight, he had indisputably recognized the rich steward's daughter,—that it was his acquaintance Gertrude who had passed by them. "Nay, nay," said Alice; "what would induce a girl of her habits,—so proud, forsooth, and always so finely dressed,—to be wandering here at such an hour? How could she trust herself all alone in these woods? You forget that the witches—God protect us from them—have power to assume any form they please; and though you had recognized the features of the steward's daughter, this affords no proof whatever that we are in safety."

During this discourse, Rudolf had, without molestation, brought his trembling bride home to her father's cottage; and, for his part, resolved to think no more of that evening's adventures. On Alice, however, it had made an impression far too deep to be forgotten; but to her who was the cause of all this—to Gertrude the steward's daughter,—the consequences were still more fearful and insupportable. Rudolf had, indeed, been perfectly in the right, when he thought that he recognized her; nor was this the first time that, at the rising of the crescent moon, she had come forth in disguise, and chosen the lonely road towards the mountains. In this unhappy girl was indeed realized the poet's image of the wounded hart, that flies restless through the fields and woods, trying in vain to escape from the torment which the hunter's barbed arrow had inflicted. After their first meeting, a long interval had elapsed before she was aware of the difficulties she had to encounter in her plan of gaining his affections; and when the truth was at last discovered, her attachment had already acquired too great an ascendancy to admit of its being successfully resisted. Besides, had this been possible, the will, alas! was wanting, even as much as the power to effect so laudable a purpose. Gertrude was neither pious nor resigned, and, with her father's encouragement, she made every possible attempt to break the bonds of affection between Rudolf and Alice, till, finding that calumny and threats were in vain, she determined to avail herself of other methods. It was very certain that many extraordinary events and changes had happened in their neighbourhood, which could not be referred to natural causes; and it was also well known to her that there were individuals, especially five or six old women, against whom, indeed, no legal proofs had hitherto been brought; yet, every one was firmly convinced that these persons had it in their power to ruin the fortunes of all whom they regarded with dislike. At such a time, it was precisely a character of this description to whom Alice wished to have recourse, nor had she failed to discover one who was ready to become her confidante, and aid her detestable schemes. Accordingly, they had already been at work together, and, but that the lovers were always guarded by the blessed cross and rosary round their necks, and were in heart so pious and innocent, the complete wreck of Alice's worldly hopes might very soon have been accomplished.

CHAPTER II.

Fruitless as all such endeavours for some time proved, Gertrude's unhappy passion remained unconquerable; and at length when it occurred one day at church, that the betrothing of our hero and heroine was proclaimed, and their names read aloud, the full conviction of her misfortune in all its terrors came upon her, so that, after an ineffectual struggle with her emotions, she fainted, and was carried out by her friends. This, of course, excited attention. When the service was over, and the community lingered as usual in the market-place, there were many persons eager to tell what they had heard of Gertrude's disappointed hopes,—the violent conduct of her father,—and the despair by which she would, of course, be overcome, now that Alice's marriage was irrevocably fixed. Female neighbours were, of course, not wanting, who repeated all this at the steward's house; and Gertrude, as if it were not enough to feel that all her fond expectations were for ever baffled and dispersed, had the mortification to find that she was made a subject of raillery, or affected commiseration through the whole village.

Through that fatal Sunday, in all the bitterness of her grief and disappointment, she waited impatiently for the sinking of the sun, and then hastened forth, in this direful emergency, to take counsel from her wicked confidante. Wrapt in her mantle, she had stolen out in the twilight from her father's house; had unobserved reached the witch's cottage, which was situated in a rocky ravine of the mountains, and, with great vehemence, demanded that the long promised aid should instantly be granted her, if all were not to be given up and lost. Grinning with an abominable aspect of confidence and composure, the old woman recommended her to have patience, declaring, at the same time, that she was then employed on certain incantations, which, when completed, would enable her to meet all the wishes of her young friend, as the stars had of late been unusually propitious. The utmost that she required at this moment, in order to succeed, was to be allowed to pluck seven hairs from Gertrude's beautiful tresses. With these words she stretched out her long bony arms like the talons of a fiend, and forced her guest down on a low root of a tree that served in place of a chair. But at the first touch of the old hag Gertrude started up and screamed aloud, so that it was not without violence that the sorceress, laughing scornfully at the poor girl's pain, effected her purpose. Having obtained the seven hairs, she instantly led Gertrude (who was now stunned and speechless) to the door, thrust her out with resistless force, and turning the key in the lock, called aloud, that she might come again when the now crescent moon was at full, but not sooner.

Yet it was not till after a long interval that Gertrude was able to move from the door of this unhallowed abode. Her head felt violently painful, and a nameless horror, such as she had never before experienced, had quite overpowered her. In the cottage, all was now silent; the twilight had already faded away, and in her gloomy desolation she stared at the black Alpine cliffs, that rose like gigantic spectres between her and the dusky heaven. A mysterious murmuring pervaded the wood;—even the breaking of the light lake waves on the shore, seemed to her disturbed imagination fraught with some terrible meaning. At length she hastened down along the path leading through the ravine; but after she had turned the corner of the cliff, and the slant moonbeams fell on her way, every moment she seemed to behold some horrid apparition; the bats shrieked and whirled in circles round her head,—even the rustling of a leaf made her tremble. Then, too, on approaching close to the banks of the lake, through the thicket of elder trees, she actually heard whispering voices, and saw the outlines of a human form. She went on,—she recognized the tall commanding figure,—the well-known accents of Rudolf,—of the youth whom she yet so fervently loved, and had lost perhaps for ever. It was he, the dazzling hero for whose sake alone she wished to live, and Alice was in his arms! At that moment she uttered the hollow cry that was heard by them with so much terror, and then rushed homewards to the village.

Thereafter, with what impatience did the miserable girl count every day and every hour, till the coming of the full moon, that only promised her new anxieties and desperate encounters, while, with the dawn of each revolving day, the betrothed lovers met in their calm happiness and delight, looking forward, no less, with rapture to the evening, as it would bring them one day nearer to their appointed marriage. At last the full moon rose in her glory over the mountains, and Gertrude, having wrapt herself in her mantle so that no one could recognize her, hastened out, taking the loneliest path up the hills, when, on arriving at the cottage, the door was open as if prepared for her reception. In the witch's apartment, there was no light but that of the moon,—now flickering and uncertain, for clouds, driven rapidly by the wind, often came across her splendour. Behind, in the rock against which the cottage leaned for support, there was a small narrow gateway, forming the entrance to that mysterious cavern where the old woman carried on her incantations, while the front room wore the appearance of extreme poverty, and the negligent simplicity of a Swiss *paysanne*. Gertrude now looked at her hostess, and was once more seized with a fit of extreme horror and apprehension; for every feature in that visage, always forbidding, seemed tonight supernaturally distorted, and fraught with unutterable meaning. The hag, perhaps, was aware of that effect which she had produced, for she grinned as if in scorn and mockery, at the same time advancing to the inner doorway, which she opened, and Gertrude, without venturing a word, watched for the result. In the interior of the cave a fire was visible, on which stood a boiling kettle. The sorceress brought a pair of bellows, with poker and tongs to rouse the flames, in which task Gertrude advanced to assist her, but was instantly repulsed. "Fool," cried the old woman, "if thou should'st now dare to cross this threshold, thy life would be the forfeit. Remain where thou art unless I summon thee!"

Gertrude then stood trembling at the entrance;—the kettle boiled more fiercely, and a thick stupefying vapour mounted in wreathes to the ceiling, while the visage of the old woman, shown by the lurid glare of the faggots, became so repulsive and intolerable, that Gertrude was obliged to desist from gazing at her. At length the words "Now—now! Look yonder!" roused her attention, and through the dark wreathes of smoke which had collected in a distant corner of the cave, she beheld a luminous spot that always increased in size and brightness, till it assumed the form of a large mirror. Therein, after some time, she distinguished the well-furnished interior of a room, where a man was sitting at a table, busily employed in cleaning a musket and other military accoutrements. This man was Rudolf,—not his mere picture,—but himself,—as vividly and unquestionably before her, as she had seen him but a few days ago. Two children were also visible; one of whom played on the floor, the other slept in a cradle near the fireplace. At last, the door of the apartment opened; the figure of a woman entered, in whom, at the first glance, Gertrude recognized herself even as if she had seen her own reflection in an ordinary mirror. This figure went directly up to Rudolf, (who saluted her with every sign of confidence and affection,) then took her place by the fire, lifted the younger child from the cradle, and laid it on her bosom, while the father looked round on them with an expression of delighted emotion.

At this scene, Gertrude's heart beat high, and her eyes gleamed. She it was—the wife of Rudolf—and *her* children were *his*. A cry of joy and exultation escaped from her lips; but, at that moment, with a frightful crash, the whole illusion vanished from her sight. The old woman seized her by the arm, and forced her from the gateway, which was violently closed. She then broke forth into a torrent of reproaches, on account of the cry which the poor girl had uttered at a time when she should have been silent as the grave. Gertrude, however, allowed the old hag to scold on, without making any remonstrance, only asking now and then—"will it ever be so—shall I ever be his wife?" "Thou hast already seen it," answered the witch: "for the present, let this suffice, and trouble me with no farther questions." With these words, she forced the girl, as before, out of her cottage, adding, that, as she had behaved that night with such inexcusable folly, she should never come thither again unless she were sent for. This interdiction was, indeed, of little consequence, for had not Gertrude already beheld the veil lifted from futurity, and herself established as the wife of Rudolf! What could she wish for more in this world? She now walked home as if treading in air, and quite absorbed in her own dreams, though in what manner such happiness was ever to be realized, she could not even conjecture, for his marriage with Alice was now near at hand, and no stratagem or hindrance occurred by which she could obtain a farther delay. Yet, notwithstanding all this, she continued to rely on the witch's divinations, sometimes also reflecting with complacency on her own pre-eminent wealth and beauty, and on Rudolf's good sense, which might enable him before the marriage had taken place, to see the rash folly of his choice. All the interval, however, she watched with miserable and wasting anxiety for every word of news that could be gathered from the neighbours, still clinging to the hope, that, sooner or later, some occurrence must take place by which her utter misery might be averted.

Such was her impatience, that, notwithstanding the old woman's injunctions, she had already been twice at the cottage on the mountain, but whether its owner were really absent, or only in bad humour, remained unexplained. The door was always firmly closed against her, nor, when she called aloud, could she obtain any answer. At length only two days remained of the interval that must elapse before Rudolf's marriage; and, moreover, Gertrude had been informed that the witch's hovel had been found with the door open, empty and deserted, so that she had certainly left her habitation without any intention to return. With bitter self-abasement and regret, Gertrude now felt convinced, that, in addition to her other misfortunes, she had been basely deceived; that the hag had only mocked at her vain credulity, and, in her malice, would rejoice at the pangs thus inflicted. It is not then to be wondered at, if, under circumstances such as these, the unhappy girl eagerly embraced an offer made by a female friend, who wished for her as a travelling companion to a town at considerable distance, in which there resided a sister of Gertrude's mother. If thus stationed at her aunt's house, she would at least be freed from the influences of a scene, where every object reminded her of her once cherished hopes, and, above all, she would be spared the torture and humiliation of being present at Alice's wedding festival.

Next morning, then, she found herself with her friend, moving along in their small caleche, and once more, when they had arrived on the opposite shore of the lake, she looked, through tears of bitter envy and regret, on the well-known wooded mountains, where she could distinguish the smoke rising from Rudolf's dwelling—that flourishing little farm, where, after another day, her hated rival would be established in all that happiness which the affection of the handsomest and best husband in the whole canton could bestow—once more she renounced, and cursed in her heart the witch who had so wickedly deceived her with false hopes, and in a state of the deepest melancholy and despondence, she arrived at the dwelling of her aunt.

In due time, she was tormented there by a description of Rudolf's marriage festival,—how dazzling and handsome the bridegroom had appeared in his hussar dress at the church of the Benedictin Convent, and how meekly and modestly the bride had conducted herself in her grand attire of white silk, embroidered with pearls! Then there was an account of the grand banquet which followed the wedding, and, above all, an encomium on the generosity of Rudolf, who had given next day an entertainment to a large number of the poorer class, and bestowed on each individual a present of some article of dress, with a small sum of money. In short, it seemed that, where-ever Gertrude took refuge, she could not escape the poisoned arrows that were aimed against her. Her pride was more than ever wounded; her heart was crushed; and yet, notwithstanding all this, her unhappy passion remained unabated and unconquerable.

Meanwhile, however, circumstances occurred, which tended in some degree to abstract her attention, and afford her the means of pastime. A very wealthy ironsmith, (or *hammermeister*, in the language of the Swiss frontier,) who had given up business, and now lived as a man of independent fortune, often came to the house in which Gertrude was stationed; and though she had now rather lost the first bloom of youth, and assumed a haughty capricious demeanour, yet he did not like her the less for these characteristics. Indeed, as to her temper, which repelled all other suitors, the idea was rather flattering to him, (for he was exceedingly vain,) that he should be able to obtain the favourable ear of one whom others looked on even with a kind of awe, not very consistent with the feelings of true love. Besides, she was the daughter of the Baron's land-steward, and would have a large dowry, which, in his estimation, formed no slight inducement to continue his addresses; and, finally, he made a formal proposal, intreating that her aunt would speak in his behalf. Gertrude took the affair into consideration;—the man was advanced in years;—his person was neither promising nor agreeable;—moreover, his abode was on the Alps, at a remote distance from her native village. These were formidable objections—but then his wealth—the idea that she, too, ought by this time to have secured a husband—and the lurking wish to prove to the world, above all, to the proud youth who had deserted her for a goatherd's daughter, that she could form a more important connection, determined her to accept the offer now made. Only her triumph must be complete, and she therefore proposed it to her suitor as an indispensable condition, that he must give up his farm on the mountains, and come to reside at her birthplace. The wish to be near her parents and other friends served as a pretext for this arrangement, and as to her own views, she scarcely even dared to confess them to herself. In truth, she only wished, by means of her husband's fortune and her own dowry, to humble the man by whom she had been rejected, and to cast her hated rival completely into the shade.

Of course, then, the villagers were all taken by surprise, when, after the lapse of a few weeks, the steward's daughter returned as the wife of the far-famed *hammermeister*, who was well known to be one of the richest freemen in the canton. Immediately she took possession of the handsomest house that could be obtained for a high rent, and provided herself with the most costly furniture and extravagant dresses. Every one talked of this great news, sometimes laughing at the rapid change in her affections, and sometimes admiring her extraordinary good fortune. Only the two individuals aimed at, on whom all this was designed to have made a deep impression, were perfectly indifferent, indeed totally ignorant, as to what was going forward. Rudolf and Alice were too happy within their own domestic sphere to think of their neighbours, and had lately been occupied with plans for a new farming establishment; so that it was not till a whole fortnight had passed by, and people had almost given over the subject, that Alice heard on a Sunday at church of Gertrude's marriage. At this she would have sincerely rejoiced, had she not been informed that the bridegroom was old and ugly; but, on her return home, she communicated the news to her husband, who scarcely made any reply. Afterwards, as they were sitting hand in hand before their house-door, watching the glories of the evening sun as he sank behind the Alps, and the lake reflected his golden radiance, their hearts expanded in rapture and in silent gratitude to Heaven;—Gertrude and her wealthy husband were by them utterly forgotten.

It fared very differently, however, with the wife of the *hammermeister*, for she could never forget Rudolf. According to all outward appearances her circumstances were brilliant and prosperous. Their house, as we have already said, was one of the best in the village;—their domestic economy was richly provided; and from every fair her husband brought her home new furniture, costly jewels, and embroidered gown-stuffs. However, the worm of envy and concealed love still gnawed at her heart. As often as she saw Rudolf by accident at church, or at any holiday festival, she was dreadfully agitated; and at such moments felt always a burning pain in her head, where the old hag had, now nearly a twelvemonth ago, plucked the seven hairs, when she visited at the cottage. In health and temper she became gradually changed, so that her discontent was visible to everyone; and when at last the birth of a fine boy seemed to complete the happiness of Rudolf and his wife, her torments increased so as to be quite insupportable. Just at this time, it was said that the old witch had again been seen at the cottage. Huntsmen and foresters, who were always the first to bring intelligence of any such occurrence, declared that they had found traces of her wonted nightly orgies within the Druid's circle on the hill-top. Gertrude treasured up all these intimations, and there arose in her heart a violent longing to visit the frightful old hag, if it were only to put her to the question, and reproach her for the vile delusions and false prophecies of which she had been guilty. For a while this wish was combated in her mind by better impulses, or by the conviction that she would but incur new disappointments; till at last the wish prevailed over all other considerations. Gertrude went to the abode of the old woman, where the door was no longer closed against her. On the contrary, she was invited to visit there as often as her domestic duties would permit; and her whole situation seemed in a short time to have assumed a new and promising aspect.

CHAPTER III.

Gertrude's endless caprices and uncertain temper, which had often rendered her presence intolerable to her husband, and to everyone else in the household, now quite disappeared. At holiday meetings, too, she seemed always tranquillized by a kind of inward confidence; she entered cheerfully into the amusements of her friends, and looked with an expression of unaffected kindness on Alice, whom she often invited to share her seat in the church. Of course, our heroine was incapable of answering coldly or rudely, if the *hammermeister's* wife afterwards wished to enter into conversation, nor could she dwell on former injuries, if she saw any token of repentance, and a desire to atone for the past. At last, this intercourse was carried so far, that one fine Sunday, Gertrude, who had frequently praised the beautiful situation of Rudolf's farm, accompanied his wife on her walk all the way home. This first visit was short; but it was followed by others that were longer. Alice thought herself obliged to return these visits; but went as seldom as possible,—for, to leave Rudolf and her child, even but for an hour, was to her like giving up all the world. Besides, he had, from the beginning, warned her against making too intimate an acquaintance with one who had betrayed such evil intentions; and this alone would have deterred Alice from making any nearer advances,—for Rudolf's wishes were to her powerful as any law. But then her husband was obliged at last to give up his suspicions; the *hammermeister's* wife seemed so polite and kind, without any effort or exaggeration, from which he could have guessed that she had selfish views. It was said that her worldly circumstances were now even better than at the time of her marriage; and he was so willing to believe that even the most wicked and perverted heart might become changed, and seek to compensate for past errors, that his dislike had been gradually conquered, and he did not offer any objections when he saw the two friends together.

Only one circumstance sometimes disquieted him, and almost roused his former suspicions. This was, the rumour that occasionally came to his ears of Gertrude's having been discovered in a renewed intercourse with the old hag that lived in the cottage above his farm, and every one believed that this woman was a notable sorceress. Yet these rumours were so little confirmed by evidence, Gertrude's conduct was so specious and plausible, that he did not venture to draw any fixed conclusion. Besides, she always contrived to make her visits to Alice when he was not at home, so that he seldom thought of the matter. Of course, too, this caution had the effect of preventing the least approach of jealousy, which might otherwise have completely dissolved the friendship of the two young women.

Towards the return of spring, Rudolf was obliged, on account of the state of his affairs, to make a journey of considerable length, and Alice thought with great pain on the separation that awaited her. On this change Gertrude built her cherished hopes and plans more firmly than ever; but, of course, her outward conduct continued guarded and circumspect. The day came at last, when Rudolf was obliged to depart; and, as his return could not be expected before the month of May, many a long hour of widowed solitude hung over Alice, so that Gertrude made her visits as frequent as possible, in order, as she said, to divert her friend's attention. The labours of the spinning-wheels at night had now ceased; both men and women servants were almost always in the fields; and now it was that Gertrude, in these lonely evenings, began to acquire a complete ascendancy over the unsuspecting Alice, who was best amused by the relation of long wonderful stories, of which the former, as it soon appeared, had a store quite inexhaustible. Above all, they spoke of extraordinary dreams, forebodings, and apparitions, in which Alice, was a firm believer; but when such legends had been discussed, the *hammermeister's* wife went on to speak of other mysteries, which for her auditor, seemed almost to open a new world. She insisted that there were certain mortals who could make themselves invisible, or appear in different places at the same time,—that they were able to pass over a vast extent of country in a single moment,—even to call up the dead from the grave, and force them to reveal all secrets, past, present, and to come.

Pretending great caution, and under promise of secrecy, she made Alice acquainted with some adventures that had happened to her during the preceding year, when she was on a visit to her aunt, who, according to the hints that she gave, significantly enough, was one of the initiated in these occult sciences. At this disclosure, Alice could not help betraying that her curiosity was roused, and though she shuddered almost at every word which her companion now uttered, she still asked one question after another, till at length Gertrude ventured to inform her, that it was very possible to become an eye-witness of all these wonders, without any participation in the guilt (if there were guilt) by which they were attended. "But," said Alice in an anxious tone, "how can this be proved? Could any mortal be a looker on, without incurring all the risk of these mysteries?"—"Why not?" answered Gertrude. "Certainly there are precautions to which a spectator might have recourse, and there are limits which even the supernatural powers thus invoked dare not infringe. Prudence and care are no doubt absolutely required. We must not rashly step over the prescribed circle, nor be led astray, either by our curiosity or terror. Above all, it is indispensable to avoid speaking aloud. Only let such rules be observed, and there cannot be the slightest danger. For example, you see that I am here, as well and cheerful, moreover as sincere a Christian as you are, yet I have more than once been a witness of such incantations, and were I to describe what I have seen, it might, indeed, appear to most people a mere dream of a disordered brain."

Now, it should be understood, that Alice, like most mountaineers, had been from her earliest youth fond of such marvellous stories. Every word that Gertrude uttered was only adding fuel to the flame of her own heated imagination. All those wonders of which she had formerly dreamed, seemed about to be realized, and though she dared not say at once that she would be glad to have ocular proofs, yet many little artifices, by which she always led Gertrude back to the same subject, whenever they were left alone, plainly betrayed how deep was the impression that had thus been made on her mind. At length, her deceitful friend ventured to advance one step farther, giving her to understand, at first, by slight hints and afterwards in direct terms, that she had been occasionally more than an idle spectatrix at these ceremonies; moreover, that she herself was acquainted with many spells and precepts by which natural means might be used for supernatural effects and though, at this intimation, Alice evidently drew back and shuddered, yet, still she became tranquillized, when she reflected that Gertrude's behaviour, for a long time, had been quite irreproachable; her husband's farming establishment was so successful, that it seemed as if a blessing rested on their house, and, whatever had been her design on Rudolf twelve months ago, yet no one could deny that she was a regular attendant at church, and appeared there always as a devout Christian. After this conversation, therefore, she not only kept up her intercourse with Gertrude, but was always more and more deeply drawn into the snare.

Now, the latter end of March and most of April had past away; Rudolf was expected home, within, at farthest, about ten or twelve days; and Alice's heart heaved with delight to think that she would so soon behold her husband and the father of her darling child. Gertrude too was on the alert, full of confident anticipations that her vile plans were at the point of being fulfilled, and reminding herself at the same time, that not a moment was to be lost, and no method left untried to complete her purposes. So it happened, that, on a mild pleasant evening in the end of April, the two friends were sitting together at the door of the farm house, and for some time Rudolf's return, and the preparations that Alice had made to welcome him, formed the only subject of their conversation. Now, however, the colours began to fade on the landscape, and distant objects were lost in confused masses, till at length the stars had, one by one, shone out and were reflected in the Giessbach, which, after thundering like a cataract over the mill-wheels, passed before them in its quieter course to join the waters of the lake. In the dense thickets on the shore, and on the slope of the mountain, it was already dark night, and fire-beetles hovered round them with their silent green light,—Gertrude all the while seeming to watch these winged lamps with great earnestness, so that now and then an exclamation of surprise or anxiety betrayed how much her attention was excited. Alice was much struck when she observed this, and her thoughts involuntarily returned to her old subjects—of supernatural incantations,—till suddenly a clear ball of fire rose from the elder-tree thickets on the hillside, came towards Gertrude, hovered for some time right before her, then moved rapidly away and fell into the mill race, where it was extinguished with a hissing noise in the water. "Aye, indeed," said Gertrude, "I expected no less! I shall not fail to come."

At these words, Alice started up affrighted, and stared at her companion. "What means all this?" said she, crossing herself, and keeping at a distance;—"Foolish girl," said the other, "why should you be alarmed; it means only, that I am invited to the grand festival of the first of May?"—"On Wallpurgis' night," said Alice with increasing fear, "and you would venture to go then?" "I cannot well act otherwise," said Gertrude, "for to neglect such an invitation, if it has been received, would be very seriously resented; to accept it may be attended with much entertainment."—"Good Heaven, *you* Gertrude," answered Alice, "you would go to the Blocksberg mountain, where the devil holds his court,—where all the demons"—"Hush, hush!" said Gertrude shaking her head, "what foolish representations are these? It is easy to perceive that you repeat only what you have heard, and that your information has been derived from people who are absolutely ignorant of this matter. There is nothing so frightful or dangerous as you suppose—of this I can positively assure you." "Were you then already there?" said Alice: "Once," replied Gertrude, "a year ago; my aunt took me with her." "Your aunt," said Alice, "was she *here* then? I must have heard of her coming." "You force me to laugh at you," answered Gertrude, "she certainly was here, but only for a moment; nor did she arrive in her caleche with post-horses as you perhaps expect. She took me away in the night in a very different carriage, that goes fast and sure enough; nor were we seen by any mortal." "You rode on the fire-shovel perhaps," said Alice, "or the hearth-broom." "Alice," said Gertrude, "don't speak so foolishly I beg of you—just like the ignorant common people; yet why should I vex myself, or wish to explain the matter to you? Such things, in short, are what they are, and to you cannot be of any consequence; for that you will not travel with me I am very certain."—"Of that, indeed, you may rest assured," replied Alice, "but, after all, I should like to see how you set out on your journey."—"Nothing can be more easy," rejoined the other; "but it is better to say no more on the subject. You are by nature far too timid, and, to confess the truth, such adventures are safe only for those who are stout-hearted and resolute."

With these words, she paused abruptly, seeming to wish that the conversation should end there. For some time, Alice remained silent; but what she had seen and heard tonight was far too wonderful to be forgotten. She could not refrain from asking more questions, and at last gained so much confidence, that she wished to hear some description of what really happened at the grand meetings on the Blocksberg mountain,—whereupon Gertrude gave such a magnificent account of a fairy banquet, at which all the guests appeared in glittering dresses, and were enlivened by the most ravishing music, that the picture thus drawn could not fail to remain impressed in the most glowing colours on Alice's recollection. Some days had yet to pass away before Wallpurgis' Night, and Gertrude's visits were not so frequent, being interrupted, as she said, by preparations for her journey. But, meanwhile, whatever she said at their short meetings was artfully contrived to heighten her friend's curiosity, especially as she insisted that the grand assembly might be seen by an unconcerned spectator without the slightest danger—especially without any risk of becoming a less devout Christian than before—of which, indeed, Alice always had her friend as a living proof before her.

All this, however, deeply and slyly as it had been planned by Gertrude, failed to obtain the wished-for object; for Alice was far too pious to engage in any such enterprise, and, above all, would never have undertaken such a formidable voyage, without the knowledge and consent of her husband. Only this much she thought that she might safely allow herself—to behold her friend set out in her nondescript vehicle; or, if neither traveller nor carriage were to be seen, it would be a strange thing to hold conversation with one who remained all the while invisible. So it was agreed upon that Gertrude, on her journey, should knock at Alice's window, when her friend would look out for a moment, and convince herself that the account she had received was not a mere fable.

The night of the first of May had at length arrived, and the full moon was in the sky, illumining all the silent country with her enchanting radiance. Alice had retired as usual, but lay sleepless on her lonely bed, while alternate thoughts of her absent husband, and of Gertrude's wonderful stories, conflicted in her mind. Then a small clock which stood in her room struck slowly eleven. Alice felt an ice-cold shuddering, as from some undefined danger, pervade every limb, and just as the clock ceased to strike, she heard a slight knocking at the window. "That must be Gertrude," said she; but now it seemed also as if she heard an audible voice, the tones, perhaps, of some guardian spirit, that said to her, "Hush—hush!—make no answer!" But the knocking was repeated, and the clear moonlight threw into the room the shadow of some one that stood at the window. "She is not invisible, at all events," said Alice, "and it would be rather unkind, after she has taken all this trouble, not to answer her signal." She rose, therefore, put on hastily most of her usual attire, and opened the lattice, at which Gertrude stood magnificently dressed, but in glaring unusual colours. "You see I have kept my promise," said she, with a strange unnatural smile. "I am here, and my carriage too is in waiting."—"Nay, I see no carriage," answered Alice; "you are on foot."—"What nonsense!" said the other; "of course, I have alighted; but if you will come to the threshold of the front door, you will see our equipage standing yonder at the corner of your field." "You promise me, then, that there is no danger?" said Alice.—"What a needless question!" answered Gertrude. "How can it make any difference to you whether you stand at the door or the window?" Again Alice heard the same voice of admonishment—"Do not—do not go!" She went, however; but, determining not to cross the threshold, stretched out her neck at the half-open door, and actually descried some dim object stationed as her friend described; but to which she could not attribute any distinct form. She saw, however, that, instead of horses, there were two enormous monsters, shaped like bats, that waved their black leathern wings, as if with impatience, in the chill night air. Gertrude, meanwhile, had put her arm round Alice's waist, as if to bring her into the proper position to see this detestable equipage, when, all of a sudden, the poor girl felt herself seized, as by the grasp of an irresistible giant or demon. In vain did she shriek aloud, and implore her friend to have compassion; she was forced out of her house towards the field. The carriage advanced to meet them; and in an instant she found herself seated in it by Gertrude's side, when they directly mounted up into the air. Louder and louder she now screamed for mercy; but in vain. Her senses forsook her for a space, and, when she revived, she could only descry the moonlight gleaming on the lakes of her native land, at an immeasurable distance beneath. Now she began to feel for the cross and rosary, which she had unfortunately left on her bed, and would have implored every saint in the calendar for aid; but Gertrude, aware of what was passing in her mind, laid her hand anxiously on her lips, "Remember—remember your lessons," said she; "not a word—not a name must be pronounced here that would bring us into danger. Be silent, for you are in my power; and every attempt of yours to escape will only end in your destruction." Alice obeyed; for she was but too well convinced of the horrible truth which she had now heard. As she looked downwards on the awful realm of space, and beheld from afar, towns, seas, and mountains, as in a map,—or lost them all in one indefinite even surface,—every nerve of her frame vibrated with terror, so that she could not have spoken. With bitter self-reproach and repentance, she thought of her husband's repeated warnings against forming such a connection, which might have saved her from falling into the power of this accursed sorceress. She reflected, too, what dreadful agitation he must encounter,—what despair awaited him if he returned home and did not find her there;—above all, when she remembered her forsaken helpless child, her inmost heart was agonized, so that she had not strength even to moan or weep.

How long they had travelled Alice knew not; but, suddenly, she was aware of a detestable noise in the atmosphere—a whizzing of wings, and screaming of many voices. It seemed at once as if the before empty space were filled with monstrous owls and bats with human faces, besides a thousand nameless forms, all so hideous that she was glad to shut her eyes for protection,—in silence committing her spirit to Heaven and the glorified saints; for, as to sublunary life, she believed that it was lost to her for ever. "Now, then, we are at our journey's end," cried Gertrude; and, at these words, our heroine felt that the violent motion of the carriage decreased, and they sank gradually downwards. Alice opened her eyes, and, by a red glaring light, like that from the hot embers of a furnace, she beheld the summit of a woody mountain, which seemed to be in flames, and yet nothing was consumed; the tall fir trees stood unscathed amid the lurid radiance,—not a leaf nor blade of grass seemed to be injured.— Meanwhile, on a fiery platform, surrounded by a circle of moss-grown stones, were visible a multitude of hideous shapes, whirling vehemently in the dance; others were floating and chasing each other in waltzes through the air, accompanied, instead of music, by a noise of hissing, howling, and whistling, so intolerable, that Alice lost both sight and hearing. Forgetting, too, all the directions that had been forced on her, she exclaimed, in a loud voice, "Jesus—Maria!" At that instant, with a tremendous clap of thunder, the whole spectacle vanished away. She was enveloped in thick darkness, and felt herself again falling, sinking through the air. She thought that death was now inevitable,—recommended herself to the mercy of Heaven,—and lost all self-possession.

CHAPTER IV.

The morning had arisen in all its gentlest beauty and luxuriance, for it was on the 2nd of May, the month of sweet songs, flowers, and blossoms. The sun mounted up over the fir-tree woods, with his beams chasing away the last vapours of the night that had lingered in the meadows, and all nature seemed to rejoice. Then, behold! under the shelter of a green hedge, there lay a hapless female wanderer, our poor deluded Alice, who also was awoke by the mild genial influence of spring, and lifted up her heavy eyes, to look over a wide level country, with houses, towns, and church-spires indeed, but where all was strange, and she could not distinguish a single object that she had ever seen till now. She wondered even at her own existence, could not carry on any connected train of thought, nor could have explained how or from whence she had come hither.

It required a long time before she was sufficiently collected to make remarks on the new country in which she was thus placed; but, at last, she observed that there was a smooth high road running through fertile meadows and fields, and leading to a town of considerable size, with more than one church tower; but this place was far distant, and even among the houses and hamlets, there was not one which seemed nearer than half a German mile. Then she was so exhausted, that she scarcely knew how it would be possible to reach any of those dwellings, and still less what story she could tell to account for her present distress, or to protect herself from being seized, and perhaps imprisoned as a mischievous vagrant. Some resolution, however, must be taken. She rose up with great difficulty, and tottered for a while along a narrow foot-path. Here it chanced that a good-humoured peasant-lad came to meet her, driving a flock of geese across the fields, and Alice summoned up courage to address him, begging to know the name of the nearest hamlet, and of the large town at a distance? His answer, though he spoke in German, was in an accent to her so strange and unusual, that she could hardly understand him. She next inquired to what sovereign the country belonged, and, on his answering, remembered that she had heard it sometimes from her husband at the time of his campaign against the Swedes, and that she had always supposed the distance to this prince's domains to be very great.

The lad meanwhile had passed by with his flock of geese, and Alice was left there quite confounded, and as irresolute as before; but she tried once more to rouse her spirits, and walked on towards the village. It was vain, however, to hope that she could reach it, and once more, in her desolation and feebleness, she threw herself down on the grass, and began to weep bitterly.

Soon after, the sound of approaching steps excited her attention, and, looking up, she saw a man advanced in years, dressed in black, with a dignified calm countenance, who, on coming opposite to her, stood still, as if from a benevolent wish to assist the distressed. She begged him to tell her how far she had yet to go in order to reach the hamlet of which the boy had told her the name,—then ventured to ask how far it was from hence to her native town? But the man could give her no information. "Or, how far, then," said she, "to Linz on the Danube?" "Oh! my child," said he, "that must be two hundred long leagues;" whereupon Alice became deadly pale, and a moan of despair broke from her, inmost heart. The stranger seemed much interested. "Whence com'st thou my dear child?" rejoined he; "and what brought thee into our country, where thou art an absolute stranger?" But what account could the poor girl have given, that would not have seemed a mere groundless fable, and, therefore, have excited suspicions against her? The whole weight of her misfortune seemed as if, for the first time, to fall on her mind. Again she threw herself on the grass, and wept more bitterly than ever. The old man, however, would not leave her, and repeated his questions. "I am schoolmaster of this parish," said he; "I know most of the inhabitants, and if I were but sure who, and what you are, I might, perhaps, be able to obtain you relief." Alice felt the necessity of preparing some story to which he would listen, but was afraid to speak without more reflection. "Have but a little patience," said she, "and I shall tell you all; but just now I cannot speak. I shall soon be better."—"Well, daughter," said he, "I am sorry that I may not stay with you now, for my duties call me hence, but, in half an hour, I shall pass this way again, and if I should overtake you on the road, we shall speak farther."

During this interval, Alice, with that love of truth which was inherent in her nature, felt that it was almost impossible for her to contrive any narrative that would be listened to. Most ardently did she wish to tell all that had really happened to her; but then, the dread that she would incur both hatred and suspicion,—that, in consequence, she would never more behold her husband and child, overcame her scruples, and when the schoolmaster returned, she informed him, that she had been engaged as a servant by an English family at Linz, who intended to make a long but rapid journey through Vienna, Braunschweig, and other towns, then across the north of Germany towards the sea-coast;—that, not being able to bear the fatigue of travelling, she had fallen sick, and they would not wait till she recovered, but had unkindly deserted her. She was now better in health, and wished to make her way homewards, but without money, and distrusted by every one, found this impossible. It was more, perhaps, by means of her innocent looks, and even by the tones of her voice, than by this story, that she won the confidence of the old schoolmaster. "My dear child," said he, "I should indeed be glad if it were in my power to enable you to reach home; but the distance is too great—even if I wished myself to go thither I have not enough of money. But where are the people now, that left you so cruelly?" Alice had luckily remembered, that the prince whose name she had heard from the boy driving the flock of geese, possessed a large town named Braunschweig, and answered, that all she knew of them was, that they intended to go thither; but she could not hope that they would remain there for any length of time, or that it would benefit her to inquire after them. "But," added she, "if it were possible to find any one who would employ me as a servant, I might at least earn enough to support my life. I am but a poor farmer's daughter, well accustomed to labour, and not afraid of any task that could be imposed on me."—"In truth," said the old man, after having looked at her for a while with still greater attention, it seems as if Providence had sent you hither at this time with some especial purpose. I am schoolmaster in the village, as you have heard already. My house is that one with the lime-trees before it, which you can see even from this distance. Now, the day before yesterday, we lost a woman-servant, who had attended us faithfully for seventeen years, and my wife has herself become so frail and old, that such an event made her quite inconsolable. This morning, just in the nick of time, we are provided with another, the best, as I think, that we could have found in the world—so, in God's name, let us make a trial together, and if there should be faults on either side, I trust, after all, we shall not quarrel."

To Alice, these words sounded, indeed, like a direct interposition of Providence, for now she could not say that she was utterly forsaken; she had at least found one individual who received her with friendly kindness and sympathy. So she rose up, and, as fast as her extreme weariness would allow, followed the old man to his house. His wife, indeed, on their arrival, made some objections as to the youth and extraordinary beauty of the girl, but the schoolmaster contrived to evade all those scruples, and, in a very short time, Alice proved, by her conduct, that their benevolence was not thrown away on one unworthy of protection. Never, before, had they known any servant so patient, so industrious, and so faithful. As far as it was possible, she took from the old woman all the cares of the household, read every wish even by the expression of her eyes, and by her punctual obedience and scrupulous good order, became almost like a guardian angel in the house that had so hospitably received her. In a few months, therefore, her situation was completely altered. Instead of being looked on as a servant, she was rather treated like a beloved daughter, and she, on her part, began to respect the good old couple, as if they had been her own father and mother.

Fortunate as her situation proved with these worthy people, she was yet wholly unable to conquer her own deep sorrow, and that longing which she always felt after the objects of her affection that were so far remote. In the silence and solitude of night she wept unobserved; and prayed unceasingly, that God, in his infinite mercy, would compassionate her sufferings, and point out some way by which she might retrace her steps to Switzerland. Evermore the thoughts irresistibly recurred of Rudolf's terror and affliction, of the suspicions that he and all the inhabitants of the canton would entertain on account of her disappearance—of the black designs that Gertrude, perhaps even now, continued to cherish, and the cruel fate that might hang over her forsaken child. Those tormenting reflections were all sharpened by her own self-reproaches, and only the omnipotent arm of Providence upheld the poor trembling exile, enabling her still to place her confidence in that power who chastises where he loves, and who will not suffer the already bruised reed to be crushed.

Thus passed over two long melancholy years, and all the inquiries she had set on foot, or letters that she had dispatched, remained unanswered and in vain. No way seemed left to her of obtaining news from Switzerland, and still less was there any possibility, without money or credit, of returning thither. But at the end of this time, after severe illness, Alice's old mistress died, and was followed soon by the disconsolate widower, who was not able to remain in the world without that faithful companion, to whose presence he had been so long accustomed. Alice had continued to serve them with the utmost attention to their last moments, and had closed their eyes in death, so that she now found they had left her enough, besides her stipulated wages, to enable her to make the long wished-for journey to her native land. Hope, to which she had been so long a stranger, once more dawned in her mind; and the mere possibility of again beholding Rudolf, was an impression so delightful, that she thought of nothing else, and did not lose a day in putting her plans into execution. She obtained proper information as to the route that she must pursue, and, in short, after some laborious weeks travelling, sometimes with the mail-waggon, sometimes on foot in company with good people to whom she had been recommended, she at length beheld the snow clad tops of the Alps once more rise at a far distance on her view; and the thought, "Yonder lives thy husband and child, and thou wilt soon behold them again", was so overpowering, that she burst into tears and almost fainted, so that her travelling associate, an old citizen's wife, had much trouble in again restoring her to any degree of composure.

She had determined to make out the remainder of the way, from this last station to her birthplace, quite alone, and on foot. For, in truth, she knew not what changes might have taken place, or what people would now think of her, and she would gladly, at first, have remained unknown as a stranger. These doubts and fears increased as she drew near her journey's end, so that she could not move along with her wonted rapidity. Now, at last, she had past through a rocky narrow ravine, which alone lay between her and the sight of the wide gleaming lake, and her former beloved habitation. With every step, her agitation increased, till behold!—the beautiful expanse of waters—the well known landscape—the wooded cliffs, and smiling village were unrolled, as if by magic, before her!—As yet, she could not, on account of the sheltering woods, discern her own house, but the smoke of the chimneys was rising over the trees, marking the place where Rudolf and her child now lived, if indeed they yet survived. Once more, quite overpowered, she threw herself weeping on the ground, and prayed long and fervently for support in the trials that perhaps awaited her. Feeling her strength quite exhausted, she determined to make inquiries, and to beg some refreshment at the nearest house that had a promising appearance, and luckily observed one, where there was seated, with her spinning-wheel at the door, a good-humoured old woman, surrounded by a little party of children, who looked kindly at the handsome stranger, remarking, no doubt, both her unusual dress, and the traces of care and anxiety which were so visible on her countenance. A jar of milk and some brown bread were immediately brought out, and Alice was requested to sit down on the stone bench with her hostess, where the varied objects in the beautiful landscape soon afforded a commencement for their conversation. On inquiring who lived at the farm, whence the smoke was rising over the woods, and hearing Rudolf's name, Alice ventured to ask many questions regarding him, pretending that she had known that handsome young Swiss, when he was a cavalry soldier in the Pappenheim cuirassiers. She, herself, was born in the neighbourhood of Prague, and now came in search of some friends of her late husband's who lived at St. Gilgen. The old woman kindly answered all her queries, and especially as to Rudolf said, that he was living in his usual way, with his wife and two children.

"His wife," exclaimed Alice, turning deadly pale. "He has then married again?" "Not that I know of," said the old woman, "unless he had a wife before when he was abroad in the wars. Soldiers indeed are not very scrupulous about such matters." "And to whom then is he now married?" said Alice. "She was a girl of this neighbourhood," answered the woman—"and they have now been man and wife several years." "Two years perhaps?" faltered Alice. "Oh longer than that," replied the other—"their youngest child runs about and speaks by this time." Alice was petrified with astonishment. She knew not what to conclude from such assertions; and her hostess, thinking that perhaps Rudolf had formed some connection with this handsome young girl when he was in foreign states, looked with increasing interest on the poor sufferer.—She, therefore, in her turn, proposed many questions, of which Alice, in her confusion, scarcely observed the proper drift; but when she had in some degree recovered, begged to know whether Rudolf now lived happily with his wife? "On the contrary," answered the old woman, "people talk of them all over the country,—she is said to be so ill-natured and whimsical, that the good young man's life will end in absolute martyrdom." A strange feeling of blending triumph and compassion gave Alice new strength; but through the rest of the conversation, all that she heard only served to perplex her the more, though she had, alas! learned enough to crush every lingering hope that might have remained of future happiness. Before taking leave, it occurred to her that she ought to ask some questions about Gertrude, the wife, as she said, of a very rich *hammermeister*. "How is this?" said the old woman, "you seem to be well acquainted in our country?"—"My husband was often in Switzer land with his relations," answered Alice, "ant from him I used to hear of the inhabitants in your neighbourhood. Tell me then, how is the rich flaunting wife of the wealthy ironsmith?" "Lack-a-day," replied the other, "it must have been a great while since you heard of her, for she has been long since dead."

"Dead?" exclaimed Alice with horror, "how or where did she die?"—"As to this Gertrude of whom you speak," answered her hostess, "she was always a very strange young woman,—and people said, that she was devoted to those terrible arts for which we faithful Christians know not even a name. But you understand me,—one would not speak willingly of such matters, and besides, nothing was ever proved against her, so that it would be very wrong to decide absolutely against one's neighbour. It is enough to tell you, that, for several years, she was in the habit of going into the lake to bathe. It was said that she did this to preserve her beauty, and that the water was before-hand enchanted by the many spells and exorcisms that she pronounced over it. So it happened about two years ago, as people said, that she went out before sunrise, as was her wont, and the servant maid was to wait for her at some distance in the woods. But then we are told that she never appeared again,—the servant became alarmed and ran to look for her mistress, but she was absolutely gone,—her clothes were lying on the shore, but she herself could nowhere be discovered. Whether she was naturally drowned in the lake, or the evil one, God protect us! had overpowered her in the midst of these incantations, it is impossible to prove! The *hammermeister* made every possible search for her body, but in vain? It is not unlikely,—for the lake has deep unexpected places,—that the unhappy woman had fallen into one of these, and been drawn down by a whirlpool. Other conjectures have also their foundation—but, in short, she has never since that day been seen among us."

Alice shuddered in silence. She thought that, in this dreadful fate of Gertrude, she could read the just interposition of avenging Providence; and when she had recovered some appearance of composure, and thanked the old woman for her courtesy, she proceeded on her last painful stage to that home, at which she had hoped to find perfect happiness, but where she must now appear in disguise, and perhaps could remain but a few moments before leaving it for ever. Still, however she must once more behold her husband and her child, though it were for the last time in this world. The way was yet long, her strength was exhausted, and she walked slowly and laboriously. At length, she saw her own beloved dwelling-place; she had turned the corner of the thicket—the rivulet on whose banks she had so often sat with Rudolf saluted her with its accustomed murmur,—the farm-yard, the garden and trees were all as she had left them; and on drawing near to the door, she heard from within the plaintive accents of a child's voice,—perhaps her own child! On entering the court, she observed there a female figure employed on some household-work at the fountain, but she was bending down over her labour, and Alice could not see her features; so she glided onwards to the half open door, looked in, and, good Heaven, there sat Rudolf, her own dear husband,—but, leaning his head thoughtfully on his hand, looking very pale and disconsolate. All reflection and caution forsook her at this sight, and, with a loud exclamation of blended sorrow and delight, she flew into his arms. But Rudolf angrily forced himself from her embrace. "What means all this?" said he; "why these foolish pretences? and why have you drest yourself out so absurdly?" Alice felt as if she had been struck by a thunderbolt. This reception, at once so cold, and yet so natural, as if he perfectly well knew to whom he was addressing himself, confounded her more than aught that she had yet encountered, so that she could do nothing but wring her hands, and look up to him imploringly. Her husband, however, took no other notice of her than by exclaiming "Pshaw! let us have no more of this mummery!"—and turned away in wrath towards the window. "Alas! Rudolf," said she, "have you no better words for me than these, after two long years of such unhappy separation?" "Two years of separation, forsooth!" answered he, "half an hour ago, you went out to the fountain in the court, and now you come back in a strange dress? To say the truth Alice, your conduct all this morning has been by no means in keeping with this fine scene, and, in short—but I shall not vex myself more about the matter. Away with you to your task, for here you have no business at this hour." "Oh, Rudolf, Rudolf!" answered Alice, "what monstrous deception must have been practised against you. It is now two long years and three months since I had the happiness of seeing you! Never since the fatal Wallpurgis' night—" "Darest thou yet speak of that time?" replied he; "aye, from that night, as thou well know'st, thou hast been changed, and I have been a miserable injured husband!" "It was not I—it was not I,"—cried Alice with increasing animation and courage. "No, Rudolf, I have never done ought to vex you, and, moreover, I was far far from hence.—Alas! have you then quite forgotten your once dear Alice?" With these words she stretched out her arms towards him. The tears that now flowed from her eyes,—her tone of voice and whole expression of countenance, moved him to the very heart.—"Good God!" cried he, "it seems at this moment as if old times were indeed revived,—Alice, is it possible!—and do you indeed still love me?"

At that moment the door opened, and behold her second self,—another Alice, in person the same, only different in dress, stepped into the room. "The saints defend us!" cried Rudolf, "Have I then two wives?" But Alice, who had cherished her own suspicions, shrieked aloud,—ran to a large tub of water that stood in the doorway, and, having made the sign of the cross, sprinkled some drops on the mysterious apparition; whereupon the latter, who had seemed mutually terrified, started aside—rushed with a horrid scream out at the door, and in her flight, both Rudolf and Alice thought they recognized the form and features of Gertrude.

She had vanished. The husband and wife looked at each other trembling and astonished. Yet, in Alice's heart, that had been so long wounded and depressed, tranquillity was soon renewed, and Rudolf too began to understand the vile illusions by which his life had been rendered so wretched. With rapture he flew to embrace his beloved wife. "Can it then be true?" said he; "am I so blest as once more to fold in my arms my own good, faithful, and beautiful Alice?"—She was now weeping for joy, so that she could not answer—and Rudolf too was quite overpowered by his conflicting emotions. At length was revealed, to his astonishment and horror, the whole story of Alice's unfortunate intercourse with Gertrude,—her violent abduction at midnight,—the witches' dance on the Blocksberg, and her abode in the schoolmaster's house. Every word that she uttered served more and more to convince him that there never had been in his wife's character even the least shade of change, and that the passionate wayward being who had embittered his life for many years, had only been some malicious and disguised evil spirit. Then, too, he began his narrative; how, two years ago, he had come home after that frightful Wallpurgis' night,—found his wife engaged in her household occupations, and his house in the best order,—so that no suspicion could possibly have arisen in his mind. Soon after, however, the supposed Alice's character seemed completely changed. In place of her wonted mildness and humility, there was evident a haughty impatience, which would not bear with the least contradiction, nor allow to any one in the house the slightest indulgence. From daybreak to nightfall the scolding and quarrelling were incessant. Even her affection for him, though more vehement than ever, had yet assumed a new character, by which he was exceedingly disconcerted; nor would it ever have been in his power to clear up these mysteries, had not the talkative propensities of an old woman-servant led her to disclose that her mistress had gone out secretly on Wallpurgis' night with the wife of the rich *hammermeister*, and that she did not return till next morning, then gliding in at the back-door of the garden, and stealing quietly into her chamber. "From that hour," added the old woman, "her temper has been so much changed that I have never been able, for one day, to satisfy her by my services." Rudolf was horror-struck by the suspicions which now crowded on his mind; and when he sat gazing on those features, that reminded him of happy days, now for ever past, his conflicts were almost insupportable. At length he came to the resolution of calling her to account regarding her excursion on Wallpurgis' night; and the manner in which she answered his inquiries, proved but too plainly that his suspicions had been well founded. After that conversation, all appearance of love and attachment between this most unhappy couple had quite vanished. Alice seemed to live for no other purpose but to torment her husband, and if there were any sign of returning affection, it was expressed only by the most furious jealousy. Her conduct towards the children was equally unaccountable and capricious. The elder, though amiable and engaging, she always hated and persecuted;—the younger, who—

"You have another child, then," cried Alice, when Rudolf came to this part of his narrative. "Yes,—I knew it!" A feeling of strange perplexity came over her, and she looked wildly through the room. "Yonder it lies in the cradle," said her husband, and Alice ran to it; but the cradle was empty, for the child had vanished unnoticed by them at the same moment with its mother. More than ever astonished, they gazed silently on each other, but now the elder boy, holding by his nurse's hand, came into the room. Alice rushed forward, and clasped her own dear child in her arms with rapture, and with gratitude to Heaven for that infinite mercy which had thus restored to her all she held dear in this world.

For the future, Rudolf's worldly fortune became more prosperous than it had ever been. The sufferings of their past years afforded them an inexhaustible subject for conversation and pious reflections. It should be told also, that a few days after Alice returned, some fishermen found the long-sought-for remains of the *hammermeister*'s wife in the lake, and brought them to her husband. Report said, that they were much astonished to perceive, that the body, after an interval of more than two years, seemed as fresh and unchanged, as if the accident of her death had happened only yesterday. The widower, according to use and wont, made a magnificent funeral, and it was said, that he was rather rejoiced to find, by this unquestionable proof, that she was really dead, and could never return to his house again.

THE SUITABLE SURROUNDINGS
Ambrose Bierce

First published in San Francisco Examiner *(14 July 1889)*

Ambrose Gwinnett Bierce (1842–c.1914) has been called both "a consummate artist"[*] (from 1892) and "a literary eunuch, his utterances the windy spasms of an uneasy frog"[†] (from 1895). As I'm having fun finding these quotes, here are two more from the same sources; his stories are either "unique in contemporary literature" or they are the "most complete literary failure of this century".

Bierce was born in Ohio in 1841, was a "printer's devil"[‡] at the age of fifteen and during the Civil War fought for the Union (where he was known as the "Boy Major"). He received a brain injury when he was shot in the head at the Battle of Kennesaw Mountain and was discharged from the army in 1865. After the war he lived in San Francisco and wrote for *The Argonaut*. He moved to London in 1872, gaining a considerable reputation for his journalism and other writing. His first published work was in 1873, a collection of stories and poetry called *The Fiend's Delight* (as by "Dod Grile"). Two other books, both under the "Dod Grile" name, followed: *Nuggets and Dust Panned Out in California* (1873) and *Cobwebs from an Empty Skull* (1874). He was employed by Empress Eugenie of France to edit *The Lantern*, a paper that was used to fight her political battles. Falling out with her, he returned to America in 1885 and thus began a truly extraordinary career where he worked hard to earn the enmity of many, working

---

[*] Ambrose Bierce: "Something About Authors and Publishers", *The Daily Picayune*, 24 April 1892.

[†] William Greer Harrison, "The Degeneracy of Ambrose Bierce", *The San Francisco Call and Post*, 20 October 1895.

[‡] A young apprentice at a printing company.

at the *San Francisco Examiner*, owned by William Randolph Hearst, and taking potshots at political and societal figures with gleeful abandon, the fallout from one of which cost Hearst his hopes of becoming the country's President.

As a critic Bierce could be savage; as Richard O'Connor quotes in his biography *Ambrose Bierce* (Little, Brown & Co., 1967), one example of his cutting wit read "The covers of this book are too far apart." Bierce's greatest fictional work, the collection *Tales of Soldiers and Civilians* was published under his real name in 1891. It contained an embarrassment of riches, with the stories "A Horseman in the Sky", "An Occurrence at Owl Creek Bridge", "Chickamauga", "An Inhabitant of Carcosa" (an influence on Robert W. Chambers; *The King in Yellow*), "The Middle Toe of the Right Foot" and "The Suitable Surroundings", all collected within. It is *The Devil's Dictionary* for which he will be most remembered, a satirical series of dictionary entries that began life in the March 1881 issue of *The Wasp*. He subsequently wrote seventy-nine columns for *The Wasp*, ending with his entry on the word "lickspittle" in August 1886. He wrote a couple of entries under the title "The Cynic's Dictionary" when he worked for Hearst, but then rested the series for sixteen years. It finally appeared in book form in 1906 as *The Cynic's Word Book*, but it wasn't until 1911 that *The Devil's Dictionary*, volume seven of a twelve-volume set of the collected works of Bierce, was published.

Ambrose "Bitter" Bierce, also known as "the wickedest man in San Francisco" and "the Maupassant of the West", disappeared in 1914. He was said to have left the States to join Pancho Villa's army in Mexico. He vanished as completely as the characters of the sketches he once wrote for the Hearst newspapers under the heading "Mysterious Disappearances".

"The Suitable Surroundings" starts on a midsummer's night with an inquisitive boy who thinks he sees a dead man sitting at a table in the centre of a room. What transpires is a puzzle of a story that's not what it seems, and is also a brilliant tale that grapples with the question: how scary can a story really be?

THE NIGHT.

ONE midsummer night a farmer's boy living about ten miles from the city of Cincinnati, was following a bridle path through a dense and dark forest. He had been searching for some missing cows, and at nightfall found himself a long way from home, and in a part of the country with which he was but partly familiar. But he was a stout-hearted lad, and, knowing his general direction from his home, he plunged into the forest without hesitation, guided by the stars. Coming into the bridle path, and observing that it ran in the right direction, he followed it.

The night was clear, but in the woods it was exceedingly dark. It was more by the sense of touch than by that of sight that the lad kept the path. He could not, indeed, very easily go astray; the undergrowth on both sides was so thick as to be almost impenetrable. He had gone into the forest a mile or more when he was surprised to see a feeble gleam of light shining through the foliage skirting the path on his left. The sight of it startled him, and set his heart beating audibly.

"The old Breede house is somewhere about here," he said to himself. "This must be the other end of the path which we reach it by from our side. Ugh! what should a light be doing there? I don't like it."

Nevertheless, he pushed on. A moment later and he had emerged from the forest into a small, open space, mostly upgrown to brambles. There were remnants of a rotting fence. A few yards from the trail, in the middle of the clearing, was the house, from which the light came through an unglazed window. The window had once contained glass, but that and its supporting frame had long ago yielded to missiles flung by hands of venturesome boys, to attest alike their courage and their hostility to the supernatural; for the Breede house bore the evil reputation of being haunted. Possibly it was not, but even the hardiest sceptic could not deny that it was deserted—which, in rural regions, is much the same thing.

Looking at the mysterious dim light shining from the ruined window, the boy remembered with apprehension that his own hand had assisted at the destruction. His penitence was, of course, poignant in proportion to its tardiness and inefficacy. He half expected to be set upon by all the unworldly and bodiless malevolences whom he had outraged by assisting to break alike their windows and their peace. Yet this stubborn lad, shaking in every limb, would not retreat. The blood in his veins was strong and rich with the iron of the frontiersman. He was but two removes from the generation which had subdued the Indian. He started to pass the house.

As he was going by, he looked in at the blank window space, and saw a strange and terrifying sight,—the figure of a man seated in the centre of the room, at a table upon which lay some loose sheets of paper. The elbows rested on the table, the hands supporting the head, which was uncovered. On each side the fingers were pushed into the hair. The face showed pale in the light of a single candle a little to one side. The flame illuminated that side of the face, the other was in deep shadow. The man's eyes were fixed upon the blank window space with a stare in which an older and cooler observer might have discerned something of apprehension, but which seemed to the lad altogether soulless. He believed the man to be dead.

The situation was horrible, but not without its fascination. The boy paused in his flight to note it all. He endeavoured to still the beating of his heart by holding his breath until half suffocated. He was weak, faint, trembling; he could feel the deathly whiteness of his face. Nevertheless, he set his teeth and resolutely advanced to the house. He had no conscious intention,—it was the mere courage of terror. He thrust his white face forward into the illuminated opening. At that instant a strange, harsh cry, a shriek, broke upon the silence of the night,—the note of a screech owl. The man sprang to his feet, overturning the table and extinguishing the candle. The boy took to his heels.

THE DAY BEFORE.

"Good-morning, Colston. I am in luck, it seems. You have often said that my commendation of your literary work was mere civility, and here you find me absorbed—actually merged—in your latest story in the *Messenger*. Nothing less shocking than your touch upon my shoulder would have roused me to consciousness."

"The proof is stronger than you seem to know," replied the man addressed; "so keen is your eagerness to read my story that you are willing to renounce selfish considerations and forego all the pleasure that you could get from it."

"I don't understand you," said the other, folding the newspaper that he held, and putting it in his pocket. "You writers are a queer lot, anyhow. Come, tell me what I have done or omitted in this matter. In what way does the pleasure that I get, or might get, from your work depend on *me?*"

"In many ways. Let me ask you how you would enjoy your dinner if you took it in this street car. Suppose the phonograph so perfected as to be able to give you an entire opera,—singing, orchestration, and all; do you think you would get much pleasure out of it if you turned it on at your office during business hours? Do you really care for a serenade by Schubert when you hear it fiddled by an untimely Italian on a morning ferryboat? Are you always cocked and primed for admiration? Do you keep every mood on tap, ready to any demand? Let me remind you, sir, that the story which you have done me the honour to begin as a means of becoming oblivious to the discomfort of this street car is a ghost story!"

"Well?"

"Well! Has the reader no duties corresponding to his privileges? You have paid five cents for that newspaper. It is yours. You have the right to read it when and where you will. Much of what is in it is neither helped nor harmed by time, and place, and mood; some of it actually requires to be read at once—while it is fizzing. But my story is not of that character. It is not the 'very latest advices' from Ghost Land. You are not expected to keep yourself *au courant* with what is going on in the realm of spooks. The stuff will keep until you have leisure to put yourself into the frame of mind appropriate to the sentiment of the piece—which I respectfully submit that you cannot do in a street car, even if you are the only passenger. The solitude is not of the right sort. An author has rights which the reader is bound to respect."

"For specific example?"

"The right to the reader's undivided attention. To deny him this is immoral. To make him share your attention with the rattle of a street car, the moving panorama of the crowds on the sidewalks, and the buildings beyond—with any of the thousands of distractions which make our customary environment—is to treat him with gross injustice. By God, it is infamous!"

The speaker had risen to his feet, and was steadying himself by one of the straps hanging from the roof of the car. The other man looked up at him in sudden astonishment, wondering how so trivial a grievance could seem to justify so strong language. He saw that his friend's face was uncommonly pale, and that his eyes glowed like living coals.

"You know what I mean," continued the writer, impetuously, crowding his words—"You know what I mean, Marsh. My stuff in this morning's *Messenger* is plainly sub-headed 'A Ghost Story.' That is ample notice to all. Every honourable reader will understand it as prescribing by implication the conditions under which the work is to be read."

The man addressed as Marsh winced a trifle, then asked with a smile: "What conditions? You know that I am only a plain business man, who cannot be supposed to understand such things. How, when, where should I read your ghost story?"

"In solitude—at night—by the light of a candle. There are certain emotions which a writer can easily enough excite—such as compassion or merriment. I can move you to tears or laughter under almost any circumstances. But for my ghost story to be effective you must be made to feel fear—at least a strong sense of the supernatural—and that is a different matter. I have a right to expect that if you read me at all you will give me a chance; that you will make yourself accessible to the emotion which I try to inspire."

The car had now arrived at its terminus and stopped. The trip just completed was its first for the day, and the conversation of the two early passengers had not been interrupted. The streets were yet silent and desolate; the house tops were just touched by the rising sun. As they stepped from the car and walked away together Marsh narrowly eyed his companion, who was reported, like most men of uncommon literary ability, to be addicted to various destructive vices. That is the revenge which dull minds take upon bright ones in resentment of their superiority. Mr. Colston was known as a man of genius. There are honest souls who believe that genius is a mode of excess. It was known that Colston did not drink liquor, but many said that he ate opium. Something in his appearance that morning—a certain wildness of the eyes, an unusual pallor, a thickness and rapidity of speech—were taken by Mr. Marsh to confirm the report. Nevertheless, he had not the self-denial to abandon a subject which he found interesting, however it might excite his friend.

"Do you mean to say," he began, "that if I take the trouble to observe your directions—place myself in the condition which you demand: solitude, night and a tallow candle—you can with your ghastliest work give me an uncomfortable sense of the supernatural, as you call it? Can you accelerate my pulse, make me start at sudden noises, send a nervous chill along my spine, and cause my hair to rise?"

Colston turned suddenly and looked him squarely in the eyes as they walked. "You would not dare—you have not the courage," he said. He emphasized the words with a contemptuous gesture. "You are brave enough to read me in a street car, but—in a deserted house—alone—in the forest—at night! Bah! I have a manuscript in my pocket that would kill you."

Marsh was angry. He knew himself a man of courage, and the words stung him. "If you know such a place," he said, "take me there tonight and leave me your story and a candle. Call for me when I've had time enough to read it, and I'll tell you the entire plot and—kick you out of the place."

That is how it occurred that the farmer's boy, looking in at an unglazed window of the Breede house, saw a man sitting in the light of a candle.

THE DAY AFTER.

Late in the afternoon of the next day three men and a boy approached the Breede house from that point of the compass toward which the boy had fled the preceding night. They were in high spirits apparently; they talked loudly and laughed They made facetious and good-humoured ironical remarks to the boy about his adventure, which evidently they did not believe in. The boy accepted their raillery with seriousness, making no reply. He had a sense of the fitness of things, and knew that one who professes to have seen a dead man rise from his seat and blow out a candle is not a credible witness.

Arrived at the house, and finding the door bolted on the inside, the party of investigators entered without further ceremony than breaking it down. Leading out of the passage into which this door had opened was another on the right and one on the left. These two doors also were fastened, and were broken in. They entered at random the one on the left first. It was vacant. In the room on the right—the one which had the blank front window—was the dead body of a man.

It lay partly on one side, with the forearm beneath it, the cheek on the floor. The eyes were wide open; the stare was not an agreeable thing to encounter. The lower jaw had fallen; a little pool of saliva had collected beneath the mouth. An overthrown table, a partly-burned candle, a chair, and some paper with writing on it, were all else that the room contained. The men looked at the body, touching the face in turn. The boy gravely stood at the head, assuming a look of ownership. It was the proudest moment of his life. One of the men said to him, "You're a good 'un"—a remark which was received by the two others with nods of acquiescence. It was Scepticism apologizing to Truth. Then one of the men took from the floor the sheets of manuscript and stepped to the window, for already the evening shadows were glooming the forest. The song of the whip-poor-will was heard in the distance, and a monstrous beetle sped by the window on roaring wings, and thundered away out of hearing.

THE MANUSCRIPT.

"Before committing the act which, rightly or wrongly, I have resolved on, and appearing before my Maker for judgment, I, James R. Colston, deem it my duty as a journalist to make a statement to the public. My name is, I believe, tolerably well known to the people as a writer of tragic tales, but the somberest imagination never conceived anything so gloomy as my own life and history. Not in incident: my life has been destitute of adventure and action. But my mental career has been lurid with experiences such as kill and damn. I shall not recount them here—some of them are written and ready for publication elsewhere. The object of these lines is to explain to whomsoever may be interested that my death is voluntary—my own act. I shall die at twelve o'clock on the night of the 15th of July—a significant anniversary to me, for it was on that day, and at that hour, that my friend in time and eternity, Charles Breede, performed his vow to me by the same act which his fidelity to our pledge now entails upon me. He took his life in his little house in the Copeton woods. There was the customary verdict of 'temporary insanity.' Had I testified at that inquest—had I told all I knew, they would have called *me* mad!

"I have still a week of life in which to arrange my worldly affairs, and prepare for the great change. It is enough, for I have but few affairs, and it is now four years since death became an imperative obligation.

"I shall bear this writing on my body; the finder will please hand it to the coroner.

"JAMES R. COLSTON.

"P. S.—Willard Marsh, on this the fatal fifteenth day of July, I hand you this manuscript, to be opened and read under the conditions agreed upon, and at the place which I designate. I forego my intention to keep it on my body to explain the manner of my death, which is not important. It will serve to explain the manner of yours. I am to call for you during the night to receive assurance that you have read the manuscript. You know me well enough to expect me. But, my friend, it *will be after twelve o' clock.* May God have mercy on our souls!"

"J. R. C."

Before the man who was reading this manuscript had finished, the candle had been picked up and lighted. When the reader had done, he quietly thrust the paper against the flame, and despite the prostestations of the others held it until it was burnt to ashes. The man who did this, and who placidly endured a severe reprimand from the coroner, was a son-in-law of the late Charles Breede. At the inquest nothing could elicit an intelligible account of what the paper contained.

FROM THE "TIMES."

"Yesterday the Commissioners of Lunacy committed to the asylum Mr. James R. Colston, a writer of some local reputation, connected with the *Messenger*. It will be remembered that on the evening of the 15th inst. Mr. Colston was given into custody by one of his fellow-lodgers in the Baine House, who had observed him acting very suspiciously, baring his throat and whetting a razor—occasionally trying its edge by actually cutting through the skin of his arm, etc. On being handed over to the police, the unfortunate man made a desperate resistance and has ever since been so violent that it has been necessary to keep him in a strait-jacket. Most of our esteemed contemporary's other writers are still at large."

A MIDSUMMER NIGHT'S MARRIAGE
J. Meade Falkner

First published in The National Review *(March–August 1896)*

John Meade Falkner (1858–1932) was an English author, born on 8 May 1858 in Manningford Bruce, Wiltshire. His father, the village curate, was a reclusive scholar. On his fifth birthday, his mother taught him Latin. On his sixth, his father taught him Greek. He went to school at The Thomas Hardye School in Dorchester (founded 1579). The family moved to Weymouth when JMF was ten, with Falkner attending Weymouth Grammar School. On leaving there he went to Marlborough College and there he wrote his first poetry. He went to Hertford College to read Modern History and learned several more languages in addition to his classical ones. JMF became the personal secretary working for Andrew Noble, the head of engineering and armaments firm Armstrong Mitchell & Co. He would soon have to step up and become the head of the household; his mother died in 1871 and his father died in 1887, killing off any family income as it was based on a marriage settlement. JMF put his two brothers through Cambridge University and his sisters through art school. 1894 saw the publication of his first book, the non-fiction *Handbook for Travellers in Oxfordshire*. The next year saw the publication of his first novel, the incredible *The Lost Stradivarius*. He wrote "A Midsummer Night's Marriage" in 1896 and followed that with *Moonfleet* (1898). In 1899, aged forty, he married Evelyn Violet Adye, who was twenty-nine. They had no children, and the pair moved into Divinity House in Durham. In 1903 Arnold published another novel, *The Nebuly Coat*, and his last work of fiction was 1916's *Charalampia*, originally published in *Cornhill Magazine*. He died at home on 22 July 1932 and was cremated, his ashes buried in Burford churchyard. After his death it was revealed he had an estate of £215,524 and had bequeathed £500 to the pope. A rare book collector, JMF's library was sold after his death, raising £8,010 (approximately £706,500 in today's money).

"A Midsummer Night's Marriage" is only one of two short stories by Falkner and one I first read when it was published in *The Lost Stradivarius* (Tartarus Press, 2000). It's one of those incredibly written pieces that you can return to time and time again. It's a strange tale because it is about religion and worship, two things that I run away from, but it's also the story of a young man who, on St. John's Eve in 1816, crosses space and time and finds himself in the same place 236 years earlier. Then it all goes horribly wrong. I'm thrilled to be reprinting this story; twenty-five years is long enough for it to have slipped back into obscurity, so I've gone and put a ring on it (you'll see what I've done there in a bit).

I

MR. Anthony Santal, a gentleman-commoner of Christchurch, Oxford, was a person of some distinction, being young, handsome, and possessed of large landed property at Minsteracres, in Derbyshire. He had been deprived in early youth both of father and mother, but had attained his majority in the year 1816, and entered on the enjoyment of his estate.

It was on the last day of the summer term in that year that Mr. Santal, whilst walking in the High Street at Oxford, noticed in the window of a jeweller's shop a gold signet ring exposed for sale. Its solid and antique construction arrested his attention, and he entered the shop and enquired its history and price. The jeweller stated that the ring had been dug up at some village in the north of Oxfordshire, and had been brought to him by a labourer. It bore an incised coat of arms of which Santal was shown an impression; and the man added that a competent antiquarian had blazoned it heraldically as *Barry nebuly of six argent and sable*, showing that the wavy bands by which the shield was crossed were alternately silver and black. He had not been able to ascertain to what family these arms belonged, but there was cut on the inside of the ring a motto, *Beando Beatior*, which was, he gathered, to be translated *In blessing thou shalt be blessed*. Santal's fancy was attracted by the ring, and as the price asked by the jeweller was by no means excessive, he brought it forthwith, and with a youthful fancy, put it on the third finger of his left hand, which it fitted tolerably well.

He had determined to make the return journey from the University to his home on horseback this summer instead of by stage-coach as was his custom; and as the distance from Oxford to Minsteracres was long enough to occupy several days, he was to take with him a riding servant to carry his mails. He left Oxford on the evening of the 22nd of June, 1816, and passed the first night at Woodstock. Late on the afternoon of the 23rd he found himself on the confines of Warwickshire; and desiring to see Laffontine Abbey, which lay a little off the main road, he struck across the meadows to the ruins, but sent his servant forward to the village of Winterbourne, where an inn called the Bejant Arms had been recommended to him as a good resting-place for the night.

The remains were sufficiently picturesque to induce him to make a pencil sketch of them, for he was more than a tolerable draughtsman. His picture so engrossed his thoughts that he paid little attention to the extreme sultriness of the air, or to the continual mutterings of distant thunder, until a heavy raindrop fell on his paper, and he looked up to see the sky behind him black with ominous thunder-clouds.

The storm broke with unusual fury, and though he found shelter in the ruins both for himself and for his horse, two hours elapsed before he ventured to resume his journey. It was now past ten o'clock and the thunder and rain had ceased, but the rising wind swept masses of cloud across the sky, and the night was growing exceedingly dark. Santal was anxious to lose no time in pushing on to Winterbourne, and took what he thought was a short cut back to the high road, but after a quarter of an hour's riding found himself in miry tillage fields, and perceived that he had lost his path. As he picked his way carefully through the darkness, he met with a belated peasant who at first seemed alarmed and endeavoured to pass on, but on Santal speaking to him, excused himself by saying that it was St. John's Eve when spirits walked, and that he had not known what to think of a horseman met in so lonely and unusual a spot. He told Santal that Winterbourne was still eight miles distant, but led him to a lane which would bring him direct to his destination. Santal gave him money and set out at a brisk trot, but he heard the man shouting after him directions to be very careful in fording a brook which crossed the road a mile from Winterbourne.

After riding for three-quarters of an hour he saw a wide sheet of water gleaming before him, and recognized in it the ford of which the man had spoken. But on coming to the brink he hesitated to cross, for the heavy rain had evidently swollen the stream, so that it had overflowed its banks and was now crossing the road in a raging torrent. The breadth of the water was at least twenty yards; and though white posts had been placed on either side to mark the ford, they were in the middle almost entirely covered.

Glancing round in some doubt, he saw on the right hand, among trees, the lights of a house; and turning his horse towards it determined to enquire there as to the depth of the water, and if he found it impassable to ask shelter for the night. The lights were at no great distance, and the undulating turf, studded at intervals with large trees, convinced him that he was riding through a park; though he had noticed neither paling nor any other enclosure. The sky had grown a little lighter, and he was soon able to make out against it the huddled outline of a large house; but although he was certainly approaching the front of it, he could not distinguish any road or drive. In a moment more he pulled up before a projecting porch with an arched doorway in the centre of the house, and dismounting, knocked on the heavy oak door with the butt of his riding-whip.

His attention was now engrossed by the behaviour of his horse. Ever since entering the park the animal had showed signs of terror and excitement, frequently stopping short, starting aside, and making obstinate endeavours to turn back. The butt of Santal's whip had scarcely sounded on the door when it swung slowly open as if his coming had been awaited; but at the same moment his horse reared with such suddenness as to snap the rein, and, breaking loose, rushed madly away into the darkness. In wheeling round the animal struck its master with its flank, and flung him violently to the ground.

For a moment Santal was stunned, but almost immediately gathering himself up he saw standing before him in the porch a sober-faced man, dressed entirely in black, and having the appearance of a lackey. Santal was about to ask to whom the house belonged, and to beg that a servant might be sent to look for the runaway horse, when the man, without speaking, turned back into the house and beckoned to him to follow.

On this invitation Santal entered, and noticed that the hall was bare except for a few oak settles, and a quantity of pikes, helmets, and armour which hung on the walls. The floor was strewn with sprigs of evergreen shrubs, and there was a smell in the air of resin and spices with which the trodden leaves mingled a peculiar odour. Following his conductor, he passed through the corridor and entered a lofty banqueting hall or dining-room, with a large oriel window opening on to a dais at the far end. Here were oaken tables on which were placed trenchers of various kinds of cakes and fancy bread, cold meats, tankards of liquor, and drinking-cups. The room was entirely empty, though the tables showed that the company had but recently left it; and Santal was surprised to see that the panelled walls were festooned at intervals with bunches of black crape. Again he essayed to question his guide; but the man left the room, saying that he would fetch his mistress.

A few moments elapsed, and then through a side door, which opened on to the dais, there entered a very beautiful girl of 18 or 19 years. She was tall in stature, and her pale face and red eyes showed signs of recent weeping. Her dress was of pure white silk; she wore a lace stomacher, and a mass of flaxen hair was confined in a net of heavy gold thread. She walked straight towards Santal, and said, speaking in a low but very clear and musical voice, "You are welcome, sir, to such hospitality as our poor house can offer. You come at a sorry time, and it is but a sorry greeting that we can give you. I pray you be seated and eat, though these are but funeral meats; for we are tomorrow to lay my poor father's body in the grave, and are even now engaged in devotions for the repose of his soul."

With that she motioned him to be seated, and sinking herself on a bench, hid her face in her hands and wept bitterly. Santal was deeply moved, and his sorrow and sympathy overcoming his astonishment, he tried every means to comfort and console her, but she remained for some minutes immersed in grief. After a time she collected herself sufficiently to lift her head and to enter into conversation with him. She took from him his heavy riding cloak, hanging it over the back of an oaken settle; and then pressed him to eat and drink. "For the hospitality of my father's house," she said, "hath never failed, nor shall it now, though you be the last to whom it shall ever be offered." She took from the table a curiously wrought bottle, and, filling a silver beaker with wine of a deep golden colour, said, "Drink this; it is old Pascaret and came from Laffontine Abbey; it will save you from chills, and from our sorrow palling on you." Santal thought of Laffontine Abbey as he had seen it a mass of ruins that very evening, and it seemed to him that the wine must indeed be strangely old.

Bowing to his hostess, he drank deep; the generous liquor warmed him; he felt a strange strength and gladness move through every limb, and the incidents and fatigues of the evening became scarce remembered things. While he humoured her by partaking of the food she set before him, he learnt so much of her history, without unduly pressing her or appearing to ask questions, as informed him that she was Cecilia Bejant, only child to the late Roger Bejant, who had died two days before.

She filled his silver cup again, and when he drained the second draught he saw how wonderfully beautiful she was. The great room was but faintly lighted; there were only a few candles of wax placed here and there, but one stood on the table opposite her, and the light fell full on her face. Her hair was of the lightest flaxen, her eyes were liquid blue, and her countenance wore an air of unmistakable distinction.

Santal drained a third draught and felt a new fire coursing in his veins, and knew that it was love. She spoke again in her low, clear voice; and now she no longer kept her head bowed but raised it, looking at him as she spoke, and their glance meeting, he gazed into the depth of her eyes, and read there answering love. She told him that to the bitterness of her father's death was added the bitterness of leaving her home, and going as an outcast, she knew not whither. All the estates passed by entail to a distant cousin who would have her marry him, and whom she hated; and then she hid her face again and sobbed as though her heart would break.

They were alone in the shadowy hall, and Santal felt an infinite pity steal over him. He moved nearer and sat by her side. "Lady," he said, and his own voice sounded strange to him and like another's, "do not grieve as one without hope. I, Anthony Santal, will give you a home: I will be your protector, and you shall be my wife." He put his arm about her and drew her to him. She did not resist, but rather moved towards him, and a great tenderness mastered him as he felt her young form pressed against him. She hid her face on his breast, and he bent down and kissed very reverently the flaxen hair, and then raised the tear-stained face to his and kissed her on the lips. So she sat, locked in his arms; it seemed a minute; and yet it seemed a lifetime, for the event of a lifetime had happened to him, and his old life stood far away.

They spoke little, and no one entered to interrupt their sweet fancies; but at length the tinkling of a bell, heard faintly from within, roused their attention. The girl rose, and taking her lover by the hand, led him through several passages to another part of the house. They reached at length a Gothic archway, and passing through, Santal found himself in a chapel. Here was a strong scent of incense, and the air was heavy with the fume. A few candles shining through the haze gave a look of unreality to the objects on which their light fell, and left the greater part of the building wrapped in vague gloom. In the aisle there was placed a coffin, supported on tressels, and covered with a rich pall. There were a number of persons present, all kneeling, motionless, and apparently devoutly following the service which a priest was conducting at the altar, his low monotonous chanting seeming only to intensify the stillness. The girl loosed her hand from Santal's, and, motioning him to one of the benches towards the west, on which only one man was sitting, she passed on up the aisle, and knelt on a fald-stool which had evidently been placed for her near the head of the coffin. Santal copied the attitude of his neighbours, and fell on his knees: indeed, the strange solemnity of the scene was well calculated to inspire feelings of sorrow and reverence to the exclusion of all ordinary thoughts and everyday concerns. The low chanting of the priest was only varied at long intervals by his reciting in a louder voice the versicle *"Subvenite Sancti Dei, occurrite Angeli Dei,"* to which the congregation responded in a deep murmur, *"Suscipientes animam ejus."*

Santal's attention was at first engrossed in the service that was going forward, and in the effort to distinguish the words of the Latin prayers that the priest was reciting. But after a while the monotony wearied him, his thoughts wandered, and he began to observe his surroundings more accurately. He perceived that the forty or fifty persons present were all men, and all habited in black gowns, and that the priest kneeling at the altar wore a black cope with a Calvary embroidered in scarlet on the back. The altar itself was draped with purple, having on it four lighted candles and a silver crucifix in the centre. Beside the coffin also were lighted wax candles, of a taper shape, three on either side, in tall silver candlesticks; and by the candles stood mutes gowned in black, whose heads were bowed in an attitude of grief, and entirely veiled in hoods or cowls. The coffin itself was placed with the feet to the east, and covered with a black pall, bordered with silver, and embroidered with a coat of arms, many times repeated. Except for the candles on the altar and those which stood by the coffin, there was no light in the chapel, but he could see that there was over the altar a large window of the Gothic style, divided by stone mullions; and that the roof was lofty with much ornate timber-work, although the details were lost in obscurity. High up on the walls were suspended helmets, frayed banners, and funeral hatchments with elaborate coats of arms, which the faint light did not permit of his distinguishing.

And still the monotonous chanting went on, and at intervals rose the versicle, *"Subvenite Sancti Dei, occurrite Angeli Domini,"* and the motionless, kneeling mourners responded, *"Suscipientes animam ejus."*

The figure of Santal's betrothed, for so he now regarded her, kneeling with her flaxen hair and white dress against the pall of the coffin, caught the light from the candles and shone out curiously from the surrounding gloom. She reminded him of kneeling statues of alabaster that he had seen on ancient funeral monuments; her head was bent, and she was absorbed in her devotions. Then his eye wandered from the bowed form to the pall, and he saw that the coat of arms embroidered on it was a plain shield, crossed by wavy bars of silver and black alternately. The tall silver candlesticks which stood at the side of the coffin flung a light sufficiently strong to enable him to decipher the motto repeated in Gothic characters under each shield, and he found it to be "Be and o Beatior." This discovery at once arrested his thoughts and brought them back for a moment to the realm of ordinary life, for he remembered that the gold ring that he had bought at Oxford was charged with similar arms and motto. He took it off his finger and examined to make sure. There were the same wavy bars across the shield, and on the inside the same inscription, "Be and o Beatior," which he now recognized as a motto punning on the name of Bejant, in the manner of heraldic equivoque. He had no doubt that the ring had in the past belonged to some member of that family; but he had scarcely time to reflect on the curious coincidence which had led to his being present at the obsequies of a Mr. Bejant so soon after its purchase, when the priest brought his prayers to a close, rose from his knees, and turned round to face the congregation. He took a book from the altar and began to read from it a Latin exhortation. As he read Santal had an opportunity of studying his face, and was much struck by the beauty of his features and by the sanctity of his expression. He was a tall man in the prime of life, with a clean-shaven face, and black hair which showed no signs of a tonsure. His complexion was very pale, and his thin and emaciated countenance gave indication of his having lived a life of abstinence and self-denial.

So much impressed was Santal by the dignity of his appearance that he turned to the man sitting by him on the bench, and asked him in a whisper the priest's name. His neighbour was a little man, past middle age, but wearing a wig of flowing hair. His eyes were bright, and twinkled beneath bushy and overhanging eyebrows. He turned towards Santal, and looked at him with a glance in which surprise was mingled perhaps with suspicion: "I am sorry," he said, speaking in a constrained and deprecatory tone, "I am sorry that I too am a stranger here. You see in me but a poor surgeon-barber who am come over from Banbury to balm Master Bejant, and will return thither as soon as I have made the affidavit that the body is properly buried." There was something in his tone that made Santal say, "You need not fear that I ask from any unworthy motive, being betrothed as I am to this dead gentleman's daughter."

The little man's manner changed, and he said, becoming at once much more kindly and communicative, "I did not know, sir, that you were one of us, or that you had the honour to be betrothed to Mistress Cecilia Bejant. The priest whose name you ask is the saintly Theodore Brady of the Society of Jesus, and Vicar-Apostolic of His Holiness the Pope. He is come here from Mr. Fermor's of Arlaston, where he has been lying in concealment these three months past. You will pardon my former caution, but it is best to be careful in giving to strangers the name of a man who may be hailed to the gallows for what he is doing this night." Santal allowed his surprise at what he had heard to appear on his face, and the little man added, "If you are indeed betrothed to his daughter you will know that Master Bejant was a recusant, and that though he must perforce be buried tomorrow in the parish graveyard, he died in the bosom of our Blessed Mother, the True Church, and fortified with all her holy rites. Were I in your place," he went on, "and affianced to so fair a lady, I would not let the sun go down again before I married her, for we live in troublous times. None can tell what may befall, and there is one standing by her side even now that is like to have her by foul means, if he cannot have her by fair." As he spoke he looked across the aisle, and Santal, following his glance, saw a young man standing close beside Cecilia, and having his eyes continually fixed upon her. He was a coarse and ill-favoured fellow enough, and Santal knew him at once for that cousin of whom Cecilia had already spoken.

A sudden flush of anger came over him, and while they talked the kneeling girl turned her head and looked at him. He thought she half-motioned to him to join her, and with a new resolution he rose and walked up the nave towards her. She moved a little and made room for him at the fald-stool, and he knelt beside her. None of the black-robed mourners took any notice, appearing either not to perceive or to be indifferent to his presence. The priest had fallen again to monotonous prayer, only raising his voice at intervals to recite the versicle, "*Subvenite Sancti Dei, occurrite Angeli Domini,*" and Santal found himself repeating with the rest the antiphon—"*Suscipientes animam ejus.*" Among the murmur of deep voices he could distinguish the thin tones of the little surgeon-barber. He held Cecilia's hand in his and felt it deathly cold, and as their heads bent together over the desk he whispered to her, telling her that he was resolved to ask the priest to marry them that night, and asking her consent. She did not answer, and he urged upon her the expediency of such a step; saying that he dared not leave her even for a day unprotected, and repeating the phrase of the surgeon-barber, that "they were living in troublous times," though he did not know the meaning of it. She said nothing, nor did she look at him, but he felt the grasp of her hand tighten, and knew that he had her consent.

The most solemn part of the service was approaching; an altar ministrant rung a silver bell, and the black-robed worshippers sunk their heads still lower at the elevation of the Host. Strangely moved, Santal bowed his head with the rest, and for a moment in the wave of devotion which swept over the whole congregation all sense of present things was lost.

When he looked up again he saw that daybreak was near at hand, for the great window over the altar was growing light with a pale radiance. The flame of the candles burnt fainter and yellower, and the figure of the priest and the crucifix before which he stood grew darker against the brightening sky. Though the windows were shut, Santal fancied he could feel the cooler breath of morning mingling with the heavy incense-laden air of the chapel, and there was a little sprig of ivy projecting across a side pane, which by its constant tapping against the glass showed that a breeze was moving outside.

The mass was ended, the priest slowly turned and raised his hand in the parting benediction, yet none of the congregation stirred; it seemed as though they were expecting something more to come.

Santal rose from his knees, and taking Cecilia by the hand led her up the aisle to the altar-steps. "Father," he said, addressing the priest, "this noble lady and I desire that you will join us in marriage before these honourable gentlemen and before the world." The priest showed no sign of surprise at the request, but only motioned to them to kneel at the altar-rail. No voice was raised among those present, and no one moved except the ill-favoured cousin, who left his place and drew a little nearer. The pair knelt together, but Santal's thought was so bewildered that he scarcely took notice of the service that the priest had begun to read, until he heard the question—"Wilt thou take Cecilia here present for thy lawful wife according to the rites of our Holy Mother, the Church?" He answered, "I will," and his bride making a like response, the service went on. In a few moments the priest joined their hands, and Santal repeated slowly after him—"I, Anthony, take thee, Cecilia, to be my wedded wife if Holy Church will it permit, to have and to hold from this day forward, for better, for worse, for richer, for poorer, in sickness and in health, till death do us part, and thereto I plight thee my troth."

The priest instructed him in a low voice that he must put into his bride's hand a piece of gold and of silver, and on her finger a ring. He took from his purse a guinea and a shilling, and placed them in the white hand stretched towards him; and for a ring he drew from his third finger the gold ring with the Bejant Arms that he had bought in Oxford, and slipped it on to the thumb of her left hand, saying as he did so—"With this ring I thee wed; this gold and silver I thee give; with my body I thee worship; and with all my worldly goods I thee endow."

Then the priest turned to the congregation and said in a clear voice, "Sirs, ye are all witnesses that this man hath taken this woman to be his lawful wedded wife, and that the bond which hath this day been tied cannot again be loosed in life, but that they are sealed one to another till death shall them part."

It was at this moment that Santal, turning round, saw for the first time the countenances of the other worshippers. They wore a fixed gaze as though not cognizant of the scene that was being enacted, and he was suddenly aware of a ghastly contrast between their white faces and black dresses in the low light of the rising sun. He was conscious, at the same time, that the ill-favoured cousin had moved a little nearer to him. The priest read a few more prayers, and then, holding his hands over them, gave them the benediction, and Santal was about to rise from his knees when he felt a heavy hand laid on his shoulder.

11

It was his servant's hand that was placed on his shoulder and that shook him vigorously. He woke and found the man standing by him with the landlord of the inn at which he had intended to pass the night. They had sat up late for him on the previous evening, and when he did not arrive, had at length come out to look for him. It was not till after sunrise, however, that their search was rewarded, and they had discovered him in the ruined chapel of an old and dismantled house, near Winterbourne, sleeping heavily, with his head on the broken altar-step.

Santal managed to walk back with them to the inn at Winterbourne, but only with considerable difficulty, for his exposure had affected him strangely, and he felt that sickness and extreme prostration which generally accompanies the return of consciousness after the administration of a powerful anaesthetic. For some hours he lay in a semi-stupor, and his state was such that his servant considered it advisable to seek medical advice. The village practitioner, who was shortly in attendance, bled him and prescribed a febrifuge. He enquired of the servant the particulars of his master's attack, and being informed of what had happened, said that the exposure could not account for such a condition, and that Mr. Santal had undoubtedly been drugged. He put some searching questions in an attempt to discover how any drug could have been administered; but his patient ridiculed the idea, saying that his time was fully accounted for up to his being knocked down by the horse in its efforts to break loose; and that his present seizure must be attributed to a violent fall and subsequent exposure in a semi-stunned condition. The doctor, however, would not abandon his position, and remarked drily to the landlord that boys would be boys; hinting that Mr. Santal had fallen among bad company on the way; and professing to be able to diagnose from certain symptoms that the drug had been administered in the medium of wine.

The young man's vigorous constitution soon rallied, and, though he kept his bed the next day, his head was clear and he was able to listen with interest to the account given him by his servant and the landlord of their search for him. The delay in his arrival had not at first aroused their anxiety, as they concluded that he had taken shelter somewhere from the storm; but when twelve o'clock struck, and still nothing was seen of him, they began to think that some misadventure had occurred. It was shortly after midnight that the sound of hoofs called them to the door of the inn, where they came upon a riderless horse with a rein broken, and the saddle turned upside down. The servant at once recognized his master's horse, and a fresh cause for alarm was found in the dripping saddle, and the state of the animal, which showed that it had been in the water. The landlord concluded at once that Mr. Santal had chosen the by-road from Laffontine instead of the highway, and had been carried away in attempting to cross the flooded stream. They proceeded to the ford with lanterns, and the subsidence of the water allowing them to cross soon after daybreak, they found hoof marks on the sodden turf, which showed where the horse had turned off across the meadow on the previous night. Guided by these tracks, they reached the porch of a ruined house, well known in the neighbourhood as Bejant Place, and entering, came first upon a riding cloak flung on a heap of fallen timbers in the dismantled hall; and shortly afterwards found Mr. Santal himself lying prostrate on the altar-steps of a chapel attached to the house. The landlord said that the family of Bejant were formerly lords of Winterbourne Manor, and had built Bejant Place in the reign of Elizabeth; but their waning fortunes had forced them to abandon their residence shortly after the close of the Civil Wars, and it was now little more than a ruined shell. The inn where Santal lay was called after them, the Bejant Arms, and their shield, with the wavy bars of silver and black, could be seen swinging on the signboard from his bedroom window.

Santal was thus enabled to trace the origin of some of the fancies which had filled his dream; but he was left to wonder at the coincidence of his having purchased in Oxford a ring which had undoubtedly belonged to some member of that family in whose house he was destined to pass so strange a night.

The dream had left so vivid an impression that he could not easily shake it off, and more than one circumstance contributed to intensify the idea of reality that it had produced on his imagination. He missed from his finger the ring itself, and remembered with a smile, and yet with sadness, the important part it had played in his vision. He had little doubt that he had in sleep actually removed it from his hand, and that it would be found somewhere in the chapel; and he was scarcely surprised that a guinea and a shilling should also be missing from his purse.

His indisposition caused Santal to modify his plans; and instead of proceeding directly on his journey he retained his rooms at the Bejant Arms, and remained nearly a week at Winterbourne. After he was sufficiently recovered to leave the house he several times visited the ruins of Bejant Place. The stream was now sunk to a mere brook and might have been crossed even without the aid of the stepping-stones which bridged it. From the further bank a broad expanse of undulating greensward, dotted here and there with old elms, led up to the house. This stretch of turf had once formed the pleasure park of Bejant Place; and as The Park it was still known, though the fences had long ago been removed, and it was now used as a common pasture by the villagers. Santal found that the house, when viewed in the less romantic hues of daylight, was indeed, as his landlord had told him, little better than a ruin. It had been entirely dismantled at some comparatively remote period, the staircases throughout and the floors in part had been removed, and the rooms stripped of their panelling and even of their fireplaces. He entered by the projecting stone porch, and found no difficulty in retracing his steps or in identifying the various chambers which he had actually visited; but he wondered as he remembered the fantastic properties and persons with which his imagination had equipped them. The walls from which the panelling and plaster had been stripped, the cracked and broken stuccoes of the ceiling, the gaping holes whence the fireplaces had been removed, and the cobwebbed or shivered casements combined to produce a scene of desolation which reached its culmination in the chapel.

Here the collapse of the roof had left a few scarred and jagged rafters projecting from the walls in perilous and threatening positions, while the tiles and beams had in their fall shattered the flagging of the floor below and littered it with *débris*. A wreck of mullions and tracery still remained in the east window, and Santal saw waving in the wind outside the same sprig of ivy that he had noticed in his dream. There was no trace of seats or any other fittings, but at the east end the rising steps marked the position which the altar had once occupied. He examined the place carefully in the expectation of finding his ring and the money that he had lost, but his search was entirely unsuccessful.

Besides the ruins of Bejant Place, Santal visited with much interest the parish church of Winterbourne, which lay facing the inn at the opposite side of the village green. On the south side of the church was a chantry built by some of the old lords of the manor, and known as the Bejant Aisle. It was separated from the rest of the church by oak screen-work, and in it were many monuments of the family. Among these memorials was a raised altar-tomb of elaborate workmanship, on which lay a full-length alabaster figure of a man clothed in the fantastic plate-armour prevalent at the close of the sixteenth century. Round the edge of the tomb ran an inscription in brass showing that the figure represented one Roger Bejant, who "was interred 24th of June, 1580."

The name, and still more the day of his burial, arrested Santal's attention, but his surprise was increased a hundredfold by the discovery of a plain tablet of brass let into the wall hard by, which recorded the death, in the same year, of "Cecilia, onely child to Roger Bejant, Esq., aged 18," with a rhyming inscription—

> Stay, passenger, and solace with a tear
> Th' unhappy child that here lies buried near,
> Who when shee saw that cruel fate laid low
> The onely succor she on earth did knowe,
> Droop't down and in the tombe with him was laid
> A faultlesse daughter and a spotlesse maid.

The coincidence of these names with those which his dreaming imagination had conjured up, was so startling as to lead him for a moment to doubt his reason, and to consider whether he had not on that night in the old manor-house been permitted to see rehearsed by ghostly actors a scene which had actually occurred more than two centuries before. He dismissed the idea as absurd almost before it was formed, and was constrained eventually to believe that he must in some archaeological work have once read a description of these monuments. The knowledge that the inn at which he hoped to pass the night was called the Bejant Arms, had very possibly revived his dormant recollection of such a description, and led him to attach the names of persons who had once existed to the phantoms of his dream. It was a lame and unsatisfactory explanation, but he could conceive no better, and though he taxed his memory to the utmost to recall the fact of his having ever read anything of the kind, it was without success. Neither could he determine at what precise point his dream had begun, but it seemed probable that he had never properly recovered consciousness after being knocked down by his horse, and had entered the house and wandered from room to room in a half-stunned condition.

A MIDSUMMER NIGHT'S MARRIAGE

III

After completing his university course, Mr. Santal's time was spent in improving his property of Minsteracres, and in efforts to ameliorate the conditions of his tenants. His genuine concern for the welfare of his neighbours and fellow-men in general gained him a wide respect and esteem; nor did he neglect to inform his mind by foreign travel and diligent study. Among such a variety of engrossing occupations it may well be supposed that so trivial a matter as a dream, if not dismissed from his mind, was at least no longer viewed with the exaggerated importance with which a youthful imagination had at first invested it. It was true that he had not entirely dismissed the subject from his thoughts, but when it recurred to him it was merely as a romantic memory, or as a source of curious but unprofitable speculation.

Yet it is possible that his strange experience had influenced his life more than he himself ever recognized, and that the image which his memory still retained of the singular and pathetic beauty of the lady of his dreams had rendered him fastidious and indifferent to ordinary charms. Eight years had passed since his nocturnal adventure, but he was still unmarried. This was the more unfortunate as the whole of his estates were so rigidly entailed that it was not in his power to devise any portion, and should he die without issue, they must pass to a distant connection of another name. His legal advisers and his own sentiment had combined to point out that it would be a matter for deep regret if so fine a property should pass out of the family with whose name it had been long identified. For some time, however, he had paid little attention to so remote an eventuality; and it was not until he was nearing his thirtieth year that his inclination, running in the same direction with his interests, decided him to marry. His affections had become engaged to a Miss Willoughby, the only child of a neighbouring landowner. The first time that he saw her was in winter as she stood leaning against a mantelpiece and looking down at the fire. The yellow light of some candles in sconces on the wall fell on her white dress and flaxen hair; and at the sight of the white-robed figure with bowed head, Santal was suddenly conscious of a strange fascination mixed with foreboding, for she recalled to him that other white-robed and grief-bowed form that he had pictured in his dream. The attraction between them was mutual, and the match was in every respect a suitable one, as the lady was possessed of great personal attractions, and would eventually inherit a considerable property. Yet when Santal first spoke openly to her of his love, the foreboding returned upon him with greater force, and it was only with a correspondingly increased effort that he was able once more to shake it off.

There being no reason for any delay, the marriage was arranged to take place in June, and the preparations for the event went rapidly forward. But as the day drew near, Santal, who had hitherto felt all the ardour that passion could inspire in the most youthful and enthusiastic of lovers, found himself becoming a prey to unaccountable apprehensions. It was not that his affection for his betrothed had in any way cooled, but his mind was filled with gloomy prognostications of impending evil, which assumed vague and Protean forms. Among these fancies the memory of his adventure eight years before at Winterbourne returned again and again to his mind, with a sense of depression which the subject by no means warranted. The image of Cecilia Bejant, as he had seen her in her youth and her sorrow, rose continually before him, and assumed that place in his mind and thoughts to which Miss Willoughby alone had a right. He became at last unable to banish the remembrance of his dream-love even in the presence of his affianced bride, nor could he at times divest himself of the idea, absurd though he felt it to be, that in the part he was now playing he was a traitor to both.

He received the congratulations and merry speeches of his friends with a heavy heart, and when they talked of festivities to be held at Minsteracres in honour of his wedding, he could only respond by false smiles and evasive answers. He felt, in fact, as an unhappy man might feel who, being smitten with some secret but fatal disease, listens to his friends talking gaily of a future which he can never hope to share. So harassed did he become by morbid feelings that he was led to consult his family physician, who, however, made light of the matter, attributing his symptoms to a disorder of the digestion, brought about by undue anxiety as to the important change of life which he contemplated. The doctor gave him a prescription, bidding him hope for an entire recovery as soon as the wedding should have removed all cause for his present solicitude.

So far, however, from the near approach of this event putting a term to his anxiety, the morning of his marriage found him in a condition at once depressed and excited. The bride was accompanied by her father, and there was a large gathering of friends of the contracting parties in the little church of Brant Willoughby. The villagers thronged round as closely as was consistent with their respect for their superiors; and the children, to do honour to the marriage, had strewn the aisle with flowers and sprigs of evergreen shrubs. The peculiar scent of these last as they were trodden underfoot recalled vividly to Santal's memory the great hall at Bejant Place, strewn with evergreen and scented with spices on a very different occasion.

The bride and bridegroom knelt together at the altar-rails, and the minister began the exhortation with which the marriage service opens. During the reading of this long address Santal felt his irrational disquietude increase, and in spite of the solemnity of the occasion, and his firm resolve not to allow such fancies to get the better of him, it was only with difficulty that he could control his nervousness sufficiently to prevent it from being perceived by others. The congregation were attentive and quiet, but he could hear at the back of the church the rustling and disturbance caused by a place being found for some late comer. The concluding portion of the address was at length reached—"*Therefore if any man can show any just cause why they may not lawfully be joined together let him now speak or else hereafter for ever hold his peace*"—and the minister was proceeding to the next sentence when a startling event took place. A man at the back of the church had risen in his place, and was saying, in a calm and clear voice, "I forbid this marriage."

At the first sound Santal had turned. He felt neither the surprise nor anger that such an interruption would ordinarily have occasioned, but it came, on the contrary, almost as a relief to his suspense. This he recognized at once as the evil that he had dreaded for weeks without being previously able to define its nature. It was as if he had been taking part in some stage play, and that the final catastrophe was now approaching in which his *role*, however unpleasant, was not unexpected. The voice of the man speaking woke a responsive chord in his memory, and the clear and deliberate intonation seemed perfectly familiar to him. He looked at the speaker and saw a tall man in the prime of life, dressed in an ecclesiastical habit of black cloth. He was clean-shaven, and his regular but emaciated features wore an air of peculiar sanctity.

A painful silence had fallen upon the congregation, and all eyes were fixed on the intruder. He spoke again—"I forbid you to proceed, for this man is already married." The minister who was performing the ceremony looked in amazement from Santal to the speaker, and from the speaker to Santal. The latter had said nothing, but the bride burst into tears, and her father stamped angrily on the floor. "Let us have a truce to this fooling; the man is mad; let him be led out of the church," said Mr. Willoughby.

Santal was pale and silent, but yet showed no surprise, and the clergyman put an end to the scene by asking the contracting parties and the objector to step aside for a moment to the vestry, so that the matter might be more quietly discussed. When they had entered the vestry, the clergyman asked the stranger what was the reason for his conduct, and what were the allegations he made. "I allege," he said, "that on the 24th day of June, in the year 1816, I married this man in the chapel at Bejant Place, with all the rites of Holy Church, to Cecilia, daughter to the late Roger Bejant, Esq., and that she is still his lawful wife." A shock of surprise and alarm ran through all the listeners except Santal, and Mr. Willoughby broke in—"You are a rogue and a vagabond, and a vile traducer. What proofs do you bring? What is your name?" "I am no rogue nor vagabond," the stranger answered, "but Theodore Brady, a servant of the Society of Jesus, and Vicar-Apostolic of His Holiness the Pope; and now reside with Mr. Fermor of Arlaston, in Warwickshire. I have no proofs to offer, but none are needed. It is for this gentleman," pointing to Santal, "to deny what I say; and if he is content to deny it, then I am content to be esteemed indeed the traducer which you call me." This turned the attention of all to Santal. They expected that he would have given an immediate and indignant denial, but he stood with his head bowed down, and uttered not a word. The bride touched his arm and turned her face appealingly to his. "Anthony," she said, "speak to me; tell me this is false." There was a little pause, and then Santal raised his head and said, speaking in a profound silence, "I cannot deny it, for all that this gentleman has said is true."

Then followed a scene of much excitement, and the party which had so joyously assembled broke up amid mingled tears and indignation. The bride's father, after overwhelming Santal with reproaches, took his daughter by the arm and hurried her away, refusing to allow her to question her lover further or to see him in private, as she had desired. The accused himself seemed as one dazed. Except the one short admission, he had uttered no word at all, and had accepted the abuse which Mr. Willoughby had cast at him without any effort at justification. When the assembly had dispersed, he called for his saddle-horse, which stood by waiting, mounted, and rode away on the road to London. The stranger who had caused the catastrophe disappeared during the general confusion that followed it, and when Mr. Willoughby sent to enquire for him in order to gain a more precise knowledge of Mr. Santal's prior marriage, he was nowhere to be found.

From what afterwards transpired, Mr. Santal himself seemed to have been entirely crushed by so terrible a blow. He abandoned both his habits and his home, nor did he ever again see his seat of Minsteracres. He took away with him only one servant, the same man who had attended him on his journey from Oxford eight years before. It was to Winterbourne that he now repaired, and took up his quarters at the Bejant Arms, where he hired permanent lodgings.

About two months after the scene at the church he received a letter from Mr. Willoughby couched in conciliatory terms, and informing him that the writer was prepared entirely to forget the past, and to accept Mr. Santal as his son-in-law, on receiving from him an assurance that there was no truth in the odious charge which had been brought against him. Mr. Willoughby was convinced, the letter said, that the person who had interrupted the marriage was an impostor. He had caused the fullest enquiries to be made and had referred the matter to the chief authorities of the Roman Catholic Church in England. They agreed that there was in their orders no priest of the name of Theodore Brady, and that so far from the man being the present Vicar-Apostolic, he had impudently assumed the style of a former vicar, who had suffered martyrdom under Queen Elizabeth.

The address which he had given was also proved to be false, for the Fermor family with whom he had represented himself to be living at Arlaston, had moved from that seat many years ago, and the house itself was so completely a thing of the past, that even its site could no longer be identified. Mr. Willoughby had also discovered that the chapel at Bejant Place, where the marriage was alleged to have taken place, was a ruin, and that the Bejants themselves were extinct. This being so, the writer believed the whole story to be false, and was anxious to accept Mr. Santal's assurance to that effect. There would have been, he added, no room at any time for even the slightest suspicion had not colour been lent to the accusation by Mr. Santal's own unfortunate admission, an admission which he was now convinced must be attributed solely to the sudden shock having bewildered him. His daughter had been ailing ever since the rupture, and he earnestly begged that for her sake, as much as his own, Mr. Santal would give the assurance that he sought, and in this case their marriage could at once be celebrated.

The perusal of this letter occasioned Mr. Santal much pain, and his sorrow was immeasurably increased by a note which was enclosed from Miss Willoughby, in which she assured him in the warmest terms of her unaltered love and confidence. He wrote to Mr. Willoughby in reply, thanking him for his courtesy, but regretting that it was not in his power to give the assurance asked for, as the priest's statements were in substance true. He expressed the greatest remorse that he should be the cause of so much suffering to Mr. Willoughby's family, but begged them to believe that the facts, if fully understood, would show him to be perhaps less guilty than now appeared. He could not explain further, but Mr. Willoughby would understand that he was quite ready to afford the only satisfaction which a gentleman could offer, either to Mr. Willoughby himself or to any other person nominated by him. So the matter unhappily ended, and neither side ever held any further communication with the other.

Two years elapsed, and Mr. Santal was still at the Bejant Arms, but sadly changed. His once robust health had completely given way, and his state was such as to cause the greatest anxiety to those few friends who saw him from time to time. He felt most keenly the terrible stain which rested upon his honour, and the breaking off of his marriage seemed to have entirely crushed his spirits. He grew thin and weak, and would sit the greater part of the day in a listless attitude with his hands before him. If he went out, it was generally only to visit the ruins of Bejant Place, where, if report spoke truly, he not unfrequently passed the entire night; indeed, his chief solace consisted in haunting that spot. The image of Cecilia Bejant was ever present with him, and grew at length so beloved that he looked forward with longing to his end, believing that in death he would be permitted to rejoin his lost bride. His eccentric habits gained him among the lower classes the reputation of being a harmless madman, while those of his own rank avoided all contact with him as one about whom hung some dishonourable mystery.

In June of the third year of his residence at Winterbourne, he fell ill. A severe cold, contracted, it was said, by a night spent in the ruined chapel of Bejant Place, took such effect upon a frame already reduced to great weakness that the doctor who was called in at once pronounced his case to be serious, if not hopeless. It was the same general practitioner who had visited Santal eight years before at Winterbourne. He was quite familiar with the story of the interrupted wedding, and had seen in it confirmation of his previous theories as to Santal's adventure at Bejant Place. He had talked the matter over continually with his village cronies, and always averred that

Santal had been drugged on that night and decoyed into illicit company. The man who had interrupted the wedding with Miss Willoughby and afterwards disappeared, might have been, he thought, a hedge-priest who had actually assisted at some mock marriage of Santal on that very night. He found in his patient's own mental attitude the greatest obstacle to his recovery, for Santal seemed to have entirely abandoned his hold on life. The issue justified the worst apprehensions, and on the 20th of June, near the date on which he had first visited Winterbourne, Mr. Santal breathed his last.

Shortly before his death he had been received into the communion of the Church of Rome, a proceeding which was considered by those who were aware of it as a further proof of his eccentricity. He left strict instructions with his servant that he should be buried on the south side of the church, and as near the Bejant Aisle as might be: but the clergyman of the parish objected to this being done as Mr. Santal had died a Roman Catholic. On finding, however, that Santal had left a substantial benefaction to the parish, he eventually consented to the burial being made in that position; but only on the understanding that the body should not be taken into the church, and that the Protestant form of service should be read at the graveside. To this the servant readily agreed, having, indeed, no reason to make any opposition.

This man was sincerely attached to his master, and would not leave the dead body. But he had come to regard with superstitious fear the strange habits and especially the nocturnal visits to Bejant Place which Santal had affected towards the close of his life. On the night before the burial he did not remain with the corpse, saying it was St. John's eve, and the night on which those spirits walked who had undone his master. He lit candles round the body and persuaded the landlord to sit up with him below stairs, and they kept watch together through the night as they had done on that same date ten years before. Both dozed off, however, towards morning, but woke together imagining that they heard a monotonous murmur as of low chanting proceeding from the room above. It must, however, have been a dream, for on going upstairs they found the candles still burning and the body undisturbed.

When the time of the funeral arrived there were gathered at the graveside a group of sympathizing villagers who wished to pay a last token of respect to Mr. Santal's memory; for though they deemed him mad, they had always found him willing to listen to their complaints and anxious to use his wealth in helping them in time of need. The coffin had been carried from the inn to the graveside, and there rested on trestles; and the little crowd about it waited patiently for the appearance of the minister. After a time a report spread that the minister was ill; and this was shortly confirmed by the arrival of a female servant from the rectory, who said that her master had been seized with faintness, and would not be able to perform the service. Those in charge of the funeral were at a loss what to do, when a stranger who had joined the group of spectators stepped forward and offered to take the minister's place.

He was, he said, a Roman Catholic priest, as indeed his black habit showed, and as he understood that Mr. Santal had died in the True Faith, he would read over him the service for the burial of the dead according to the Roman rite. No objection was raised by the onlookers, and the priest, a tall and ascetic-looking man in the prime of life, stood on the heap of earth which had been removed from the grave, and performed the service. The spectators listened with wonder, but with reverence, to the monotonous Latin prayers which he recited until all was complete. At the conclusion of the ceremony he gave no benediction, but merely ejaculated in a fervent tone the versicle from the burial service—"*Subvenite Sancti Dei, occurite Angeli Domini.*" He looked round as though expecting a response, but the spectators, who understood nothing, remained silent. Only a little man at the back of the group, with shaggy eyebrows and bright eyes, whom no one had hitherto observed, but who was no doubt a Catholic, replied in a thin voice with the antiphon—"*Suscipientes animam ejus.*"

THE LOOKING-GLASS
Walter de la Mare

First published in The Riddle and Other Stories *(Selwyn and Blount, 1923)*

Walter John de la Mare (1873–1956), "the Laureate of Dreamland", was a man of letters, a poet, children's author and writer of some of the best ghost stories published in the English language. Born to James Edward de la Mare, a banker, and Lucy Sophia, Walter and his siblings—he had two brothers and four sisters, one of whom died in infancy—grew up in Charlton. His father died when he was four years old and his mother's influence left a deep impression on him. The family subsequently moved to London and he was educated at St. Paul's Cathedral School where he became the founder and editor of *The Chorister's Journal*. Upon leaving school at the age of fourteen he became a clerk for the Anglo-American Oil Company, a place he would remain for the next twenty years. In his spare time he would write short stories and poems and gained success with publications in magazines such as *Pall Mall Magazine*, *The Sketch* and *The Cornhill Magazine*. These early efforts were written under the pseudonym "Walter Ramal".

De la Mare married (Constance) Elfrida Ingpen in 1899 and went on to have four children, two boys and two girls.

His first publication, a poetry collection titled *Songs of Childhood*, was published in 1902, followed by his first novel, *Henry Brocken* in 1904. By the time his second novel, *The Return* (1910), had been published, he was out of the oil business and was writing full time. His 1913 book of rhymes, *Peacock Pie*, established him as "the true inheritor of the nursery rhyme"[*] and from there his career really took off. A real novel of the unusual, *Memoirs of a*

---
[*] Miss Victoria Sackville-West.

Midget, was published in 1921 to great acclaim, with many critics considering it a masterpiece. Two collections, *Two Tales* and *The Connoisseur and Other Stories* came out in 1925, the same year as his debut fairy play *Crossings*, appeared at the Lyric, Hammersmith. Dame Alice Ellen Terry made her last appearance and Phyllis Calvert made her first. De la Mare successfully juggled his writing career between poetry, children's writing and genre writing, with some of his greatest ghost stories, "Seaton's Aunt" and "All Hallows", written during this imaginative time.

His wife was diagnosed with Parkinson's in 1940 and died three years later. He was awarded the Order of Merit in 1953 and in 1955 he was awarded an honorary membership of the American Academy of Arts and Letters, but due to illness was unable to attend, with the American Ambassador presenting it to one of De la Mare's sons on his behalf.

De la Mare had suffered from a coronary thrombosis in 1947 and it was this that killed him in 1956, dying two months after the National Book League arranged an exhibition of his manuscripts, books and pictures to commemorate his 83rd birthday. His ashes are buried in St. Paul's Cathedral. In a slightly backhanded compliment, the *Birmingham Post*'s obituary stated: "He was concerned with the creation of atmosphere [...] we hardly remember characters or plot."

"The Looking-Glass" is one of De la Mare's most straight-forward stories, yet it's one that becomes curiouser and curiouser. Alice is talking to a woman in the garden behind her house. But who is this mysterious interlocutor? Subtle, unsettling, with the most perfect use of absence in fiction.

For an hour or two in the afternoon, Miss Lennox had always made it a rule to retire to her own room for a little rest, so that for this brief interval, at any rate, Alice was at liberty to do just what she pleased with herself. The "just what she pleased," no doubt, was a little limited in range; and "with herself" was at best no very vast oasis amid its sands.

She might, for example, like Miss Lennox, rest, too, if she pleased. Miss Lennox prided herself on her justice.

But then, Alice could seldom sleep in the afternoon because of her troublesome cough. She might at a pinch write letters, but they would need to be nearly all of them addressed to imaginary correspondents. And not even the most romantic of young human beings can write on indefinitely to one who vouchsafes *no* kind of an answer. The choice in fact merely amounted to that between being "in" or "out" (in *any* sense), and now that the severity of the winter had abated, Alice much preferred the solitude of the garden to the vacancy of the house.

With rain came an extraordinary beauty to the narrow garden—its trees drenched, refreshed, and glittering at break of evening, its early flowers stooping pale above the darkened earth, the birds that haunted there singing as if out of a cool and happy cloister—the stormcock wildly jubilant. There was one particular thrush on one particular tree which you might say all but yelled messages at Alice, messages which sometimes made her laugh, and sometimes almost ready to cry, with delight.

And yet ever the same vague influence seemed to haunt her young mind. Scarcely so much as a mood; nothing in the nature of a thought; merely an influence—like that of some impressive stranger met—in a dream, say—long ago, and now half-forgotten.

This may have been in part because the low and foundering wall between the empty meadows and her own recess of greenery had always seemed to her like the boundary between two worlds. On the one side freedom, the wild; on this, Miss Lennox, and a sort of captivity. There Reality; here (her "duties" almost forgotten) the confines of a kind of waking dream. For this reason, if for no other, she at the same time longed for and yet in a way dreaded the afternoon's regular reprieve.

It had proved, too, both a comfort and a vexation that the old servant belonging to the new family next door had speedily discovered this little habit, and would as often as not lie in wait for her between a bush of lilac and a bright green chestnut that stood up like a dense umbrella midway along the wall that divided Miss Lennox's from its one neighbouring garden. And since apparently it was Alice's destiny in life to be always precariously balanced between extremes, Sarah had also turned out to be a creature of rather peculiar oscillations of temperament.

Their clandestine talks were, therefore, though frequent, seldom particularly enlightening. None the less, merely to see this slovenly ponderous woman enter the garden, self-centred, with a kind of dull arrogance, her louring face as vacant as contempt of the Universe could make it, was an event ever eagerly, though at times vexatiously, looked for, and seldom missed.

Until but a few steps separated them, it was one of Sarah's queer habits to make believe, so to speak, that Alice was not there at all. Then, as regularly, from her place of vantage on the other side of the wall, she would slowly and heavily lift her eyes to her face, with a sudden energy which at first considerably alarmed the young girl, and afterwards amused her. For certainly you *are* amused in a sort of fashion when any stranger you might suppose to be a little queer in the head proves perfectly harmless. Alice did not exactly like Sarah. But she could no more resist her advances than the garden could resist the coming on of night.

Miss Lennox, too, it must be confessed, was a rather tedious and fretful companion for wits (like Alice's) always wool-gathering—wool, moreover, of the shimmering kind that decked the Golden Fleece. Her own conception of the present was of a niche in Time from which she was accustomed to look back on the dim, though once apparently garish, panorama of the past; while with Alice, Time had kept promises enough only for a surety of its immense resources—resources illimitable, even though up till now they had been pretty tightly withheld.

Or, if you so preferred, as Alice would say to herself, you could put it that Miss Lennox had all her eggs in a real basket, and that Alice had all hers in a basket that was *not* exactly real—only problematical. All the more reason, then, for Alice to think it a little queer that it had been Miss Lennox herself and not Sarah who had first given shape and substance to her vaguely bizarre intuitions concerning the garden—a walled-in space in which one might suppose intuition alone could discover anything in the least remarkable.

"When my cousin, Mary Wilson (the Wilsons of Aberdeen, as I may have told you), when my cousin lived in this house," she had informed her young companion one evening over her own milk and oatmeal biscuits, "there was a silly talk with the maids that it was haunted."

"The house?" Alice had inquired, with a sudden crooked look on a face that Nature, it seemed, had definitely intended to be frequently startled; "The house?"

"I didn't say the *house*," Miss Lennox testily replied—it always annoyed her to see anything resembling a flush on her young companion's cheek, "and even if I did, I certainly *meant* the garden. If I had meant the house, I should have used the word house. I meant the garden. It was quite unnecessary to correct or contradict me; and whether or not, it's all the purest rubbish—just a tale, though not the only one of the kind in the world, I fancy."

"Do you remember any of the other tales?" Alice had inquired, after a rather prolonged pause.

"No, none"; was the flat reply.

And so it came about that to Sarah (though she could hardly be described as the Serpent of the situation), to Sarah fell the opportunity of enjoying to the full an opening for her fantastic "lore." By insinuation, by silences, now with contemptuous scepticism, now with enormous warmth, she cast her spell, weaving an eager imagination through and through with the rather gaudy threads of superstition.

"Lor, no, *Crimes*, maybe not, though blood is in the roots for all *I* can say." She had looked up almost candidly in the warm, rainy wind, her deadish-looking hair blown back from her forehead.

"Some'll tell you only the old people have eyes to see the mystery; and some, old or young, if so be they're ripe. Nothing to me either way; I'm gone past such things. And *what* it is, 'orror and darkness, or golden like a saint in heaven, or pictures in dreams, or just like dying fireworks in the air, the Lord alone knows, Miss, for I don't. But this I *will* say," and she edged up her body a little closer to the wall, the raindrops the while dropping softly on bough and grass, "May-day's the day, and midnight's the hour, for such as be wakeful and brazen and stoopid enough to watch it out. And what you've got to look for in a manner of speaking is what comes up out of the darkness from behind them trees there!"

She drew back cunningly.

The conversation was just like clockwork. It recurred regularly—except that there was no need to wind anything up. It wound itself up overnight, and with such accuracy that Alice soon knew the complete series of question and answer by heart or by rote—as if she had learned them out of the Child's Guide to Knowledge, or the Catechism. Still there were interesting points in it even now.

"*And what you've got to look for*"—the *you* was so absurdly impersonal when muttered in that thick, coarse, privy voice. And Alice invariably smiled at this little juncture; and Sarah as invariably looked at her and swallowed.

"But have *you* looked for—for what you say, you know?" Alice would then inquire, still with face a little averted towards the black low-boughed group of broad-leafed chestnuts, positive candelabra in their own season of wax-like speckled blossom.

"Me? *Me?* I was old before my time, they used to say. Why, besides my poor sister up in Yorkshire there, there's not a mouth utters my name." Her large flushed face smiled in triumphant irony. "Besides my bed-rid mistress there, and my old what they call feeble-minded sister, Jane Mary, in Yorkshire, I'm as good as in my grave. I may be dull and hot in the head at times, but I stand *alone*—eat alone, sit alone, sleep alone, think alone. There's never been such a lonely person before. Now, what should such a lonely person as me, Miss, I ask you, or what should you either for that matter, be meddling with your May-days and your haunted gardens for?" She broke off and stared with angry confusion around her, and, lifting up her open hand a little, she added hotly, "Them birds!—My God, I drats 'em for their squealin'!"

"But, why?" said Alice, frowning slightly.

"The Lord only knows, Miss; I hate the sight of 'em! If I had what they call a blunderbuss in me hand I'd blow 'em to ribbings."

And Alice never could quite understand why it was that the normal pronunciation of the word would have suggested a less complete dismemberment of the victims.

It was on a bleak day in March that Alice first heard really explicitly the conditions of the quest.

"Your hows and whys! What I say is I'm sick of it all. Not so much of you, Miss, which is all greens to me, but of the rest of it all! Anyhow, *fast* you must, like the Cartholics, and you with a frightful hacking cough and all. Come like a new-begotten bride you must in a white gown, and a wreath of lillies or rorringe-blossom in your hair, same pretty much as I made for my mother's coffin this twenty years ago, and which I wouldn't do now not for respectability even. And me and my mother, let me tell you, were as close as hens in a roost… But I'm off me subject. There you sits, even if the snow itself comes sailing in on your face, and alone you must be neither book nor candle, and the house behind you shut up black abed and asleep. But, there; you so wan and sickly a young lady. What ghost would come to you, I'd like to know. You want some fine dark loveyer for a ghost—that's your ghost. Oo-ay! There's not a want in the world but's dust and ashes. That's my bit of schooling."

She gazed on impenetrably at Alice's slender fingers. And without raising her eyes she leaned her large hands on the wall. "Meself, Miss, meself's *my* ghost, as they say. Why, bless me! it's all thro' the place now, like smoke."

What was all through the place now like smoke Alice perceived to be the peculiar clarity of the air discernible in the garden at times. The clearness as it were of glass, of a looking-glass, which conceals all behind and beyond it, returning only the looker's wonder, or simply her vanity, or even her gaiety. Why, for the matter of that, thought Alice smiling, there are people who look into looking-glasses, actually see themselves there, and yet never turn a hair.

There *wasn't* any glass, of course. Its sort of mirage sprang only out of the desire of her eyes, out of a restless hunger of the mind—just to possess her soul in patience till the first favourable May evening came along and then once and for all to set everything at rest. It was a thought which fascinated her so completely that it influenced her habits, her words, her actions. She even began to long for the afternoon solely to be alone with it; and in the midst of the reverie it charmed into her mind, she would glance up as startled as a Dryad to see the "cook-general's" dark face fixing its still cold gaze on her from over the moss-greened wall. As for Miss Lennox she became testier and more "rational" than ever as she narrowly watched the day approaching when her need for a new companion would become extreme.

Who, however, the lover might be, and where the trysting-place, was unknown even to Alice, though, maybe, not absolutely unsurmised by her, and with a kind of cunning perspicacity perceived only by Sarah.

"I see my old tales have tickled you up, Miss," she said one day, lifting her eyes from the clothes-line she was carrying to the girl's alert and mobile face. "What they call old wives' tales I fancy, too."

"Oh, I don't think so," Alice answered. "I can hardly tell, Sarah. I am only at peace *here*, I know that. I get out of bed at night to look down from the window and wish myself here. When I'm reading, just as if it were a painted illustration—in the book, you know—the scene of it all floats in between me and the print. Besides, I can do just what I like with it. In my mind, I mean. I just imagine; and there it all is. So you see I could not bear *now* to go away."

"There's no cause to worry your head about that," said the woman darkly, "and as for picking and choosing I never saw much of it for them that's under of a thumb. Why, when *I* was young, I couldn't have borne to live as I do now with just meself wandering to and fro. Muttering I catch meself, too. And, to be sure, surrounded in the air by shapes, and shadows, and noises, and winds, so as sometimes I can neither see nor hear. It's true, God's gospel, Miss—the body's like a clump of wood, it's that dull. And you can't get t'other side, so to speak."

So lucid a portrayal of her own exact sensations astonished the girl. "Well, but what is it, what is it, Sarah?"

Sarah strapped the air with the loose end of the clothes-line. "Part, Miss, the hauntin' of the garden. Part as them black-jacketed clergymen would say, because we's we. And part 'cos it's all death the other side—all death."

She drew her head slowly in, her puffy cheeks glowed, her small black eyes gazed as fixedly and deadly as if they were anemones on a rock.

The very fulness of her figure seemed to exaggerate her vehemence. She gloated—a heavy somnolent owl puffing its feathers. Alice drew back, swiftly glancing as she did so over her shoulder. The sunlight was liquid wan gold in the meadow, between the black tree-trunks. They lifted their cumbrous branches far above the brick human house, stooping their leafy twigs. A starling's dark iridescence took her glance as he minced pertly in the coarse grass.

"I can't quite see why *you* should think of death," Alice ventured to suggest.

"Me? Not me! Where I'm put, I stay. I'm like a stone in the grass, I am. Not that if I were that old mealy-smilin' bag of bones flat on her back on her bed up there with her bits of beadwork and slops through a spout, I wouldn't make sure overnight of not being waked next mornin'. There's something in me that won't let me rest, what they call a volcano, though no more to eat in that beetle cupboard of a kitchen than would keep a Tom Cat from the mange."

"But, Sarah," said Alice, casting a glance up at the curtained windows of the other house, "she looks such a quiet, *patient* old thing. I don't think I *could* stand having not even enough to eat. Why do you stay?"

Sarah laughed for a full half-minute in silence, staring at Alice meanwhile. "'Patient'!" she replied at last," Oo-ay. Nor to my knowledge did I ever breathe the contrary. As for staying; you'd stay all right if that loveyer of yours come along. You'd stand anything—them pale narrow-chested kind; though me, I'm neether to bend nor break. And if the old man was to look down out of the blue up there this very minute, ay, and shake his fist at me, I'd say it to his face. I loathe your whining psalm-singers. A trap's a trap. You wait and see!"

"But how do you mean?" Alice said slowly, her face stooping.

There came no answer. And, on turning, she was surprised to see the bunchy alpaca-clad woman already disappearing round the corner of the house.

The talk softly subsided in her mind like the dust in an empty room. Alice wandered on in the garden, extremely loath to go in. And gradually a curious happiness at last descended upon her heart, like a cloud of morning dew in a dell of wild-flowers. It seemed in moments like these, as if she had been given the power to think—or rather to be conscious, as it were, of thoughts not her own—thoughts like vivid pictures, following one upon another with extraordinary rapidity and brightness through her mind. As if, indeed, thoughts could be like fragments of glass, reflecting light at their every edge and angle. She stood tiptoe at the meadow wall and gazed greedily into the green fields, and across to the pollard aspens by the waterside. Turning, her eyes recognized clear in the shadow and blue-grey air of the garden her solitude—its solitude. And at once all thinking ceased.

"The Spirit is *me*: *I* haunt this place!" she said aloud, with sudden assurance, and almost in Sarah's own words. "And I don't mind—not the least bit. It can be only my thankful, thankful self that is here. And that can *never* be lost."

She returned to the house, and seemed as she moved to see—almost as if she were looking down out of the sky on herself—her own dwarf figure walking beneath the trees. Yet there was at the same time a curious individuality in the common things, living and inanimate, that were peeping at her out of their secrecy. The silence hung above them as apparent as their own clear reflected colours above the brief Spring flowers. But when she stood tidying herself for the usual hour of reading to Miss Lennox, she was conscious of an almost unendurable weariness.

That night Alice set to work with her needle upon a piece of sprigged muslin to make her "watch-gown" as Sarah called it. She was excited. She hadn't much time, she fancied. It was like hiding in a story. She worked with extreme pains, and quickly. And not till the whole flimsy thing was finished did she try on or admire any part of it. But, at last, in the early evening of one of the middle days of April, she drew her bedroom blind up close to the ceiling to view herself in her yellow grained looking-glass.

The gown, white as milk in the low sunlight, and sprinkled with even white embroidered nosegays of daisies, seemed to attenuate a girlish figure, already very slender. She had arranged her abundant hair with unusual care, and her own clear, inexplicable eyes looked back upon her beauty, bright it seemed with tidings they could not speak.

She regarded closely that narrow, flushed, intense face in an unforeseen storm of compassion and regret, as if with the conviction that she herself was to blame for the inevitable leave-taking. It seemed to gaze like an animal its mute farewell in the dim discoloured glass.

And when she had folded and laid away the gown in her wardrobe, and put on her everyday clothes again, she felt an extreme aversion for the garden. So, instead of venturing out that afternoon, she slipped off its faded blue ribbon from an old bundle of letters which she had hoarded all these years from a school-friend long since lost sight of, and spent the evening reading them over, till headache and an empty despondency sent her to bed.

Lagging Time brought at length the thirtieth of April. Life was as usual. Miss Lennox had even begun to knit her eighth pair of woollen mittens for the annual Church bazaar. To Alice the day passed rather quickly; a cloudy, humid day with a furtive continual and enigmatical stir in the air. Her lips were parched; it seemed at any moment her skull might crack with the pain as she sat reading her chapter of Macaulay to Miss Lennox's sparking and clicking needles. Her mind was a veritable rookery of forebodings, flying and returning. She scarcely ate at all, and kept to the house, never even approaching a window. She wrote a long and rather unintelligible letter, which she destroyed when she had read it over. Then suddenly every vestige of pain left her.

And when at last she went to bed—so breathless that she thought her heart at any moment would jump out of her body, and so saturated with expectancy she thought she would die—her candle was left burning calmly, unnodding, in its socket upon the chest of drawers; the blind of her window was up, towards the houseless by-road; her pen stood in the inkpot.

She slept on into the morning of May-day, in a sheet of eastern sunshine, till Miss Lennox, with a peevishness that almost amounted to resolution, decided to wake her. But then, Alice, though unbeknown in any really conscious sense to herself, perhaps, had long since decided not to be awakened.

Not until the evening of that day did the sun in his diurnal course for a while illumine the garden, and then very briefly: to gild, to lull, and to be gone. The stars wheeled on in the thick-sown waste of space, and even when Miss Lennox's small share of the earth's wild living creatures had stirred and sunk again to rest in the ebb of night, there came no watcher—not even the very ghost of a watcher—to the garden, in a watch-gown. So that what peculiar secrets found reflex in its dark mirror no human witness was there to tell.

As for Sarah, she had long since done with looking-glasses once and for all. A place was a place. There was still the washing to be done on Mondays. Fools and weaklings would continue to come and go. But give her *her* way, she'd have blown them and their looking-glasses all to ribbons—with the birds.

MIDSUMMER AT STONEHENGE
J. Britten Austin

First published in When Mankind Was Young *(Doubleday, Page and Co., 1927)*

Frederick Britten Austin (1885–1941) was born in Mile End, London. He was a clerk at the Stock Exchange and while working there saw several of his short stories published—his first novel, *The Shaping of Lavinia*, was published in 1911. He joined the London Rifle Brigade as a private on the day the Great War was declared and within four weeks was promoted to second lieutenant.

His main interest was warfare: the first of his books (naturally influenced by the horrors he saw) on this theme was *In Action: Studies of War* (1913). Another book, *The War God Walks Again* (1926), sounded warnings about modern developments in warfare. In 1927 Austin turned to history with *A Saga of the Sword*, which dealt with warfare from the Neolithic times to the tanks of 1916.

The work for which he would be most remembered is his Napoleonic study, *The Road to Glory: A Biographical Novel of Napoleon* (1935), a book one could absolutely see director Stanley Kubrick owning. An eccentric character, Austin protested the building of electricity pylons near his Sussex home by moving to Paris. He moved back to the UK after the fall of Paris in May 1940, losing all of his personal possessions and library. He arrived back in England broken physically, and died at the Royal West Infirmary, Weston-Super-Mare the following year of a seizure. He was 55. A month after his death it was revealed that he had been added onto the Civil List for services to literature.

"Midsummer at Stonehenge" is by far my pick of this anthology. As with Neil M. Gunn's non-genre short "The Moor", which I used in *Scotland the Strange* (British Library, 2023), this historical tale wears the "weird" label extremely well. The story feels like mist creeping up on you and it really does take you back in time. It is beautifully evocative, and I really hope you fall in love with this important, lost work.

WOLFHOUND, the cattleman, driving before him a selection from his herd, and Wheatear, his wife, trudged cheerfully in the long straggling procession of men, women, children, and animals which followed the deep-worn track over the swelling, treeless chalk downs. (For so many thousands of years had those tracks been trodden by so many myriads of feet, that even now, after the lapse of nearly four thousand subsequent years, they may instantly be recognized by their excessively hard surface where the turf grows thin.) Away on either side, clearly distinguishable in the bright early-morning sunshine, other similar processions moved across those bare uplands, converging on a point that was still far distant. They, like the noisily merry train where Wolfhound and his wife sang with fresh young voices, had also that morning issued from their great hill-top fortresses, protected by chalk embankments of colossal height and cunning complexity, wherein not only they but their cattle had been sheltered from the dangers of the night. Only within the last generation or two had those mighty walls been heaped up. A new menace had added itself to that of the fierce packs of wolves, swarming in the low-level forests, against which, for many centuries, the unwalled hillside platforms, raised too high and too steeply for the upward-leaping wolf to reach, had given their cattle adequate security. Of late years, a strange and formidable people, coming from across the narrow seas to the eastward, had harried in swift and terrible raids this primitive skin-clad folk who lived peacefully and industriously under the divine if alien theocracy of the sacred Children of the Sun. It was, however, a menace not for the moment imminent—thanks to its last hard-fought repulse, five years back—and neither Wolfhound nor Wheatear gave any thought to it as they pursued their way happily over those abruptly elevated chalk downs which are the skeletal frame of southern England, stretching northeastward from Dorsetshire to Salisbury Plain, and thence dividing into three great ridges thrust far into Norfolk, Kent, and Sussex. They—and those other processions—were journeying toward the great annual Sun-worshipping on that vast nodal plateau where, with immense labour, a new orthodoxly circular temple of colossal stones had recently been raised. That religious ceremony, drawing to itself pilgrimages from all over that lofty flint-bearing chalk formation, lifted high above the almost impassable forests thick around it, which then was—and for many ages had been—alone conveniently habitable, was also the occasion, as everywhere such religious festivals were in ancient times, for a great annual fair.

Wolfhound and Wheatear, equally with their companions, looked forward eagerly to that excitement, rare in the dull drudgery of their lives. Not only would there be the thrill of the great Sun Sacrifice, there would be that subtle, stimulating intoxication arising from an immense concourse of people (for such today, in the modern Anglo-Saxon world, men flock in their thousands to football and baseball matches), there would be a fascinatingly lavish display of all sorts of tempting and unheard-of novelties brought from unknown lands, there would be feastings and drinkings and love-makings, there would be who knew what of unexpected experience or adventure. As, under that already hot summer sun, they drove before them the cattle destined for the great market, carried on their heads or on a few pack ponies the skilfully home-made commodities they hoped to exchange for jet or amber or good bead money, they laughed and joked together, crudely—and, it must be confessed, coarsely; their sense of humour reacting only to its most primitive stimulus.

There was, for example, Round-Paunch (as with many others, his doubtless prettier original designation had long ago been forgotten in a nickname derived from a physical characteristic). At last year's Sun-worshipping, Round-Paunch had succumbed to the attractions of some strange-looking foreign dancer women, and had been discovered by his outraged spouse lying face downward in the mud, intoxicated to an insensibility impervious to her blows and kicks, and completely stripped of every article of value. He was now reminded of the occurrence, with a variorum commentary of suppositions as to what had really happened to him which goaded him to a highly amusing fury and which finally provoked his wife to unite with him, in shrill virago wrath, for his defence. There was also Black-Cow, the good-looking, strappingly built young wife of Weasel, the thin, squint-eyed, lame flint-knapper. She also was reminded of an episode in her domestic history with a realistic wit which exasperated her to furious *tu quoque* retaliations. For had she not been seen slipping surreptitiously into the long hut of the Sun priest novices, what time her morose husband was quarrelsomely gambling with knucklebones inside the skin tent of a seller of barley beer? This revived memory of what Black-Cow angrily screamed was an unworthy suspicion caused Weasel—most humorously—to attempt to beat her in a paroxysm of jealous rage while she dodged away from him, vituperating appallingly scandalous accusations against the men and women who yelled with laughter. And then there was Water-Lily, the demure, shy one, against whom no one could ever rightfully adduce the least misbehaviour, but to whom the most outrageous conduct at the previous Sun-worshipping was now gleefully imputed, while she protested vehemently, ludicrously at the point of tears. And then there was Forest-Cat, she whom Thick-Neck, the herdsman, had refused to marry after the last Sun-worshipping.

So they went on, joyously, mile after mile over the bare downs shimmering in the heat haze of the summer sun, in just such an interchange of primitively ribald jocularities as pass between a string of African tribesmen padding along to one of their great jungle-surrounded fairs in this present year of grace. Wheatear was earnestly recommended to keep a sharp eye on Wolfhound—he was exactly the sort of lad to go off with one of those fortune-telling women. And Wolfhound was similarly warned to keep a vigilant watch over his wife's fidelity—not only were those Sun priests terrible fellows, but there were all manner of jugglers and tumblers to be feared, not to mention the strange-looking traders who came from beyond the sea and who were unscrupulous corrupters of morals. How, for example, did Red-Poppy get that fine piece of amber at last year's Sun-worshipping?

Red-Poppy's reply was vigorously indecorous, but Wolfhound and Wheatear only smiled at each other in a happy mutual confidence. Not long had they been wedded. They had been betrothed at last winter's fire festival, when they had leaped hand-in-hand together through the flames and smoke of the fiercely hot pyre. And they had been married—leaping together once more through the flames, amid the acclamations of the tribe—at the spring fire festival, on the eve of the day when (a date regulated by the all-wise Sun priest) the cattle were released from their winter enclosures on the hill-top. (On that occasion, the terrified cattle had also been driven through the flames, to make them one with the fire god high in the sky and thus immune from pestilence and the ravages of the wolves that were so accursedly numerous in the low-lying adjacent forest.) Very happy were Wolfhound and Wheatear together in the newness of their wedded bliss. Their conical hut of skin-covered poles, in the village of such congregated within the colossal gleaming white chalk walls of the settlement, was to them a transfigured temple of miraculous felicity, of the strange and inexhaustible ecstasy of mutual love. They kept it quite uncommonly clean, vied with each other in bringing wild flowers—she from the narrow hillside terraces of ploughland where she hoed the corn; he from the low-lying cattle pastures cleared from the woodland—wherewith to decorate it, each in delightful surprise for the other. Robustly youthful she was, with strong straight bare limbs issuing from her short skin tunic, with honest eyes in a face freckled by constant exposure to the weather. And he was athletically muscular—could he not wrestle with his own cattle, throw them to the ground with a powerful cunning twist on their long, almost straight horns?—candid and pleasing in his primitive simplicity of soul. Very happy they were as, for the first time as a wedded couple, they journeyed together to the excitements of the great Sun-worshipping, feeling in that bright morning that all the world was happy, too.

Nevertheless, despite those other distant processions trailing across the bare downs, by no means all the world was going to the fair. On the great boulder-strewn stretches to either side of them, they could see the spearmen-guarded slave gangs at work. Some, in crude white gashes of freshly excavated chalk, were digging the shafts of flint mines, where, twenty feet down, they would toil crouchingly and perilously in the low radiating galleries to extract the precious silex. Others were labouring at the alluvial deposits of tin ore and gold left strewn by past glacial periods all over this rough and elevated land. (You will look as vainly for those metals there today as you would in those prehistoric goldfields worked for ages by the ancient Egyptians.) None of that tin ore was smelted in the country, nor did Wolfhound have any idea of such a process or know what ultimately became of it. The peculiar black stone which the superior Sun People were so eager to find, and which the slave gangs bore back each day in the great heavy lumps they smashed from the rock, passed out of his knowledge when the slave porters hoisted to their shoulders the poles of the stretchers on which it was heaped and wound their way in long procession down to the distant sea. Thither, to a like mysterious destination, also went the yellow metal washed and sieved from the pay dirt by other miserable slaves. Very sacred was that metal, participating of the nature of the Sun God himself, and fearsomely taboo for any but the Sun People—themselves all sublimely kin to the luminary—to possess. Wolfhound, a free man and no slave, would have shrunk with superstitious horror from the touch of it.

To Wolfhound and his joyous fellow travellers these surrounding activities were too familiar to merit even a passing thought. Slaves were slaves. As for the exalted Sun People whom he and his like docilely and superstitiously obeyed, he was content to regard them as incomprehensibly mysterious, as untouchable incarnations of that almighty Sun God whom they had taught his own remote ancestors to worship with appropriate ceremony. (Nevertheless, privately, on no account to be discovered to them, he cherished certain other gods—having the more comfortably intimate natures of stone, or tree, or rare running water—of even more primitive antiquity;

sometimes, too, when safely unobserved, he would make not inefficacious supplications to the wise old bull who was the leader of the herd, and was surely also himself a god.) Already for many centuries, perhaps even for more than a thousand years, although he had no conception of such a period of time, the Sun People had been established in the land where one of their sublime race was a god-incarnate king. From time immemorial, they had set the local folk searching for the peculiar black rocks, for the grains of sun metal, which they valued so highly and which they dispatched none knew whither.

Mysterious they were to him, and hardly less mysterious are they to us. Who were these people who, from India to Scandinavia, on a route that is a sea route along the coasts of the Mediterranean, the western coast of France, the sea-encompassed land of Britain, the bleak islands of the Hebrides, have left the megalithic temples of their astronomically scientific Sun worship? Always those temples are in the vicinity of ancient alluvial tin and gold workings. They sought for metals, yet the use of metals was unknown in the lands they dominated. Conversely, far away, in Babylonia, in Egypt, in Crete, bronze-using civilizations had flourished already for a thousand years; but to them the distant tin-bearing Atlantic islands, whence, nevertheless, came to them that indispensable ten per cent, alloy which converts soft copper into hard enduring bronze, were as utterly unknown and unsuspected as was America to the Europe of the Middle Ages.

Who were the people who controlled both halves of this great double and doubtless sacred secret, preserved through a score of centuries? Not yet had appeared those Phœnicians who later were to found Sidon and Tyre and, in their turn, for hundreds of years, to keep inviolate the inherited or spied-out secret of the sea route to the Tin Islands; not until after the fall of the ancient Cretan sea empire were their ships to become the common carriers of the Mediterranean world; nor did they ever do more than trade precariously on the coasts where their then vanished predecessors had established a despotic theocracy comparable only to those of Egypt and

Peru. The hypothesis of a lost Atlantis, which would explain many enigmas of that far-distant past, is today as scientifically unpopular as was the belief in the real existence of Troy until Dr. Schliemann dug it up and revealed it as an incontrovertible fact. Whence-ever they came, it is at least certain that these mysterious Children of the Sun maintained, for many centuries, mid-route entrepôts in the vicinity of Cadiz and on the coast of Portugal, whither their little crude ore-ladened ships came from the stormy North, and whence they departed again through the sunny Mediterranean to Crete, to Egypt, to the primitive Syrian ports that pertained to Babylonia, to Troy which commanded the Dardanelles gate to the swarming nomad tribes on the Black Sea. They guarded with amazing fidelity perhaps the greatest secret ever kept by man, and their secrecy still envelops them.

To the cattle-raising, agricultural, semi-savage people over whom they held sway, they bore the same relation as to their Peruvian subjects did the curiously similar Inca race of three thousand years later. They were a divine fact, beyond impious question, divorced from the brotherhood of common men in a destiny whose glory and whose recurrent tragedy belonged to the high affairs of gods. Wolfhound and the simple folk who trudged with him across those now English downs where the shepherds attribute to the Devil the mighty earthworks of old, if they dropped to more serious talk from their joyously anticipative jokes and laughter, discussed only whether this year their ruler the Sun King himself would be sent in the appropriate vehicle of consuming flame to reabsorption in the great deity whence he derived his nature, or whether—as for many years past had been the case—one of his sons, partaking of his divine substance and therefore equally efficacious, would go in his stead. In their primitive logic, there was nothing of wanton cruelty in the awful and annual sacrifice. On the one hand, the human incarnation of the god could not reasonably be suffered to fall into a senile decrepitude and thus, by sympathetic extension, so to enfeeble the luminary that his light and heat would fail and the earth cease to bring forth. On the other hand, the dispatch to Him of his earthly representative in the full vigour of his human strength must obviously reinvigorate the deity, as was equally obviously essential from time to time. Over all the primitive world (and the belief and custom yet survive in certain parts of Africa), it was the tragic, inescapable privilege of the king-god, or god-king, to die for his people.

But Wolfhound and Wheatear were only of the earthborn common herd. Their humble human love was unmenaced by the divinely awesome horror they would see—were even naïvely eager to see—consummated. She smiled at him, the honest eyes in her freckled homely face happy and proud in this first wedded journeying together to the great Sun-worshipping. He smiled back, in an impulse to kiss her that had—unless he wanted to excite the ribald mirth of their coarsely humorous fellow pilgrims—to be postponed. He shouted to the clumsily jostling bullocks he drove before him, secretly pledged himself to buy for her, from the proceeds of their sale, a really nice pair of jet ear pendants at the great fair.

For one night they had camped, united with other bands of similarly bound travellers, in a star-canopied bivouac of many fires. Food they had brought with them. Water they had obtained from one of the cunningly constructed dew ponds distributed over these fountainless uplands, far too lofty for the sinking of a well—unfailing reservoirs fed from no visible source which, paradoxically, *dried up* if a streamlet of rain water should happen to flow into them.* A merry night it had been, with much drinking of the barley

---

* Excavate a hollow considerably larger than the proposed pond. Cover the whole of the cavity with a thick layer of very dry straw. Cover the straw with a layer of fine, well-puddled clay that has no cracks, and make quite sure that the clay effectively laps over the straw all round the margins. Strew the clay closely with stones. And then, in the times even of greatest drought, your pond will steadily fill with water. That was the way Neolithic man did it—and he evidenced a surprising grasp of a subtle little problem in thermo-dynamics; if a stream should flow into the pond, it will wear down the clay margin and wet the straw; when the straw is wet, the clay is no longer insulated from the heat of the earth, and no longer will atmospheric moisture condense upon it. Q.E.D. Neolithic man—or those primitive scientists who did his thinking for him, as our scientists do the thinking for most of us—could and did apply a quite remarkable mastery of not a few abstrusely exact sciences.

beer they brought in the heavy skins. Round-Paunch had been caught kissing Red-Poppy, and Little-Wren, his wife, had sprung at her rival like a wildcat, initiating a clawing, screaming stand-up fight that was uproariously applauded by the circle of laughing, shouting spectators. Red-Poppy had emerged from that fight with her face badly scratched, muttering to herself (as she went off to find her own husband, careless of her in a private drinking bout at the other end of the camp) that she would at the first opportunity visit the Wise Man and have the death magic made for her adversary. This threat, being reported to Little-Wren, caused that lady to sit down abruptly, as though already stricken, and howl with terror, for Red-Poppy, young as she was, had a bad reputation, and was notoriously a frequenter of magicians, if not already a witch herself. And then Little-Wren and her somewhat disturbing panic fear (it gave one an uncanny shudder) had been forgotten in the diversion caused by Weasel, the husband of Black-Cow. The little squint-eyed lame flint-knapper, having imbibed with exceeding freedom of the barley beer, had solemnly insisted on singing, from end to end, one of those long, semi-religious traditional ballads in which each verse accumulates and repeats all that has gone before—highly popular mnemonics that hid in a riddle the Sun priest-told story of cosmic creation; our children still repeat "The House That Jack Built," one among several debased survivals. As Weasel's singing voice at the best of times was a matter for general mockery, and as he was far too drunk to remember correctly the complicated succession of piled-up events—a circumstance that angered him furiously, and exasperated him into commencing over and over again, with hiccuping stubbornness, at the beginning—his performance had elicited shrieks of delighted mirth from his rapidly collected audience. And then, finally convinced that his now almost empty beer skin was ineffectual as an aid to memory, he had renounced the effort and, bursting into tears, had solemnly recounted to a circle that rocked with laughter the familiar story of his domestic infelicity with Black-Cow. At the termination of which, some humorous fellow had suggested that it might, perhaps, be profitable to ascertain what his virtuous spouse was doing at the moment.

Weasel, in a sudden excruciatingly comic ferocity (he could scarcely stand on his feet), had promptly embraced the idea and, supported by a couple of hypocritical sympathizers and followed by a joyously expectant throng, had reeled off into the darkness. And presently from that darkness had issued piercing screams and an awful uproar. But Wheatear had lain apart from all this coarsely rustic orgy. Closely wrapped in the warm skins Wolfhound had tucked about her, she had stared for a while at the bright stars high above the dark shoulder of the down, wondering which of them it were best to pray to for a continuance of the miraculous happiness of true wedded love. And then she had stretched out her hand to where Wolfhound lay beside her and slipping her fingers into his had slid into naïvely happy dreams of the marvels of tomorrow's fair.

They had come in sight of it in the afternoon of the following day. The vast, treeless, undulating plain was covered with a great temporary encampment where the small nucleus of permanent habitations was indistinguishable. In the centre of that far-stretching agglomeration of huts and tents, the imposing circular temple of colossal white stones gleaming in the sun rose dominant on a swelling rise of the ground, the thin smoke of the sacred fire twisting skyward from the altar marked by the great overtopping Trilithon whitin its midst. Familiar though it was to most of them, the pilgrims hailed it with a shout of awe and wonder, pointing it out to each other with eager gestures. Wheatear squeezed her husband's hand as they momentarily stopped to gaze at it from afar, smiled at him with her honest eyes. There, tomorrow, the Sun deity would manifest himself at the midsummer maximum of his glory, radiating for all the world—but most particularly for those present—a divine guarantee of fertility in herd and field and wedded love. To him would belong the first-born he would infallibly soon procure for them—even as that first-born calf of the year, trotting long-shanked with Wolfhound's half-dozen bullocks, was his—but, as did everyone else (except in times of pestilence or famine, when, of course, the great angry god must be appeased with his full rightful dues), they would ransom the babe with many gifts to the severe Sun priest who saw to it that his god was not treated with calamity-bringing niggardliness. At next year's Sun-worshipping she would surely come with the craved-for infant at her breast, even as Brown-Owl, Cornflower, Evening-Star, and many other envied women came now in that long train of skin-clad worshippers. Wolfhound smiled back at her, sharing to the full her intense desire (unhappy and doomed to poverty was the household that had not many children).

"We will make great prayers, little mother of many babes," he said fondly, calling her by a name of good omen as he reciprocated her squeeze of his hand. "I give a bullock as well as the calf. Next year our first-one shall cry in the arms of the priest and shall be given back to us.—Haste now, let us go on with the others."

Already, in fact, the chattering, gesticulating procession was streaming past them, hurrying toward that vast far-stretching encampment whence a clamour of multitudinous voices was fitfully audible.

They reached it, added themselves to it on its outskirts, making an encampment of small skin-covered shelter huts of their own. The cattle that were for the market were penned within one of the many hurdle enclosures prepared for the purpose, tallied for by the notched stick given by a half-caste representative of the Sun People. And then, driving before them the calf and the selected best bullock, Wolfhound and Wheatear set out for the great Temple.

To approach it, they had to pass through the bewildering, dusty tumult of the fair. From the roughly constructed temporary huts and booths which lined the intersecting narrow roadways running in all directions, traders of every sort and of many diverse races vehemently harangued the swarming mob which drifted slowly along with here and there a traffic-obstructing halt before some merchant whose wares were more than usually attractive or whose strange or clamantly forceful personality irresistibly arrested its attention. Here it was a vendor of amber beads, outlandishly foreign with his long fair hair and blue eyes, his face congested with the effort of out-shouting his rivals in the vociferated praise of the fascinating long strings he held up to view or ran in a rivulet through his fingers from hand to hand. There it was a native maker of crudely shaped, coarsely fired pottery, standing amidst a close-packed array of pots and cups and vases which marvellously he did not break, spinning first one and then another on his fingers, clashing them together, while at the top of his voice he proclaimed the surpassing excellence of every article he sold. Farther on, a dealer in knives and axes held up, in loudly ejaculated admiration of his own products, the beautifully shaped smooth-polished tools and weapons of heavy stone which were the closest possible imitations of those rare unprocurable bronze models that it was rigidly taboo for any but the most superior of the Sun People to possess. (Nor were those bronze axes and knives, which came from far-off Mediterranean smithies direct to the proudly exclusive nobility of the Sun, recognized by the ignorant common people as being of metal, or in any way connected with the tin ore which was so freely exported. They thought they were made of some magic kind of stone—a magic rightfully reserved to a divine race.) Elsewhere, in a shrill duet of garrulous eloquence, a man and a woman held up between them lengths of the expensive linen cloth which only the Sun People and the wealthier of the common people could afford to wear as a garment. Beyond was a dealer in magic charms, garbed in a long robe embroidered with strange devices that awed the vulgar crowd collected around him; from him could be purchased—far cheaper, he assured them, than their local Wise Men could supply them—amulets which guaranteed the cattle against pestilence, amulets which provided the wearer with supernatural strength, amulets which were an absolute specific against blindness or toothache or the body sores not uncommon among a people who rarely washed, amulets which ensured to married folk the spell-bound fidelity of their respective spouses, which conferred everlasting youth, which made certain of a man-child for those who desired such. (Wheatear very nearly stopped Wolfhound to beg him to buy one of these last, but Wolfhound at that moment was engaged in a furious altercation with a man in the crowd who had been butted in the back by their bullock.) Everywhere, mingled with these merchants, were the glowing, seductive-smelling furnaces of the honeycake makers, the thronged benches and booths of the sellers of barley beer, the jugglers, the contortionists and dancers, male and female, performing with thudding drums and screaming fifes, the singers and bagpipe players who added their quota to an immense collective din that deafened the ears and confused the senses. For one among the divine progeny of the Sun, this great religious festival might be a supreme and ghastly tragedy. But what mattered to earthborn human beings the remote destinies of gods? For the merchants and showmen it was quite frankly an occasion to make the biggest profits of the year, and they exploited it vigorously to the full. For those simple-souled cattle breeders and agriculturists swarming between the booths it was an occasion to make holiday, to saturate themselves with unimagined marvels, to relax joyously for unwonted delights in that spontaneous release from normal inhibitions which is strangely sanctioned by the congregation of a multitude united in a common thirst for pleasure. Awful are the many gods man has devised for himself, but in all ages he has managed somehow to accommodate them to his elemental need to live and be happy, to make of their solemn and even dreadful rituals an excuse for trade and feasting.

 Wolfhound forced a vehemently disputed way through the press for his bullock and his calf, for Wheatear and himself. Not until they had made their pious offering could they tarry for the enjoyments of the fair. It was a long and slow journey, hindered by all manner of obstacles, beset by many temptations. In the whole world, did one ever see so many wondrous things gathered together? Happy the women who would wear those richly dyed linen robes, who would possess those fascinatingly attractive long necklaces of strung shells, those pendants of magic-imbued jet! Happy the man who would acquire that glassy-polished greenstone axe! Presently, they would come back to this cake stall and eat—no, this other one seemed even more appetizingly set out—or this one? Make way there, in the crowd—make way! Clumsy fool! Son of an unmarried mother! Have I not a right to drive my calf and my bullock to the Temple? To the Temple, I tell thee! where thou shouldst have taken the offering thou hast drunk in the beer tent!

Touch them not—they are sacred—they are already dedicate to He-Who-Must-Not Be-Named! Make way, there—make way! Look where thou goest, O woman—yea, cattle have horns, even like thy husband. My calf!—Smite not my calf who is first-born and sacred! May the Angry One wither thy crops! And to thee, too, O Pig-face! Make way there! Beerskin, make way! Yea, I see thee—thou art dead and corrupt. Ho, temple scavengers! Remove me this hill of stinking flesh! Make way! Make way! Didst thou see that girl dancer bending her body back so that her head touched her heels? And that giant black man—he comes assuredly from the abode of demons—breathing flames of fire from his mouth? Here will we come back and eat. Didst ever see such honey cakes? Presently, presently. Make way there—make way! Is there no end to this accursed multitude? Make way!—Blind and deaf, make way!

Thus, adding their shouts to the vociferated clamour of the crowd, they struggled through the narrow congested street between the booths where the competing merchants broke off in their cheap-jack salesmanship to scream vituperations at each other. At last, choked with dust, streaming with perspiration, they emerged from the stifling heat of the jostling mob to the bare gentle slope where, surrounded by its great circular embankment of gleaming white chalk, the great Temple was vivid against the blue summer sky.

Not directly to it, however, did they take their offerings. A little way distant from it, on the slope where the booths were not allowed to intrude, the Sun priests had established a temporary depot for the receipt of this great annual influx of the Sun God's income. Thither streamed a continual succession of skin-clad peasants driving before them their dedicated cattle, as Wolfhound and Wheatear drove their calf and bullock, bringing on their heads great pots of grain, skins of barley beer, the pelts of wild animals, whatever was specifically typical of their wonted industry. Wolfhound and Wheatear handed over their cattle to a businesslike young Sun Priest, his linen robe embroidered with the sacred solar symbol of concentric rings about an inmost dot, tonsured in the fashion of Sun priests the world over (did not St. Jerome adjure his ecclesiastics not to shave their heads in the manner of the priests of Isis and Serapis?); received in exchange a conventionally solemn assurance of divinely guaranteed felicity. The young priest was overwhelmed with the pressure of business, could not spare time for more than a most perfunctory blessing, particularly as at that moment a wealthy cattle breeder approached, driving before him a double-hand tally of fine cows. Secretly a little disillusioned, though neither would on any account have confessed the sacrilegious thought, they saw their precious calf and bullock driven away by a short-tempered Sun servant, saw them driven, with many others, to the great cattle enclosure at some distance from the Temple. Thence they would in due course go to join the sacred herds of the Sun God which pastured innumerably on the fattest lands all over the country. Surely, they would now get their hearts' desire! Wheatear smiled bravely at her husband. Poor they were, and a bullock as well as a calf was a recklessly generous contribution from their scanty possessions; the fact was depressingly vivid to them now that the animals had definitely gone. Surely the great benevolent Sun God, sublimely of more penetratingly sympathetic understanding than his overworked, heat-exasperated priests—only junior ones, it was to be remembered—would take note of the relative splendour of their offering, would vouchsafe them prosperity, would grant them the plumpest, the sturdiest of man-children! It would have been heartbreaking to doubt it.

Wolfhound put his strong arm round his wife.

"In thy arms he shall be at the next Sun-worshipping," he said, "and all women shall envy thee, little one—the first of many to make proud the husband to whom thou art the only woman with a face that smiles."

Wheatear looked fondly up at him with her honest eyes, spoke with a simple sincerity:

"If He-Who-Must-Not-Be-Named shall will it, man of my heart."

And as she spoke, she wondered secretly whether this grandiose and definitely masculine deity who ruled the sky was indeed the most efficacious to invoke for this particular purpose, whether the crude, obesely feminine little stone statuette which her mother kept concealed in her hut (it had been handed down through uncountable generations) was not more likely to concern itself sympathetically and potently with her specifically woman's prayer. At any rate, when they returned, she would make the experiment—furtively, with those uncouth hidden rites which her mother had already whisperingly suggested to her—saying nothing to Wolfhound, who, as a man, might not be given the least hint of these traditional woman's mysteries. A great wrath fell upon the woman who revealed them to the other sex. She was forever barren. She smiled at him, spoke with a perfidy excused by her love for him, by the urgency of their common heart's desire, covering her wicked thought, repeated the pious formula of the Sun priests, intolerant of the primitive cults they had supplanted.

"There is no God but the one God who flames in the heaven and wheels forever about the earth. To Him alone I pray, and He alone gives increase."

Wolfhound devoutly, as was proper, repeated the formula after her, at the same time thinking to himself that an additional supplication or two to the wise old bull who was the leader of his herd might be a judicious reinforcement of divine assistance—but this was a man's mystery, not to be disclosed to chattering women. The Sun priests were unpleasantly severe in the matter of exacting fines. He changed the subject abruptly lest—as, uncannily, she sometimes did—she should read what was in his mind.

"Look! The people are gathering on the wall. Let us go and see. Perchance He-Who-Must-Not-Be-Named passes to the Temple."

They hastened toward the circular double embankment of upcast chalk where already an increasing throng was posting itself, obviously as spectators. He helped her up the short slope, down again, and up to the second and slightly higher crest. Thence they had a clear view into the arena which was the most sacred spot in all their land.

Majestic in its crude simplicity of colossal stones, the Temple reared itself not a hundred feet away from them. An outer ring of thirty vast, smoothly wrought monoliths, standing twelve feet out of the ground and four feet apart, was linked together by a continuous lintel of great blocks invisibly keyed on to the uprights. Within that ring was another circle of smaller but still huge rough-hewn single stones (perhaps possessing an already ancient sacred history, they had been brought with incredible labour from far-off Pembrokeshire in the wilds of Wales; by water to the river at West Amesbury and thence dragged on rollers by great teams of men up the easiest gradient to the lofty plain). Encompassed all about by that double circle was a horseshoe of five vast lintel-joined trilithons, the central and tallest of them twenty-five-and-a-half feet high, overtopping all the rest. And within that was another horseshoe of the smaller Welsh single blocks enclosing the great horizontal flat stone which was the altar whereon burned the never-extinguished sacred fire. The opening of that double horseshoe was accurately oriented to the northeast, to the precise spot on the horizon where, on the longest day, the Sun God would rise in his awesome blinding brilliance. There was no detail in that edifice, from the number of its outer ring of uprights (thirty days had the solar month, in Egypt as in Peru) to the horseshoe-shape of the central sanctuary, which had not a symbolical esoteric significance.

Nor was that all. To the circular earthwork, in an exact prolongation of the northeastern axis of the Temple, led a great sacred avenue, likewise between embankments of thrown-up chalk, which was a union of two such roads, one conducting from the distant river, the other issuing from the earthwork-walled enclosure, half a mile to the northward, that was the residence of the god king. In the centre of that avenue, a few yards before it passed into the circular earthwork around the Temple, was erected an immense roughly hewn monolith, of far greater antiquity than the oldest temple on this site, a survival indeed from an infinitely more primitive worship and thus excessively sacred. That stone, meticulously in alignment from the horseshoe-enclosed altar to the sunrise of midsummer morn, stands yet where for millenniums it has stood, bearing still the name that the rough Saxon tribesmen of two-and-a-half thousand years later gave it— the Hele-Stone, from the verb *helan*, "to conceal," because, on the longest day, to a man standing within the then-ruined circle, the sun rose hidden behind it. And just on the threshold of the circular earthwork, where the sacred avenue led into it, was another great flat block, level with the earth, known to this day from immemorial if vague tradition as "the Slaughter Stone." Two other sacred rough-hewn monoliths stood—and stand—within the earthwork; from the point of view of the priest officiating at the great altar, and looking between the trilithons, one marked the rising of the sun at the winter solstice and the other its setting on that shortest day. That esoteric priesthood, reserving to itself its now unfathomable stores of knowledge, could boast of a remarkable proficiency in by no means simple mathematics.

As Wolfhound and Wheatear stood with the throng of eagerly chattering spectators on the circular earthwork, the sun was sinking to the west behind them, and the smooth massive blocks of the great Temple glowed golden against the still blue sky. They contemplated it with an immense awe, the almost supernatural product—quite recent though was its construction on the site of a yet older temple—of intelligences immeasurably superior to their own. Other such temples existed and still exist all the way from Portugal to the remote Orkneys, but this was the most magnificent of them all—and the last of that series, though they knew it not who thus looked upon its freshness of neatly hewn stone, marvellously wrought with only crude stone implements, ever to be built. A few hundred miles away, across the North Sea, was even then accumulating the storm that should sweep the Sun People out of existence, out of the very memory of man.

But Wolfhound and Wheatear were happily unaware of that future fury of death and barbarous horrors. To them, that temple was established for eternity, was for them—as the Sun priests told them—the sacred navel of the world, a place of holy and perpetual peace within whose hallowed confines no weapon might ever be brought. Did it not exist, the sun would cease to shine and the world would be frost-withered in the bleak darkness of an endless winter night, for on its altar burned the sacred fire which magically kept the great luminary aglow. Great indeed was the awe with which they contemplated it.

The chatter of the expectant throng was suddenly hushed. From down the sacred avenue came a blast of raucous horns. They craned forward with eager interest. He-Who-Must-Not-Be-Named was coming to the sunset sacrifice. The procession approached. In front marched the men blowing harshly on the long, slightly curved bulls' horns which themselves had a mystic significance. Behind them came an array of priests, their white linen robes embroidered with the symbols of the sun, swinging the smoking pierced potter-ware censers which contained embers of the sacred fire, and chanting a hymn that was immemorially old. In rear of them, two by two, came the superior priests, old men, with venerable beards and small gold ornaments on their heads; very awe-inspiring they were in their slow-paced solemnity, but their dignity was forgotten in the sardonic majesty of the high priest who followed singly after them, his linen robe gold-emblazoned with esoteric geometrical signs, a cone of beaten gold upon his head, his long beard white as snow. And behind him, loftily borne on a litter hoisted on the shoulders of four men, came—blazing with flashing gold—the incarnation of the Sun God upon earth, he who with the Sun God himself could not be directly designated, could only be cautiously and obliquely referred to as He-Who-Must-Not-Be-Named. Those who marched by his litter, waving poles terminated by the mystic symbols of cone and circle, swastika and equilateral triangle, and the especially sacred *tau*, piously averted their eyes from his insupportable divinity. The throng upon the earthwork did likewise. They cast themselves prostrate in a murmur of awed worship, refraining from direct gaze lest they should be stricken blind, or haply dead, by his effulgence. To them he was nothing less than the very god himself. They did not see that almost pathetically human anxiety-haggard face under the great ray-aureoled headdress of solid gold, had no hint of the terror gripping the soul of that man already well past middle age whose destiny was caught in the fatal destiny of a divinity. They did not know—as he, faint with apprehension under his heavy magnificence, knew too well—the tortuous, merciless intrigues of the inner hierarchy of superior priests, the secret debate which had already determined—although (and it was that which consumed him with a mouth-parched fever) he did not know the result—the continuance or not of his earthly life.

For thirty years he had been a strong ruler, had governed the land in a stern autocracy that had severely maintained the privileges of the divine Sun People, had enforced a peaceful prosperity wherein the earthborn common herd was well content. But now—he could no longer deceive himself—his mind was no longer so vigorous and so penetrating as of old, no longer were his decisions informed by that cunning shrewdness, that ruthless statesmanship, which had been the admiration of the venerable subtle-brained priests (in his heart he cursed them) who dominated, by immemorial right, in his council house of carved and painted wood, which had kept him on the great throne, covered with plates of beaten gold and backed with a golden sun radiating its glory, for a term of years unparalleled by any of his recent predecessors. A long life of unrestrained indulgence— was he not divine, all things permitted unto him?—had suddenly claimed its toll. Invaded by a paralysing lassitude that terrified him with an increasing terror, but from which only spasmodically could he emerge, he craved for repose, for an unworried idle enjoyment of his unbounded prerogatives. Delightful indeed was that newest Bride of the Sun, she who was little more than a child and was so exquisitely timorous with him whose awful divinity she did not question—he thought of her little hands and feet, of her innocent eyes, of the long hair she let down for him to comb amorously with his shaking fingers, and it was like a new fire within him. Perhaps, even yet—? No, at the council gathering yesterday he had not been able to endure the interminable accumulation of public business, had broken up the solemn conclave in a sudden exasperation, had perceived, with a shock of renewed alarm, the piercing eyes of the hypocritically deferential high priest fixed on him from under their bushy white brows, in an expression he could not, would not allow himself to, divine. Perhaps that episode had settled his fate! If only he could recall it, live yesterday over once again!—He would make a big effort, a superhuman effort, to keep his brain awake and keen. He shuddered.

That business he had so petulantly refused further to consider was of the highest import to the State. Carefully though they concealed the menace from the earthborn multitude, the Sun People had become acutely aware of a formidable danger threatening them from over the narrow sea to the eastward. The swarming myriads of wild tribesmen who dwelt by the great rapid river that finally emptied itself in a dozen channels through low-lying marshland were ominously once more collecting their canoes, and since their last invasion they had been lavishly supplied—taking in flank the work of a thousand years—with bronze weapons by unscrupulous traders from the Mediterranean. To repel them would demand the fiercest energies of the Sun ruler. Would he be equal to it? Would he be allowed the opportunity? Whom, this year, would the pointing finger of the Sun God designate for sacrifice?—himself?—or, as heretofore he had always arranged (how easily these solemn mummeries *could* be arranged!), one of his many sons? He had already (as he always did) indicated to the high priest which son he would prefer to see selected by the god—that son whom not a week since his spies had discovered in intrigue against him. The sardonic, taciturn old priest had suavely replied (precisely as always hitherto) that doubtless the Sun God, the source of all blessings, would take note of the desire of his sublime incarnation upon earth. Perhaps he would be vouchsafed yet one more year of life, of sweet existence (how inexpressibly soothing was the touch of that child Sun Bride's finger-tips upon his brow!). But as, blazing with a gorgeous magnificence of solid gold, he was borne into the sacred enclosure, he feared—he feared—he almost screamed with fear.

Behind him marched, splendidly apparelled, of all ages, from grown men to little children, the several score of his sons. They also were pale and haggard-looking with suppressed anxiety and excitement. Within twelve hours, one of them would be either a victim or a king. And behind them trooped, singing with sweet voices, the great company of Sacred Virgins of the Sun—of divine blood, all of them, from whom the Sun King drew his many wives, to whom his sons also could alone be wedded.

They passed into the circle, grouped themselves around the Temple for the sunset sacrifice.

Then, when the great luminary had dropped below the horizon, they marched back in exactly similar solemn procession down the sacred avenue.

The throng of spectators arose from its pious prostration. Wolfhound and Wheatear joined hands, ran joyously down the slope toward the undiminished clamour of the great fair. They would have several hours of naïvely happy enjoyment amid its wonders. Not until midnight would the sacred ceremonies commence, the colossal annual fire be kindled within the Temple.

That midnight hour was already long past. The great stone uprights of the sacred edifice were silhouetted around the intense incandescence of the fire whose heat and light would reinforce that of the divine luminary now at its season of maximum potency, would most efficaciously reinvigorate it for that annual winter struggle with the inimical powers of darkness which would henceforth imperceptibly begin. Outside the building, an unbroken ring of priests circled endlessly, chanting their hymns of encouragement and praise, swinging the censers which contained each a particle of the sacred fire, assisting by their upward motion the sun itself to mount once more into the sky. And in a great golden throne, facing the northeast where that sun would rise, the Sun King himself sat motionless, his features like those of a dead man in the glare of the many torches which surrounded him, making—as was fitting—night into factitious day around his presence. Near him stood his divine sons, in an ordered group, and at a little distance the Virgins of the Sun mingled their voices with those of the chanting priests.

All around, on the walls of the circular embankment, the massed faces of the spectators reflected back that central brilliance of illumination. They were the lucky ones, the early comers. Behind them, on every side, an immense crowd packed itself solidly over the undulating plain, participating, with superstitious awe, in this great worship whose incidents they could not directly see. Wolfhound and Wheatear had come with the first, however. They stood (Wheatear gripping him tightly in her excitement; to be actually present at the sacrifice was an absolute guarantee of all she craved for) jammed in the press on top of the chalk wall. They had a clear view over the part of the circle that would be most important; could see, plainly discernible in the glow of the great fire, the immense primitive monolith standing alone in the first few yards of the sacred avenue leading straight to the northeast, exactly aligned with the inner horseshoe of the Temple over the great flat threshold stone of grim tradition. *There* would occur the thrilling culmination of this annual rite.

That culmination became swiftly imminent. The sky overhead was already pallid, had almost lost its stars. The great fire within the Temple ceased to be a source of light, the torches around the Sun King were ineffectual tongues of smoky yellow flame. Yet a little longer period of waiting— long, and yet curiously short in the retrospect—and the crystalline dull blue of the overhead sky was irradiated with a greenish light on the northeastern horizon. That greenish light became primrose based with a thin line of burnished gold. High up, a small floating cloud was suddenly dyed blood-red.

It was the appointed moment. Amid a murmur from the close-packed throng, a new chanting from the priests and Sun Virgins, the Sun King descended from his throne, advanced across the circle to where the high priest stood among a small group of the most ancient priests. Behind the divine ruler came his sons in a single file of mingled ages—all were equally liable. The high priest raised his arms and intoned a consecrated phrase of ritual. The Sun King answered him in an antiphonic similarly ritual phrase, resigning, as he proclaimed, unto the wisdom of the Sun God the choice of that one of his divine race whose earthly life should be reabsorbed into his fiery essence for his greater and undying glory. The sons of the King reaffirmed it in a chorus of diversely toned voices, some of them piping pathetically in their extreme youth. The high priest made solemn and appropriate answer. Placing himself at their head, he led them forward to the space between the Temple and the entrance to the sacred avenue. Then, quitting them, he posted himself at one side of the sacred threshold stone, a young and vigorous acolyte taking up his position at the other.

Again the chanting of the priests and virgins changed to a new and wilder litany. To that barbaric music, the long file headed by the Sun King commenced to move slowly round in a serpentine procession that formed itself into a figure-of-eight, between the Temple and the avenue. The course of that ritual figure passed over the sacred threshold stone, and each individual, as he stepped on the great slab, stopped for a moment and turned himself toward the northeast. The chanting of the priests increased suddenly in vehemence. On that northeastern horizon appeared the first intensely vivid thin segment of the rising sun.

Round and round in its serpent-indicating ritual figure-of-eight went that procession in which the little children ran to keep up with their elders, that procession in which one of them was doomed. Higher and higher rose the bright blood-red disk of the sun. Already, the great stone circle projected a vague-edged shadow which prolonged itself, over the packed mass of spectators, to infinity. Already, from that primitively sacred rough-hewn monolith, a similarly infinite vague shadow commenced to define itself, a shadow that passed just to one side of the horizontal slab where those marchers stopped each for his moment—a moment that became at every instant more dangerous. The close-packed watchers on the wall held their breaths in heart-gripping suspense. The priests and virgins chanted louder and ever louder, adjuring the great Sun God to make his choice.

Higher and higher climbed the sun. More and more definite stretched the long shadow cast by the monolith. And as it acquired precision, it shortened—shortened rapidly, while at the same time it moved laterally with an almost imperceptible but steady approach toward the slab where yet each successive member of that intertwining procession halted for a moment to make obeisance. Wolfhound, watching with fascinated intentness, felt a sharp pain in his arm; it was the grip of Wheatear's fingers upon it, convulsively strong in the emotion of that more and more imminent tragedy for which as yet the victim was undesignated. To whom would point that more and more clearly revealed slowly moving finger of doom, the very finger of the Sun God himself? It had contracted now almost to the slab, upon which the eldest son of the Sun King stood for his brief gesture of worship. Would it be he? No. He passed on. Another son stood upon the fatal slab—and He-Who-Must-Not-Be-Named, following close behind, stared at him in agonized expectation. This was the son whose intrigue he had discovered. The shadow had already begun to encroach upon the stone. The grim-visaged old high priest made an almost imperceptible gesture. The young man passed on. He-Who-Must-Not-Be-Named stood, himself, upon the slab. The shadow was full upon it, its extreme tip touched his feet. He looked down, perceived it, screamed—screamed again as the young acolyte sprang at him with a downward thrust of a stone knife.

The next instant—while from the altar stone within the great circle the Sun appeared to blaze poised upon the very summit of the monolith—while the priests and virgins chanted at the top of their voices—a half dozen of the younger priests hurried his sagging body into the Temple, hurled it upon the great fire.

Three days later, Wolfhound and Wheatear journeyed happily homeward from the delights of the great fair which had continued, in a riot of unrestrained joyousness—was not the world safe for yet another year?—after that tragic Sun-worshipping which had seen the replacement of one worn-out Sun King by another, younger and more vigorous. No qualm of compunction troubled them as they went, along with Round-Paunch and Little-Wren, with Weasel and Black-Cow and Red-Poppy and Water-Lily and all the others of their original company, over the swelling, treeless downs. What to them was the death of divine kings? Far, far distant—so distant as to be unknown to them—were the days when common folk such as they were liable to divinity, to immolation for the good of the world. Dynasties had usurped that tragic privilege and to such as they it would have been sacrilege to challenge it. Wolfhound and Wheatear had meritoriously assisted at the most important of religious rites, and they went joyously back to their little hut in the chalk-walled hill fortress, confident that all they had prayed for would be granted to them.

It is to be hoped that they lived happily ever after, seeing not that dreadful time—which occurred not very long subsequently—when the fierce bronze-weaponed foemen from the Rhineland swept over those downs and obliterated the Sun People forever. Much later, those relentless warriors, who were the first of men to speak the Aryan tongue in these islands, were themselves exterminated by the Goidels, who afterward were the ancient Irish and the Gael. And after them, equally ruthless, came the Brythons, whom Julius Cæsar eventually conquered in his avarice, for party political purposes, of what had then become the richest pearling station in the ancient world.

AUTHOR'S NOTE

The reader who is seriously interested in Stonehenge and its enigmatic builders may be referred to an imposing list of authorities. They are remarkably unanimous—in their flat contradiction of each other. Whatever theory he adopts, the earnest searcher after that deep-buried truth will have to make a quite considerable use of his imagination, as I have done.

THE BLACK STONE
Robert E. Howard

First published in Weird Tales, *November 1931*

Robert Ervin Howard (1906–1936) was an American pulp author, credited for inventing the sword and sorcery genre with his creation, Conan the Barbarian. Born in Texas, he spent his early years reading, but felt hemmed in by incessant bullying and the strict teachers at school. His loves growing up were reading, writing and boxing, a sport that was culturally important at the time. He started writing at nine years old, influenced by the works of Jack London and Rudyard Kipling. By sixteen he was sending stories to pulp magazines, and after several rejections his first two stories were published in the December 1922 issue of *The Tatler*. It wouldn't be until 1924 that he sold his first of many stories to *Weird Tales*, a caveman story titled "Spear and Fang". His first cover story for the magazine was "Wolfshead" two years later in 1926. During this time Howard drifted from job to job, finally settling at a drugstore, where, trying to supplement his income, he worked himself ill.

In 1928 and 1929 Howard broke through, creating the characters of Solomon Kane and Kull of Atlantis, the latter character earning the most he had ever been paid for a story. In 1930 he became friends with H. P. Lovecraft and his stories took on a Cthulhu-esque flavour, exploring old gods, their followers and occasionally straying into scenes of lurid violence ("The Black Stone" takes us into this tranche of his writing). The market for pulp magazines took a hit during the Great Depression and Howard, like many other writers, saw the market contract, with many publications folding. In 1931 his savings were wiped out.

Weird Tales still struggled ever onwards and Howard came up with the character that would make his name, Conan the Barbarian. He was an instant hit with the readers of *Weird Tales*, and it wasn't long before a

British publisher, Dennis Archer, asked him to write a Conan novel. *The Hour of the Dragon* was never published by Archer, as the company had gone into liquidation just as the book was finished, and it would end up being serialized in *Weird Tales* instead. It was finally published in one volume in the US by Gnome Press in 1950 as *Conan the Conqueror*.

Howard then became obsessed with the Western genre, and a collection called *A Gent from Bear Creek* was to be published by British publisher Herbert Jenkins. At the moment he was making the transition from the pulp market to the book market, it all fell apart. His mother, who had been poorly for decades with tuberculosis, slipped into a coma. Howard asked his mother's nurse if she would regain consciousness. On being told no, he walked out to his car, took his borrowed gun from the glove box, and shot himself in the head. He died eight hours later; his mother died the next day.

So, you've been given a hint about the gruesomeness contained in "The Black Stone", but don't let that put you off. In a departure from Howard's ultra-macho characters, our bookish and learned narrator sets off for Hungary due to a mention of "The Black Stone" which piques his curiosity. Our narrator ends up near the monolith on Midsummer's Day and at that point the story manages to outdo Conan the Barbarian for barbarianism. Don't say you've not been warned.

"They say foul beings of Old Times still lurk
In dark forgotten corners of the world,
And Gates still gape to loose, on certain nights,
Shapes pent in Hell."

—JUSTIN GEOFFREY

I READ of it first in the strange book of Von Junzt, the German eccentric who lived so curiously and died in such grisly and mysterious fashion. It was my fortune to have access to his *Nameless Cults* in the original edition, the so-called Black Book, published in Düsseldorf in 1839, shortly before a hounding doom overtook the author. Collectors of rare literature are familiar with *Nameless Cults* mainly through the cheap and faulty translation which was pirated in London by Bridewall in 1845, and the carefully expurgated edition put out by the Golden Goblin Press of New York in 1909. But the volume I stumbled upon was one of the unexpurgated German copies, with heavy leather covers and rusty iron hasps. I doubt if there are more than half a dozen such volumes in the entire world today, for the quantity issued was not great, and when the manner of the author's demise was bruited about, many possessors of the book burned their volumes in panic.

Von Junzt spent his entire life (1795–1840) delving into forbidden subjects; he travelled in all parts of the world, gained entrance into innumerable secret societies, and read countless little-known and esoteric books and manuscripts in the original; and in the chapters of the Black Book, which range from startling clarity of exposition to murky ambiguity, there are statements and hints to freeze the blood of a thinking man. Reading what

Von Junzt *dared* put in print arouses uneasy speculations as to what it was that he dared *not* tell. What dark matters, for instance, were contained in those closely written pages that formed the unpublished manuscript on which he worked unceasingly for months before his death, and which lay torn and scattered all over the floor of the locked and bolted chamber in which Von Junzt was found dead with the marks of taloned fingers on his throat? It will never be known, for the author's closest friend, the Frenchman Alexis Ladeau, after having spent a whole night piecing the fragments together and reading what was written, burnt them to ashes and cut his own throat with a razor.

But the contents of the published matter are shuddersome enough, even if one accepts the general view that they but represent the ravings of a madman. There among many strange things I found mention of the Black Stone, that curious, sinister monolith that broods among the mountains of Hungary, and about which so many dark legends cluster. Von Junzt did not devote much space to it—the bulk of his grim work concerns cults and objects of dark worship which he maintained existed in his day, and it would seem that the Black Stone represents some order or being lost and forgotten centuries ago. But he spoke of it as one of the *keys*—a phrase used many times by him, in various relations, and constituting one of the obscurities of his work. And he hinted briefly at curious sights to be seen about the monolith on Midsummer's Night. He mentioned Otto Dostmann's theory that this monolith was a remnant of the Hunnish invasion and had been erected to commemorate a victory of Attila over the Goths. Von Junzt contradicted this assertion without giving any refutory facts, merely remarking that to attribute the origin of the Black Stone to the Huns was as logical as assuming that William the Conqueror reared Stonehenge.

This implication of enormous antiquity piqued my interest immensely and after some difficulty I succeeded in locating a rat-eaten and mouldering copy of Dostmann's *Remnants of Lost Empires* (Berlin, 1809, "Der Drachenhaus" Press). I was disappointed to find that Dostmann referred to the Black Stone even more briefly than had Von Junzt, dismissing it with a few lines as an artefact comparatively modern in contrast with the Greco-Roman ruins of Asia Minor which were his pet theme. He admitted his inability to make out the defaced characters on the monolith but pronounced them unmistakably Mongoloid. However, little as I learned from Dostmann, he did mention the name of the village adjacent to the Black Stone—Stregoicavar—an ominous name, meaning something like Witch-Town.

A close scrutiny of guide-books and travel articles gave me no further information—Stregoicavar, not on any map that I could find, lay in a wild, little-frequented region, out of the path of casual tourists. But I did find subject for thought in Domly's *Magyar Folklore*. In his chapter on *Dream Myths* he mentions the Black Stone and tells of some curious superstitions regarding it—especially the belief that if any one sleeps in the vicinity of the monolith, that person will be haunted by monstrous nightmares for ever after; and he cited tales of the peasants regarding too-curious people who ventured to visit the Stone on Midsummer Night and who died raving mad because of *something* they saw there.

That was all I could gleam from Dornly, but my interest was even more intensely roused as I sensed a distinctly sinister aura about the Stone. The suggestion of dark antiquity, the recurrent hint of unnatural events on Midsummer Night, touched some slumbering instinct in my being, as one senses, rather than hears, the flowing of some dark subterraneous river in the night.

And I suddenly saw a connection between this Stone and a certain weird and fantastic poem written by the mad poet, Justin Geoffrey: *The People of the Monolith*. Inquiries led to the information that Geoffrey had indeed written that poem while travelling in Hungary, and I could not doubt that the Black Stone was the very monolith to which he referred in his strange verse. Reading his stanzas again, I felt once more the strange dim stirrings of subconscious promptings that I had noticed when first reading of the Stone.

*

I had been casting about for a place to spend a short vacation and I made up my mind. I went to Stregoicavar. A train of obsolete style carried me from Temesvar to within striking distance, at least, of my objective, and a three days' ride in a jouncing coach brought me to the little village which lay in a fertile valley high up in the fir-clad mountains. The journey itself was uneventful, but during the first day we passed the old battlefield of Schomvaal where the brave Polish-Hungarian knight, Count Boris Vladinoff, made his gallant and futile stand against the victorious hosts of Suleiman the Magnificent, when the Grand Turk swept over eastern Europe in 1526.

The driver of the coach pointed out to me a great heap of crumbling stones on a hill near by, under which, he said, the bones of the brave Count lay. I remembered a passage from Larson's *Turkish Wars*: "After the skirmish" (in which the Count with his small army had beaten back the Turkish advance-guard) "the Count was standing beneath the half-ruined walls of the old castle on the hill, giving orders as to the disposition of his forces, when an aide brought to him a small lacquered case which had been taken from the body of the famous Turkish scribe and historian, Selim Bahadur, who had fallen in the fight. The Count took therefrom a roll of parchment and began to read, but he had not read far before he turned very pale and without saying a word, replaced the parchment in the case and thrust the case into his cloak. At that very instant a hidden Turkish battery suddenly opened fire, and the balls striking the old castle, the Hungarians were horrified to see the walls crash down in ruin, completely covering the brave Count. Without a leader the gallant little army was cut to pieces, and in the war-swept years which followed, the bones of the noblemen were never recovered. Today the natives point out a huge and mouldering pile of ruins near Schomvaal beneath which, they say, still rests all that the centuries have left of Count Boris Vladinoff."

I found the village of Stregoicavar a dreamy, drowsy little village that apparently belied its sinister cognomen—a forgotten black-eddy that Progress had passed by. The quaint houses and the quainter dress and manners of the people were those of an earlier century. They were friendly, mildly curious but not inquisitive, though visitors from the outside world were extremely rare.

"Ten years ago another American came here and stayed a few days in the village," said the owner of the tavern where I had put up, "a young fellow and queer-acting—mumbled to himself—a poet, I think."

I knew he must mean Justin Goeffrey.

"Yes, he was a poet," I answered, "and he wrote a poem about a bit of scenery near this very village."

"Indeed?" mine host's interest was aroused. "Then, since all great poets are strange in their speech and actions, he must have achieved great fame, for his actions and conversations were the strangest of any man I ever knew."

"As is usual with artists," I answered, "most of his recognition has come since his death."

"He is dead, then?"

"He died screaming in a madhouse five years ago."

"Too bad, too bad," sighed mine host sympathetically. "Poor lad—he looked too long at the Black Stone."

My heart gave a leap, but I masked my keen interest and said casually: "I have heard something of this Black Stone; somewhere near this village, is it not?"

"Nearer than Christian folk wish," he responded. "Look!" He drew me to a latticed window and pointed up at the fir-clad slopes of the brooding blue mountains. "There beyond where you see the bare face of that jutting cliff stands that accursed Stone. Would that it were ground to powder and the powder flung into the Danube to be carried to the deepest ocean! Once men tried to destroy the thing, but each man who laid hammer or maul against it came to an evil end. So now the people shun it."

"What is there so evil about it?" I asked curiously.

"It is a demon-haunted thing," he answered uneasily and with the suggestion of a shudder. "In my childhood I knew a young man who came up from below and laughed at our traditions—in his foolhardiness he went to the Stone one Midsummer Night and at dawn stumbled into the village again, stricken dumb and mad. Something had shattered his brain and sealed his lips, for until the day of his death, which came soon after, he spoke only to utter terrible blasphemies or to slaver gibberish.

"My own nephew when very small was lost in the mountains and slept in the woods near the Stone, and now in his manhood he is tortured by foul dreams, so that at times he makes the night hideous with his screams and wakes with cold sweat upon him.

"But let us talk of something else, *Herr*; it is not good to dwell upon such things."

I remarked on the evident age of the tavern and he answered with pride: "The foundations are more than four hundred years old; the original house was the only one in the village which was not burned to the ground when Suleiman's devils swept through the mountains. Here, in the house that then stood on these same foundations, it is said, the scribe Selim Bahadur had his headquarters while ravaging the country hereabouts."

I learned then that the present inhabitants of Stregoicavar are not descendants of the people who dwelt there before the Turkish raid of 1526. The victorious Moslems left no living human in the village or the vicinity thereabouts when they passed over. Men, women and children they wiped out in one red holocaust of murder, leaving a vast stretch of country silent and utterly deserted. The present people of Stregoicavar are descended from hardy settlers from the lower valleys who came into the upper levels and rebuilt the ruined village after the Turk was thrust back.

Mine host did not speak of the extermination of the original inhabitants with any great resentment and I learned that his ancestors in the lower levels had looked on the mountaineers with even more hatred and aversion than they regarded the Turks. He was rather vague regarding the causes of this feud, but said that the original inhabitants of Stregoicavar had been in the habit of making stealthy raids on the lowlands and stealing girls and children. Moreover, he said that they were not exactly of the same blood as his own people; the sturdy, original Magyar-Slavic stock had mixed and intermarried with a degraded aboriginal race until the breeds had blended, producing an unsavoury amalgamation. Who these aboriginies were, he had not the slightest idea, but maintained that they were "pagans" and had dwelt in the mountains since time immemorial, before the coming of the conquering peoples.

I attached little importance to this tale; seeing in it merely a parallel to the amalgamation of Celtic tribes with Mediterranean aborigines in the Galloway hills, with the resultant mixed race which, as Picts, has such an extensive part in Scotch legendry. Time has a curiously foreshortening effect on folklore, and just as tales of the Picts became intertwined with legends of an older Mongoloid race, so that eventually the Picts were ascribed the repulsive appearance of the squat primitives, whose individuality merged, in the telling, into Pictish tales, and was forgotten; so, I felt, the supposed inhuman attributes of the first villagers of Stregoicavar could be traced to older, outworn myths with invading Huns and Mongols.

The morning after my arrival I received directions from my host, who gave them worriedly, and set out to find the Black Stone. A few hours' tramp up the fir-covered slopes brought me to the face of the rugged, solid stone cliff which jutted boldly from the mountainside. A narrow trail wound up it, and mounting this, I looked out over the peaceful valley of Stregoicavar, which seemed to drowse, guarded on either hand by the great blue mountains. No huts or any sign of human tenancy showed between the cliff whereon I stood and the village. I saw numbers of scattering farms in the valley but all lay on the other side of Stregoicavar, which itself seemed to shrink from the brooding slopes which masked the Black Stone.

The summit of the cliffs proved to be a sort of thickly wooded plateau. I made my way through the dense growth for a short distance and came into a wide glade; and in the centre of the glade reared a gaunt figure of black stone.

It was octagonal in shape, some sixteen feet in height and about a foot and a half thick. It had once evidently been highly polished, but now the surface was thickly dinted as if savage efforts had been made to demolish it; but the hammers had done little more than to flake off small bits of stone and mutilate the characters which once had evidently marched in a spiralling line round and round the shaft to the top. Up to ten feet from the base these characters were almost completely blotted out, so that it was very difficult to trace their direction. Higher up they were plainer, and I managed to squirm part of the way up the shaft and scan them at close range. All were more or less defaced, but I was positive that they symbolized no language now remembered on the face of the earth. I am fairly familiar with all hieroglyphics known to researchers and philologists and I can say with certainty that those characters were like nothing of which I have ever read or heard. The nearest approach to them that I ever saw were some crude scratches on a gigantic and strangely symmetrical rock in a lost valley of Yucatan. I remember that when I pointed out these marks to the archeologist who was my companion, he maintained that they either represented natural weathering or the idle scratching of some Indian. To my theory that the rock was really the base of a long-vanished column, he merely laughed, calling my attention to the dimensions of it, which suggested, if it were built with any natural rules of architectural symmetry, a column a thousand feet high. But I was not convinced.

I will not say that the characters on the Black Stone were similar to those on that colossal rock in Yucatan; but one suggested the other. As to the substance of the monolith, again I was baffled. The stone of which it was composed was a dully gleaming black, whose surface, where it was not dinted and roughened, created a curious illusion of semi-transparency.

I spent most of the morning there and came away baffled. No connection of the Stone with any other artefact in the world suggested itself to me. It was as if the monolith had been reared by alien hands, in an age distant and apart from human ken.

I returned to the village with my interest in no way abated. Now that I had seen the curious thing, my desire was still more keenly whetted to investigate the matter further and seek to learn by what strange hands and for what strange purpose the Black Stone had been reared in the long ago.

I sought out the tavern-keeper's nephew and questioned him in regard to his dreams, but he was vague, though willing to oblige. He did not mind discussing them, but was unable to describe them with any clarity. Though he dreamed the same dreams repeatedly, and though they were hideously vivid at the time, they left no distinct impression on his waking mind. He remembered them only as chaotic nightmares through which huge whirling fires shot lurid tongues of flame and a black drum bellowed incessantly. One thing only he clearly remembered—in one dream he had seen the Black Stone, not on a mountain slope but set like a spire on a colossal black castle.

As for the rest of the villagers I found them not inclined to talk about the Stone, with the exception of the schoolmaster, a man of surprising education, who spent much more of his time out in the world than any of the rest.

He was much interested in what I told him of Von Junzt's remarks about the Stone, and warmly agreed with the German author in the alleged age of the monolith. He believed that a coven had once existed in the vicinity and that possibly all of the original villagers had been members of that fertility cult which once threatened to undermine European civilization and gave rise to the tales of witchcraft. He cited the very name of the village to prove his point; it had not been originally named Stregoicavar, he said; according to legends the builders had called it Xuthltan, which was the aboriginal name of the site on which the village had been built many centuries ago.

This fact roused again an indescribable feeling of uneasiness. The barbarous name did not suggest connection with any Scythic, Slavic or Mongolian race to which an aboriginal people of these mountains would, under natural circumstances, have belonged.

That the Magyars and Slavs of the lower valleys believed the original inhabitants of the village to be members of the witchcraft cult was evident, the schoolmaster said, by the name they gave it, which name continued to be used even after the older settlers had been massacred by the Turks, and the village rebuilt by a cleaner and more wholesome breed.

He did not believe that the members of the cult erected the monolith but he did believe that they used it as a centre of their activities, and repeating vague legends which had been handed down since before the Turkish invasion, he advanced the theory that the degenerate villagers had used it as a sort of altar on which they offered human sacrifices, using as victims the girls and babies stolen from his own ancestors in the lower valleys.

He discounted the myths of weird events on Midsummer Night, as well as a curious legend of a strange deity which the witch-people of Xuthltan were said to have invoked with chants and wild rituals of flagellation and slaughter.

He had never visited the Stone on Midsummer Night, he said, but he would not fear to do so; whatever *had* existed or taken place there in the past, had been long engulfed in the mists of time and oblivion. The Black Stone had lost its meaning save as a link to a dead and dusty past.

It was while returning from a visit with this schoolmaster one night about a week after my arrival at Stregoicavar that a sudden recollection struck me—it was Midsummer Night! The very time that the legends linked with grisly implications to the Black Stone. I turned away from the tavern and strode swiftly through the village. Stregoicavar lay silent; the villagers retired early. I saw no one as I passed rapidly out of the village and up into the firs which masked the mountain slopes with whispering darkness. A broad silver moon hung above the valley, flooding the crags and slopes in a weird light and etching the shadows blackly. No wind blew through the firs, but a mysterious, intangible rustling and whispering was abroad. Surely on such nights in past centuries, my whimsical imagination told me, naked witches astride magic broomsticks had flown across this valley, pursued by jeering demoniac familiars.

I came to the cliffs and was somewhat disquieted to note that the illusive moonlight lent them a subtle appearance I had not noticed before—in the weird light they appeared less like natural cliffs and more like the ruins of cyclopean and Titan-reared battlements jutting from the mountain-slope.

Shaking off this hallucination with difficulty I came upon the plateau and hesitated a moment before I plunged into the brooding darkness of the woods. A sort of breathless tenseness hung over the shadows, like an unseen monster holding its breath lest it scare away its prey.

I shook off the sensation—a natural one, considering the eeriness of the place and its evil reputation—and made my way through the wood, experiencing a most unpleasant sensation that I was being followed, and halting once, sure that something clammy and unstable had brushed against my face in the darkness.

I came out into the glade and saw the tall monolith rearing its gaunt height above the sward. At the edge of the woods on the side toward the cliffs was a stone which formed a sort of natural seat. I sat down, reflecting that it was probably while there that the mad poet, Justin Geoffrey, had written his fantastic *People of the Monolith*. Mine host thought that it was the Stone which had caused Geoffrey's insanity, but the seeds of madness had been sown in the poet's brain long before he ever came to Stregoicavar.

A glance at my watch showed that the hour of midnight was close at hand. I leaned back, waiting whatever ghostly demonstration might appear. A thin night wind started up among the branches of the firs, with an uncanny suggestion of faint, unseen pipes whispering an eery and evil tune. The monotony of the sound and my steady gazing at the monolith produced a sort of self-hypnosis upon me; I grew drowsy. I fought this feeling, but sleep stole on me in spite of myself; the monolith seemed to sway and dance, strangely distorted to my gaze, and then I slept.

I opened my eyes and sought to rise, but lay still, as if an icy hand gripped me helpless. Cold terror stole over me. The glade was no longer deserted. It was thronged by a silent crowd of strange people, and my distended eyes took in strange barbaric details of costume which my reason told me were archaic and forgotten even in this backward land. Surely, I thought, these are villagers who have come here to hold some fantastic conclave—but another glance told me that these people were not of the folk of Stregoicavar. They were a shorter, more squat race, whose brows were lower, whose faces were broader and duller. Some had Slavic or Magyar features, but those features were degraded as from a mixture of some baser, alien strain I could not classify. Many wore the hides of wild beasts, and their whole appearance, both men and women, was one of sensual brutishness. They terrified and repelled me, but they gave me no heed. They formed in a vast half-circle in front of the monolith and began a sort of chant, flinging their arms in unison and weaving their bodies rhythmically from the waist upward. All eyes were fixed on the top of the Stone which they seemed to be invoking. But the strangest of all was the dimness of their voices; not fifty yards from me hundreds of men and women were unmistakably lifting their voices in a wild chant, yet those voices came to me as a faint indistinguishable murmur as if from across vast leagues of Space—or *time*.

Before the monolith stood a sort of brazier from which a vile, nauseous yellow smoke billowed upward, curling curiously in an undulating spiral around the black shaft, like a vast unstable serpent.

On one side of this brazier lay two figures—a young girl, stark naked and bound hand and foot, and an infant, apparently only a few months old. On the other side of the brazier squatted a hideous old hag with a queer sort of black drum on her lap; this drum she beat with slow, light blows of her open palms, but I could not hear the sound.

The rhythm of the swaying bodies grew faster and into the space between the people and the monolith sprang a naked young woman, her eyes blazing, her long black hair flying loose. Spinning dizzily on her toes, she whirled across the open space and fell prostrate before the Stone, where she lay motionless. The next instant a fantastic figure followed her—a man from whose waist hung a goatskin, and whose features were entirely hidden by a sort of mask made from a huge wolf's head, so that he looked like a monstrous, nightmare being, horribly compounded of elements both human and bestial. In his hand he held a bunch of long fir switches bound together at the larger ends, and the moonlight glinted on a chain of heavy gold looped about his neck. A smaller chain depending from it suggested a pendant of some sort, but this was missing.

The people tossed their arms violently and seemed to redouble their shouts as this grotesque creature loped across the open space with many a fantastic leap and caper. Coming to the woman who lay before the monolith, he began to lash her with the switches he bore, and she leaped up and spun into the wild mazes of the most incredible dance I have ever seen. And her tormentor danced with her, keeping the wild rhythm, matching her every whirl and bound, while incessantly raining cruel blows on her naked body. And at every blow he shouted a single word, over and over, and all the people shouted it back. I could see the working of their lips, and now the faint far-off murmur of their voices merged and blended into one distant shout, repeated over and over with slobbering ecstasy. But what that one word was, I could not make out.

In dizzy whirls spun the wild dancers, while the lookers-on, standing still in their tracks, followed the rhythm of their dance with swaying bodies and weaving arms. Madness grew in the eyes of the capering votaress and was reflected in the eyes of the watchers. Wilder and more extravagant grew the whirling frenzy of that mad dance—it became a bestial and obscene thing, while the old hag howled and battered the drum like a crazy woman, and the switches cracked out a devil's tune.

Blood trickled down the dancer's limbs but she seemed not to feel the lashing save as a stimulus for further enormities of outrageous motion; bounding into the midst of the yellow smoke which now spread out tenuous tentacles to embrace both flying figures, she seemed to merge with that foul fog and veil herself with it. Then emerging into plain view, closely followed by the beast-thing that flogged her, she shot into an indescribable, explosive burst of dynamic mad motion, and on the very crest of that mad wave, she dropped suddenly to the sward, quivering and panting as if completely overcome by her frenzied exertions. The lashing continued with unabated violence and intensity and she began to wriggle toward the monolith on her belly. The priest—or such I will call him—followed, lashing her unprotected body with all the power of his arm as she writhed along, leaving a heavy track of blood on the trampled earth. She reached the monolith, and gasping and panting, flung both arms about it and covered the cold stone with fierce hot kisses, as in frenzied and unholy adoration.

The fantastic priest bounded high in the air, flinging away the red-dabbled switches, and the worshippers, howling and foaming at the mouths, turned on each other with tooth and nail, rending one another's garments and flesh in a blind passion of bestiality. The priest swept up the infant with a long arm, and shouting again that Name, whirled the wailing babe high in the air and dashed its brains out against the monolith, leaving a ghastly stain on the black surface. Cold with horror I saw him rip the tiny body open with his bare brutish fingers and fling handfuls of blood on the shaft, then toss the red and torn shape into the brazier, extinguishing flame and smoke in a crimson rain, while the maddened brutes behind him howled over and over that Name. Then suddenly they all fell prostrate, writhing like snakes, while the priest flung wide his gory hands as in triumph. I opened my mouth to scream my horror and loathing, but only a dry rattle sounded; a huge monstrous toad-like *thing* squatted on the top of the monolith!

I saw its bloated, repulsive and unstable outline against the moonlight, and set in what would have been the face of a natural creature, its huge, blinking eyes which reflected all the lust, abysmal greed, obscene cruelty and monstrous evil that has stalked the sons of men since their ancestors mowed blind and hairless in the treetops. In those grisly eyes were mirrored all the unholy things and vile secrets that sleep in the cities under the sea, and that skulk from the light of day in the blackness of primordial caverns. And so that ghastly thing that the unhallowed ritual of cruelty and sadism and blood had evoked from the silence of the hills, leered and blinked down on its bestial worshippers, who groveled in abhorrent abasement before it.

Now the beast-masked priest lifted the bound and weakly writhing girl in his brutish hands and held her up toward that horror on the monolith.

And as that monstrosity sucked in its breath, lustfully and slobberingly, something snapped in my brain and I fell into a merciful faint.

I opened my eyes on a still white dawn. All the events of the night rushed back on me and I sprang up, then stared about me in amazement. The monolith brooded gaunt and silent above the sward which waved, green and untrampled, in the morning breeze. A few quick strides took me across the glade; here had the dancers leaped and bounded until the ground should have been trampled bare, and here had the votaress wriggled her painful way to the Stone, streaming blood on the earth. But no drop of crimson showed on the uncrushed sward. I looked, shudderingly, at the side of the monolith against which the bestial priest had brained the stolen baby—but no dark stain nor grisly clot showed there.

A dream! It had been a wild nightmare—or else—I shrugged my shoulders. What vivid clarity for a dream!

I returned quietly to the village and entered the inn without being seen. And there I sat meditating over the strange events of the night. More and more was I prone to discard the dream-theory. That what I had seen was illusion and without material substance, was evident. But I believed that I had looked on the mirrored shadow of a deed perpetrated in ghastly actuality in bygone days. But how was I to know? What proof to show that my vision had been a gathering of foul spectres rather than a mere nightmare originating in my own brain?

As if for answer a name flashed into my mind—Selim Bahadur! According to legend this man, who had been a soldier as well as a scribe, had commanded that part of Suleiman's army which had devastated Stregoicavar; it seemed logical enough; and if so, he had gone straight from the blotted-out countryside to the bloody field of Schomvaal, and his doom. I sprang up with a sudden shout—that manuscript which was taken from the Turk's body, and which Count Boris shuddered over—might it not contain some narration of what the conquering Turks found in Stregoicavar? What else could have shaken the iron nerves of the Polish adventurer? And since the bones of the Count had never been recovered, what more certain than that the lacquered case, with its mysterious contents, still lay hidden beneath the ruins that covered Boris Vladinoff? I began packing my bag with fierce haste.

Three days later found me ensconced in a little village a few miles from the old battlefield, and when the moon rose I was working with savage intensity on the great pile of crumbling stone that crowned the hill. It was back-breaking toil—looking back now I can not see how I accomplished it, though I laboured without a pause from moonrise to dawn. Just as the sun was coming up I tore aside the last tangle of stones and looked on all that was mortal of Count Boris Vladinoff—only a few pitiful fragments of crumbling bone—and among them, crushed out of all original shape, lay a case whose lacquered surface had kept it from complete decay through the centuries.

I seized it with frenzied eagerness, and piling back some of the stones on the bones I hurried away; for I did not care to be discovered by the suspicious peasants in an act of apparent desecration.

Back in my tavern chamber I opened the case and found the parchment comparatively intact; and there was something else in the case—a small squat object wrapped in silk. I was wild to plumb the secrets of those yellowed pages, but weariness forbade me. Since leaving Stregoicavar I had hardly slept at all, and the terrific exertions of the previous night combined to overcome me. In spite of myself I was forced to stretch myself on my bed, nor did I awake until sundown.

I snatched a hasty supper, and then in the light of a flickering candle, I set myself to read the neat Turkish characters that covered the parchment. It was difficult work, for I am not deeply versed in the language and the archaic style of the narrative baffled me. But as I toiled through it a word or a phrase here and there leaped at me and a dimly growing horror shook me in its grip. I bent my energies fiercely to the task, and as the tale grew clearer and took more tangible form my blood chilled in my veins, my hair stood up and my tongue clove to my mouth. All external things partook of the grisly madness of that infernal manuscript until the night sounds of insects and creatures in the woods took the form of ghastly murmurings and stealthy treadings of ghoulish horrors and the sighing of the night wind changed to tittering obscene gloating of evil over the souls of men.

At last when grey dawn was stealing through the latticed window, I laid down the manuscript and took up and unwrapped the thing in the bit of silk. Staring at it with haggard eyes I knew the truth of the matter was clinched, even had it been possible to doubt the veracity of that terrible manuscript.

And I replaced both obscene things in the case, nor did I rest or sleep or eat until that case containing them had been weighted with stones and flung into the deepest current of the Danube which, God grant, carried them back into the Hell from which they came.

It was no dream I dreamed on Midsummer Midnight in the hills above Stregoicavar. Well for Justin Geoffrey that he tarried there only in the sunlight and went his way, for had he gazed upon that ghastly conclave, his mad brain would have snapped before it did. How my own reason held, I do not know.

No—it was no dream—I gazed upon a foul rout of votaries long dead, come up from Hell to worship as of old; ghosts that bowed before a ghost. For Hell has long claimed their hideous god. Long, long he dwelt among the hills, a brain-shattering vestige of an outworn age, but no longer his obscene talons clutch for the souls of living men, and his kingdom is a dead kingdom, peopled only by the ghosts of those who served him in his lifetime and theirs.

By what foul alchemy or godless sorcery the Gates of Hell are opened on that one eerie night I do not know, but mine own eyes have seen. And I know I looked on no living thing that night, for the manuscript written in the careful hand of Selim Bahadur narrated at length what he and his raiders found in the valley of Stregoicavar; and I read, set down in detail, the blasphemous obscenities that torture wrung from the lips of screaming worshippers; and I read, too, of the lost, grim black cavern high in the hills where the horrified Turks hemmed a monstrous, bloated, wallowing toad-like being and slew it with flame and ancient steel blessed in old times by Muhammad, and with incantations that were old when Arabia was young. And even staunch old Selim's hand shook as he recorded the cataclysmic, earth-shaking death-howls of the monstrosity, which died not alone; for a half-score of his slayers perished with him, in ways that Selim would not or could not describe.

And the squat idol carved of gold and wrapped in silk was an image of *himself*, and Selim tore it from the golden chain that looped the neck of the slain high priest of the mask.

Well that the Turks swept that foul valley with torch and cleanly steel! Such sights as those brooding mountains have looked on belong to the darkness and abysses of lost aeons. No—it is not fear of the toad-thing that makes me shudder in the night. He is made fast in Hell with his nauseous horde, freed only for an hour on the most weird night of the year, as I have seen. And of his worshippers, none remains.

But it is the realization that such things once crouched beast-like above the souls of men which brings cold sweat to my brow; and I fear to peer again into the leaves of Von Junzt's abomination. For now I understand his repeated phrase of *keys!*—aye! Keys to Outer Doors—links with an abhorrent past and—who knows?—of abhorrent spheres of the *present*. And I understand why the cliffs look like battlements in the moonlight and why the tavern-keeper's nightmare-haunted nephew saw in his dream, the Black Stone like a spire on a cyclopean black castle. If men ever excavate among those mountains they may find incredible things below those masking slopes. For the cave wherein the Turks trapped the—*thing*—was not truly a cavern, and I shudder to contemplate the gigantic gulf of aeons which must stretch between this age and the time when the earth shook herself and reared up, like a wave, those blue mountains that, rising, enveloped unthinkable things. May no man ever seek to uproot that ghastly spire men call the Black Stone!

A Key! Aye, it is a Key, symhol of a forgotten horror. That horror has faded into the limbo from which it crawled, loathsomely, in the black dawn of the earth. But what of the other fiendish possibilities hinted at by Von Junzt—what of the monstrous hand which strangled out his life? Since reading what Selim Bahadur wrote, I can no longer doubt anything in the Black Book. Man was not always master of the earth—*and is he now?*

And the thought recurs to me—if such a monstrous entity as the Master of the Monolith somehow survived its own unspeakably distant epoch so long—*what nameless shapes may even now lurk in the dark places of the world?*

THE WITHERED HEART

G. G. Pendarves

First published in Weird Tales, *November 1939*

G. G. Pendarves was the pseudonym for the English writer Gladys Gordon Trenery (1885–1938). Information on Gladys is scarce, but what is known about her is that she was born in Liverpool and lived in Birkenhead. She achieved a pass certificate for piano held under the auspices of the Royal Academy of Music and the Royal College of Music and would go on to qualify as a music teacher in her own right at twenty-two. Her first short story was "The Kabbalist" under the "G. G. Pendarves" name, published in the November 1923 issue of *Hutchinson's Mystery-Story Magazine*. She had two stories published in the same magazine in January and September of 1924, and sold "The Devil's Graveyard" to *Weird Tales*, which was published in 1926. From there her career took off, but her debut collection wasn't published until fifty years after her death, and several of her stories appeared posthumously in *Weird Tales*, including "The Withered Heart". She died on 1 August 1938 at Sunset House, Parkgate, Cheshire, and was buried two days later at Rake Lane Cemetery, Wallasey.

Some confusion arose when I was researching Gladys. Richard Dalby's *The Virago Book of Stories* (1987) reprints "The Return" (1924) by "Marjory E. Lambe" and accredits it to being written by "G. G. Trenery" with the assumption that "Lambe" is another one of Trenery's pseudonyms. While Lambe and Trenery/Pendarves both had tales called "The Return" (Trenery's was written in 1927) they are *completely* different and by different people. At the time of writing, the sources I used had the "Lambe" story as being written by Trenery/Pendarves. It's sad to note, however, that Marjory E. Lambe was a real author in her own right. Marjory Elizabeth Sarah Lambe was born in June 1900, and died in Lewes in 1985. Her married name was Bidwell. As Marjory E. Lambe she wrote the novel *Crag's*

Foot Farm in 1931, and she also wrote prolifically under the names Mary Ann Gibbs (historical romance) and Elizabeth Ford (crime and mystery) throughout the twentieth century. While never accusing Richard of anything (it would be interesting to see what his source was!) this is a good place to give Marjory her proper due and I hope I can use her story "The Return" in a future anthology. My research on the discrepancies between the two stories has now been added to ISFDB and other reference sites.

DEAR JOHN,

If a fifteen years' friendship means anything to you, come at once. Sorry to hustle you like this, good old slow-worm that you are, but we've simply got to go into session about this thing before the month's out. The Ides of March are on Tuesday next, May 31st, this year.

My whole future is at stake and you've got to come and help. It's a very very queer thing, and Jonquil and I don't agree at all about it. I wish to heaven we'd found the box earlier and had more time to argue it all out. I see Jonquil's point of view, of course, and feel in a way bound to carry on for her sake, but—well, you know my views about playing round with anything like magic and necromancy. Jonquil says I'm morbid, still—Oh, well! come and see us through it.

RAFE.

MAY 27TH, 1938.

I TRIED to pretend to myself that I couldn't go, that I wouldn't go! But even as I made these protestations inwardly, I was giving instructions to the boy, Joe, who daily and conscientiously thwarts my best efforts to grow flowers, fruit and vegetables. For a quarter of an hour or so my foredoomed struggle went on.

"—and Joe! that gallon of weed-killer is for the whole lawn, don't pour it over one dandelion root.

"It's merely one of his latest ideas, he gets them like measles. I won't be fooled into rushing off and leaving my garden just now.

"Joe! if you let that dog bury his bones in the new seedling-bed, I'll kill you when I get back and bury you with them.

"All rubbish about his future! Another few weeks would make all the difference here! Why next Tuesday?"

"Don't forget the quassia for the gooseberries, Joe!

"—and what the devil has magic to do with his future? No! I won't go! I won't waste—"

By this time I was in the potting-shed, kicking off my heavy shoes and scrambling hastily into another and cleaner pair. Like iron to a magnet, I was drawn to the house where my mind continued to carry on acrimonious debates while my body intelligently took no notice of my mental disturbance and obeyed my will.

I packed a bag, interviewed my old housekeeper who expressed her disapproval of my plans by serving up watery coffee and an India-rubber omelette for my lunch, and set off within the hour with parting instructions to expect me back in God's good time.

It would have been more fitting to have said in the devil's own time. So far, however, no tinge of the saturnine malice which had, after a lapse of two centuries, begun to manifest itself, darkened the joyful anticipation of seeing my friend, Rafe Dewle.

I clambered into my old Austin-twelve and set her battered bonnet northwards. Those last hours on the open road when life was still free and untainted! Never, never again shall I experience anything like them. Knowledge has crippled imagination since then—evil polluted every spring of happiness.

On Shap Fells I stopped to cool my engine. Around me, yellow gorse breathed out its honey perfume; bumble-bees fussed to and fro as I lay stretched out on the heath and watched white cloud-feathers drift in the blue above. I slept for a brief spell on the warm breathing earth with the thin lonely call of curlews in my ears and the sense of hoary guardian hills all about me.

In sleep, the first faint brush of evil touched me. I dreamed that I journeyed on—on into a dark valley where, amidst mist and darkness and confusion, I felt the approach of invisible and threatening hosts. Yet I must go on swiftly—swiftly! Someone was waiting. Someone was in danger. I must hurry, hurry, hurry!

I woke to find my sunlit hemisphere all dark and angry. The great hills reared up threateningly into thunderous cloudbanks. Gusts of wind scattered the golden gorsebloom and whistled the coming storm along over shivering grass and heather.

With a sense of urgent fear left by my dream I started my car and dropped by long winding loops of road down to the valley, and, as I tore along leafy green lanes toward Keswick this fear persisted. Once past the town, I drove even more quickly, cutting across the head of Borrow-dale under dark Helvellyn's shadow and along the unfrequented road which led to *Braunfel*.

The rambling old manor house lay some twelve miles from town. I'd known it well when Rafe and I were boys together. His people had been wealthy landowners before 1914. The war took their men. The lean following years took their money and lands. *Braunfel* was on its last legs, financially, and I wondered why Rafe hadn't sold up before his marriage. I couldn't reconcile what little I knew of Jonquil French with the austere bare life that Rafe's inheritance offered. Their meeting and the marriage that so swiftly followed had been romantic and impassioned, a sort of Lochinvar affair; for Rafe had snatched her from another and very wealthy suitor almost at the church doors.

So characteristic of him and that hot Magyar blood of his! Even the lovely spoiled Jonquil French had succumbed to it. But for how long?

His letter indicated the thin end of a wedge to my mind. I'd met his bride in London and had not particularly liked her—not the wife for Rafe at all. I'd no idea what was the mysterious "thing" the pair disagreed about, of course, and I wished he'd been more explicit. Planning a good sensational story for me, no doubt. He loved being melodramatic.

At last I could see the bulk of *Braunfel* ahead, grey in shafts of pale clear light piercing a curtain of rain. About it, wide untended meadows stretched. Behind, the bare face of the fell, where only stumps remained of the great fir forest that had been so beautiful a background to the ancient house. War victims, those sheltering lovely trees! And no plantations showed their young green promise for the future. How gaunt *Braunfel* appeared! Not only that—it was positively sinister. I tried in vain to put the thought away. There was a look of boding grimness hanging over the massive pile that even neglected lands and bare scarred hillside could not wholly explain.

My old car splashed along the last mile of muddy lane between high ragged hedges. The road turned and twisted like a sea-serpent. Preoccupied and depressed, I took a sharp angle and put on my brakes with a curse. A tall and very agile figure seemed to leap from right under the Austin's bonnet.

"Rafe! What the deuce—"

"Hello! Hello! you old mud-turtle! I forgive you—don't apologize!"

He opened the car-door, slid his long legs under the dashboard, put an arm about my shoulders and grinned in the old familiar way.

"You're a marvel, John. I didn't really count on your coming until tomorrow, but I got so restless thinking you might turn up that I've been hanging round for the last hour here. Never been so glad to see your solemn old mug in my life!"

My heart grew light at sight and sound of him. Marriage had not altered him as far as his friendship and affection were concerned; they were mine still, perfectly unchanged, the warmest, strongest tie I had in the world.

I grunted and glowered up at his face, dark as a gipsy's, lighted up with the inner fire that burned so strongly in him. I never knew man, woman, or child with so glowing, so intense a quality.

"Same old mad March hare!" I grumbled. "I'd hoped marriage might have given you a grain or two of sense. I suppose you realize you've practically ruined my garden for the next six months by dragging me up here?"

"Splendid! I have made a hero of you!"

He burst out into a wild barbaric song and yelled and yodelled until I drowned him with my car's horn. The noise was insane. We broke down and laughed like hyenas at last and I drove on feeling younger than I'd ever expected to feel again—my twenty-eight years had weighed heavily since Rafe's marriage.

Saturday, May 28th. Once under the steep gabled roofs of *Braunfel*, my bubble of delight was pricked. The sight of Jonquil French—Jonquil Dewle I should say—brought back the formless fear of my queer dream on Shap Fell. Why the sight of a girl like a princess in a fairy-tale should depress a man, I didn't know. Jealousy? No, neither of Rafe nor of his exquisite bride.

I had been jealous, afraid she'd come between us: I knew now most emphatically that she had not. Nor did I envy him. A woman has never yet roused the passionate thrill of joy I feel at sight of a perfect flower. It's no use arguing with me, I can't help it; that's the way I'm made.

"Mr. Fowler—John, I mean! How *perfect* that you've come! What a relief! You simply can't imagine what a time I've had lately. How lovely and large and shy you look! Isn't he too perfect, Rafe?"

"Certainly not. I refuse to live with two perfect beings. John's a mere man like myself."

She blew him a kiss, pirouetted round the dark panelled room like a little red flame blown on the wind, dropped on one knee before me and raised her hands in an attitude of prayer.

"Dear, dear John! You *are* perfect! Oh, if you could only see yourself. Just like a lovely solemn pine tree planted in the middle of our library. Please, please may I kiss you—I really must."

In a flash she was on her light dancing feet, her arms about me, her pleading face upraised. I bent a stiff reluctant head, received a moth-like touch on my lips and watched her and Rafe clasp each other in ecstatic amusement.

"I take it back, darling." Rafe wiped his eyes. "He certainly is—perfect."

"Well, now you've settled that, perhaps you'll start explaining things. You haven't brought me here to point out the singular beauty of my character?"

"No," chuckled Jonquil. "But you wouldn't be of any use to us unless you were such a perfect wise old owl."

Her smile glanced like the sun on running water.

"Not time to explain before dinner. It's a long, sad tale. Rafe will take you up to your nice large draughty room, and when you hear a sound like a bull being massacred—come down for dinner. Rafe's invented a patent bugle-thing he uses when I'm late for meals; he's too lazy to walk the half-mile upstairs."

Left to myself in a bedroom whose size and dignity made me feel something like a small dry ham-sandwich on a platter designed for the traditional boar's head, I pushed open a diamond-paned lattice window, slumped down on the broad uncushioned seat beneath it and glared out at the cobbled garth below. Pigeons kept up a low bubbling complaint from roofs of stables and outbuildings—ruinous affairs, minus doors and windows, their slates and stones stained with centuries of rain, their woodwork grey and cracked, weeds, moss and lichen a green-gold signal of defeat.

It wasn't the garth, or the many evidences of poverty elsewhere that worried me, however, as I sat listening to the *broo! broo broo* of the pigeons. It was the thought of Jonquil.

It was impossible to do more than put into mere words her remarkable beauty, and what are words when it comes to a young, living, exquisitely made creature like her? She had crisp red-gold curls, eyes of changing deep warm brown that reminded me of wallflowers in sunlight, a milk-white skin, and body so light and quick in movement, so sure in poise, so extraordinarily expressive of her every mood that she seemed winged—a brilliant tropic bird darting and flashing to and fro.

But it was the will behind her laughing eyes that frightened me. Her will—blind, ignorant, unyielding, a terrible weapon in her reckless hands!

Abruptly, my dream possessed me again... I was hurrying along that dark valley into mists and darkness and confusion—someone needed my help—I must hurry, hurry, hurry. And now Jonquil was beside me, her hand on my arm, her voice laughing, persuading, telling me to come back, come back, come back—she hindered me—I could not shake off her detaining hand. Her clear laugh prevented my hearing what my ears were straining for. I only knew I must hurry, hurry, hurry—in the gathering darkness ahead someone needed me…

It wasn't until after leaving the dinner-table, graced no longer by Queen Anne silver and Waterford glass, that I realized the significance of Jonquil's inclusion in my disturbing and recurring dream.

Rain and wind turned the May night to chill discomfort. Rafe lighted the big library fire, piled up fir-cones and logs until a heartening blaze warmed a respectable area of the lofty room with its mouldering books, threadbare rugs and worm-eaten oak.

Stimulated by tobacco, whisky, and Rafe's company I began to discount my boding fears again—but not for long. Jonquil was as eager as Rafe seemed reluctant to enlighten me. He yielded to her importunity at last, lifted down an iron casket from a high bookshelf and set it on a heavy table near the fire.

"There you are, lady and gentleman!" he made an exaggerated showman's gesture. "This is the Luck of *Braunfel* and guaranteed to supply your heart's desire. To make its magic work you need a nice round full moon, a strong belief in ghosts and devils, and a bottle of my best whisky inside you. These will qualify you to commune with a Benevolent Gent who died two hundred years ago in the hope of an extraordinary Resurrection from the Dead."

His nonsense wasn't well received. The sight of that twelve-by-eight inch box filled me with a nasty crawling sensation of horror. I set down my glass and stared at it in silence.

Jonquil ran up to the table, tried to pull the box from beneath Rafe's long brown fingers.

"It's not fair—it's not fair to tell him like that! You're trying to prejudice him. Let *me* show him! Let *me* tell him!"

Instantly he became the bland infuriating nurse with a spoiled child, patted her shining coppery curls with one hand and imprisoned her impatient fingers with his other.

"Now! Now! Now! Remember there's a little visitor here, darling! Don't forget your pretty manners!"

He kissed and put her back in a chair with another admonitory pat on the head.

"This is my Ancestor! My Benevolent Gent—hereafter known as B.G., and I will not be intimidated by a woman with red hair!"

I knew Rafe well. He was stalling now. It was a very old habit of his to approach anything he deeply disliked with idiotic badinage. Well, he might deceive Jonquil, but not me. So I sat tight and waited. My hands and feet grew cold in spite of the hot cheerful fire. I was most acutely awake, my eyes on Rafe's face, when that cursed dream of mine recurred... a dark long valley stretched between us... he faded, dissolved into distance and smoky dark confusion...

"John! What is it?"

I found myself on my feet, blinking stupidly down into Jonquil's alarmed face. Rafe was staring at me across the table, his mouth open in surprise.

"Cramp?" he inquired. "Must have been a bad twinge. I never heard you yell like that before."

"Cramp!" I echoed feebly, then pulled myself together. "No—it's a tooth—going to have it out."

I mumbled apologies, filled my glass, drank and felt considerably better. My mind cleared.

"Let's get down to business." I waved my pipe toward the box on the table. "I want to know where *I* come in. Let's have the story straight, mind!"

"John, you *are* such a darling! When you look at me like that through those enormous specs I feel just like a criminal before a judge."

Jonquil sat very stiffly and raised a hand as if to take an oath:

"I promise not to interrupt—unless I *have* to."

She tucked her little green slippers under her, curled up in the corner of a settee, and assumed an air of child-like innocent patience. I watched her with a pang. She was so sure of herself. She knew so exactly what she wanted—and intended to get it at all costs.

"Well?" My voice was brusque with anxiety as I turned to Rafe. "Bring out the skeleton in the cupboard."

His lips twisted in a rather doubtful smile.

"Queer you should say that. It's not exactly a skeleton, but it is part of a dead body."

"What? Your Ancestor, did you say—was he embalmed?"

"His heart was."

He lifted the casket's heavy lid as he spoke. A breath of thin cold air blew across my face and neck as I leaned forward to watch. I hated to see him standing over that beastly box; there was something so repulsive and ominous about it that my flesh crept when his fingers touched its rusty lid. Intuition told me that he did more than open a lid—he opened a door to something deadlier than plague.

It was a relief to my taut nerves to see him take out two tangible objects and set them on the table. One was a fat little book, fastened with broad brass clasps and bound in solid leather. The other—I got to my feet and went to examine it more closely.

My gorge rose at sight of the dark dried thing. I've seen mummies, and some were hideous enough. I've prowled about laboratories and examined scientific specimens preserved in fluids, and many were fairly revolting to a mind and imagination like mine. But this little horror, black and withered, with a strange metallic sheen! In amazement I drew still closer, unable to credit my sight. Then I straightened up with a jerk and glanced at Rafe.

"It's living! It beats—the thing beats!"

He nodded—"Since 1738, according to his tombstone date."

I saw he shared my revulsion. I forced myself to touch the heart, and drew back in horror at finding the dark withered bit of muscle was warm.

Jonquil clapped her hands. "You see! You see! Now perhaps you'll persuade Rafe to do it. Oh, he must—he must!"

She could contain herself no longer and flashed across to us. There wasn't a vestige of fear in her eager face as she put out a delicate exploring hand and touched the withered heart. Her faith in it, her strong will to test it, lent the dreadful thing power, and I saw it swell under her fingers—saw the throbbing pulse beat stronger, fuller.

"No! Don't!"

Rafe's voice sharply admonished her. His hand snatched back her own. She looked from him to me and laughed, but the red-brown eyes were bright with impatient anger.

"How exasperating men are! You look like two old hens with a duckling! I didn't think you'd be afraid too, John."

She gave me a stormy scornful glance. Next moment she was curled up in her corner again, sudden as a puff of wind.

"John, darling!" her voice was honeysweet now; "that's a heart of gold. Quite literally a heart of gold for Rafe and me—if he chooses! Oh, I see what you're thinking. You're a sentimentalist like Rafe. I'm not. *His* heart won't reduce the Bank's overdraft, you know. *That*,"—she flicked an airy hand toward the table—"that heart will."

I caught Rafe's glance at her and sharply realized his carefully concealed unhappiness. His shining tower of romance was fast changing to an old house in need of repair. The solitary countryside where he and she would walk in dreams was being reduced to an estate whose every hedge and gate and meadow clamoured for money—money—money! I'd never felt the pinch of my own straitened circumstances before, but now I hated myself—I'd have given anything to put things right for Rafe. And I hated Jonquil too—unreasonably, fiercely, for making him unhappy.

I didn't answer her. I was watching Rafe as, with swift distasteful touch, he took up the repulsive little heart, restored it to its metal box and dropped the lid with a clang.

Then he picked up the squat leather book and I followed him to the fireside.

I was convinced he was as much relieved as I to have that beastly heart out of sight.

"Don't tremble in your shoes, old man! I'm not going to read this tome right through. It's full of queer stories and experiments that don't concern our problem directly. This is the really juicy bit that does."

He drew a stiff yellowed crackling sheet from a pocket of the book's cover and unfolded it with a flourish.

"This is the apple of discord in the house of Dewle! This is the bee in Jonquil's bonnet! This is what's muting the family lute! *A scrap of paper*—a thing capable of starting anything in the world—wars, duels, murders—all the trouble that is, or ever will be."

"A cheque for £1,000,000 is a scrap of paper I'd love to see—with your name on it, dearest!"

"It was only £100,000 this morning," he reminded her. "Even a B.G. has limits, you must remember."

"And those that don't ask, don't get," she retorted with a flirt of her red curls.

"Well, we'll see what John thinks of my ancestor, Count Dul's *billet-doux*." He gave me a swift glance. "There's a preliminary but I'll spare you about his grave. It's been lost for generations, but Jonquil discovered it after reading this."

I could see the black thick lettering through the semi-transparent paper as Rafe held it up. He seemed to know it pretty well by heart, to judge by the way he galloped through the closely written lines:

> *This document concerns only those in whose veins my blood doth run, and who bear the ancient name of Dul. Let any such read these words with faith to believe and courage to obey, and to them will I grant the wish that lies most closely to their heart, be it for life beyond mortal span, for riches, for fame, or for the sweet delights of love. Let him who would seek my aid ask in the full knowledge that I, Count Dul, have power to give him his desire.*

> *For his part, he must most strictly observe such instructions as are writ hereafter, failing not in any particular. Let him take careful heed therefore to obey.*
> THE DEED MUST BE DONE UPON A CERTAIN NIGHT *and that the first night of a month of June when the moon is at the full between its second and third quarters.*
> I MUST BE SUMMONED BY ONE WHO STANDS BESIDE MY GRAVE *and in such words as are graven upon the inner side of the Box in which this document shall be discovered, together with the Book and my Heart.*
> AT THE FIRST LINE OF THE CONJURATION MY KINSMAN SHALL LIGHT A FLAME *and it shall be of oil poured out in a black bowl and set at the foot of the grave.*
> AT THE SECOND LINE HE SHALL SPRINKLE EARTH UPON THE GRAVE *and it shall be earth which fire has made bitter, and rain has washed, and the four winds blown upon.*
> AT THE THIRD LINE HE SHALL SET MY HEART AT THE HEAD OF THE GRAVE; *then, kneeling beside it, he shall cut his left hand until his blood drops from it upon the heart.*
> LASTLY HE SHALL SUMMON ME IN A LOUD VOICE AND PRONOUNCE HIS WISH. *And I shall hear him. And I will come to him. And whatsoever boon he asks, it shall be his.*

Rafe stopped reading as abruptly as he'd begun, and held out the paper. "You can read the Conjuration yourself. It's a bit melodramatic to declaim aloud just now."

I read in silence, then sat staring into the fire. The touch of the paper, its crabbed evil lettering and the hateful words themselves filled me with loathing.

"Well?" Rafe continued. "How's that for an ancestor? Jonquil's convinced that if I do my little song and dance he'll come rushing back from—well, this Book leaves no doubt from *where*—with a Present for a Good Boy under his ghostly arm."

"Yes, I'm convinced he would."

"Oh, John! You dear! You absolute darling!" cried Jonquil. "You *do* think there's something in it? You really and truly do! Oh, I'm thrilled. Rafe's been so exasperating about it. Now he'll simply *have* to give in."

"I didn't say that I agreed with you," I interrupted.

She sat up with a jerk, scattering cigarette ash over the satin iridescence of her dress. Black cold rage possessed me, brain and body. I knew I'd never make her understand—spoiled lovely little materialist that she was. Superstition urged her to snatch at this promised wealth. Ignorance blinded her to the hideous risk.

"You don't agree with me? You've just said you believed the Count could and would return!"

"Yes. I believe that."

"Well?" Her face grew radiant again. "Then you're just teasing! You *are* on my side, after all."

"No. Once and for all, I'm utterly against you. The man that wrote that promise and left behind him that foul thing"—I pointed to the box on the table—"must have been the devil's own brother."

"Oh-h-h!" wailed Jonquil. "You're not going to talk about demons and dangers and unholy powers, too! Rafe's been croaking like a raven for three whole days—and now you!"

"Go to it, old man!" urged Rafe. "She won't take it from me, but perhaps you can make her see it's not just money for jam."

I knew I couldn't move her, but I tried—explained, reasoned, argued, all to no purpose.

"It's no use trying to frighten me. You believe Count Dul can be brought back," she repeated for the twentieth time, "and that he could make Rafe a rich man. That's enough for me. He's only a ghost, poor thing! Perhaps he was just a harmless eccentric old man. Wouldn't make a will. Wanted to give it himself to his descendants."

"Harmless! What about that heart of his—beating two hundred years after his death? D'you think unaided human knowledge could leave *that* behind? Count Dul will surely return if the door is opened to him. But it's forbidden. The dead may not—*must* not return."

"I can't see why not. You don't actually know any more than I do myself. You've read a lot of stuffy books and believe everything in them. I haven't. I'm unprejudiced. I'm willing to take risks."

"You mean to let Rafe take them."

Rafe, who'd sat listening with a queer twisted smile, laughed out at this.

"Hear! Hear! Exactly. Is *she* to do a pantomime scene at midnight by the grave of a disreputable old nobleman? No! Is *she* to chat with a two-hundred year old devil-worshipper in the moonlight? No! Is *she* asked to shed her good red blood on a thing that looks like a bit of cat's meat? No!"

"Well, Rafe, darling! It probably *is* all nonsense and I'm tired of arguing about it. Still—"

She jumped up from the settee and stood before the fire, facing the two of us.

"John has helped me, after all." She dropped me a mocking curtsy. "Yes, you dear old Solomon! You've helped enormously. Now I feel absolutely certain there *is* something in it, or you wouldn't be so worried.

"You know, darling," she turned to Rafe, "you promised to be guided by John's opinion. He's given it. He completely believes in your ancestor. And so do I—now! I'll never forgive you if you don't take a chance and try this thing out."

"Jonquil!" I was on my feet now, almost incoherent with fury. "What I believe in is the risk—the damnable risk of trying such a thing. You only believe in the money you want and shut your eyes to anything else. D'you suppose for a moment that dead Thing has waited two centuries to give you a fortune?"

She burst out laughing. "John, if you could only see yourself! You look like one of the Minor Prophets in action! There's a picture in the National Gallery that exactly—"

"Rafe!" I was almost shouting now. "*You* know enough, if she doesn't, to realize the wicked insanity of doing such a thing. D'you remember Harland

and the sticky end he came to? And Browning who's gibbering away in an asylum? They happen to be men we know personally, but think of the hundreds of others who've been fools enough to think necromancy's a mere parlour game—who've deliberately walked into hell! It's hushed up—such cases always are. People are called mad, or reputed dead of heart attacks, etc. The truth is too beastly to publish."

"There's a good deal in what you say." Rafe had assumed a poise of amused detachment now. "I've not delved into occult lore as you have, old man. I dislike what I know, however. Still, Jonquil's attitude of 'nothing venture, nothing win' has a lot to recommend it."

She flew to him, took his hand in both her own.

"Oh! I knew, I *knew* you'd be an angel! You really mean to try it out?"

His answering look at her eager lovely face, his gesture as he rumpled her flaming aureole of hair, was sufficient for me. She'd won. My hot angry opposition had decided him, had pushed him into doing so. And I cursed myself for a pompous muddle-headed fool. I'd tilted the balance down—down to hell. If I'd kept calm and laughed at Count Dul, made light of the whole affair, Jonquil's belief might have faded. I'd lost my temper with her—lost my best chance by forcing Rafe to take her part...

My dream enveloped me in its swirling vapour... I was driving furiously down that long desolate valley—in the cloudy smothering darkness I heard a voice—Count Dul! Count Dul! Count Dul! The piercing cry was echoed by howls of laughter from the swirling mists—I drove on—on—someone needed me—someone I loved, needed me...

Sunday, May 29th. I spent a night of wretched anger and self-reproach and misery, interspersed with lapses into the haunting terror of my dream.

Rafe found me at eight a.m., empty pipe between my teeth, sitting on the stone parapet of a bridge, my thoughts dark and cold as the water I watched so gloomily.

"Not worth the usual penny, I can see!"

Rafe came to perch beside me.

"Still, there's some excuse for you. Enough to make anyone broody—my estate! Reminds me of the hymn, 'Change and decay in all around I see.'"

He patted me on the back.

"Cheer up, Jacko! And don't worry about the way things have turned out. This way—or another! What odds? I'm tremendously bucked up to have you here, and I'm bent on enjoying myself while I can. Forget Tuesday night—forget it! After all, you never know."

His look, his voice, his friendly touch cheered me. After all, as he said, one never *did* know! It was a relief to let myself be bluffed by his absurdly high spirits. Depression slipped off like a wet cloak as we tramped home for breakfast as carefree as if the pair of us had nothing more on our minds than a boat-race, or a thesis to be finished.

Jonquil appeared in high feather at the breakfast table—adorable with Rafe, mockingly sweet with me. And, of course, she scarcely talked of anything but Count Dul—how and when and where and what was going to happen about the wealth with which the family fortune was to be restored.

Rafe refused to be serious for even a moment about the B.G., as he called the Count. He was in the unreasoning fey mood that always seized him before any special test in our college days.

"I think the date's a mistake," he remarked. "The old boy meant April 1st."

I didn't remind him that the last night of May, this year, was peculiarly fitted for Count Dul's return. He knew considerably more than he acknowledged of ceremonial magic. It was unlikely that the significance of next Tuesday's date had escaped him. Together, as students, we'd read the Fourth Book of *Philosophia Occulta*, and the works of Pirus de Mirandola, and the *Grimoire* of Pope Honorius.

Above all, he'd read the book which Count Dul had left behind him. I'd borrowed and read it too, from cover to cover, and it was plain that Rafe's ancestor had, after many experimental essays, followed the teachings and practises of the infamous Lord of Corasse. These entailed observance of astronomy and, according to them, such a purpose as the return of the dead could only be accomplished at certain rare conjunctions of the stars and moon and planets. Rafe must be aware of these facts.

"Perhaps," Jonquil's face sparkled with excitement, "perhaps it will be priceless old jewellery he brought from Hungary. Count Dul was the first of your family to settle in England, wasn't he, Rafe?"

"He came because he was pushed," he replied. "They found he'd smuggled emeralds mined in the High Tatra Alps. He escaped from a particularly spectacular death connected with rope and four horses by a miracle—and, tradition records, by the aid of the devils he served."

"Emeralds!" breathed Jonquil, her eyes two deep pools of ecstasy. "How I adore emeralds! I shall keep the very most beautiful for myself, Rafe. You can sell the rest if I have just one perfect stone to wear."

"Certainly, Madam!"

He whipped out a notebook and pencil and assumed a businesslike air.

"Let me see, now! What size and colour does Madam prefer? I would not like to order something unsuitable. Oval, round, or square? Green or rose-red?"

"Rose-red," she took him up promptly. "A very very large square-cut stone set as a pendant with diamonds."

He licked his pencil and printed her order laboriously.

"You can take off that superior smirk, my child," he assured her. "There are such things as rose-red emeralds."

Their discussion went on to the end of the meal. Then she announced that we were all going to climb Hawes Fell.

"I've found a black bowl for the oil. All we need now is the earth."

"Earth! Climb up five hundred feet on a good Sabbath day of rest! Your breakfast has flown to your head, child. Think again—what about my untilled acres?"

"Doesn't it say the earth must be bitter with fire, and washed with rain, and blown on by the four winds? Very well, then. Wasn't there a heath-fire on Hawes Fell last month? It's as black as soot now and soaked in rain, and every wind in the world blows up there."

She'd made up her mind. It was to be earth from Hawes Fell, and the remainder of the day was spent in getting it.

Tuesday Night, May 31st. Tuesday morning—afternoon—night. At last, Tuesday night.

Rafe and I stood waiting for Jonquil in the library. It was after eleven p.m. In a few minutes we should set out across the fields to where Count Dul's grave lay. From the Book he'd left it was clear that in England, as in his own native country, the Count had been excommunicated by the Church and his body buried therefore in unconsecrated ground. It was Jonquil's indefatigable curiosity that had discovered the grave with its broken headstone in one of Rafe's outlying meadows. It was this initial discovery that had first determined her to carry out the remainder of the Book's instructions.

"Who actually found the metal box?" I asked now.

The constraint between Rafe and myself on this last day had made me desperate. He'd steadily avoided being alone with me until now, although I'd persistently sought such opportunity, for today Jonquil had, for the first time, weakened in her project.

Too obstinately proud to say outright she was afraid, she'd endeavoured in roundabout ways to get Rafe to change his mind. He'd refused to rise to her bait, brushed aside her every tentative move toward cancelling the date he'd determined to keep with his B.G.

But her wavering had given me a gleam of hope. Perhaps I might persuade him out of his insanely dangerous rendezvous even now. I felt sure Jonquil had given me this last chance to do so.

"Was it you who found the box?" I repeated.

He gave me a queer slanting look, half speculative, half sad.

"It found me," he laughed. "Slipped from the top of a bookshelf. I haven't the slightest recollection of seeing it in the house before. Never heard my father mention it. Must have been pushed out of sight somehow—it fell with a crash right at my feet and the Book and the B.G.'s heart rolled on the floor."

"Rafe! Don't go on with this. Even Jonquil doesn't want it now. You know—you surely know the risk. Why will you—"

He caught my eye, and changed colour. I saw he was trying to bring himself to answer me, and waited. He began to speak in quick, almost stammering words.

"Yes, I know the risk. I know, old man, but—I must go on now. It's been heaven—these last six months with Jonquil—heaven! But it can't last. We married in haste, but I'm damned if I'll let her 'repent at leisure.' It's a million to one I'll come through—with money, or without it, tonight, but—she'll remember I've tried."

"Rafe! You can't… you won't—"

"I will. It's easier to die than to lose her. I can face any hell but that."

"But she's going to—to lose you. And she's afraid of that now. She'd be glad—thankful if you gave up."

He smiled, as he'd smiled a thousand times when I'd missed some obvious point.

"Dear old chap! You don't know Jonquil. She's temperamental—just working up to the proper gooseflesh mood for tonight's orgy. No use, John! I'd never live it down if I failed her now. She's a child, an adorable child. I've had more than most men—and I'm choosing the easiest way out."

Jonquil's light step sounded on the uncarpeted old stairway.

"Ready?" her shining curls appeared round the door. "It's after eleven o'clock. We ought to start."

We went out to the great, echoing hall; our feet, on the old-fashioned red tiles, clanked dismally.

"This the picnic basket?" Rafe took up Count Dul's box from an oak chest. "Got the champagne and oysters, dear? Right! Let's start."

The night was cool, almost cold. Wind stirred in the treetops. Tall solemn elms on either side of the avenue whispered uneasily as we passed between their double ranks. Overhead a brilliant sky of stars, and a proud moon sailing in full majesty.

I wondered if any remote world up there was like the one I trod; if any other beings knew such bitterness and horror and evil as we did on our earth. I wondered if I could go on living here—alone, when Rafe—when Rafe—

Suddenly my dream blotted out moon, stars, and earth... I had reached the end of that awful valley—breathless, spent from long pursuit—before me a broken pathway descended to the lip of a yawning chasm. And along that path, walking with steady purposeful tread, a man's tall figure loomed. Rafe—it was Rafe! In agony I stumbled after him...

My dream blew like mist from across my vision. I was back in a country lane with Rafe and Jonquil, under the full moon's menace, the moon that would presently light Count Dul from hell.

"Here's our field-path." Jonquil turned aside to an old stile of flat stones laid with gaps between to keep cattle from crossing.

We followed her, cut across a field to another stile and across it to the desolate overgrown rocky bit of wasteland that was our objective. In another minute Jonquil stopped and pointed.

"There! There it is!"

The white merciless moon showed up every grass-blade and flower and stone of the hummock before us. Nature had flung a poisonous pall over the dead, and even the moon's glare could not blanch the blotched evil of henbane, viper's bugloss and deadly nightshade, or the scarlet-spotted fungus on Count Dul's grave. A cracked and sunken headstone leaned awry at the head of it. The worn lettering showed only a few words of whatever inscription had been cut two hundred years ago—COUNT DUL... DIED 1738... A WARNING TO ALL WHO READ...

Rafe looked at his watch, glanced up at the moon as it climbed to its fateful meridian. He'd doffed his armour once more. With mocking brilliant smile he looked down on the horrible grave and airily kissed his hand.

"Rafe!" Jonquil's brows went up in anxiety. "You *must* be serious."

"Darling! I'm sure the B.G. wouldn't like it. Think what a gay old dog he was in his time. Think how much he must have enjoyed himself to have tried for two centuries to get back again. Must make his little trip enjoyable, you know! About time I got to the front door to meet him. I suppose it's no use arguing any more—you won't go home?"

"For the hundredth time—no, dearest! You might take my rose-red emerald and run off with some other pretty lady."

She was looking up into his face and, even to my jaundiced eyes, was a sight to stir the blood of any man. For a second, Rafe's devil-may-care mask dropped, his dark burning eyes and drawn features showed such anguish that I started forward with a cry. This was my dream… his tall figure—so dear, so obstinate, so tragic—moving steadily onward to the edge of an abyss…

At once he recovered himself. Behind the brilliant smile he turned to me I read entreaty. He wanted me to take Jonquil away. He was in terror of what she would see and hear, in terror that she might be endangered too. But I knew also, and it was the only poor comfort I had left, that he wanted me—needed me as he and I always needed each other in a tight corner.

No one on earth—nor from hell—should move me from that graveside, and I confess I was glad that Jonquil should be there also. I wanted to spare her nothing.

I hoped if Rafe did not survive that she too would be destroyed.

I don't know how much of my thoughts he read, but in any case she wouldn't have left with me. He turned away, opened the metal casket, lifted out of it the withered pulsing heart and set it down at the head of the grave under the deeply sunken headstone.

My fascinated gaze was held by the horrible little thing. I saw it throb and quiver to the beat—beat—beat of whatever infernal power quickened life in it. I saw its dark withered walls gleam in the moonlight like tarnished copper.

At the other end of the grave, Rafe uprooted a clump of spotted henbane, set down a small black bowl and poured oil into it.

Jonquil's small hands clasped in excitement. She watched with dancing eyes, her curls ruffled about her eager flowerlike face.

Rafe glanced at his watch again, smiled once more at Jonquil. He didn't look toward me—I was thankful for it.

"Now for my old B.G. Stand back! Stand back, there!" he waved an imperious hand. "Make way for the Count Dul—make way—"

He took from his pocket the crackling parchment on which the conjuration was written, its black lettering very plain in the moonlight, ran his eye over it for the last time, although I was certain every word of it was stamped deep in his memory.

His voice rang out as I'd heard it ring on the playing-fields when we were boys together:

> *For your sightless eyes—this Flame!*

He stooped to set alight the oil in the black bowl.

> *For your fleshless bones—this Earth!*

He scattered dry dark soil from the basket.

> *For your withered heart—this Blood!*

He knelt, held out his left hand and slashed it with a knife until blood dripped upon the heart. Then he got swiftly to his feet. His loud voice challenged the dead:

> *Wake from your sleep, Count Dul!*
> *Rise from your grave, Count Dul!*
> *Return from the dead, Count Dul!*
> *Give me wealth—wealth for my boon!*

My body was turned to ice, my feet rooted to the ground, my whole being concentrated on Rafe's tall rigid figure standing at the graveside—at the mouth of hell.

His last word echoed and reverberated like an organ-note; louder—louder it swelled and boomed, until the quiet night hummed and quivered, and the poisonous grave-weeds slowly withered, blackened, lay in dust, until the earth beneath them cracked widely open and the burning oil shot up into a red roaring fire that was cold as wind off an ice-field and seemed to lick the stars.

It froze the tears on my cheek. It chilled even the unbearable anguish in my heart.

The heart—in the red name's brilliance—shone, incandescent, fiercely alive, then vanished.

In that moment the flame sank to earth again, the noise of its burning ceased—silence far more ominous fell, while overhead the great moon looked down in passionless survey.

The grave yawned widely open; from its void rose a wisp of dark smoke that turned and wreathed and twisted and coiled in ever denser volume as it swelled and blew and eddied to and fro above the gaping grave, blind, purposeless, uncertain. Then a nucleus formed in the vaporous evil, a dull purplish-red heart-shaped glowing core about which the dark mist swiftly formed and re-formed to a tall swaying pillar—an imperceptibly growing outline—a recognizable human body whose white face of damnation stared into Rafe's, whose awful rotted hands reached out to touch, to hold, to bind him fast.

And now I could not distinguish Rafe from the smothering infernal Thing itself. It swirled about him. It covered head and hands and feet from sight. When he moved, he moved within the enveloping darkness. When his face turned to me I saw only the dreadful livid face of the dead.

Still I was frozen there, unable to speak, to move, to do more than see and hear the Thing that now moved forward with fixed pale staring eyes and loose dark lips that mouthed and laughed and whispered as it came.

I could not turn to look at Jonquil. I felt her arms about me, clutching—I felt her warm soft body pressed to mine, her face against my cold and empty heart. I heard her long shrieks echoing above the thin dry whisper of the Thing that steadily advanced—nearer—nearer.

It halted beside us. Now I could see Rafe's tortured eyes, his face and form behind the clouded horror that enfolded him—he was shut up inside it like a chrysalis in a dark cocoon. He was Count Dul—Count Dul was Rafe!

Next moment Jonquil was plucked from my side. Her body was flung down on the dew-wet earth, her curls gleamed as two hands met about her throat, choking a last thin cry...

The Thing that killed her rose and moved back to the grave. Now I could see Rafe more distinctly beneath the wavering cloud of evil. His dreadful garment grew thin, and patchy, drifted from him, lost density and outline as it hovered over the open grave.

And the grave's darkness sucked it down out of sight, back to the hell from which it came.

The yawning hole closed up. The ugly weeds grew rank again upon the hummock. A sunken headstone leaned awry at its end.

In the same moment, I was released and ran stumbling over the long grass to where Rafe lay huddled.

A month later. Rafe was not dead. But he would have died—he *would* have died if that devil hadn't barred his way out!

By some infernal miracle, and after lying unconscious for a week, Rafe woke to full possession of his faculties. No memory was spared him of that fatal resurrection, or of Jonquil's unthinkable end.

He lives to remember it hour after hour, day after day, week after week.

For another two months his torture will endure. Then he will be hanged. That much is certain. He confessed to the murder of his wife and stands trial next week. He'll plead guilty and there'll be practically no defence. Neither he nor I mean to confess a word of the actual truth. It would condemn him to years and years of life as a criminal maniac—remembering—remembering...

A murderer—and a millionaire! Oh, yes! Count Dul kept his promise. A will turned up when the Chief Inspector of Police was going through Rafe's papers in the library—the thing toppled off a bookcase at the inspector's feet. It stated that the count had left a legacy buried in the cellars of *Braunfel*.

The police dug it up. Emeralds! An astounding collection which was photographed and written up in every rag in the country.

The finest gem was a great rose-red emerald, cut square and set with diamonds as a pendant.

I burned the Book and the Conjuration. I threw the metal box into Lake Derwent water. But I couldn't find the heart—I went over every inch of the grave and all round it.

Rafe takes this as a sign Count Dul's power is expended. I'm thankful that he doesn't understand.

I know that devil will return somehow—somewhere! Jonquil's death means life for him. Her will to live is added to his own.

When Rafe dies, he will look for her—and never find her. Never. She is one with the Count now, part of his thought, his will, his enduring evil.

Whether I can learn his secret, learn enough to meet him—and destroy him—I don't yet know.

When I am left alone, it will be all that remains worth doing in a world of fear and shadows.

MAY DAY EVE
Nick Joaquin

First published in Philippines Free Press (1947)

Nickomedes "Nick" Marquez Joaquin was born in May 1917 in Pacò, Manila. His father was an attorney and colonel of the Philippine Revolution, and his mother was a public school teacher. At ten he was given a library card for the National Library and discovered Stevenson, Dumas and Dickens. His father lost the family fortune and died not long after, when Nick was only twelve. He dropped out of Mapa High School and worked as an apprentice in a bakery in Pasay, and then as a printer's devil in the composing department of the *Tribune* newspaper. His first poem about Don Quixote was published in the *Tribune* in 1934, while his first short story, "The Sorrows of Vaudeville", was published in the *Sunday Tribune Magazine* in 1937. He continued to write during the war and on the other side of it wrote the stories that would define him, "Summer Solstice" and "May Day Eve". In 1950 he joined the *Philippines Free Press*, as a proofreader and copywriter, before becoming a staff writer and finally its literary editor and associate editor until 1970.

His first novel, *The Woman Who Had Two Navels*, was published in 1961. His other main role from 1961 to 1972 was his appointment to the Board of Censors for Motion Pictures. His love of films was a large part of who he was, and while there he did not cut or ban any films, believing in the intelligence of the moviegoers. In 1976 Joaquin was named National Artist of the Philippines, the highest recognition the state could give an artist. However, he tried to keep his distance from the state as much as possible. His second novel, *Cave and Shadows*, was published in 1983, and until 2000 he was a prominent biographer of famous Filipinos. He died of a heart attack at his home in San Juan in April 2004, aged eighty-six. In 2017, Penguin Classics published a collection of Nick Joaquin's stories as *The Woman Who Had Two Navels and Tales of the Tropical Gothic*.

THE old people had ordered that the dancing should stop at ten o'clock but it was almost midnight before the carriages came filing up to the front door, the servants running to and fro with torches to light the departing guests, while the girls who were staying were promptly herded upstairs to the bedrooms, the young men gathering around to wish them a good night and lamenting their ascent with mock sighs and moanings, proclaiming themselves disconsolate but straightway going off to finish the punch and the brandy though they were quite drunk already and simply bursting with wild spirits, merriment, arrogance and audacity, for they were young bucks newly arrived from Europe; the ball had been in their honour; and they had waltzed and polka-ed and bragged and swaggered and flirted all night and were in no mood to sleep yet—no, caramba, not on this moist tropic eve! Not on this mystic May eve!—with the night still young and so seductive that it was madness not to go out, not to go forth—and serenade the neighbours! cried one; and swim in the Pasig! cried another; and gather fireflies! cried a third—whereupon there arose a great clamour for coats and capes, for hats and canes and they were presently stumbling out among the medieval shadows of the foul street where a couple of street lamps flickered and a last carriage rattled away upon the cobbles while the blind black houses muttered hush-hush, their tiled roofs looming like sinister chessboards against a wild sky murky with clouds, save where an evil young moon prowled about in a corner or where a murderous wind whirled, whistling and whining, smelling now of the sea and now of the summer orchards and wafting unbearable childhood fragrances of ripe guavas to the young men trooping so uproariously down the street that the girls who were disrobing upstairs in the bedrooms scattered screaming to the windows, crowded giggling at the windows, but were soon sighing amorously over those young men bawling below; over those wicked young men and their handsome apparel, their proud flashing eyes, and their elegant moustaches so black and vivid in the moonlight that the girls were quite ravished with love, and began crying to one another how carefree were men but how awful to be a girl and what a horrid, horrid world it was, till old Anastasia plucked them off by the ear or the pigtail and chased them off to bed—while from up the street came the clackety-clack of the watchman's boots on the cobbles, and the clang-clang of his lantern against his knee, and the mighty roll of his great voice booming through the night: "*Guardia sereno-o-o! A las doce han dado-o-o!*"

And it was May again, said the old Anastasia. It was the first day of May and witches were abroad in the night, she said—for it was a night of divination, a night of lovers, and those who cared might peer in a mirror and would there behold the face of whoever it was they were fated to marry, said the old Anastasia as she hobbled about picking up the piled crinolines and folding up shawls and raking slippers to a corner while the girls climbing into the four great poster beds that overwhelmed the room began shrieking with terror, scrambling over each other and imploring the old woman not to frighten them.

"Enough, enough, Anastasia! We want to sleep!"

"Go scare the boys instead, you old witch!"

"She is not a witch, she is a maga. She was born on Christmas Eve!"

"St. Anastasia, virgin and martyr."

"Huh? Impossible! She has conquered seven husbands! Are you a virgin, Anastasia?"

"No, but I am seven times a martyr because of you girls!"

"Let her prophesy, let her prophesy! Whom will I marry, old gypsy? Come, tell me."

"You may learn in a mirror if you are not afraid."

"I am not afraid, I will go!" cried the young cousin Agueda, jumping up in bed.

"Girls, girls—we are making too much noise! My mother will hear and will come and pinch us all. Agueda, lie down! And you, Anastasia, I command you to shut your mouth and go away!"

"Your mother told me to stay here all night, my grand lady!"

"And I will not lie down!" cried the rebellious Agueda, leaping to the floor. "Stay, old woman. Tell me what I have to do."

"Tell her! Tell her!" chimed the other girls.

The old woman dropped the clothes she had gathered and approached and fixed her eyes on the girl. "You must take a candle," she instructed, "and go into a room that is dark and that has a mirror in it and you must be alone in the room. Go up to the mirror and close your eyes and say:

> *Mirror, mirror,*
> *show to me*
> *him whose woman*
> *I will be.*

If all goes right, just above your left shoulder will appear the face of the man you will marry."

A silence. Then: "And what if all does *not* go right?" asked Agueda.

"Ah, then the Lord have mercy on you!"

"Why?"

"Because you may see—*the Devil!*"

The girls screamed and clutched one another, shivering.

"But what nonsense!" cried Agueda. "This is the year 1847. There are no devils anymore!" Nevertheless she had turned pale. "But where could I go, huh? Yes, I know! Down to the sala. It has that big mirror and no one is there now."

"No, Agueda, no! It is a mortal sin! You will see the devil!"

"I do not care! I am not afraid! I will go!"

"Oh, you wicked girl! Oh, you mad girl!"

"If you do not come back to bed, Agueda, I will call my mother."

"And if you do I will tell her who came to visit you at the convent last March. Come, old woman—give me that candle. I go."

"Oh, girls—come and stop her! Take hold of her! Block the door!"

But Agueda had already slipped outside; was already tip-toeing across the hall; her feet bare and her dark hair falling down her shoulders and streaming in the wind as she fled down the stairs, the lighted candle sputtering in one hand while with the other she pulled up her white gown from her ankles.

She paused breathless in the doorway to the sala and her heart failed her. She tried to imagine the room filled again with lights, laughter, whirling couples, and the jolly jerky music of the fiddlers. But, oh, it was a dark den, a weird cavern, for the windows had been closed and the furniture stacked up against the walls. She crossed herself and stepped inside.

The mirror hung on the wall before her; a big antique mirror with a gold frame carved into leaves and flowers and mysterious curlicues. She saw herself approaching fearfully in it: a small white ghost that the darkness bodied forth—but not willingly, not completely, for her eyes and hair were so dark that the face approaching in the mirror seemed only a mask that floated forward; a bright mask with two holes gaping in it, blown forward by the white cloud of her gown. But when she stood before the mirror she lifted the candle level with her chin and the dead mask bloomed into her living face.

She closed her eyes and whispered the incantation. When she had finished such a terror took hold of her that she felt unable to move, unable to open her eyes, and thought she would stand there forever, enchanted. But she heard a step behind her, and a smothered giggle, and instantly opened her eyes.

"And what did you see, Mama? Oh, what was it?"

But Doña Agueda had forgotten the little girl on her lap: she was staring past the curly head nestling at her breast and seeing herself in the big mirror hanging in the room. It was the same room and the same mirror but the face she now saw in it was an old face—a hard, bitter, vengeful face, framed in greying hair, and so sadly altered, so sadly different from that other face like a white mask, that fresh young face like a pure mask that she had brought before this mirror one wild May Day midnight years and years ago...

"But what was it, Mama? Oh, please go on! What did you see?"

Doña Agueda looked down at her daughter but her face did not soften though her eyes filled with tears. "I saw the devil!" she said bitterly.

The child blanched. "The devil, Mama? Oh... *OH!*"

"Yes, my love. I opened my eyes and there in the mirror, smiling at me over my left shoulder, was the face of the devil."

"Oh, my poor little Mama! And were you very frightened?"

"You can imagine. And that is why good little girls do not look into mirrors except when their mothers tell them. You must stop this naughty habit, darling, of admiring yourself in every mirror you pass—or you may see something frightful some day."

"But the devil, Mama—what did he look like?"

"Well, let me see... He had curly hair and a scar on his cheek—"

"Like the scar of Papa?"

"Well, yes. But this of the devil was a scar of sin, while that of your Papa is a scar of honour. Or so he says."

"Go on about the devil."

"Well, he had moustaches."

"Like those of Papa?"

"Oh, no. Those of your Papa are dirty and greying and smell horribly of tobacco, while these of the devil were very black and elegant—oh, how elegant!"

"And did he have horns and a tail?"

The mother's lips curled. "Yes, he did! But, alas, I could not see them at that time. All I could see were his fine clothes, his flashing eyes, his curly hair and moustaches."

"And did he speak to you, Mama?"

"Yes... Yes, he spoke to me," said Doña Agueda. And bowing her greying head she wept.

"Charms like yours have no need for a candle, fair one," he had said, smiling at her in the mirror and stepping back to give her a low mocking bow. She had whirled around and glared at him and he had burst into laughter.

"But I remember you!" he cried. "You are Agueda, whom I left a mere infant and came home to find a tremendous beauty, and I danced a waltz with you but you would not give me the polka."

"Let me pass," she muttered fiercely, for he was barring her the way.

"But I want to dance the polka with you, fair one," he said.

So they stood before the mirror; their panting breath the only sound in the dark room; the candle shining between them and flinging their shadows to the wall. And young Badoy Montiya (who had crept home very drunk to pass out quietly in bed) suddenly found himself cold sober and very much awake and ready for anything. His eyes sparkled and the scar on his face gleamed scarlet.

"Let me pass!" she cried again, in a voice of fury, but he grasped her by the wrist.

"No," he smiled. "Not until we have danced."

"Go to the devil!"

"What a temper has my serrana!"

"I am not your serrana!"

"Whose, then? Someone I know? Someone I have offended grievously? Because you treat me, you treat all my friends like your mortal enemies."

"And why not?" she demanded, jerking her wrist away and flashing her teeth in his face. "Oh, how I detest you, you pompous young men! You go to Europe and you come back elegant lords and we poor girls are too tame to please you. We have no grace like the Parisiennes, we have no fire like the Sevillians, and we have no salt, no salt, no salt! Aie, how you weary me, how you bore me, you fastidious young men!"

"Come, come—how do you know about us?"

"I have heard you talking, I have heard you talking among yourselves, and I despise the pack of you!"

"But clearly you do not despise yourself, señorita. You come to admire your charms in the mirror even in the middle of the night!"

She turned livid and he had a moment of malicious satisfaction.

"I was not admiring myself, sir!"

"You were admiring the moon perhaps?"

"Oh!" she gasped, and burst into tears. The candle dropped from her hand and she covered her face and sobbed piteously. The candle had gone out and they stood in darkness, and young Badoy was conscience-stricken.

"Oh, do not cry, little one! Oh, please forgive me! Please do not cry! But what a brute I am! I was drunk, little one, I was drunk and knew not what I said."

He groped and found her hand and touched it to his lips. She shuddered in her white gown.

"Let me go," she moaned, and tugged feebly.

"No. Say you forgive me first. Say you forgive me, Agueda."

But instead she pulled his hand to her mouth and bit it—bit so sharply into the knuckles that he cried with pain and lashed out with his other hand—lashed out and hit the air, for she was gone, she had fled, and he heard the rustling of her skirts up the stairs as he furiously sucked his bleeding fingers.

Cruel thoughts raced through his head: he would go and tell his mother and make her turn the savage girl out of the house—or he would go himself to the girl's room and drag her out of bed and slap, slap, slap her silly face! But at the same time he was thinking that they were all going up to Antipolo in the morning and was already planning how he would manoeuvre himself into the same boat with her.

Oh, he would have his revenge, he would make her pay, that little harlot! She should suffer for this, he thought greedily, licking his bleeding knuckles. But—Judas!—what eyes she had! And what a pretty colour she turned when angry! He remembered her bare shoulders: gold in the candlelight and delicately furred. He saw the mobile insolence of her neck, and her taut breasts steady in the fluid gown. Son of a Turk, but she was quite enchanting! How could she think she had no fire or grace? And no salt? An arroba she had of it!

"No lack of salt in the chrism
At the moment of thy baptism!"

He sang aloud in the dark room and suddenly realized that he had fallen madly in love with her. He ached intensely to see her again—at once!—to touch her hand and her hair; to hear her harsh voice. He ran to the window and flung open the casements and the beauty of the night struck him back like a blow. It was May, it was summer, and he was young—young!—and deliriously in love. Such a happiness welled up within him the tears spurted from his eyes.

But he did not forgive her—no! He would still make her pay, he would still have his revenge, he thought viciously, and kissed his wounded fingers. But what a night it had been! "I will never forget this night!" he thought aloud in an awed voice, standing by the window in the dark room, the tears in his eyes and the wind in his hair and his bleeding knuckles pressed to his mouth.

But, alas, the heart forgets; the heart is distracted; and Maytime passes; summer ends; the storms break over the rot-ripe orchards and the heart grows old; while the hours, the days, the months, and the years pile up and pile up, till the mind becomes too crowded, too confused: dust gathers in it; cobwebs multiply; the walls darken and fall into ruin and decay; the memory perishes… and there came a time when Don Badoy Montiya walked home through a May Day midnight without remembering, without even caring to remember; being merely concerned in feeling his way across the street with his cane; his eyes having grown quite dim and his legs uncertain—for he was old; he was over sixty; he was a very stooped and shrivelled old man with white hair and moustaches, coming home from a secret meeting of conspirators; his mind still resounding with the speeches and his patriot heart still exultant as he picked his way up the steps to the front door and inside into the slumbering darkness of the house; wholly unconscious of the May night, till on his way down the hall, chancing to glance into the sala, he shuddered, he stopped, his blood ran cold—for he had seen a face in the mirror there—a ghostly candlelit face with the eyes closed and the lips moving, a face that he suddenly felt he had seen there before though it was a full minute before the lost memory came flowing, came tiding back, so overflooding the actual moment and so swiftly washing away the piled hours and days and months and years that he was left suddenly young again: he was a gay young buck again, lately come from Europe: he had been dancing all night: he was very drunk: he stopped in the doorway: he saw a face in the dark: he cried out… and the lad standing before the mirror (for it was a lad in a night gown) jumped with fright and almost dropped his candle, but looking around and seeing the old man, laughed out with relief and came running.

"Oh, Grandpa, how you frightened me!"

Don Badoy had turned very pale. "So it was you, you young bandit! And what is all this, hey? What are you doing down here at this hour?"

"Nothing, Grandpa. I was only… I am only…"

"Yes, you are the great Señor Only and how delighted I am to make your acquaintance, Señor Only! But if I break this cane on your head you may wish you were someone else, sir!"

"It was just foolishness, Grandpa. They told me I would see my wife."

"Wife? What wife?"

"Mine. The boys at school said I would see her if I looked in a mirror tonight and said:

> *Mirror, mirror,*
> *show to me*
> *her whose lover*
> *I will be.*"

Don Badoy cackled ruefully. He took the boy by the hair, pulled him along into the room, sat down on a chair, and drew the boy between his knees. "Now, put your candle down on the floor, son, and let us talk this over. So you want your wife already, hey? You want to see her in advance, hey? But do you know that these are wicked games and that wicked boys who play them are in danger of seeing horrors?"

"Well, the boys did warn me I might see a witch instead."

"Exactly! A witch so horrible you may die of fright. And she will bewitch you, she will torture you, she will eat your heart and drink your blood!"

"Oh, come now, Grandpa. This is 1890. There are no witches anymore."

"Oh-ho, my young Voltaire! And what if I tell you that I myself have seen a witch?"

"You? Where?"

"Right in this room and right in that mirror," said the old man, and his playful voice had turned savage.

"When, Grandpa?"

"Not so long ago. When I was a bit older than you. Oh, I was a vain fellow and though I was feeling very sick that night and merely wanted to lie down somewhere and die, I could not pass that doorway of course without stopping to see in the mirror what I looked like when dying. But when I poked my head in what should I see in the mirror but... but..."

"The witch?"

"Exactly!"

"And did she bewitch you, Grandpa?"

"She bewitched me and she tortured me. She ate my heart and drank my blood," said the old man bitterly.

"Oh, my poor little Grandpa! Why have you never told me! And was she very horrible?"

"Horrible? God, no—she was beautiful! She was the most beautiful creature I have ever seen! Her eyes were somewhat like yours but her hair was like black waters and her golden shoulders were bare. My God, she was enchanting! But I should have known—I should have known even then—the dark and fatal creature she was!"

A silence. Then: "What a horrid mirror this is, Grandpa," whispered the boy.

"What makes you say that, hey?"

"Well, you saw this witch in it. And Mama once told me that Grandma once told her that Grandma once saw the devil in this mirror. Was it of the scare that Grandma died?"

Don Badoy started. For a moment he had forgotten that she was dead, that she had perished—the poor Agueda; that they were at peace at last, the two of them, and her tired body at rest; her broken body set free at last from the brutal pranks of the earth—from the trap of a May night; from the snare of summer; from the terrible silver nets of the moon. She had been a mere heap of white hair and bones in the end: a whimpering withered consumptive, lashing out with her cruel tongue; her eyes like live coals; her face like ashes… Now, nothing!—nothing save a name on a stone; save a stone in a graveyard—nothing! nothing at all! was left of the young girl who had flamed so vividly in a mirror one wild May Day midnight, long, long ago.

And remembering how she had sobbed so piteously; remembering how she had bitten his hand and fled and how he had sung aloud in the dark room and surprised his heart in the instant of falling in love: such a grief tore up his throat and eyes that he felt ashamed before the boy; pushed the boy away; stood up and fumbled his way to the window; threw open the casements and looked out—looked out upon the medieval shadows of the foul street where a couple of street lamps flickered and a last carriage was rattling away upon the cobbles, while the blind black houses muttered hush-hush, their tiled roofs looming like sinister chessboards against a wild sky murky with clouds, save where an evil old moon prowled about in a corner or where a murderous wind whirled, whistling and whining, smelling now of the sea and now of the summer orchards and wafting unbearable Maytime memories of an old, old love to the old man shaking with sobs by the window; the bowed old man sobbing so bitterly at the window; the tears streaming down his cheeks and the wind in his hair and one hand pressed to his mouth while from up the street came the clackety-clack of the watchman's boots on the cobbles, and the clang-clang of his lantern against his knee, and the mighty roll of his great voice booming through the night: *"Guardia sereno-o-o! A las doce han dado-o-o!"*

THE SALE OF MIDSUMMER
Joan Aiken

First published in The Sixth Ghost Book, *edited by Rosemary Timperley (Barrie & Jenkins, 1970)*

Joan Aiken (1924–2004) was an English author and children's writer of over one hundred books. She was born in Rye to Pulitzer Prize-winning poet Conrad Aiken and mother Jessie MacDonald, who was also an author. Her father left home when Joan was very young and when she was five her mother remarried, to another writer, Martin Armstrong. By the age of seven Aiken was reading Edgar Allan Poe and at twelve she was sent to boarding school, where she discovered the two books that would influence her more than any other, *The Midnight Folk* and *The Box of Delights* by John Masefield. She found it difficult to make friends, so she immersed herself in her writing. At eighteen years old she had her first short story accepted for publication and a few years later she married Ronald Brown, a journalist with whom she had two children. Her first collection of stories, *All You've Ever Wanted*, was published by Jonathan Cape in 1953, followed by the companion collection *More Than You Bargained For* in 1955. Her first novel (one that she wrote when she was seventeen), *The Kingdom and the Cave*, was published in 1960. Her second novel and the book for which she would become famous (and still the one most remembered for), *The Wolves of Willoughby Chase*, was started in 1952, but had to be put aside when her husband became gravely ill. He died in 1955, and Joan took on a job as an editor at *Argosy*, then at the advertiser J. Walter Thompson to keep a roof over her family's head.

Her story "Jugged Hare" was published in the inaugural *Pan Book of Horror Stories* in 1959. *Wolves* was finally published in 1962. The instant success of the book meant that she could give up her job in advertising and dedicate her life to writing full time. Her debut (and in this humble editor's eyes, greatest) collection, *The Windscreen Weepers and Other Tales of Horror and Suspense*, was published in 1969. In the same year her novel *The Whispering Mountain* won the Guardian Children's Book Award and in 1972 she won an Edgar Allan Poe award for her Cornish-set novel *Night Fall*. In 1982 she wrote a "how to" guidebook for young adults wanting to become authors called *The Way to Write for Children*. In 1976 she married the American painter Julius Goldstein (d. 2001). Later work saw her write a sequel to Jane Austen's *Mansfield Park* and complete an unfinished Jane Austen work, *The Watsons and Emma Watson*.

In 1999 she was awarded an MBE for services to children's literature. Joan died at home aged seventy-nine and a memorial service for her was held at St. James's Church, Piccadilly on 13 May 2004. Regarding her thoughts on the supernatural she had this to say: "I don't think I'd be scared of the supernatural, but then I have never really encountered it. I think I would be more interested than scared if I did."

"The Sale of Midsummer" is sublime and sees Aiken at her evocative best. The chance to include her work thrills me. It's also a dream of mine to one day edit her complete supernatural works. In this classic tale the village of Midsummer is up for sale. But what truth is there to the legend that there's a version of Midsummer that exists for only three days each year?

THE van, which was labelled Modway Television, chugged up a long, steep hill, slipped thankfully into top, and ran down through fringes of beechwood bordering a small star-shaped valley which lay sunk in the top of the downs. Presently the trees ended and sunny curves of cowslip-studded grass began; ahead, clustered elms half revealed a few grey stone roofs.

"This ought to be it," Andrew said, looking at his map. "There's a village green; that'd be the best place to leave the van. I'll take the mike and you take the camera, Tod, and we'll wander."

"What shall I do?" asked Bill, the van driver.

"Find the pub and get their recipe for cowslip wine. It's a speciality of the place."

"That'll suit me fine."

Among the elms grouped in pairs through the village there were also lime-trees, and the scent of lime-blossom plus cowslip meadow was almost overpowering. The village drowsed in it; a solitary dog barked, a cuckoo called, nobody was about in the street or on the green.

"Quiet sort of place," Bill said, mopping his forehead. He parked the van on the grass verge and walked off towards the inn, The Fan-tailed Pheasant, pausing incredulously to stare at the sign. It depicted a pheasant with a most improbable tail, two feathers curved like a pair of washing-tongs.

Andrew picked up his microphone and looked about for material. A rhythmic thudding drew his eyes in the direction of a low wall. Beyond it lay a paddock shaded by walnut trees where a girl in shirt and jeans was schooling a pony. When the two men approached a wicket gate in the wall and stood by it, the rider trotted towards them inquiringly.

"Very photogenic," murmured Tod, as his camera whirred. The girl was black-haired and her grey eyes seemed to reflect all the light from the sky; she was rather pale and had a long, graceful neck. "Can I do something for you gentlemen?" she asked, dismounting.

"Excuse our troubling you—is this Midsummer Village?" Andrew asked.

"Certainly. Where else could it be?"

"You live here?"

"All my life, of course."

"Do you know that the village is up for sale, that the Trust which owns it is obliged to raise money by selling off this parcel of land?"

"Of course. Everybody in the village knows."

"And that the highest bid has come from Carrock, the millionaire, who has announced his intention, if he gets it, of turning it into a garden city?"

"Yes?" Her luminous eyes turned each of her responses to a question.

"Are you at all perturbed about this?" Andrew asked, slightly impatient at her lack of reaction.

"Perturbed." She turned the word over in her mind. "If I were at all perturbed," she said at last, "it would be for the man—Carrock. He is trying to buy a dream. He is bound to be disappointed."

Her pony tossed its head and snorted. She dropped the reins on its neck and let it go free.

"Of course you are familiar with the legend of Midsummer Village—that it is so beautiful it exists for only three days each year?"

"You were lucky in picking your day to come here, weren't you?" she said, and smiled slightly. He heard a little grunt of satisfaction, or anguish, from Tod with the camera.

"There must be some tale in the village to account for this belief?" Andrew said. "Can you tell us?"

She leaned against the wall, twirling a walnut leaf.

"Certainly. It originated in the eighteenth century when Morpurgo, the Poet Laureate, came to live here. He had been a fine poet, but by the time he became Laureate he was an old man. He slept all the year round and woke only for three days in the summer to compose an ode for the Queen's birthday and earn his tun of wine. He had been crossed in love—in his youth he wanted to marry a beautiful girl called Laura who was so devoted to her twin brother that she had sworn she would never take a husband. Some say Morpurgo slept all year to forget his unappeasable grief. He was struck by lightning one summer day in his garden and died in his sleep."

"Did he never marry?"

"Oh yes, he married," the girl said rather scornfully. "He married a woman called Edith, a farmer's daughter thirty years younger than himself. As she had a smattering of witchcraft—nearly everyone knew a bit about it in those days—the tale goes that she put a spell on the whole place, that it should come alive only for three days every summer while Morpurgo was awake, writing his poem."

"Sleeping Beauty stuff," Tod muttered.

"And that is the legend of Midsummer Village?"

"That's the legend," the girl said, twirling her leaf. Then she threw it aside and clucked to the pony, which came to her willingly.

"Well, thank you very much," Andrew said, and they left her to her schooling, though both men looked back at her several times.

"Now who?" said Tod.

"Here's an old boy; looks like the Squire."

An elderly man, upright, tall, and grey-headed, was approaching them.

"Might I trouble you for a few moments, sir?" Andrew inquired.

"By all means," said the man, though he gazed with a certain dislike at the camera and microphone.

"It's about this sale of Midsummer Village—have you any views on the matter, sir?"

"Naturally I have views," the elderly man said disdainfully, "though I doubt if they are of interest to the community at large. If this person, Carrock, who has the impertinent intention of buying our home, should care to pay us the common courtesy of a visit before completing his purchase, I shall be delighted to give him my views."

"Of course you are familiar with the legend of Midsummer Village?"

"Of course I am," the man said more graciously. "I shall relate it to you. It concerns a beautiful girl, the daughter of a farmer here in the valley. Both her parents died when she was in her teens and she ran the farm single-handed."

"When did all this take place, excuse me, sir?"

"In the reign of Henry VIII. The girl, Edith, her name was, made a success of the farm. Her neighbours said the ghost of her father drifted beside her constantly, advising and instructing. No doubt he felt it was the least he could do, as he had made her promise not to marry."

"Why?"

"He came of a very old family, descended from the Danes, and he couldn't bear that the last of the line should change her name. He held her to her promise, though she was in love with a young man in the village. You can't argue with a ghost. She stayed single. She was famous for her butter and eggs, and her fine pigs and her cowslip wine. In any case it is doubtful if the man would have married her—he was considerably above her in birth and had a twin sister to whom he was very devoted."

"What became of the farmer's daughter?"

"In the end, oddly enough, a man came to live in the village who bore the same name as her father—and so, though she didn't love this man, she married him."

"Was he a poet?"

"I am hardly qualified to pronounce on that," the elderly man said fastidiously. "On her deathbed, after many years of married life—she was struck by lightning one summer day and died shortly after—it is said that Edith cried out, 'I have been alive only on three days in my life: the day I met him, the day he kissed me, and the day I lost him.' She was not referring to her husband. Since then, according to legend, the village exists for three days only in every year." He looked round complacently at the lichened roofs and the towering elms. Grey cloud had begun to cover the sky but on the village the sunlight still lay like concentrated gold.

"That's a most interesting tale, thank you, sir," Andrew said. The elderly man inclined his head slightly as they moved off with their equipment, and then he took a notebook from his pocket and strolled away, writing in it.

"Now who?" said Tod.

A woman was coming towards them. She carried a large basket of cowslips and their colour was reflected in her massive coil of yellow hair.

She smiled at them in a friendly way and asked if she could help them, in a voice soothing and agreeable as the warmth from a baker's oven.

"We wondered if you'd care to give us your views on the sale of Midsummer Village?" Andrew said.

"Well, yon Carrock's on a fool's errand, isn't he?" she said, and laughed.

"Are you familiar with the legend of the village?"

"Of course," she said. "We're all brought up on it. My father used to tell it to me when I was a little thing. There was this young chap, Samuel Cutaway, oh, way back in the time of Henry the Seventh. He was to have been a monk but they dissolved the monasteries. Samuel fell in love with a farmer's daughter but she hadn't any time for him. On account of this he went voyaging off with some of those early explorers and came back at the end of seven years with a pocket full of gold and a foreign bird. He became parish priest of the village here. He was a philosopher, he used to write essays. When he first heard the bird, in Africa it was or maybe Australia, the song of it so bewitched him that he said while a man was listening to it he could explain the whole riddle of the universe. He brought the bird back with him. Some say it was a lyre bird, others a hoopoe."

"So did he explain the riddle of the universe?"

"He never got the chance," she said laughing. "The bird wouldn't sing in this cold climate, or only for the three hottest days every summer. Samuel took to drink, a gallon of cowslip wine every day in memory of the farmer's daughter who'd slighted him. And with every glass he drank he declared he would have been the greatest mind of his age if only the bird could be made to sing all the year round. So they say the village only exists now on the three days in summer when the bird would sing and he was listening to it and finding his answer to the riddle of the universe. If you'll excuse me, gentlemen, I must leave you now. I have to meet a friend."

"Thank you for your story," Andrew called after her as she hurried away.

"Here's the vicar," Tod muttered in his ear. "He's sure to be full of opinions."

The vicar was a spare-looking man with a thin mouth, who gazed at them in faint disapproval while Andrew explained the reason for their presence.

"Have you any views on the sale of Midsummer Village, sir?"

"I? Views? Certainly. The Trust have no right to sell Carrock has no right to buy. You should not sell times, or lives, or seasons."

"And the legend of the village—you know it, sir?"

"Naturally. It concerns a brother and sister who lived here in the reign of Charles the First."

"Twins?"

"Yes, twins. You know the tale?" the vicar said sharply.

But Andrew merely looked attentive, and so the vicar told his story.

"This pair, Laura and Esmond Fitzroy, were so devoted to one another that they swore never to marry. But Esmond had a scientific bent and became more and more engrossed in studies until at last he retired to live in a tower—you may see it over there—" The vicar gestured towards a crumbling grey ruin among the beech woods. "His was a mind far in advance of his age. He achieved early discoveries in the uses of electricity, could make copper wires glow by magic, according to contemporary reports, and had a metal mast affixed to the roof of his tower, down which he received mysterious messages from celestial regions. The sister became jealous because he neglected her for his research—she was not intelligent, poor thing, merely had a talent for taming animals—so she put it about that he was in league with the devil. The villagers besieged him in his tower. He kept them at bay for three days—during which time he said he was receiving messages from on high telling him how to preserve the village for ever—and before they managed to drag him out there was a violent storm and the tower was hit by lightning. Esmond was killed and everybody said it was a judgment."

"What became of the sister? You said her name was Laura?"

"Oh, she married." The vicar dismissed her with brief contempt. "The legend goes that, out of revenge for his sister's betrayal, Esmond caused the village to disappear, and return for three days only each summer."

"That is extremely interesting, and thank you, sir," Andrew said.

"Glad to be of service." The vicar gave Andrew his card which was inscribed, The Rev S. E. Cutaway.

They left him and went along to drink cowslip wine at The Fan-tailed Pheasant where Bill was already enwreathed in more than a breathalyser's bouquet.

Coming out half an hour later they saw the fair-haired woman whom they had already met strolling towards them, deep in conversation with a man in postman's uniform. She waved to them and, when they were within speaking distance, called:

"I forgot to tell you that he married."

"Who did? The philosopher with the singing bird?"

"Yes. He married, late in life, a girl who became so annoyed with his excuse of not being able to write unless the bird was singing that she swore she'd train it to sing all the time. She did, too. She had a way with animals."

"I suppose she also had a twin brother who died?"

"That's right, love. Well, I must be getting along to make my hubby's dinner. Goodbye, Esmond dear," said the fair-haired woman. She smiled at the postman and they kissed; she walked swiftly through a pair of large iron gates leading to a house among trees.

"And do you believe that this village exists on three days only each summer?" Andrew asked.

The postman, who was young and black-haired, grinned at him mockingly.

"I'd have an easy job if that were so, wouldn't I?" he said.

"But what do you think?"

"I'm not paid to think. I finished with thinking a long time ago."

With a casual flip of his hand the postman walked off towards a small combined village store and sub-post-office.

"Well? What did my brother have to say?"

Andrew turned at the voice and saw the girl they had interviewed first.

"Have they told you some good stories?" she asked teasingly "Shall you have to come back, do you think?"

"I—I'd like to," Andrew began uncertainly.

"Next time you come I'll show you my house, and my pets. But you have to pick your day, remember! Now I must hurry—there's going to be a storm."

"She's right," Tod said when she left them. "We'd best load up quick."

Andrew turned to look at the girl, who was entering a gate halfway along the village street. She waved her hand.

"Careful with the driving, Bill," Tod said. "You're on the wrong side."

"Someone's greased the steering," Bill grumbled. "Listen! Don't they half have some songbirds in this village! What's that—a nightingale?"

"They sing louder when there's a storm on the way."

The van wove precariously along the village.

They were about half a mile beyond the last house, entering the beech-woods, when lightning struck the bonnet.

When Andrew next opened his eyes, he was in a hospital bed, with a drip-feed attached to his arm.

"Are the others all right?" he asked, as soon as he was able to speak.

"Shock and concussion, that's all. You were all three lucky, considering the state of the van. Now, here's your father to see you, Mr. Carrock—but he mustn't stay more than a few moments."

His father looked, as usual, prosperous, portly, and puzzled.

"Can't think why you have to gad about the country doing this ridiculous TV job," he grumbled. "If only you'd settle down and help me with

THE SALE OF MIDSUMMER

the business, this kind of thing wouldn't happen. What's the matter with you—can't I give you everything you could possibly want?"

"Not quite," Andrew said, and smiled at his father weakly. "Listen, father—about that village you want to buy—can't I persuade you to change your mind?"

"Why?"

"It isn't the sort of place that ought to be bought."

"Matter of fact," said his father, "I don't need any persuading. Went to take a look at it—nothing there but a dip in the downs, some fields and a lot of sheep. No houses. Not even ruins! Godforsaken spot. Forgotten all about it till you brought it up. Now, make haste and get better, my boy."

He gave his son an awkward, affectionate pat, and hurried out.

Andrew lay thinking about a pair of luminous grey eyes.

"I wonder which story was the true one?" he mused. "I must ask Tod what he thinks."

But Tod and Bill had no theories to offer. Shock and concussion had taken away their memory of all events before the crash, and both of them persisted in declaring that they had never discovered the village at all.

NIGHT ON ROUGHTOR
Donald R. Rawe

First published in Haunted Cornwall, *edited by*
Denys Val Baker (William Kimber, 1973)

Donald Ryley Rawe (1930–2018) was a Cornish publisher, dramatist, novelist and poet. Born in Padstow in 1930, he became a member of Gorseth Kernow in 1970, under the Bardic name of *Scryfer Lanwednoc* ("Writer of Padstow"). A letter by him, published in the *Cornish Guardian* in 1970, saw him defend the language and insist that nobody was trying to impose learning the language on those that lived there, but that it should be an optional subject in Cornish schools. This was, in his words, "an innocuous proposal by any standards".* He was a founding member of the Cornwall Heritage Trust and became Member Emeritus in 2011. His first genre story was "Night on Roughtor", published in *Haunted Cornwall* edited by Denys Val Baker (1973), followed by "In Killigarrek Wood" in *Cornish Ghost Stories*, again edited by Baker (1981). His next genre stories would not see publication until his debut collection, *Haunted Landscapes* (1994), through his Lodenek Press which he founded in 1970. In his biography he states that he had been writing ghost stories since he was nineteen. Other books Rawe self-published through Lodenek are *Padstow's Obby Oss and May Day Festivities: A Study in Folklore and Tradition* (1971) and *Cornish Hauntings and Happenings* (1984). He lived most of his life on the North Coast of Scotland and died in 2018, at the age of 87.

---

* "The Cornish Language", *Cornish Guardian*, 17 November 1970.

THREE young men from one of the most venerated universities came up the steep hill road from Trebarwith Strand. They carried towels and swimtrunks and their long hair was damp and uncombed. One smoked a heavypipe with a bowl like a small incinerator; one had a bushy ginger moustache and sideboards. The third, a dark intellectual with steel-rimmed spectacles, wore a denim shirt and cap. June bloomed benevolently round them, fresh from their finals. Thick-fingered membryanthemum hung from walls and rock-faces, and on the deep valley slope were the minute balloons of birdsfoot trefoil, yellow, and orange and shrivelling red. Viper's bugloss reared bold blue spires lower down.

"The next question is," said Browne-Smythe in his lazy cultured tones, "where do we go from here?"

"I suppose it'll have to be camping," said de Vere Ellis, viewing the scene through his glasses. "Not that I'm enthusiastic; the Cornish summer's likely to turn damp when you least want it to…"

"But where do we camp?" said Browne-Smythe, puffing slightly through his moustache. "Come on, Mac; you know the place."

"Thus speaketh the psychologist," remarked McMahon, taking the huge pipe from his mouth. "He must know where we're going. My dear chap, don't you ever feel like taking pot luck? Why not just load up the old jalopy and pitch tent wherever we get to at nightfall?"

"Any chance of camping here in the garden—or would your family object?" asked de Vere Ellis.

"Not a hope," said McMahon. "My old man's the trouble; wants it peaceful when he brings this dear old tycoon down. Sir Geoffrey Pomphrett, Bart. About ninety, as far as I can gather. Don't suppose the old boy would care, but fathers of my generation are a bit down on denims and long hair, the sort of thing."

They turned in at the gate of the villa, spread their towels and costumes out on the privet and azalea bushes to dry, and went inside.

"What time's the family comin', Mr. McMahon?" asked the woman who was sweeping out the hall and porch.

"Oh, any time after tea. About seven, perhaps," said McMahon.

"Ah well," she said, "better go up an air the beds, I s'pose."

McMahon looked at his watch.

"Half past twelve," he murmured. "What's for lunch, Mrs. Tregellas?"

"Pasties," she said as she stooped down with the pan brushing dust into it.

"Ha!" cried de Vere Ellis in his best mock-Cornish accent, "Carnish Pasties, eh? Ess, me dear, tull do."

"Not for half-hour yet, though," said the housekeeper, unamused. "They beds d'come first."

The three wandered into the lounge and amused themselves drinking beer and playing gramophone records. They had the latest hit, in which an ecstatic pop-star yelled:

> Oh darling, oh sweetest,
> My life, my all completest,
> Whatll I do without you,
> Whatll I do without you?

to an accompaniment of wailing electric guitars and shrieking trombones.

When they sat down to the meal and, with knives and forks, had consumed pasties, Browne-Smythe suddenly said to Mrs. Tregellas as she cleared away the plates, "Where would you suggest we go to camp for tonight?"

She stopped and said, "Dunno, I'm sure. Never go camping meself."

"No," said Browne-Smythe. "But what about the moors?"

"Aw, no," said Mrs. Tregellas "Not there. I wudden go there for the golden calf hisself. Not tonight, anyway."

"Oh; how's that?"

"Well, 'tis dangerous for one thing. All they marshes and holes. An besides, 'tis Midsummer's Eve."

"Come, Mrs. Tregellas," smiled McMahon. "You aren't superstitious, are you?"

"No," she said, "not more than anybody else is round here. I dun't take no account of talk about piskies an giants an ghosts, but I wudden walk through the churchyard at midnight, not fer nobody: an I wudden go up on the moors, an specially not near Roughtor on Midsummer night. Call me simple an mazed if you like—but I wudden do it, I tell ee; an if you go an do it, you'm very silly."

De Vere Ellis, who was a physicist and subscribed to those theories which explain everything in material terms, was interested.

"It's merely a question of fear," he said. "Your reason tells you that there's nothing in these stories of the supernatural; it's only your unreasonable subconscious self that makes you afraid of these things, as our professor of psychology—indicating Browne-Smythe—will tell you."

"Just one of the lingering hereditary animal instincts that are in process of disappearing, Mrs. Tregellas," Browne-Smythe assured her with faint amusement.

"Quite," went on de Vere Ellis. "We know a little too much about the subject to fear it. There's never been any ghost that couldn't be explained quite simply and reasonably. Personally, I rather enjoy disobeying superstitions; though I never walk under a ladder at any price. I once got a pot paint down my neck... Is Roughtor a hill?

"Ess," said Mrs. Tregellas. "You can see it if you walk up on to the high ground up by Lob's Cot. But if you got any ideas about camping there tonight you better put em right out of yer head. Tis dangerous, I tell ee."

"If Roughtor's only a hill, Mrs. Tregellas," said McMahon, "it must be easy to climb. It'll be a fine night: the weather forecast is good, and there's an anticyclone just now."

"No," she said folding her arms, "I dun't like it. I dun't like it wan bit."

She stared out of the window to where between the roofs of other villas there were glimpses of leaning cliff, and Gull Rock a quarter of a mile out in the torpid sheen of Atlantic waters.

"Tis no place for you," she said. "What about they Jacky Lanterns?"

"Just marsh gas," said McMahon. "Burning methane. We shan't be fooled by them any more than by Tregeagle himself."

"Who's Tregeagle?" Browne-Smythe asked, fingering his red moustache delicately.

"Oh, a giant ghost the Cornish say runs wild on the moors, shrieking and yelling—or something of the kind. Is that right, Mrs. Tregellas?"

"So the story do go," she said. "But he dun't run wild as a rule—he've got tasks to do, like baling out Dozmary Pool with a limpet shell. They put un out here on the Strand once, so they say, to bind sand into sheaves. He managed it by wetting em with water on a winters night so they froze. He's ony s'posed to run wild when he do disobey the devil. Then the hell hounds come after un. But tis ony the wind an storm really, I spose."

"Of course, of course," said de Vere Ellis as he folded his napkin.

"Still, I dun't think tis right for you three young gentlemen to go up there. Is it Roughtor you'm thinking about? Cause if tis, well all I can say is you'm all three of you furriners when it come to the point, and where none of our crowd ud set there foot after sundown you certainly never ought to. Besides, Roughtor do mean something to we people, and some ud call it near sacriledge for you to camp there."

McMahon got up, smiling. "You Cornish are all the same: living in the past, born with your heads looking over your shoulders. All these legends and mysteries are all very picturesque, but they won't get you anywhere. I consider it'll be a bit of a lark to pitch camp on Roughtor on Midsummer Night. Anyway you needn't worry, Mrs. Tregellas: my grandmother was Cornish, so I'm entitled to play the host and entertain friends, even on the holy of holies."

McMahon's father was half-Cornish, half Irish. His mother was French. He called himself an Englishman.

"Huh! A fat lot you knaw about legends, Mr. McMahon, being away up country all the year. As for whether theyll get us anywhere, well praps they wunt. P'raps we dunt want to get anywhere. Cornwall's good enough for me; tis good enough for half London in summer, seemin'ly. When my old grandmother was dying up to Tavistock they said to her, 'Well Mrs. Pengelly, you'm going to a better land'. An she looked up an said, 'Ess, theres no place like Cornwall.'"

She smiled and then went on seriously.

"But I bain't joking about Roughtor. Sneer about the past if you like; but once you get up there you'm going to find whats past idn so dead after all. Thass where tis; now go an do what you like: I been yammering here too long. Let me get on with they dishes."

Gathering up the pile of plates she marched out with the dignity of a duty done.

It was about half-past seven when they set off for Roughtor, the old Morris groaning up the hill with the weight of baggage and three university rugby forwards. At the wheel McMahon smoked placidly, the great pipe pushed out of the corner of his mouth so that it should not obscure his view. Browne-Smythe sat beside him and in the back seat de Vere Ellis held steady a rickety camp stove which threatened to discharge paraffin if allowed to move off its balance.

  Oh darling, oh sweetest,
  My life, my all completest

mooed Browne-Smythe.

"Bi-dah-bih-dah-bi-doop," supported de Vere Ellis tattooing on the stove with a spoon. "Bi-doom-doom-blah-ah-ah!"

They had the sliding roof back and the breeze never absent from the moors came flapping in. As they reached the level high ground—McMahon wrenching the gear lever producing a grinding cry from the engine—a few other cars passed them, their windscreens flashing red in the lowering sun. Down into grey narrow Camelford they went, and beyond through valleys and up hills until the road ended abruptly at a gate opening on to the moors. On the other side of the shallow valley was Roughtor with its crest broken, jagged like the backbone of a skeleton saurian.

They got out and unloaded. McMahon locked the car doors, lifted the bonnet and dismantled the petrol lead. He put it in his knapsack and shut the flange. They could not carry everything at once, so leaving Browne-Smythe stretched out on the turf guarding the gear—although there was nobody nearer than the farm a mile away—the others started off.

They reached the bottom of the valley and crossed the little bridge over the stream. Suddenly McMahon stopped.

"Hullo! What's that?"

"You mean that rumbling?"

"Yes. There's no railway line around here, is there?"

De Vere Ellis hauled out the Ordnance Survey map from the pocket of his large sheepskin jacket.

"No," he said.

They stood still, the sound rushing and eddying round them. It appeared to come from farther up the valley, so they walked a hundred yards up towards it. There they found the stream plunging over a waterfall into a narrow deep pool, a small pot-hole. This must they thought be the source of the noise; there was no other explanation. Yet as they stood there twenty yards from it across the bog they could not say with conviction that it was definitely the cause; for the rumbling swirled round them enveloping the place, coming on them from all sides, hollow and uncanny.

"Hm," grunted de Vere Ellis, and scratched his head.

"Come on," said McMahon, almost as if he were glad to go and wanted to forget it.

They climbed stolidly up the hillside, the loud burbling receding below them. The grass of the lower slopes gave way to ankle deep bracken and ling. It took them half an hour to reach the top.

Great boulders of granite and grey basalt crowded the peak. They looked for a sheltered place, but there seemed to be none. Cold evening wind hurtled across, singing between stones. They climbed across to the eastern side where they found a rock shoulder with a small cave hollowed out on the leeward side; here it was calm like the still centre in a whirlpool. This was the place to pitch the tent. They had some difficulty in wedging the poles into the rocky soil, but with exertion they succeeded.

De Vere Ellis went back to help Browne-Smythe up with the remaining gear. Left alone McMahon secured the tent. He hammered in pegs, fixed guy ropes, laid out groundsheets inside and took in all the tins and apparatus they had brought. He tried to dig a rain trench round the tent but could not manage it. Then he took a long thick peagreen scarf from his haversack, a pair of binoculars, and wandered around the summit. It was nearly dusk and the sun was going behind another tor to the west, throwing it into bold black relief.

Below him shadows were lengthening second by second, creeping across moor and marsh and up the sides of hills like vast grey ghosts. Standing on the brow overlooking the precipitous south end, he could see vague stone pillars set in a circle immediately beneath. In daylight no doubt they would look mundane enough, but here in twilight their very vagueness seemed to promise life: at any moment they might begin to shuffle and dance. A half-forgotten tale about maidens changed into stones for dancing on the Sabbath came back to him.

Westwards there was a white hill, a china claytip which by its incongruity attracted his attention. Perhaps it was a mile off, but he could not say because at every second it seemed to be at a different distance away. It was a hill without roots or foundations; a hill that lurked and loomed, having no fixed place for its being. He found it disturbingly easy to imagine it approaching, stealing nearer and then slipping away among the other tors, all fast losing their identities in the gloom.

He looked across to his left and regarded Brown Willy, the other twin Cornish mountain. It was supposed to be higher than Roughtor, but it seemed not as tall; it sprawled loosely and carelessly against the blue night, less forceful than Roughtor and more welcome. McMahon found himself wishing they had chosen it for camping site instead.

Roughtor itself, he saw, was a place to reckon with. All around him were stones erected in illogical but natural positions by men in the lost past. He found the Logan Rock, a great flat mushroom cap of stone balanced on a much smaller rock: balanced with such precision that he could rock it unaided though it had withstood aeons of wind and storm. Like all the other rocks on this precipice it was worn smooth, rutted and grooved by centuries of west wind. Roughtor was ageless, barbaric, primitive; yet primitive in a positive sense, because it possessed the elements of a civilization—although one alien and opposed to his own.

Now conflicting thoughts came to him unreasonably and without his summoning them. It was as though he stood now on the rock of eternity, and mere time was below him: in this sudden elevation of his historical perspective the millennia ago that the ancient men raised these stones and dolmens and barrows seemed no farther away than last week. He had an ill defined sense of having been there before. He felt he knew the place, he could almost have shouted out the day—or was it century?—ago that he had been there; but the half memory struggled in vain to free itself. Among these twilight thoughts, which welled up in his mind as his flesh chilled and goosed in the night wind, was an insistent discord saying he had no right to be there at all; there was too a very simple, perhaps childish fear of some dark retribution for breaking some fundamental natural law. Then again without his consciously thinking a voice spoke within his mind, so suddenly like a shout in his ear or a tap on his shoulder that he started. It was the voice of Mrs. Tregellas saying, "What's past idn so dead after all."

Real voices now called out to him. Turning he saw a torch flashing and caught a glimpse of de Vere Ellis' blazing shirt and fleecy jacket. He groped his way back around to the tent and found his two friends putting down the remainder of the gear—bedrolls and blankets.

"We saw a will o' the wisp," cried Browne-Smythe.

He spoke excitedly so that the other two recoiled silently.

"Old Bertie here started the damned thing," said de Vere Ellis in exaggerated laconic tones. "Lit a match for a smoke as we started up the hill. Must have ignited a pocket of marsh gas."

"Gave me quite a jolt, actually," said Browne-Smythe. "One second there was nothing there, and the next this kind of purple ghost was dancing like a monkey round us. Burnt out after a few minutes, of course."

They busied themselves arranging the tent. McMahon lit a couple of oil lamps and tied them to the tent poles. No one spoke; they were perhaps little fearful of betraying the fact that the place was affecting them strongly. Each knew that this night on Roughtor was going to be far less of a joke than they had imagined; but none would admit it. Conversation was therefore strained, and confined to matters of immediate concern; which was mainly the cooking of supper. De Vere Ellis made a brave show of being at home by whistling the tune of "Oh Darling, Oh Sweetest", as he fried sausages over the stove, but soon he too relapsed into moody silence.

Supper over, they prepared to turn in. It seemed to all three that they could feel the proximity of the big rock that shielded them from the wind, even within the tent. It was as though it had a personality of its own which would not permit them to forget it. Probably this annoyed Browne-Smythe; he went outside for a smoke before sleeping.

Leaving the tent he frightened several rabbits which had gathered curiously outside, attracted by the faint lamplight. They went off scuttling down across the hillside. The moon had risen, full and ominously amber. There were no clouds in the sky. Below he heard a very faint trickling sound and shining the powerful torch down into the valley between the two hills detected an answering shimmer from the stream that flowed through it. He shone the torch around to amuse himself: the beam reached well up the side of Brown Willy, and he saw a hump on the eastern end of it which appeared to be a barrow. One or two purple will o' the wisps hovered momentarily out beyond upon the marshes, and knowing what they were he smiled superciliously; then he had a great fright, for randomly turning the beam on an outcrop of rock fifty yards away he was confronted by a white face and two large horns. For a second he stood thunderstruck, the light wavering in his hand; then he heard a deep cry, half-bray and half-bleat, and a goat leaped away over the boulders.

There was no sound except for the unwavering high note of the wind. For a moment something akin to fear gripped him, and as suddenly released him. A man could go mad on these moors, he decided. The moon cast enough light to present those gaunt shapes, grey enigmas, but never enough to explain them. Browne-Smythe threw away his cigarette and went to bed.

They lay for an hour or more sleepless on the hard ground, which their sleeping-bag did little to soften. They stared up at the indistinct canvas listening to the wind, and each sensed the others were awake. Once McMahon said, trying to sound irritated, "Don't go much on the orchestrations up here,"—but neither of the others replied.

The wind did however gradually die away; it was a process so slow that their minds preoccupied with its sound were lowered and lulled to sleep as it waned. The other two had relapsed into an uneasy slumber when de Vere Ellis sat up in bed and whispered, "For God's sake, what's that?"

McMahon stirred and made a grunt of interrogation, then he too sat up and listened. There was a sound of laughing; or was it singing? It was both: a crowd of voices laughing and singing very close at hand.

There was nothing at all uncanny in the sounds; they were jolly voices that made them, and it was only the unexpectedness of hearing them that made the three stare at each other for minutes before anybody spoke again.

Browne-Smythe was awake. He did not sound afraid when he said, "Here, I'm going out to have a look." He dragged on his jeans and a pullover; the others followed suit.

When they got outside the revelry was loud and boisterous The moon was clear and white again; they climbed across the backbone rocks of the hill and were staggered by what they saw.

There were maybe fifty dancers in a circle with arms interlinked, leaping and jigging with tremendous energy around a big boulder on which sat three figures. None of the dancers seemed to be over two feet high; they were all dressed in tight garments and little pointed caps of light green or blue. Their faces even in the half-light were shining and jovial. They sang as they danced, the little men on the boulder taking in turns to sing the verse and the whole crowd joining in the chorus with a roaring flourish. What was so stupendous, when the watchers overcame their initial surprise, was that the voices which came from the tiny beings were so loud and rich, an unhesitating unrestrained bass. What they sang none of them could understand. McMahon first thought the language was Welsh; but looking back realized it could only have been Cornish.

The three watched with a kind of astonished delight, for such merriment they had never imagined. It was naive spontaneous pleasure that spelled them motionless like statues there on the great stones. None of the rollickers took any notice of them.

This went on for some minutes, and having become intoxicated with the mirth they saw before them they were totally unprepared for what happened next.

Clouds passed overhead obscuring the moon, and for a half a minute there was darkness. The singing and dancing ceased abruptly; McMahon thought he saw figures stealing hurriedly away. Then they heard another song, as vigorous as the first but higher pitched and somehow more disturbing; it contained an subtly menacing rhythm; as it approached a sense of vicious or evil intent assailed them. Then the moon was freed and showed them about twenty little men no bigger than the others, dressed in the same way except that they had dark caps of black or deep blue. But the main difference was not of dress form. These were ugly little creatures with spindly legs and square heads too large for their bodies. When the moonlight revealed them they were not so much dancing as fighting among themselves and tripping each other up in malevolent sport; but they soon saw the three humans watching them stupefied from the boulder, and with shouts of diabolical glee bounded toward them in a body.

Unable to control his actions, McMahon turned and fled. De Vere Ellis, afraid but still proud, hesitated. Browne-Smythe started to run with McMahon, but caught his foot in a crevice and fell. Four of the goblins were on him instantly, two twisting his foot, one pulling his ears and poking at his eyes, the other jabbing him with a sharp stick. De Vere Ellis took a stride toward them, sent one sprawling with a kick and clouted the others with his fists. Browne-Smythe got to his feet and they both ran.

They were going down over the hillside towards Brown Willy, but McMahon's voice shrieked out urgently, "Here! To the tent, *quickly*! We're safe here!"

The tent was not more than a hundred yards away, and they sprinted frantically across, reaching it as the crowd of little people came hopping and screeching over the rocks. They stopped ten yards away from the tent and stood around it in a ring, glowering and uttering cries of chagrin. It was as though there was a circle drawn round the tent into which they could not penetrate.

The three flung themselves down inside the tent, panting feverishly.

"Safe—safe, thank God!" gasped Browne-Smythe. He felt his scratched and torn ear, and pulled up his shirt revealing little red weals and cuts bleeding on his ribs.

McMahon was looking at the map.

"Thought so," he said relievedly, "this spot is marked Chapel here. It—this cave thing—is a chapel to Michael the Archangel, patron saint of Cornwall; so I've heard. It explains why they can't hurt us in here."

As though they had heard the name of Michael spoken, the crowd outside dispersed silently and loped back over the boulders into the night. Once again there was silence except for the wind, which seemed to be rising, and the hard breathing of de Vere Ellis and Browne-Smythe.

"I once went into the local folk lore," said McMahon. "I remember something about these things from what I heard as a boy." He grabbed a packet of cigarettes and lit one, inhaling nervously. "The first lot were piskies, I think; they don't do any harm. The second kind were spriggans, and their jokes are nothing to laugh at."

Silence again. De Vere Ellis stared dully out of the open tent entrance toward Brown Willy. Then Browne-Smythe croaked with harsh unpleasant voice, "My God—I never dreamed for a moment…" He did not finish his sentence; it was unnecessary. Words were indeed useless. A nightmare had taken on flesh and blood and had assaulted them; talking could not calm their confusion.

McMahon remembered a flask of whisky included in his pack, and took it out. He handed it around, and the fierce liquor made them a little more sanguine.

"I feel quite mystified by all this," said McMahon somehow achieving reflective detachment. "Is it possible for three people to dream the same nightmare at the same time?"

"There's no mystery," said Browne-Smythe sourly. "Those damned spriggans were tangible enough."

"Oh, forget it!" snapped de Vere Ellis, savage now that for the first time in his life his logical beliefs were violently shaken. "Forget the whole affair! Talk about it in the morning. I'm going to sleep if I can."

"Happy dreams," said Browne-Smythe, "I shan't get any."

"The blasted wind's going to stop us sleeping," said McMahon with a yawn.

The wind was increasing in power every minute. Soon it was seething and screaming across the summit, whipping in around their corner, snatching at the tent. Through it all they became aware of a dim stony creaking rising louder and faster, the sound of boulder on boulder. It was McMahon who realized what it was.

"It's the Logan Stone," he said, "rocking in the wind."

It began to rain, though not on the tent. The heavy drops went over them, protected as they were by the Chapel rock, and splashed loudly on the boulders nearby. The Logan Stone oscillated yet more wildly, a gauge of the wind's violence: clunk-clunk, clunk-clunk, like a mad thing. The tent was illuminated in a lightning flash and they saw each other half sitting up in bed with white faces. Then an enormous roll of thunder sounded immediately above them, rotating and exploding like some cosmic cannon; the rain redoubled and the windshrieks seemed to fade beside its dark drumming.

Browne-Smythe, whose bed was at the southern end of the tent nearest Brown Willy, put out his hand to secure the end flap more tightly. As he undid the knot the strings were plucked from his hand by the hurricane, and he had to half crawl outside to regain them. Then wind entered, creasing the canvas and banging the lamps against the poles. Browne-Smythe was on his hands and knees in the doorway, they saw, when the lightning blinked again, but he was making no effort to close the flap.

"What's the matter?" yelled de Vere Ellis above the wind.

Browny-Smythe turned slowly, but as he was evidently speaking in his normal voice they could not hear him. He beckoned and then pointed to something. The other two crawled over to him.

Over the south slope of Brown Willy they could just distinguish a great jet figure against the fiercely dark sky. It was of human form, but the size of a giant; it was bending and stooping and appeared to throw up its arms to the clouds and down again, as though throwing something over its shoulder. They could not be sure. They lost the figure in the darkness, thought they saw it again; then it was gone. What was it? Had they seen a real thing, or a merely trick played by the lightning and the black pregnant clouds?

"It might," said McMahon very slowly when they had retreated into the tent, "it might have been Tregeagle baling out Dozmary. The pool lies in that direction."

"Giant ghosts now—Jesus!" muttered Browne-Smythe.

Insane fear and anger rushed through de Vere Ellis. Reason was playing him false tonight. He was bewildered, his brain near numb with helpless feelings. He wanted to scream but with great effort overcame that longing, only to find that when he did so there were tears in his eyes, rolling down his face, and he had no power to stop them. It was at this moment that the other two decided to light a lamp for comfort, and hearing McMahon fumble with matches he flung himself down on the nearest bed—Browne-Smythe's—and buried his face in the bedclothes.

"Hullo, old chap," said Browne-Smythe stupidly when he saw him there. "Anything up?"

De Vere Ellis said nothing for some moments, not trusting himself to speak without betraying emotion, and then made some explanation that Browne-Smythe in a normal time would have laughed at. But he too was confounded, and accepted the tale about hitting his head on the stony ground quite seriously. Against the voice of the wind McMahon had heard nothing of this, and having lit the lamp he began grumbling that there was very little oil left in it.

De Vere Ellis raised himself and shouted discordantly, "You talk about the bloody lamp! What's the matter with you two; what d'you think this is, a boy scout's jaunt?"

No one replied for a minute, and then McMahon shouted back, "You can't accept the supernatural; that's what's the matter with you. I've seen it: I believe and keep sane. You've seen it and you won't believe it: if you don't look out you'll go out of your minds!"

There was no time to reply to this. They heard a long piercing wail rising above the wind; it was a loud bass tortured voice from some distance away, like a trumpet gone mad and possessing the strength of ten trumpets. It was followed by a sound that could only be described as a laugh: a maniacal fiendish laugh, a great gloating chuckle out of the clouds. But they hardly had time to experience fresh fear at this, for the wind without the slightest warning veered round and blew in from the east in giant gusts. The Chapel rock was now no protection; with the rain sheeting down on the canvas came stones flung by the gale. Then a guy rope snapped and the tent collapsed on top of them.

There was only one thing to do. Thunderstruck as they were they managed to uproot the other pegs and drag the whole gear to the cave. It was only shallow and left them half in, half out of the storm. They covered themselves up with blankets and the canvas.

Gathering stray items together McMahon found his big pipe and instinctively clutched hold of its familiar form. Like a child clutching a teddy bear, he thought, and realizing this saw irony; but he could not smile. He thought of his peagreen scarf, de Vere Ellis' loud shirt, Browne-Smythe's moustache: the pop record and the cigarettes and the brandy—all futile vanities now strewn abandoned like children's playthings, or hugged but no longer comforting; and they themselves were suddenly no more than terrified children, afraid of what they did not understand.

They were now facing up the valley between Roughtor and Brown Willy and so saw without hindrance the last satanic stormy episode. There was a glaring yellow flash of lightning lasting several seconds it seemed, which revealed that same dark figure towering against an inflamed sky and flying toward them down from the uplands. It was Tregeagle with his head in the cloud, whooping and screaming, running with thunderous footsteps. A hell-hound pack pursued with murderous baying.

Down between the two hills he came bellowing out tormentedly. His great thighs were level with them as he passed and his footsteps shook Roughtor itself so that loose stones fell down around them. His screams cut into them like knives, severing the roots of nerves and stabbing through the floors of sanity. At his heels those devildogs leaped, sabre fangs in cavernous jaws open for the kill. Their raucous throatings sawed the air, upward emanating like fists seizing, choking, with horror sickening them beholding. Night filled overpowering with sudden hellmighty voices, rock moor cloud abyss, two hills with terror yelling between them—were they, grovelling unbearably, the only things afraid?

Away westward they ran, echoes bellowing out among the tors even in the unabated wind, but diminishing as they went. De Vere Ellis was on his feet and ran round the Chapel rock to watch; he came back with face wet but not with rain, and gibbered for the whisky. Browne-Smythe sat moaning unintelligibly like an idiot. McMahon himself, though quivering with shock, heart racing uncontrollably, did not dare think but searched for the flask. He found it under a pile of blankets and reached out to give it to de Vere Ellis. Browne-Smythe snatched at it and they began to fight. McMahon did the only thing he could think of: he picked up a jagged stone weighing nearly half a hundredweight and snapped, "I'll brain you both if you don't sit down and shut up!"

They calmed down a little. Browne-Smythe began his dull moaning again, looking around him piteously like a whipped cur.

"Listen," said McMahon very firmly and calmly, "there's only one thing to do—stay here at all costs."

But then the gaunt baying and howling, which had never quite died away, became louder; Tregeagle and the savage yelping hell pack were returning. De Vere Ellis was on his feet in an instant, running away, scrambling frantically across the boulders. Browne-Smythe made as though to get up; McMahon leaned over and roared in his ear, "Don't be a bloody fool! This is the only place where they can't hurt you!" He put his hand on his shoulder to prevent him rising. But now they could hear the footsteps pounding. Browne-Smythe shrieked, flung himself sideways; tripped McMahon as he came at him and lashed out ferociously with his fist. He caught him on the jaw, and fled off across the rocks. McMahon fell, hit a boulder and lost consciousness.

When he came around it was dawn and the sun, spinning crimson up over the moors, shone full into the Chapel cave. The wind was now merely a faint placid breeze, the clouds high, white and motionless. A lark was singing up among them, his ceaseless wings whirring.

This much McMahon observed sleepily; then realizing he was cold he moved to cover himself and found a sickening pain shooting through his head. He had ugly cuts and bruises on his temple.

He managed to wrap himself in blankets, and slept again for several hours. He was conscious from time to time of the gathering warmth of the sun; and though he felt vaguely impressed by some recent event he was too insensible to try and remember it, or ask himself what he was doing there so early in the morning on the hillside.

When he finally awoke his head was clear, the sun was high, and he remembered not without shuddering the adventures of the night. He got up, found a rock pool and bathed his face and wound, donned an anorak which belonged to Browne-Smythe, and went off in search of the other two.

Obviously they had gone across to the north, with the object of reaching civilization. Crossing the rocky backbone of Roughtor he saw the car was still there by the gate at the end of the road.

He found Browne-Smythe in a gorse clump very near the rumbling waterfall. He was asleep and snoring stertorously. When awakened he gave no sign of recognition, and said nothing; the only sound he made, at long intervals, was the same low moaning he had made in the night. He could not walk; his ankle was broken.

For about a fortnight Browne-Smythe suffered a complete loss of memory concerning himself and the events leading up to the morning he was found on the moor. Gradually his awareness of his past life and who he was returned, but he never recalled the events of that night on Roughtor, nor would he believe McMahon, who told him about them. Yet though he refused to accept the story, the cuts and weals on his back healed leaving ugly red scars which no doctor could ever satisfactorily explain.

Although he now owns the property left him by his father, McMahon does not visit Cornwall much. He lectures at a college in the Midlands, has a flat in London and is fond of travelling abroad.

De Vere Ellis was lost for two days, wandering the moors without any sense of bearing; he declared afterwards that he was convinced he was being led in circles by something, and marvelled that he had not been drowned in a bog. He has since taken up the study of parapsychology, and is in his way something of an authority on psychical research. One day, when he feels equal to the occasion, he may go back to Roughtor; but whether to spend the night there in further research, he does not say.

WHERE PHANTOMS STIR
Mary Williams

First published in Where Phantoms Stir *(William Kimber, 1976)*

Mary Williams (1903–2000) was born in Leicestershire and went to Collegiate School, Leicester. There she took an interest in art, history and literature. When she left school, her first job was at the *Leicester Chronicle*, where she reported on social events under the name "June" and interviewed actors who appeared at the local theatre, such as Diana Wynward and Laurence Olivier. She spent some time living on the canal boat "Cressy" with L. T. C. Rolt and his first wife Angela during WWII, broadcasting on behalf of the BBC from on board. Her first novel, *Louise*, was published by London Sentinel in 1947 around the time that marriage took her away from Leicester and she moved to Wales, writing under the moniker of "Jane" of *The Abergavenny Chronicle*.

She then moved to a studio home overlooking the harbour in St. Ives, Cornwall, and continued to write short stories, with Francis Hyland becoming a champion of her work. She opened a gallery with her husband at Porthmeor Beach selling her paintings and black and white illustrations. She kept her connection with Wales, with several of her stories and illustrations featured on Welsh BBC children's programmes. She was invited to write a story ("The Lost Ones") for Denys Val Baker's *Haunted Cornwall* (1973) and the story proved so popular with readers that they flooded publisher William Kimber with letters asking to read more of her work. This resulted in her first collection for Kimber, *The Dark Land: A Book of Cornish Stories* (1975), prompting other publishers to advise Kimber against publishing a collection by a little-known writer. Kimber was not to be dissuaded, and the book sold well, especially to libraries in the UK and also in the European market.

On her ghost stories she had this to say: "I'm very happy writing ghost stories because I know they give pleasure to so many people […] living in Cornwall is ideal because it is so inspirational for a writer. The surrounding area is rather silvery in winter and very eerie on occasions, so it does help me with my imagination." Mary died in 2000, aged 97.

At first her face was merely a disc of white in the thickening waves of curling mist; then, as the light cleared momentarily, he saw the figure of a girl approaching hesitantly from the side of the lane. From what he could see of her she was wearing the current style of dress… long maxi skirt and a kind of shawl thing round her shoulders. Her pale hair caught the fleeting glow from distant bonfires where beacons blazed to honour Midsummer Eve; then as quickly, her form was taken again into the swirl of falling cloud shapes, leaving only the brief impression of delicate features and pleading stare of enormous, haunted looking eyes.

She was obviously in great distress and forgetting his own plight… for he'd been lost for hours in that bewildering district of misted moorland and winding paths… he plunged towards her, saying… "Are you all right? What is it? Can I help?"

As she moved, dispelling the fog momentarily, by a wave of her hand before her face, he saw how beautiful she was. Fey-looking, ethereal and somehow innocent, having a quality seldom found in current society. At first, mingled with astonishment and a stirring of emotions he had thought long since dead in him, he was mildly irritated. Obviously she was in need of help and obviously he had to give it… if he could. It was the last thing he wanted. No more women, he'd determined, as he'd set off for his tramping holiday in Cornwall, following his divorce from Wanda. No more involvement with desire and loss, lies and pretence, arguments and the endless reunions which had proved to be so futile. No more waste of life. Life was precious; as he, being a doctor, should know. For a brief time anyway, he'd decided to be free of emotional impact.

Yet here, in one of the remotest spots of Cornwall, he must come all unexpectedly upon this waif of a creature, marooned, apparently, as *he* was… in a benighted wasteland of barren fog-bound moor.

"Can I help?" he enquired once more, against all commonsense and better judgement.

For a moment or two there was complete silence, until she whispered, "No. No thank you. It's just…"

Her voice trailed off uncertainly as she turned from him and began moving away. He caught up with her, instinctively clutching her shoulders, swinging her round, and taking one hand in his. It was icy cold. As cold as her terrified voice when she said, "No. Leave me. It's all right. I made a mistake…"

"What mistake? What do you mean?"

"My father," she answered, her voice falling and rising on the intermittent soughing of the thin wind. "I was going to see him. But it's no use. I shouldn't have come."

From the dead finality of her tone, he knew she really believed it.

Still holding her hand he said, "But how have you got here? From where? Tell me?"

"A long way," she said. "A very long way. And I shouldn't have come. He doesn't want me."

Her head was bowed, with the silvered cloak of her hair half hiding her face.

"Look here…" he said loudly, a little harshly, to break the uncanny brooding intensity of the furred damp air around them, "look here… that's nonsense. Anyway you can't go wandering alone in… in all this. And I don't believe what you said about your father. Not for one minute. You've had a quarrel. Right. I know all about quarrels. But sometimes… just *sometimes* things can be made right again. Now… where's your home? Where do you live?"

"Up there," she answered, lifting her arm to a rising stretch of mist-wreathed land on the right. Trencabra they call it! I was there as a child and afterwards for a time. But then…" Her voice faltered. "I tell you, he doesn't *want* me anymore."

Thinking she must be some errant student who'd possibly taken off on a crazy love affair, he insisted firmly, "As I said… I don't believe it. You know the way I suppose? And he must be there or you wouldn't have come. So suppose we go up there together and find out how things stand now. Maybe I can help."

She demurred at first, but eventually gave in, going a little in front to indicate the way through the ever-shifting waves of rolling fog, which had become so dense not even a blurred glow from the distant beacons penetrated the damp curtain any more. They were climbing steeply; past great rocks which loomed pale for a moment then were as quickly obscured again… pushing through the thorned grasp of thrusting undergrowth, ever onwards and upwards, her form gaining speed and purpose now she had been forced to a decision. She couldn't have forgotten an inch of the way, he thought once… so nimble and quick she was, in locating the mere thread of path.

"Your father lives in a benighted place," he said. "What is he? Naturalist?… Writer?… Or just…?" He didn't finish. The words were torn away from him on the rising wind which moaned now with a harsh eerie voice of its own… sighing and creaking through furze, stunted bushes and round the monolith shapes emerging beast-like through the thick air.

At last he glimpsed the looming distorted shape of a building… darker and denser than the creeping fog… a monstrosity in daylight, surely, with grotesque turrets thrusting through the curdled vapour, which swirled and billowed in macabre suggestions of mal-formed shapes round skeleton peaks eventually fading into nothingness.

No more was said until they reached the doors of the house, which were already open as though to receive them. For a moment he felt hesitant, an intruder into a domain where he had no right. Then the girl plunged ahead and he instinctively followed her,… forcing his heightened senses into more normal channels by saying to himself sharply, "Pull yourself together. Your name's Charles Baines… *Doctor* Baines; there's nothing abnormal about this… it's what you wanted isn't it…? Escape from Wanda; and you've damn well found it, that's all… a chance to help a poor kid in the wilds of nowhere, make peace with her old man…"

His own mental therapy was interrupted by the girl saying, "Why don't you go back now? It would be better." But there was something in her voice begging him to stay, in spite of the suggestion.

So he went on behind her down a wide hall… stone paved, from the feel of it, smelling dank and unhealthy from the rushing fog holding the flap of cobwebs and the intermittent squelch of decay underfoot.

No object was visible, except an occasional black shape, signifying nothing of utility… just deeper darkness against the furred quality of dense air.

He wanted to ask why the hell there was no lamp, nothing to show the way to wherever it was she was taking him. Then, as though sensing his thoughts, she lifted an arm pointing to a mere drift of light filtering ahead… a trickle zig-zagging in a broken line from what must be, obviously a door. She started running light-footed as a young deer, pale, ghost-like… any lingering reluctance gone now, finally exorcized by the terrain of her birth and her belonging. He nearly lost her but was quick enough to catch the wet cloth of her coat as the door swung open, pushed by her two hands.

He followed. The interior was a surprise… or "shock" perhaps was a more adequate description. Although the wind still penetrated, flapping the costly tapestries on the wall, drifting under the luxurious rugs, lifting tassels of the rich upholstery and stirring the hundred candle-flames cradled in crystal and silver… the air was warm and comforting. A large log-fire crackled and burned from the immense fireplace. A long refectory table was laid for a meal at the far end of the room, with wine and glasses winking in the glow from the leaping flames. A party expected, obviously; which was why, probably, the girl had been so reluctant to appear.

He waited hesitantly at the door, while she hurried to a figure seated in a high-backed carved chair close to the fire. Her voice, when she spoke was a mere whisper but so clear in quality, its echoes drifted on each breath of wind… each sigh of air… round the vast stone walls and floor.

"Father… I'm here father…" The statement was a plea, like that of some small child begging forgiveness.

The head resting against the massive oak, turned towards her, and for a moment Baines was astonished. No; more than that… *shocked*. Not because of any deficiency, but by the power of profile… arrogance, and pride, exemplified in every feature… strongly carved nose and chin beneath prominent forehead and bristling lowering brows… crisply curling hair… thick red and carefully trimmed beard. A handsome man and when he got up swiftly to face her, his form loomed immense against the firelight… broad, almost burly; six feet six possibly in height, yet well proportioned, wearing a well-cut velvet jacket with the current fashionable cravat at his neck.

Not wishing at first to interrupt their greeting unless forced to, Charles waited, while the man said in a harsh voice to the girl… "*You.*"

She took an involuntary step backwards. "I *had* to. Don't you *see*, Father…?"

She clutched her damp coat to her neck, swaying uncertainly, together with the faint quiver of curtains and tremble of wind round her feet.

"I told you *never* to come here again," the father said, with controlled underlying violence. "What in the name of…." He stopped, suddenly, lifting one hand to his forehead. The girl rushed up to him, both hands pulling the sleeves of his coat, her white face lifted; anxious, imploring.

"I can't go on any more like I have…" she said. "No family… no-one to talk to…"

"Don't be a fool, Rhianna. You've plenty of company…"

"But not *mine*. They're different. They don't understand…" Her voice died into a sigh, joining all the other sighs of that great hall.

"Why on earth *tonight* of all nights?"

"It was the only day I *could* come, wasn't it?" she said quietly.

He did not reply at first, then asked heavily, "How did you find the way in all this fog? After so long and so many…?" He didn't finish the question.

He didn't have to. She turned and facing the figure at the door, said… "He helped me, I mean… when I was turning back he gave me… courage."

"*Courage!*" The great figure threw back his head and laughed; a roar of sound holding contempt, derision and a surge of savage fury. For the first time he appeared to notice the doctor those few yards away. "Well!…" The laughter died suddenly, he paused, before continuing, "He'll *need* it. If he stops here tonight."

"I'd no intention of staying," Charles managed to answer. "I only came along with your daughter to see she got here safely, in one piece. It's damned dangerous out there."

"Indeed." Heavy sarcasm flooded the voice now. "And didn't it occur to you, sir, that my daughter might have been right to turn back? That in forcing her here you could do dangerous harm?"

"I don't see…"

"No. You do *not* see. But because of your unwarrantable intrusion you *shall*. Oh you *shall*; never fear." He strode to the door, shut and locked it with a rattle and turn of a heavy key.

"Now…" he continued with a malicious smile, "suppose we prepare ourselves… for the feast…"

"The feast?"

"Yes indeed. There's a party tonight. But of course you didn't know. Never mind, never mind," he said, pacing up and down, while the girl, Rhianna, slunk back a little into the shadows. "That can soon be remedied. Rhianna…"

"Yes?" The whisper was so terrified and cowed, Baines couldn't help exclaiming, "Now I see why she was frightened. I'm sorry… I know this is not my affair… except that I'm a doctor and…"

"Doctor? Don't be a fool. *Your* kind of doctor isn't needed here, is he daughter? Is he…?"

Baines could not hear the girl's reply; but apparently it was immaterial. The man… engrossed only by himself and lust for self-power… strode to the table, pointed to a seat at the end, saying with underlying sinister amusement, "Take your place girl. Your *rightful* place. You've insisted on it. So take it... take it; and as he's here for such a short time, let your friend sit next to you."

She flung off her coat, shook her hair behind her ears, letting it flow free as the wanton moonlight over the cream woollen dress which in the fitful candlelight took on an etherealized quality, insubstantial as the cool mist blown through cracks of windows and doors; then obeying her father compliantly, she moved to the place indicated, wraith-like... a dream figure... as though conjured up by the elements of fog, air and prevailing wind itself.

Charles followed automatically, with a growing sense of unreality and gathering apprehension.

He reached for her hand as he sat beside her. It was deadly cold, the slim fingers trembling so violently he could feel the thin bones beneath the flesh. Pity filled him that anyone... anything... so defenceless and trusting... should be at the mercy of that great brute of a man, who had returned to the fire and was standing there, licked by the spitting flames to a monstrous silhouetted red shape... curling hair and beard rich and deep as that of wine or blood newly spilled. He made no move to join them but strode to the door, unlocked it and waited there, gigantic head turned to the corridor where the mist crept and billowed with the grey menace of a phantom army resurrected from the dead.

And then it came. The first wild shrieking from outside somewhere... a jubilant screaming and crying and yelling that reduced the rising mean of wind and approaching storm to a mere shadow of sound.

Shortly afterwards the first shape appeared in the doorway... a grotesque travesty bearing little semblance to human... hump-backed, hook-nosed... slit-eyed with draggled grey locks streaming and tangled over skeleton-like shoulders under torn black drapes. Others followed; grimacing, clawing, laughing obscenely in thirsty triumph, revealing long fangs of teeth, some with the snouts of pigs or beaks of hawks... lascivious hungry creatures, carrying brooms or tossed tied bundles of rag-wort, on which they must have flown that night.

Fearing to look, yet unable to tear his eyes away, Charles Baines saw them scramble and encircle the figure of their host avidly, lifting their clawed hands in unholy greed, caressing his velvet coat, grinning gloatingly, peering from red-rimmed sunken orbs into his face, while the fiendish chattering filled the air in a crescendo of tormented and tormenting greeting.

As they swarmed to the table, Charles with lurching stomach managed with an effort to look away. He knew Rhianna's terror, sensing at the same time, the approaching orgy was no surprise to her; she had known... expected it.

During a momentary cessation of sound, he lifted his head cautiously. They were settling themselves at the table, already clawing and reacting like a company of carrion crows for the food and wine so temptingly displayed. But one or two had already noticed Rhianna and from their faces... whether male or female, warlock or witch, Charles knew she had already sealed her own fate... had delivered herself as the ultimate sacrifice, in deference to a law far beyond the realism of human need and desire, having its birth in the unholy hinterland of creation... of living and the dead. Corruption and the black aftermath of evil achieved and proclaimed.

At first they paid little attention to the girl; and for them, the doctor apparently was an object merely of derisive amusement and contempt. Occasionally a calculating eye was thrown in his direction but only momentarily. It was as though he existed just as a shadow... something which could be dispelled at a word or wave of a hand if necessary.

Charles himself, began to feel nebulous and unreal... a ghostly visitant in their weird celebration. At moments only his host seemed to have substance... the fiery red of beard and burning eyes reducing the macabre assembly to vague shapes which faded and formed again in malignant disorder through the curdling light of flame and fog.

Charles did not touch the food which had an exotic though unhealthy odour and his one sip of the wine, forced on him by a nearby crone, brought a sense of revulsion and sickness which was overpowering. Rhianna tore the goblet from his hand. "Don't drink," she said, loudly enough for all to hear. "Put it *down*. For God's sake, don't touch it."

At the mention of God, there was a sudden eerie cessation of voices. The very wind seemed to die away and the mist disintegrate, as the vile corrupt faces turned in automatic suspicion towards them. The silence... for those few seconds that could have been an eternity... seemed to gather force stimulated by its own concentrated fateful purpose... before it was shattered suddenly with the renewed screaming and the mist of skeleton arms into the vortex of clutching writhing evil.

Charles, helpless and overpowered by the thickening air and swirl of chattering shapes had a brief moment of consciousness as they fell upon the girl, tearing the clothes from her body, limb by limb... until she was lifted, a naked wounded thing, high above the clamouring throng, and carried screaming from the hall. Then mercifully all was dark and he knew no more.

Morning came; clear and cool under a lowering grey sky holding no lingering trace of festivity or afterglow of beacon fires.

Charles, chilled and dazed, lay for some moments with stiffened limbs, as events slowly resolved and steadied through his head. He sat up presently and looked around. The great stones of the immediate landscape lay massed around and above him; sentinels from the past, with no sign of life or vegetation, but patches of thin turf and occasional twisted tumps of grasping undergrowth. No birdsong; no tree reached from the barren earth... and there was no sign of a dwelling, or intimation there had ever been one. Just a gaunt hill rising remote and bleak, overlooking the moorland stretches of West Penwith, dotted at intervals by the dark shapes of a ruined minestack and huddled hamlets crouched deep in the shadows of secret valleys halfglimpsed in the early light.

Still shocked, Charles struggled to his feet, flaying chest and shoulders with his arms as he had been taught to do when a boy, on mountaineering expeditions. A little warmth returned to his body, enabling both his eyes and brain to assess events more coherently.

Reason told him he had lost his way, fallen exhausted and had a nightmare. But he knew instinctively, from a deep inner sense, there was more to it than that. There *had* been a girl. He remembered acutely now, the white face in the fog… the pleading look in her great eyes which had forced him to this benighted spot… recalled, with loathing the following events with their ghastly finale.

An illusion? A temporary aberration of mind and brain following his break with Wanda? But if so, in heaven's name *why?* For years they'd existed merely in a semi-bored state of mutual dislike. He'd thanked his stars for being rid of her at last. No. Wanda did not come into it. Then… *what?* He touched his face, recalling the old tale of Rip-Van-Winkle. There was no beard there… no stubble; just a slight roughness indicating he needed a shave. Something to eat too. My God, yes. He thought, his stomach was a hollow cave as though he'd had no food for a week… only that one sip of the heady unholy stuff the… witch, crone… devil… or ghost… had forced on him before the girl's cry.

And yet… where was she? If she had really existed? And where was the house… that great turretted building she'd led him to only a few evenings earlier?

He clambered fifty yards or so to the summit of the hill, and with his eyes now strained to every detail of the barren land, thought at one point he saw her body lying, pale and ravaged under an immense standing stone which caught at that moment the first drift of silvered sunlight from the lifting horizon. He tried to remember her name but couldn't… it didn't matter. She was there… slim, defenceless, washed clean and white on the waste of reddened ground, with her hair spread cloak-like over the virgin breasts.

Half running, half stumbling, he thrust his way forward. But when he reached the place there was nothing… no girl… no sign of life, or that anyone had recently walked there… just a slim piece of rock, slightly less than life size but with a glistening look about it, of marble intermingled with granite.

He turned, with a queer feeling of desolation, and made his way down the hill to the lane threading at its base towards a huddle of cottages about half a mile away. It was a small place, with a church on the outskirts... probably serving two parishes... one small shop, two farms and a dozen or so cottages, the kind of place he thought vaguely, that would be popular with holiday-makers. Luckily for him he was right about the latter. Round a twist of the lane, bordered by a brook, he came upon a primitive looking but picturesque small place behind a well kept garden, with a board standing outside, which said, "Bed and Breakfast. Refreshments".

Well, he thought, he certainly wouldn't want to spend another night in the district, but the refreshments would be welcome, if it wasn't too early in the day.

By then the sunlight was already tipping the roofs and chimneys with gold, and when he rapped on the door it was immediately opened by a homely woman, with a cheery fresh complexion, ample bosom beneath a clean apron, and a wealth of black hair pinned in a bun on her neck.

"Of course we can give you breakfast, surr," she told him, cheerfully. "Always ready for walkers and such like. You never know when one's going to turn up. Come along here, midear, into th'parlour. I'll have it ready in 'two shakes of a lamb's tail' as they say... an' *that's* a fulish sayin' to be sure, as them who know lambs well know."

Laughing at her own good humour, she showed him into a pleasant room traditionally furnished in country Cornish style, with lace curtains at the windows, a potted plant on the low sill, mahogany table, already set with pots and cutlery. Upholstered furniture and a welcoming fire... despite the summer... burning in the grate.

"Now sit down and make yourself comfortable," she said. "I'll be back with the usual. Eggs, bacon? And cereal surr? Or porridge?"

"Cereal," he answered. "And many thanks. Bacon, too, of course and the eggs."

"Glad you have an appetite," the woman observed appreciatively. "It's good bacon we have here, the very best. Home cured. And tea of course.

Or... if it's coffee you're wanting you can have that. Sometimes furriners prefer coffee... with all respect, surr. But it's a cup of good strong tea takes *my* fancy. I must say."

"*And* mine," Charles answered quickly.

Obviously pleased, she disappeared with a rustle of skirts, shutting the door behind her, leaving Charles to reflect in solitude.

He did not have to wait long. She soon came back and after a little desultory chatter he was presently tucking in to what he described later as the best and most welcome breakfast he'd ever had.

Before he left, he touched briefly on the night's events, relating how he'd lost his way, helped a girl in distress, then, obviously, had some shock or other, been overcome by the cold and had, what must have been, some obscene and particularly disturbing nightmare on the hill.

When he'd finished there was dead silence. She did not speak until he looked up into her face, which from its previous rosy hue had distinctly paled.

"Well?" he said. "What's the matter? Have I said...?"

"Did you say *Trencabra?*" he heard the woman say in awed, almost frightened tones.

"It sounded like it... that hill, round the bend there..." indicating the direction.

She nodded slowly, while her features assumed a deadpan look of dread, of sudden, veiled fear.

"You should *never*'ve gone there... never at all," she said. "*No* one does... not locals anyway, not after sunset. And last night... *mid* summer. Oh my dear soul! How you ever got back's a miracle. It is surely."

After considerable questioning and evasive answers, he eventually got the whole story out of her.

"Of course books on them dark things call 'et a legend nowadays," she said. "But we who lives round here knows different. A long time ago 'et was... that it all happened. But not so long that it's written off in the memories of our grandfathers and those before them.

"There was a house there all right… *once*. Trencabra. Hall… owned by a great giant of a fellow… Squire Trewarris. Ambitious he was; so greedy for gold, he sold his immortal soul to the devil for it. And *that's* why…" She took a deep breath before continuing… "*that's* why every midsummer eve he has to come back from the dead and entertain the devil's crowd… with feasting and song… and…"

"Yes?"

"Human sacrifice," she answered on a lower key. "That's what happened up there all right… on Trencabra those years ago… fifty, a hundred, or a thousand years… it doesn't matter. Time's nothing in the face of Satan. As we who's bred in these parts know. Why… d'you know, even squire's own *daughter* was taken that way, poor young thing…" Her voice trailed away and when she spoke again it was on a more cheerful practical note.

"But I'm a stupid woman to be putting such things into your head," she said. "That's what Joe, my husband's always telling me. 'Don't you go trying to scare folks, Annie,' he's always saying. 'Someone might go and believe it one day. And then what?'" She laughed merrily. "But then my Joe, he's a furriner from up country. And what do furriners… even such a fine figure of a man as my Joe, bless him… know of such things?"

What? Indeed? I thought ironically as I walked away down the lane, half an hour later.

I for one, however, had already seen and knew too much; an experiment I had no intention of repeating.

In future my walks through the countryside would be strictly confined to daylight, through territory carefully chartered on the map; that is… when I settled down for the rest of my break in some civilized coastal town of shops and the usual holiday crowds.

Which is just what I did.

FOXGLOVES

Susan Price

*First published in 13 Again, edited by
A. Finnis (Scholastic, 1995)*

Susan Price (b. 1955) is a children's author, born in Dudley, Worcestershire. Her first novel, *The Devil's Piper*, was published in 1973, and her first of four collections, *Ghosts at Large*, was published in 1984. Her novel *The Ghost Drum* won the Carnegie medal in 1987. She edited one anthology, the rather cracking *Horror Stories* published by Kingfisher in 1995, which featured stories by Stephen King and Joan Aiken. Price was the first person to reprint Catherine Sinclair's "The Murder Hole" since its original appearance in *More Great Tales of Horror* edited by Marjorie Bowen in 1935. "The Murder Hole" has since been reprinted in my British Library anthology *Scotland the Strange* (2023).

"Foxgloves" was published in *13 Again*, an anthology from the infamous *Point Horror* series, a line introduced by Scholastic Books in 1986 which ran until 2005. It was a gateway into horror and also highlighted real teen issues if you could make your way through the countless slashers and monsters. *Point Horror* was rebooted in 2013 but sadly fizzled out.

"OH, give me a break!" Sean said. "It's too hot to argue." It was almost one in the morning, but all the windows stood open, and the flimsy curtains hardly moved.

Penny, sitting on the settee, folded her arms and turned away. Her mouth was tightly shut.

"I went over and said a few words. I used to work with her. What d'you want me to do—ignore her?"

"Oh! You weren't ignoring her!" Penny said.

"She was a *friend*!"

"Oh, yes. *Very* friendly."

"I can do without this," Sean said. "I'm going home, get some sleep." He started out of the room and down the hallway. He heard someone move on the landing overhead: Penny's mother or father eavesdropping.

Penny came out of the room behind him. "And I can do without you! Don't bother coming back here—ever again!"

Sean opened the front door and stepped out into the thick summer dusk. The warm air folded around him like a soft blanket, scented by the roses in Penny's front garden. Feeling as if he was amongst those roses, scratched and sore, he shouted back into the house, "I *won't* bother coming! What's the point? You've sulked all night just because I spoke to a friend, you stupid —! Good riddance!"

Penny came out on to the step and shouted after him, "Drop dead! I hope you drop dead! Just drop dead!" Before he could shout anything back, she'd slammed her front door shut.

He hurried down the road, half-running, until he had to stop because his head was swelling with heat, and his shirt was sticking to his wet body.

His throat was sore with thirst, and tight, and he felt half-choked. The hot, still air was as difficult to breathe as wool. It was mid-summer—literally. It was Midsummer's Eve, and it had been hot for weeks, the nights seeming hotter than the days. The last thing he wanted to do was walk three miles home in that heat, but he had no choice. The last bus had long gone. All because he'd hung on with Penny, hoping that her bad mood would pass. Anger helped him walk faster. Replaying the argument in his head, muttering aloud, he hurried past hedges and walls and windows with drawn curtains.

He took a short cut—a narrow gully between two streets. Overgrown bushes grew high on either side, and bindweed climbed through them, the white of its flowers shining in the dusk. His footsteps, loud and clear in the early morning quiet, echoed back from the walls and returned to his ears as shuffling steps that seemed now ahead of him, now behind. He turned and walked a few steps backwards as he checked the path behind him. No one was following him. Turning again, he caught a glimpse of something whisking into the tall nettles and weeds beside the path. Two green lights flashed briefly from the undergrowth—cat's eyes, probably.

Had it been a black cat? It was lucky to have a black cat cross your path. A pity it couldn't have crossed his path earlier that evening, though.

He walked on a pace or two, and turned in a circle to check on some slight noise behind him. Whatever made it, he couldn't tell. There was nothing to see. He hurried on, to get out of the gully and back to the street. Walking alone, late at night, wasn't one of his favourite things. He didn't like the state of prickly alertness which made him twitch at every little sound and movement, and then feel a fool because there was nothing to be afraid of.

Midsummer's Eve, too—an unlucky night to be out. It was one of the "turning days" of the year, according to his granny, like Hallowe'en, Christmas Eve and May Day. They were the days when the year turned from winter to spring, from spring to summer, from summer to autumn, and then to winter again. They were different from other days... More open. The nights were even more so. Ghosts walked on those nights that couldn't walk other nights; things were seen on those nights that couldn't be seen on other nights… On those nights, magic worked. According to Granny.

He turned in a circle again, to check on the normality of the hedges and lamp-posts around him, the parked cars, and paving stones and gates.

His granny was full of such stories. Whenever he went to see her, she seemed to remember another that he hadn't heard before, and she would swear that they were all true. Ghastly stories of the ghosts of stillborn babies coming to call away their still living but pining mothers; or the story of the ghost his great-grandad had seen when he'd been out late on Midsummer's Eve.

Ghoulies and ghosties and long-leggety beasties, he thought, trying to laugh himself out of the nervous mood that was settling on him. But that mood fed on itself, and there was no shaking it off. He turned to look behind him again. Obviously some passing ghoulie had put a jinx on him, and inspired him to give Cassie a kiss while Penny was watching. It was so stupid. He and Cassie had worked together for nearly two years, and had got on really well, always had a laugh and a joke—but he'd never been out with Cass. She was older than him, and still had the same steady boyfriend she'd had when he first met her. He couldn't honestly say that he'd never fancied Cass, just a little bit, but it had never been serious. He'd just given her an affectionate, friendly kiss on the cheek. And, because of that, Penny had gone into a major sulk that had lasted all evening, and had told him to drop dead. He hadn't realized she could be so jealous. It was flattering, he supposed… He would give her a day to calm down, and then ring her…

He came to the place where he could take the little track that led along the side of a closed fish and chip shop, and on down to the river—or he could go on along the road and through the town centre. He teetered on his feet, leaning first towards one way and then towards the other.

It would be quicker to follow the river, but from where he stood he could see the darkness that the track led into, the overhanging arch of whispering, leafy branches. The river way was also lonelier, and darker, and there would be countless little rustlings and shiverings in the undergrowth, to make him jump and sweat.

He turned towards the road, grey and drab in the street lights, but hesitated again. Always walk where it's well lit, the police said, but it was such a long, dreary trudge through the town-centre—and even at that time in the morning there would be people about. Drunks. They could be more dangerous than rustlings in the undergrowth.

He was angry with himself at his cowardice. Take the shortest way, he told himself. Get home and get to bed. The river was the shortest way. He turned down the side of the chip-shop, following a track which became a hard-trodden, narrow strip of gravelly earth with tall grass and nettles growing on either side. The trees began to lean in from the sides, and he had to duck beneath the branches. Cool leaves touched his neck. A spider's web spread its stickiness across his mouth. He wiped it away with his hands, and his fingers were plastered with a mess of sticky fibres, dust and trapped insects.

In the river lived Megs Greenteeth. Another of his granny's stories. Megs Greenteeth, with her long hair that looked like weed floating on the water, who lurked under the water near the banks of the river, and seized hold of small children who went too close. Down under the water she would drag them, and hold them there while they drowned, and then she ate them with her big green teeth. Every year she drowned two boys and two girls—had to, or she would die herself. So she never relaxed, she was always waiting… And it was Midsummer's Eve, so she would be there. Such monsters were always more alive on the year's turning nights. On Midsummer's Night, Old Megs would be able to clamber right out of the river on to the bank… And there she would be, waiting for him in the half-dark… a hunched, crouching figure, dripping water and weed, her grin showing her big, green teeth…

He was actually scaring himself. He paused where the track came out on to the river-bank. It was cooler there, under the leaves, and darker than it had been on the road. The air was full of the green scent of leaves and grass, and of the rattle and brush of grass-heads against his clothes. Ahead of him the water of the river shone with a dull grey sheen, like pewter. It was so warm that smoke-clouds of gnats still danced in the air above the water.

He peered up and down the river-bank. There was no sign of anyone or anything waiting, nor of any large head breaking the surface of the water. He laughed at himself, but it came out as a thin, nervous giggle. Of course he didn't believe that a monster named Megs Greenteeth was hiding just out of sight below the river-bank—but in the whispering quiet under the trees he had a sense of something waiting.

He set out briskly along the river path and, as he went, his hip brushed a tall foxglove and set it swaying. He glanced back at it. In the dusk its pale, fresh pink glowed, and he could even see the darker spots in the throats of the flowers. Foxgloves… Midges whirled about his head and fluttered against his face as he walked through the haze of them hovering under the trees. There was something about foxgloves, some other story his granny had used to tell him when he'd been little… She'd made silly jokes about foxes making gloves out of the flowers, but there'd also been something about woods where foxgloves grow being lucky—or unlucky. A sound of splashing in the river made him turn sharply and peer into the darkness behind him. Megs Greenteeth was coming for him!

He waited tensely, studying the darkness for any movement, and listening. And when he moved on, he was still uneasy. White moths fluttering above the grasses and shining in the dusk drew his gaze sharply. A sudden fish rising in the dark on the river's other side made him jump on his heels with fright. The assurances he tried to give himself were hollow, and only made his unease deeper. Something in him—something that made the hair shift on his arms and his neck, something that had made his heart beat quicker and his breath come faster—knew that there was reason to fear on the shadowed path under the trees.

A thick stand of hawthorn cast a stretch of the path into dense darkness, starred with a few late white blossoms. Their scent was spread wide by the warmth of the night and the dampness of the river, but he wasn't in the mood to hang around sniffing flowers. He stretched his legs and hurried to get past the bushes—and so walked hard into someone who stood in the darkness, and who reeled back with a little gasp and said, "Oh, you scared me!" A girl's voice.

Sean backed off. A pale face glimmered in the dark. "Sorry," he said. "You scared me, too. Are you all right?"

"I'm scared," she repeated and he felt again that shiver over his own skin—but before he could wonder about it, he was surprised to recognize her as Penny. He was walking on, slowly, and she walked with him and, as they emerged from the shadow of the hawthorns into the twilight of the more open path, he looked at her and saw that she wasn't Penny. Of course she wasn't—how could she be? Again there was that trickle of apprehension through his mind, which he tried to ignore. He couldn't be scared, not in front of a girl.

A pretty girl, too. It was even more impossible to be scared in front of a pretty girl. She was about the same height as Penny and had long hair like her—which explained his mistake. He tended to see Penny everywhere, mistaking any girl of similar height and colouring for her.

This girl's face shone pale in the dusk as she turned towards him. Her chin was very pointed as she lifted her face to look at him. Her mouth opened softly and her eyes seemed huge and black in the darkness. Her hair fell in heavy dark curls on to her shoulders. The dark top she wore was low-cut, and her throat and breasts gleamed too. She had a fuller figure than Penny. "Can I walk with you?" she said. "I'm feared. Let me walk with you."

To his own surprise, everything instinctive in him said, "No!" He wanted to step away from her, to hurry past her, even to run away. His reason told him that was ridiculous. She was just a girl. "What are you doing down here on your own?" His tone of voice was harder than he had intended. Her boyfriends are waiting in the bushes, he was thinking. She's been sent to bring you along to them.

In a thin little voice, she said, "I'm feared. Can I walk with you?"

The voice, and the whimper in it, instantly appealed to him. Was she simple-minded, he wondered. There was no possibility of leaving her if she was. "Course you can," he said.

She startled him then by suddenly hugging his arm in both of hers and leaning against him, close and warm and soft. Her hair fell over his shoulder and brushed against his neck. Again that shiver of fright—or revulsion—quivered through him. He found himself struggling with two distinct sets of thoughts. One set—cowardly and childish—was telling him to shove her away and run, leave her, get away. The other set—adult and reasonable—was telling him not to be so stupid, and asking him, how could he leave a frightened girl—a simple-minded girl—alone in the dark?

If she wasn't simple-minded, she was very bold. She was rubbing her chin against his shoulder and hugging his arm tight (so you can't get away!). He wouldn't want Penny, or his little sister, to behave like this.

"You're all right with me," he said, "but you should be careful who you talk to at this time of night."

She looked up at him, her face pearly in the dusk, her eyes huge. With a little wrinkle of her nose, she said, "I could see you were nice." An accent of some kind lilted from word to word.

A confusion of feelings filled him: that dread again, the sense of warning which urged him to run; but also a foolish pleasure which made him grin despite himself. "I am nice. Very nice. And so are you." She looked up at him again, and gave a little rub of her cheek against his shoulder. He'd only known her minutes. But it was nonsense to suspect her of meaning him any harm. Why should she? "I'm Sean. What's your name?"

"Essylt."

"What? That's different. Are you from abroad?"

She shook her head and her dark hair rippled and floated around her face. "No. I'm—I'm Welsh."

"Oh, that's the accent!" She was so very pretty that he was strongly tempted to try kissing her—except that he shivered at the thought. Anyway, he'd told her that she was safe with him—and what if she *was* simple-minded? Then it would be wrong of him to try anything on with her. It was nobility, he told himself, that kept him from kissing her, not fear. The path where he turned off into the back streets of Brierley wasn't far ahead.

"Where do you live?" he asked.

She drew a soft breath and hesitated before saying, "Not far."

She sounded like a child. "I'm only going as far as the dairy," he said. It was a reminder to himself as much as a warning to her, in case he should be overcome by chivalry and offer to walk her to her door. He refused to admit to the relief he felt at the idea of soon being rid of her. "Can I get you a taxi? I'll worry about you getting home otherwise."

She raised her pointed face and smiled at him. "Walk with me."

He felt a revulsion, as if at some slyness or insincerity. Glancing ahead, he saw the wall of the dairy through the trees. That was where he turned off. "There's a cab-office on the way. We can get you one there." He ducked into the darkness of the trees overhanging the path, and she went with him, clinging to his arm and pressing warmly against his side. Straightening, he walked out on to the wider track that led into the factory estate. The dairy's chain-link fence was on one side and, on the other, a little wilderness of bushes, brambles, tin cans and litter. As his feet trod on the hardness of tarmac, he felt a draught at his side, and lost the touch of her. She was gone.

He turned in a complete circle, looking all around him, at the drab concrete and tarmac, at the bushes and litter, at the dark, overhanging trees of the river-bank. Essylt was nowhere.

He opened his mouth to shout her name, and then closed it again. She had not let go of his arm and gone away… When he had ducked under the trees, she had been close beside him, holding on to his arm. There had been no slackening of her hold, no moving away. She had been there—and then she had not been there. The night around him had that curious, flat feeling—that somehow threatening feeling—that tells you a house is empty.

He turned his back on the river-bank and ran, ran with loud feet through the empty roads and past the empty buildings of the factory estate.

The hot air was hard to breathe, and he choked for breath. His head swelled with heat, his body ran with sweat, but he forced himself to stumble on until the pain in his chest and side was so bad that he fell against a wall and leaned there, gasping.

He was in a long street of small terraced houses, all of dirt-darkened brick, all with small windows and coffin-sized doors. From where he leaned he could see them stretching on and on along a dark pavement. Cars were parked at the kerb, the streetlights shining on the curves of their roofs. A ripple of light, reflected from the lamp-posts, ran down the long line of windows.

His breath roared in his ears and scoured his throat. His legs shook under him. I've seen a ghost! he thought. A Midsummer's ghost. He didn't know whether to laugh or start running again. As he was in no state to run, he laughed, a little, shaky, breathless laugh. You coward, you fool! he said to himself. Running off and leaving the girl like that, when she'd only gone back under the trees for a moment… Maybe she dropped something.

But however his brain reasoned, his body knew that he had been right to run.

He hadn't fully recovered his breath when he started walking. He didn't want to hang about there. Sweat had soaked his shirt, and he took it off as he walked, and tied it around his waist by its sleeves. His footsteps were loud and clattering in the open street, but every few feet he passed the mouth of an entry leading to the yards behind the houses. The entry caught the sound of his walking and made it boom. The entries, with their echo and their darkness, made him nervous, and he took to walking as far from them as he could, close to the cars. He set off one over-sensitive alarm, and its shriek made his heart thump again, just when it had been beginning to slow down.

A ghost! He'd really seen a ghost, just like his grandad. Not everybody could say that. Just the same, he looked behind him and—with a start—into an entry he suddenly discovered himself to be passing. Seeing ghosts might be something special, but it wasn't an experience he wanted to repeat.

Not that it had been a very frightening ghost... His body didn't agree. His skin shivered again at the mere thought of the thing he had met down by the river. Get home! Get home, as soon as possible, to brick walls and locked doors, curtained windows and electric light. He hurried on.

He reached the main road, a broad dual-carriageway, where lorries were still passing. He waited for one to pass and ran across the road, vaulting the barrier in the middle. And then he had a choice. He could go the long way round by the road—a long, dreary trudge through empty streets, which would add an hour or more to his journey. Or he could cut through the wood.

It wasn't a natural wood, but a new plantation on derelict land, an "Urban Reforestation Project". It made a long, black shape in the midsummer dusk, but something pale glowed against its darkness—a tall foxglove, swaying at one of the arched entrances to the wood. Was it lucky or unlucky to walk where foxgloves grew?

He stood on the pavement before the wood, considering. A whisper of wind through the leaves made him jump, and shiver, and turn to look behind him. What to do? He didn't want to go into the darkness of the wood—(wolves and witches sneaked through the fairy-tale woods of his mind)—even if it was only a little, tame, Council-planted wood. But if he took his short way through the wood, and hurried, he would only be among the trees for a few minutes, and then he'd be home in half an hour, at most.

If he went the long way round, by road, it would be a long hour of silent streets, and stealthy noises, and looking behind him.

He took a step towards the wood, and then stopped again. He'd met *her* under trees...

Come on, he said to himself—as he turned to look behind him again—make up your mind instead of standing here. What's it to be? A quick trot through the wood, or a long trudge by road?

The wind was still, and the leaves hung limp, making no sound. With one last look at the grey, empty road behind him he entered the wood by one of its many hard-trodden little paths, passing through an archway of trunks and leaves. He kept his hands out of his pockets, ready to act. The shortest path would take him through the wood in less than five minutes.

Just inside the wood the paths were wide, though grooved with the flow of water and uneven with roots, and he was able to walk briskly. It was darker under the trees, as their canopy of leaves shut out the light of the street-lamps and moon, and gathered in the dusk. It was much cooler, too, and there was a smell of earth and damp. The shadow of the trees had preserved puddles and muddy hollows even through the long, hot, dry spell.

But once away from the main road, where many people entered the wood, the paths became narrower, and then Sean was reminded that it's never easy to walk through a wood at night, and impossible to walk quickly. There were hollows filled with leaves to send him stumbling, and fallen branches to roll under his feet. Thin whippy branches, blended into the greyness of the dark, smacked his face or poked him in the eye. Briars snagged his clothes and, in the dark, were painful and difficult to remove. He began to curse himself for ever having come into the wood but, by then, it would have taken as much time and effort to go back as to go on.

So he went slowly, one hand held before his face to fend off branches, which projected suddenly even into broad and well-trodden paths. A narrower path turned off to his left, in the direction he needed, and he followed it. Ahead the trees were closer and darker, and he was constantly ducking or brushing leaves or twigs from his face. A booming, crashing sound from above, and a snapping of twigs made him halt, his heart thumping in his chest—he had scared up some roosting birds, which now rebuked him with the wood-pigeon's cry of, "You fool you! You fool you!"

He agreed with them, and pushed on. The path seemed to be closing ahead of him, until he found himself trying to shove his way through bushes, and being showered with dirt, his bare arms and chest thwacked with branches, or scratched. He wiped his hot face, smearing it with bark dust, and reluctantly started back the way he had come. Obviously he'd taken the wrong path. He hadn't realized that the wood was so big. He swore as he went, striking out at bushes. Just the time to get lost (on ghost-haunted Midsummer's Eve). He could have been home by now (and safe).

He found his way back, not to a broader path, but to a clearing he had never seen before. It wasn't a place easy to forget. Moonlight filtered down through the opening in the leaves above, and showed—all black and silver—an immense fallen trunk, grooved and split and grown with fungus. Another tall tree stood at the clearing's centre, its black trunk and branches glimmered over with white flowers. I'm lost, he thought, completely lost. A little cold dread crept into him and settled under his breast bone. Such huge old trees as that didn't grow up in a few years, after being planted by an Urban Reforestation Programme.

He wandered around the clearing, peering along the paths that led from it—paths that led into a thick grey of dusk and faded into darkness. His arm had been badly scratched, and he licked it, and stumbled on uneven ground, and briefly wondered if it would be best to lie down and sleep there—but no, not in that place. He couldn't sleep there. Not in that place, on that night.

A voice spoke from the darkness, and it was no imaginary voice. The sound vibrated softly against his ear-drum. "Can I walk with you? I'm feared."

A pale tower of foxglove flowers swayed as she stepped from the darkness of the bushes at the edge of the clearing. He recognized her voice, and the shape of her, the gleam of her face in the dim light, and the dark fall of her hair... The river, where he'd last seen her, was more than a mile away. He tried to back away from her, but she moved more surely in the dark than he could.

She came close, her head tilting as she looked up at him. "I'm lost and feared. Can I walk with you?" He shivered as if her voice was a feather drawn over his skin. Her manner held no hint that she remembered him, or that she remembered speaking those words before.

She came closer still and tried to take his arm, but he violently shook it free of her and took a clumsy step back. A bush behind him jabbed its many sharp twigs and branches into his back, and he had to stop. He opened his mouth to tell her to get away from him, but then remained silent. He was afraid to speak to her, as if beginning any kind of talk with her might trap him.

She came close again, and he couldn't back further, and had to stand still as she leaned against him. The touch of her body was soft and warm against his skin; not at all as he had always supposed the touch of a ghost to be. The thickness of her hair brushed his chin, and a scent came to his nose—a sweet, honey-scent of flowers, gorse-flowers. Yet he stood braced and tense against her, too scared of her even to shudder.

"I'm cold," she said, as if anyone could be cold on that night. "Keep me warm." Her head tilted its heavy, warm weight on to his shoulder, and her hair was soft on his neck. "Put your arms round me and keep me warm."

Revulsion and fear made him act. He shoved her away from him, so that he could move away from the bush and into the open space of the clearing. She was solid and warm, like a living body, and swayed away from his push like a real girl—but the shivering of his skin and the sickness in his gut told him that she wasn't. Whatever she was, she wasn't a living girl.

She moved after him: he could see the paleness of her face, throat and breast in the dusk. "Don't you like me?" she said, and her little voice, which hardly disturbed the silence, was so sad that it tugged at the pity in him. He had to make an effort to take another step away from her, and to hold out a hand to fend her off.

"I want to get to the road," he said. "That's all. You go away!"

She tried to catch hold of his hand. "Let's lie down here and keep each other warm."

Never! he thought. He was trying to watch where he put his feet, feeling for each step in the dark, fearing to stumble and fall. He kept turning his head slightly, trying to hear the sound of traffic. The wood was surrounded by roads; they must be near one. He could hear nothing but the sound of the breeze in the leaves, his own breathing, the sound of his own movements.

"You're tired," her voice came whispering. "Lie down and sleep with me. We'll keep each other warm till morning." She made a snatch and caught one of his hands between both of her own. Her hands were small, but their grip—he couldn't get free. Her fingers were clenched as tightly around his as a tree's roots clench around a stone. It was horrible enough that she—the thing—was touching him again, but he sweated with panic as he used all his strength and still couldn't break her grip. She was pulling him towards her, her pale face gleaming in the dark and her voice whispering, "Lie down with me, lie down with me—"

"No!" With his free hand, he tried to wrench her fingers open. "What are you?"

Still clinging to his hand, holding him still, she said, "I love you, I love you—Stay with me, I love you—"

"Let go!" He shook their linked hands violently. "Get away from me!"

She stilled suddenly and straightened, a dark shape against the dark background of trees. But still she clung to his hand. Her voice, when she spoke, was louder, and harder. "Don't you like me?"

"Let me go."

"Am I ugly?" she said.

He paused, remembering how pretty she had been by the river, and seeing her now, all soft in the moonlight. So like Penny, but prettier. "You're beautiful," he said, "but you're not real—are you? What do you really look like?"

"Do you refuse me?" she said.

"Let me go. I don't want you. I want to go."

She swung him from her, releasing her grip on his hands, so that he went staggering away from her. "Go then!" she cried. As he passed her, he felt a solid blow thump on to his spine, between his shoulder-blades, and her voice shrilled, "And that to take with you!"

The blow was so hard that it sent quivers of impact through his body, and knocked the breath from him. His mouth gaped as he turned back towards the girl, but he could no longer see anything of her. She might have been standing among the black shapes of the trees, watching him, but he couldn't catch even the pale sheen of her face.

He crooked one arm behind his back, straining to reach the spot between his shoulders where she'd struck him. He feared that he'd been stabbed, but he touched no knife, and could feel no wound or blood. Yet the blow went on aching, and his flesh felt bruised at every slight movement, not only on his back, but inside his chest. The pain even seemed to have seeped into bones, and spread up his neck into his head.

He had stumbled into one of the narrow paths leading from the clearing, and he reached out for support to the trees on either side. His chest was heavy, tight. His feet were disconnected from his control, and sent him half-running, staggering, almost falling. Every breath took such effort that sometimes he had to stop and lean on a tree while he dragged in air. His heart was stifled, sometimes beating ponderously slow, sometimes skittering in panic before being overcome by the solidness of his chest, which was so hard to move, it seemed to be turning into wood.

His eyes glazed with light and, finding no tree where he reached for support, he fell. The hard ground thumped him in the chest, but he had no breath to lose. He tried to get up but his wooden lungs pinched out his life.

A man on his way to work on Midsummer morning took his usual short cut to his bus-stop through the little patch of woodland. Lying in the middle of the broad path he found the boy, lying face down, his shirt tied around his waist, and a big blue-black bruise between his shoulder blades. His head, lying at the edge of the path, nudged a tall foxglove, its pale pink flowers glowing in the morning light.

THE MIDSUMMER EMISSARY
Minagawa Hiroko
Translated by Ginny Tapley Takemori

First published as "Fumizuki no Shisha" (文月の使者) in Shosetsu Subaru (小説すばる), July 1996. First published in English as "The Midsummer Emissary" in Kaiki: Uncanny Tales from Japan. Volume 3: Tales of the Metropolis, *edited by Masao Higashi (Kurodahan Press, 2012)*

Minagawa Hiroko (皆川博子) was born in 1930 in Gyeongseong, Korea, but moved to Tokyo at three months old when her father, who was an assistant professor of medicine at Gyeongseong Imperial University, opened a clinic in Shibuya, Tokyo. She entered Tokyo Women's University, majoring in foreign languages and English literature, but dropped out after two years due to illness. When her daughter decided to go to Australia for a year as an exchange student, Minagawa started writing stories, primarily exploring historical and mystery fiction. In 1970, she won the Gakken Children's Literature Award for *Kawato*. Her 1976 novel *The End of the Midsummer Festival* was nominated for the prestigious Naoki Prize. There have only been four translations of her work, three in English and one in Italian. She was one of the writers of the film *Sharaku* (dir. Masahiro Shinoda, 1995), based on her novel of the same name, about an artist in Edo-era Japan.

Ginny Tapley Takemori is a British editor and translator (Catalan, Spanish and Japanese language) now living in Japan, who has been making waves in recent years with her translations of Murata Sayaka's novels and short stories, published by Granta in the UK. Her translation of Murata's Akutagawa prize-winning novel *Convenience Store Woman* was one of the *New Yorker*'s best books of 2018 and Foyle's Book of the Year 2018. She has also published translations of the works of Nakajima Kyoko (*The Little House*, 2019) and many other early-modern and contemporary Japanese authors.

"The Midsummer Emissary" is set in the liminal space of Japan's summer, traditionally the season for telling ghost stories (*kaidan*), and a time in which spirits return from the realms of the dead to interact with the living—perhaps to celebrate with them, or to complete some purpose. Of course, not all spirits made it to their resting place, and Japanese folklore is full of tales of wandering spirits tethered to some trauma or unresolved emotion of their past life. In this tale, Minagawa evokes the notions of the "living" and the "dead", the "ordinary" and the "unordinary", the "real" and the "illusion" which all coexist. It's a strange and unfamiliar story, and a real delight to read.

I GAVE *you my finger, you know.*
   The wavering voice had come from behind him.
   He must be hearing things. Or maybe he had misheard.

He had been descending the stairs to the ferry landing at the foot of the collapsed Onnabashi bridge and was just three or four steps above the river. The well-worn stone was like a sponge, oozing water with each step. As he turned, his foot slipped, and he barely managed to stay upright. Meanwhile, the voice's owner had disappeared—not by any mysterious trick but most likely into the shadows round a bend in the alley.

He imagined her in fresh summer clothes, light and diaphanous, possibly Akashi crepe. He had the impression she was twirling a parasol. No, she wasn't carrying a parasol, or anything else. Her coiffure left the nape of her neck refreshingly exposed. And her light summer kimono had a design of irises in indigo on a white background. On her bare feet she wore geta. The straps were black, like those worn by men… Her toes and heels were white against the muddy path.

But nobody had been there when he turned around, so he must have imagined the voice. It was a little hoarse, but seductive nonetheless…

It wasn't only the owner of the voice who was out of sight; there was no sign of anybody else, either. Had the torrential rain from last night's storm washed away all the residents of Nakasu once and for all?[*]

---

[*] Nakasu was a popular entertainment district built on a sandbank supplemented by landfill in the Sumida River that flourished briefly from 1771 until 1790.

Both the Otokobashi and Onnabashi bridges had collapsed.[*] Otokobashi appeared to have been struck by lightning, his broken girders burned black. Onnabashi looked as though she had followed her lover in death, her rotten girders all twisted and boards bent over at an angle, one side submerged under water.

He had first crossed over Onnabashi to visit Nakasu three years earlier. It had already been dangerous then, with crumbling handrails and holes in the boards. That time too had been just after a heavy downpour. With both the bridges down, Nakasu would be isolated and helpless, a boat cut loose and set adrift. It had been Yumimura who had said that, hadn't it?

Last night, as he crossed over Onnabashi to Nakasu, it had never occurred to him that it might fall down.

There was a small boat moored at the ferry landing.

Turbid water lapped at the landing. The wood here was rotten too, with blackish blotches, a mix of mildew and moss. Trash drifted on the surface of the swollen river, catching on posts like the floating nests of grebes.

Perhaps the ferryman was resting somewhere waiting for customers to gather, for he was nowhere to be seen. The moored boat was half full of bilge water that made him feel sick. It looked as though it would sink the moment anyone got in it.

Last night's rain had soaked into the ground and was now rising once more in the heat of the day to make the air terribly sultry. Even the sun beating down became part of the overhead mesh of hot mist that rained down. Everything before him seemed to shimmer.

I gave you my finger. Either he had been hearing things, or he had misheard, he told himself again. He groped around in the wide sleeve of his kimono that served as a pocket and found a half-crushed cigarette box. He opened it up and found it full not of cigarettes, but of severed fingers...

---

[*] Literally, "Man Bridge" and "Woman Bridge" respectively.

Laughing at himself for being so silly, he opened the box again. Time for a smoke, he thought. It was empty, except for the crumpled silver paper. He crushed it in his hand and threw it into the water.

Just then he saw something. Mixed in with the trash caught on a post, bobbing on the waves of the river, was a woman's pillow.

It was one of those wooden box pillows shaped like the hull of a ship, to which a small cushion was fastened. The wood was coated with an alluring vermilion lacquer that had worn away here and there over the years. The cushion was quite sodden with water. The piece of paper placed over it to keep it clean had writing on it—an unsent letter, perhaps—and the black ink was blurred.

Flowing... he read, but he was unable to make out the characters that followed it.

He strained his eyes.

Black hair... That's what it said.

Hair...

Previously he would have shuddered with horror at the sight of that word alone, but now there was no longer anything to be afraid of.

Even so, that did not mean he was over his fixation with hair, and out of curiosity he reached out his hand for the pillow. It felt slimy, as if the water had dissolved the glue on it. He scooped it up in one hand. Along with the pillow, bits of straw or something like it clung to his hand. The rotten plank beneath his feet suddenly gave way, and he stumbled forward. Yet even then he hung onto the pillow and was on the point of falling in when someone caught hold of him and a voice said, "Watch out!" He hadn't noticed anyone approaching from behind.

"Such an inconvenient thing to have dropped!"

It was a middle-aged woman. Her voice was rough, quite unlike the beguiling voice that had called to him earlier. Her "praying mantis"-style chignon was secured not with an elegant coral hairpin but with a coarse black pin, and the striped weave and black satin collar of her robe looked uncomfortably hot. Her bare feet were slipped into worn geta, her toes muddy. Something black peeped out of a folded old newspaper in her bamboo handbasket and meowed.

"You take care now," she said, turning to leave.

"Oh, but… is the ferryboat running?" he queried, casting a doubtful glance at the dilapidated boat and wondering whether there even was a boatman.

"I suppose so," she answered vaguely. "Perhaps you should ask the boatman."

"There doesn't appear to be one."

"Are you in such a hurry to cross the river?"

"It's not that… it's just that I was visiting an acquaintance and was forced to stay over by last night's rain."

"Nakasu is no place for such a good-looking student, is it?" she said, gazing lasciviously at his skin. "Did you quarrel with your companion?"

"Why do you ask?"

"That thing's dripping wet, isn't it? Throwing someone's pillow into the river isn't exactly amicable."

"It was already in the river. I just saw it and fished it out."

"On a whim, I suppose." She laughed, but apparently disinclined to inquire further, said teasingly, "A fortuitous rain, perhaps," as she took her leave. Her black cat stretched its head out of the basket and meowed disdainfully. Once she had disappeared around the bend in the alley, the place was again deserted, as if all life had died out.

The paper cover over the pillow was sodden and looked as though it would rip at the slightest touch.

Flowing black hair spreading over the water.

He could barely make out the elegantly inscribed characters.

There were more words, but the paper was wrinkled from where it was tied with cords to the pillow and it was hard to read. He would have to wait until it was dry before he could smooth it out.

He cradled the pillow gently in one hand. It felt heavier than he'd imagined. A pillow used by some unknown person, and discarded in the river to boot.

The ferryboat did not appear to be about to depart any time soon. He climbed back up the stone staircase and scanned the row of houses for a tobacconist's sign.

His feet sank in deep sludge. A black boarded fence. A storehouse, its doors closed. There was what looked like some kind of store, but a scrap of yellowish cloth—it hardly qualified as a curtain—hung behind the glass door as if to indicate it was closed. Pasted onto the fence was a handbill for a movie, or perhaps it was a play. The colours were faded and the border torn, revealing the edges of older flyers beneath. Red and blue and white: even the continuous upward spiral of the candy-striped barber's pole had come to a standstill.

He peered further along the alley and finally, amidst the darkened eaves, his eyes alighted on a sign advertising tobacco and salt. He headed for it, sidestepping the puddles formed by putrid water overflowing the rotting boards over the gutter.

The glass door of the tobacconist's stood open. Household goods from toilet paper to scrubbing brushes and disposable chopsticks were arranged on a stand, and in a glass case on the left, just as the sign had said, there were several boxes of cigarettes. Behind a lattice screen on the raised tatami floor was seated an old man, his skinny body wrapped in a washed-out, threadbare summer robe that appeared held together by starch alone. In his hand was a round, flat fan with which he directed a cool breeze to his neck, but upon noticing he had a customer he stopped fanning himself and lightly raised the rim of his reading glasses. His close-cropped hair was white and his throat scrawny, yet his eyes revealed a strength that belied old age.

"Have you any Golden Bat?"

The glass case was out of the old man's reach from where he sat behind the screen, so he stood up. He was tall, the bare shins peeping from beneath the hem of his robe so fleshless they seemed barely able to support him. Nevertheless, he moved with surprisingly agility over to the case, took out a packet of Bats, and wordlessly placed them before the student.

"Some matches, too," said the student, trying unsuccessfully to open the packet with one hand. Conscious of the drips, he placed the pillow on the edge of the raised wooden floor.

The interior of the store was dark, untouched by sunlight, yet it felt sultrier within than it did outside.

"How much?" A disagreeable voice.

"What?"

"How much?" asked the old man again.

Had he mistaken the order for salt or sugar? His hearing was evidently rather poor.

"Some matches," said the student, a little louder.

The old man reached for a bamboo basket on top of the glass case. Inside were loose matchsticks the size of toothpicks, their tips painted with red phosphorous.

"How much?" The same question again.

Next to a bundle of tissue paper was a weighing scale with a small basket placed on top of it.

The old man dropped a few matchsticks into the basket.

"You sell them by weight? Don't you have any boxes?"

"Here. On the house."

The old man took a matchstick from the basket on the scale and handed it to him. Without the striking surface on the side of the matchbox, however, it would not ignite.

The old man went inside. Visible through the open door was a small tatami room with a kitchen to the right. The alcove was decorated with what appeared to be a chest for storing armour, touches of vermilion visible on the lid. The same colour ornamented a spear hanging up on the crossbeam.

The old man came right back and slid the door closed behind him, cutting off the view of the interior. He had with him an economy-sized box of matches, the sort used in kitchens. He thrust this at his customer and then took out a tobacco tray from behind the latticed screen and filled the bowl of his pipe with shredded tobacco.

He wanted someone to talk to, the student thought. The old man indicated the raised floor, as if telling him to sit down for a smoke. Not that there was anything piteous about him; on the contrary, he had the haughty air of an old-time samurai.

The old man's eyes were drawn to the writing on the sodden pillow. He adjusted his spectacles and stared at the words. "Flowing black hair… consume…" he murmured.

The student could not catch *what* was consumed but missed his chance to ask. He was about to correct the old man—"spreading over water"—when he realized it did appear to say "consume", just as the old man had said.

Flowing black hair… He had pictured a cascade of loosened black hair, but read another way it could mean "melting black hair." He was briefly seized with the vision of the words in ink on the pillow paper as numerous black strands of hair, tangled and flowing, welling up out of the paper, sidling up to him.

"It was in the river," he said needlessly. This did not explain why he had fished it out.

Really, why had he gone to such lengths? Looking at it now, it was just a filthy pillow used by goodness only knew who and permeated with female body grease and hair oil.

It had been because of that single word, "hair". That was why he had wanted it…

Such a gold- and silver-decorated red-lacquered object could only belong to a professional. There were brothels in Nakasu, too—a lustful woman, sleeping with different partners every night, probably diseased.

It wasn't Tamae's pillow, surely…?

It wasn't possible! *But what if…?* The thought weighed on him.

Even though he had tried to erase all memory of the very name Tamae from his mind…

He heard a cat's meow followed by the sound of claws scratching, and the door slid open a crack. A black paw stretched through the gap, forced the door open, and was followed by the cat's body squeezing through.

Was it the same cat as that middle-aged woman had been holding? Had that woman been from this household? He caught a fleeting glimpse of a human figure pass behind the narrow gap. Young, dressed in a white robe…

As he sat there in confusion, the cat meowed again and came sidling up to him, knocking the pillow to the ground. Just as he bent down to pick it up, the door clattered wide open and bare feet peeking out from beneath the hem of a wavy-striped kimono strode through it.

"Well, well, if it isn't the student! We meet again."

"You're the mistress of this house?"

The figure he had glimpsed a moment ago was not this woman. It had been more suited to the voice that had called to him about the finger, an unspoiled young…

The middle-aged woman seemed to like chatting even more than the old man, for she came and sat down beside him.

"I'm his daughter-in-law."

So she was the wife of the old man's son. It had clearly been many years since she had set down roots in this house. Her husband must be working elsewhere. As though reading his thoughts, she said, "My husband has another woman across the river and no longer comes home. I'm lumped with the old man." Having let slip such unnecessary personal details, she asked, "So didn't the ferryboat leave?"

"I don't know."

"That must be a very precious pillow for you to hold onto it for dear life like that."

"No, it's not that, but—"

"Would you like something cold? Eh, young man?"

"Yes, please, I would. I'm boiling."

The woman withdrew inside and reemerged carrying a tray upon which had been placed three cups of cold barley tea.

Kuzu zakura…

Immediately, his thought was turned into words.

"Would you like a *kuzu zakura* sweet?"

"No, no," he added hastily, afraid of being thought impudent.

"I just remembered the first time I came to Nakasu, a while ago. On my way to visit a friend in hospital, I was caught in a sudden downpour and took shelter beneath the eaves of a stranger's house. It was only a passing shower, but I was invited into the house to wait it out. I was cheeky enough to accept the invitation and was treated to cold barley tea and *kuzu zakura* sweets."

"How unfortunate. We're all out of sweets."

"No matter."

"Weren't there some candies in that can over there?" put in the old man, but the woman cut him short. "Those are cough sweets for old people. They're not fit to offer to a student."

She went on, "As for a hospital in Nakasu, there's only the one."

"Yes, that's the one."

"It's filthy, you know."

"It's enough to make even those of us in good health sick," he said, before realizing this was disrespectful to local people. Flustered, he said without being asked, "The sick person I went to see was called Yumimura."

The student was from Kanazawa but since passing the entrance examination into a Tokyo university he had moved to the capital and was lodging in Nezu Katamachi. He had already lost both his parents, and, lacking the money to pay for his studies, he worked during the day at a printer's so that he could attend classes in the evening.

Yumimura had lodged in the room next to his. It had been immediately obvious that this was a man with no friends. He was the sort of fellow who took pride in having a good brain and thought everyone else was stupid, and people shunned him because of this stubbornly arrogant attitude. Yet his utter aloofness was rooted in loneliness and a desperate need for attention.

Whenever he talked, he would immediately become boastful. Anything, however trivial, would be a feather in his cap, such as having managed to knock the price down even further when buying something cheap at a night stall or having argued with the local policeman. Letting Yumimura talk on and on without so much as contradicting him, the student had found himself treated as a close friend.

There came a time when Yumimura began whining about having a slight fever and a heavy feeling in his head. The student had been unable to ignore this and recommended seeing a doctor. He was diagnosed with a reoccurrence of an earlier pulmonitis, for which he needed to be hospitalized, and so the doctor referred him to the hospital in Nakasu. Packing his wicker trunk and preparing to leave the lodging house, Yumimura told him reproachfully, "It's all because you told me to see a doctor", as if he were to blame for the illness itself.

Yumimura had told him not to visit, and the student had taken him at his word and left him alone, but then a postcard arrived asking him to send a book he had left behind at the lodging house. This was just an excuse disguising the fact that Yumimura was desperate for him to visit.

For the first time in his life, the student visited Nakasu. In fact, it was the first time in his life that he had been anywhere in Tokyo outside the little triangle between his lodgings, workplace, and university, and the occasional stroll around nearby Ueno.

Little by little his story came out. The woman asked him, "And the sick man, did he get better?"

"No."

"He's been hospitalized these three years?"

"Yes."

"That's terrible. So have you come to visit him again this time?"

"Yes, well…"

"When you came, was the bridge still intact?"

"Yes, I came yesterday before the downpour."

"So you got caught in the rain and stayed over? The bridge is down, and the ferryboat isn't running. You're in trouble, aren't you?"

"No, I'm not particularly bothered."

"You're rather irresolute for someone so young! Put a little more energy and spirit into your conversation, can't you?"

"Um…" he said vaguely, raising his hand to his head.

"Don't do that!" she continued relentlessly. "It's uncouth to scratch your head. It looks cheap. You're a fine-looking student, so show some backbone."

"Have you always lived here?"

The old man nodded at his question.

"You grew up in Honjo, didn't you, Father?" said his ageing daughter-in-law. "Even so, he's from a samurai family, you know. This old man's father was from a family of shogunal vassals that lived by the Honjo canal. Come the Meiji Restoration, he fell on hard times, and as no lucky break presented itself, he ended up running this general store in Nakasu, although he was already dead by the time I came to this house as a bride."

"Were you born in Nakasu?"

"Do I look like I was born on such a miserable patch of floating weeds? I'm a daughter of Fukugawa, I'll have you know. My parents were fishmongers hawking their wares on the streets, quite different from a samurai's pedigree. My mother-in-law was really hard on me, I can tell you. She's in the grave too, now."

"Do you have children?" He asked not so much out of interest as to keep the conversation flowing.

"Just this one," she said, stroking the cat's head.

"Do you know Nakasu well?"

"Well, yes, in such a small place… I get to hear which wives have been unfaithful and with who, what sort of guy such-and-such prostitute has for her lover and even which stray cat gave birth to how many kittens. I see things for myself, too."

"Do you know who the owner of this pillow is?"

"However big my ears are," she said with a wry smile, "how could they possibly reach the owner of an old pillow?"

"In that case, do you know of a woman with cropped hair who used to go from door to door playing the moon zither? In her house, there was an extraordinarily beautiful… woman," he began, but then found himself lost for words to explain it had actually been a man. "He sold himself as a woman, even in this day and age,* like one of those boy actor-prostitutes from the Edo period… so pretty…"

Well now! The old man and his daughter-in-law exchanged a look. He also had the impression that they were looking searchingly at each other.

"The woman with cropped hair was the lady of that house where three years ago I sheltered from the rain.

"I was sheltering from the rain under the eaves of the house when a voice came from behind the latticework inviting me, 'Come and shelter inside.' I hesitated, saying it would be too presumptuous, but pressed further, I accepted the kind offer."

"Was the cropped hair one there?"

"She looked like Hōkaibō.† And, the young maiden… The truth is that I did think he was a maiden to begin with. And a bit of a flirt at that. With a name like Tamae, how could I have thought he was anything but a woman?"

Having told the student, "Come and make yourself comfortable", the woman left him with Tamae and went out.

"It was really as though she was telling us to get on with it."

Left alone with the young woman, he found it hard to breathe. He was still a virgin and hardly knew what to do with himself.

"Tamae suddenly laughed. 'I'm a man, you know!' he said casually. 'I make a living looking like this,' he went on. 'But I won't eat you, so just relax, won't you? Eh, young man?'"

In a corner of the room was a moon zither. Tamae told him that his aunt sometimes went around the streets performing.

"'Whenever that aunt of mine takes a fancy to a man her hair is in the habit of growing and winding itself around his neck. That's why she cut her hair, you know,' he explained. Then he told me his aunt was a cook at the hospital."

---

* The story is set in the Taishō period (1912–26).

† The name of a rogue disguised as a monk, the leading character of the bawdy Kabuki play *Sumidagawa gonichi no omokage* (also commonly known as Hōkaibō).

"That's the hospital your friend was in, I suppose."

"Yes."

Tamae's hair was long and raven black. Once the rain had stopped the student took his leave, but behind him he heard the sound of hair being hacked off with a knife.

"Yumimura had a large six-bed room to himself. There weren't many patients."

He had handed over the book as requested.

"But then Yumimura pulled a face. 'There it is again,' he said. 'The rasping sound of a boat's scull as it passes beneath the window. It hurts my ears.' I myself couldn't hear anything, and when I said so, Yumimura replied, 'That's why I hate it.'"

Beneath the window was a narrow alley with no sign of any river.

"'As long as I hear that scull, I can't leave hospital.' Yumimura had been admitted to hospital with pneumonia, but it seemed he'd also gone a bit strange in the head."

"The poor thing," put in the woman.

"Suddenly I felt some hair winding itself around my shoulders and chest."

The hair was long, and the more he had tugged at it the longer it had grown.

"'What are you doing?'

"'The hair...'

"Yumimura said he couldn't see any hair, and then he laughed merrily. But I knew what it was. Tamae's hair had come after me. If I could find out about the woman Tamae called aunt, I would be able to clarify which of us was mistaken. I asked Yumimura whether there was a cook with cropped hair working at this hospital, but he answered, 'There's no one like that.' Just then, I heard a rasping sound loud and clear. My flesh broke out in goose bumps. After all, I'd seen with my own eyes that there was no river beneath the window. Seeing me shudder, Yumimura again roared with laughter. 'That's the sound of the cook pushing the trolley with the evening meals!'"

"So you met the cropped-haired cook?"

The woman prompted him to continue his story, but the old man remained silent. The only sound he made was the occasional tap of his pipe against the bamboo ash receptacle.

"Yes. When I went out into the corridor to collect Yumimura's tray, there she was, pushing the trolley, although she had a towel tied around her head."

"And?" The woman urged him to continue.

"I too found myself hospitalized without further ado."

"That's terrible!" The woman frowned. "What was wrong with you?"

"Apparently there was no such thing as a cropped-haired cook at the hospital."

"There wasn't?"

"Just as Yumimura had to remain in hospital until he could no longer hear the sound of the scull, I too was hospitalized until I could no longer see the cropped-haired cook."

"What an awful thing to happen!"

"I could have died of boredom. The two of us were there side by side, felled in action. Yumimura would trace with his finger the patterns on the wall made by stains and mildew from the leaking roof."

We're surrounded by women, so we're all right, he had said. This here was Okyō's face, this was Harube. That over there was Omin. He would idle away the hours giving them all women's names.

They're all acquaintances from the whorehouse. Hey, I'm joking. It's not that I really believe anything so silly as women's faces floating up out of the wall, he'd insisted senselessly. *Don't go telling the doctor, now. He'll say they're delusions or something and delay my release even longer. The doctor doesn't understand my jokes.*

Yumimura had mentioned numerous women but not a single one came to visit him in Nakasu, and not a single postcard came for him.

"'Meeting people is such a bother,' that's what Yumimura said. 'Before coming into hospital, I told everyone not to come and visit and not to write to me either.'"

"The bluff of a vain person," the woman put in.

"Indeed."

Amongst the stains on the wall, he could see Tamae's face.

"Of course, it was just an impression I had."

Theirs had been just a passing acquaintance. It was not as though their hands had even touched, much less their lips. Tamae may even have been merely teasing him with the story about the aunt who cut her hair short to stop it from growing and winding itself about any man she was attracted to.

However hard he tried, though, the fact was he could not rid himself of the long hair entwined around his shoulders, and it was abundantly clear to him that their meals were regularly brought to them on a trolley by the cropped-haired cook, her head covered with a hand towel. Yet Yumimura insisted that there was no hair wound about him and that the cook did not have cropped hair. The doctor agreed and told the student that as long as he saw things that did not exist, he could not allow him to leave the hospital.

"Surely all you had to do was say that you no longer saw them and you could have left the hospital right away."

"But I *could* see them."

"Honest as the day is long, aren't you?" The woman became contemplative. "What if the doctor was lying? He'd have wanted to keep you in hospital as long as he could."

"I did have my suspicions."

"The hospital fees must have been no small matter."

"You see, as a self-supporting student, there was no way I could pay a doctor's fees myself, but in the case of nervous disorders, the authorities— the government or state, I'm not sure—will pay the hospital some amount for any patient unable to meet the costs of their own treatment. If the hospital has too few admissions it would have to close, and so it welcomes such patients too. And so, perhaps… well, I did have my suspicions, but then it's also possible I really was ill… If it had been any other illness, I would have had no option but to stay in bed in my lodgings, but since I could get free treatment, well, perhaps it was a blessing in disguise."

"There you go sounding wishy-washy again. You should know yourself whether you were sick or not."

"Well, it made no difference to me either way. That in itself is perhaps an illness."

"Auntie", he had tried calling the cook who brought around the meal trolley. The woman, the towel covering her head, raised the corners of her mouth in a broad smile. "Tamae's hair has wrapped itself around me. I'm in a right fix."

"He's my nephew, after all. Whenever he falls in love, his hair kicks up a fuss. Tamae and I, we're the same. There's nothing we can do about it," whispered the aunt, her cropped hair concealed beneath the towel. "If he would only cut his hair, like I did… but then he's young. The poor thing shouldn't have to look like a monk."

"He doesn't even come to see me."

"Do you want him to come?"

The student was stuck for an answer. Even if Tamae did come to visit, what if Yumimura and the doctor said they couldn't see him? It would give them another excuse to keep him in hospital longer.

"Perhaps you're not in love?"

"With Tamae? Not particularly…"

"Really! Is that all you said? Not particularly?" said the middle-aged woman reproachfully as she lightly stroked the throat of the cat on her lap.

"Yes. I do think he's beautiful, but I can't say I'm especially in love with him."

"How calm you are, saying something so cruel!"

"Cruel?" he repeated, blankly.

"Failing to reciprocate an evil spirit's love is not exactly cruel," put in the old man.

"An… evil spirit?"

"Ah," was the old man's curt reply.

"That figures, I suppose. Could the pair of them have been demons?"

"There are all kinds here in Nakasu," said the woman. "I know the people here inside out, but my contacts don't extend to spirits."

"I had actually wondered about it myself. If it's true, then I feel even worse…"

"It's nothing to get depressed about, though."

"If someone's in love with you, better a flesh-and-blood woman."

"There shouldn't be anything dubious about a flesh-and-blood man and woman, you know." The woman batted her eyelashes. Her gaze was not directed at him, however, but at the old man.

The old man was sitting with his back straight as a rod, and his expression never so much as flickered, but the student suddenly found him comical and had to suppress a smile.

"You've been released from hospital," the old man nonchalantly changed the subject, "so congratulations are in order."

The cat turned its eyes to the boy, its large black pupils thinly bordered by golden irises.

"When did you get out?"

"It'll be over a year ago now…"

"So you no longer see that hair, or the cropped-haired aunt?"

"No…"

The words written on the pillow started drifting into his vision.

Flowing black hair…

Yesterday evening…

"I'll come again," he said, preparing to leave the hospital as dazzling flashes of lightning raged continuously. "Are you leaving?" Yumimura twisted his fingers around the student's hand. "You shouldn't go out in this terrible storm."

"It doesn't bother me."

"I suppose not."

Lying on the bed as always, Yumimura toyed with the student's hand.

"Its all the same to you whether you get wet or not now, isn't it?"

The student nodded.

"I feel so lonely," Yumimura said. "I suppose you do, too."

"I'm used to it."

"Lucky you. Is it something you can get used to? Will I, too?"

"If you do, you do."

He hadn't intended to be funny, but Yumimura burst out laughing, a little too loudly, although he sounded forlorn and fearful as he said, "But I don't want to."

"So don't," the student soothed him. "It seems that not everyone has to." He changed the subject. "This room is as awful as ever."

"There are more women than before," Yumimura said, touching the stains on the wall.

The student sat on the edge of Yumimura's bed.

"I really envy you," Yumimura said. "How did you manage it?"

"It's not difficult."

"But thanks to you, things are worse now. They won't allow me to use anything resembling a rope. As for the toilet, they removed the door. I can't do anything."

"If you're set on doing it, you can tear up the bedclothes to make a rope."

"Don't be so glib! But then, you're brave."

"You don't need to be brave. It was just that I got fed up with everything. That's why I did it."

"And what about now? Do you feel better?"

"Nothing's really changed. I'm still fed up with everything, just as before, only now there's no more recourse so I guess it's worse than before."

"It's worse than being alive? So maybe there's no point in dying."

"If you get weary of living, you can always die, but once you're dead, you can't die again however sick of it you are."

Eight o'clock was lights out in the sickroom.

"It's stopped raining."

"But you'll stay with me, won't you? At least until morning?"

"Sure. I'm not in any particular hurry."

"Was it because of being hounded by that Tamae?"
"Was what?"
"The reason you hanged yourself."
"Not really."
"It must have been annoying."
"Well, a little."
"So you remained a virgin, after all. That's such a pity."
"It's probably better that way. That way I won't feel any regrets."
"But still," Yumimura persisted.
"Is that so? You were still a virgin when you hanged yourself?" put in the woman as she tickled the cat's neck. "That was a bit hasty, wasn't it? If you'd played around a bit, you'd have been bound to change your mind."
"Yumimura was a womanizer, but he still got depressed, so it doesn't make any difference either way."
"But he won't hang himself. That's the difference, isn't it?"
"But…" He flinched at the woman's forceful tone.
"Why don't you try it now? You'll regret it if you don't."
"It's already too late. I'm not bothered anyway."
"Don't be shy. Come on, get that obi off. Listen. You're just a dead man. How presumptuous of you to put on adult airs, wearing that Hakata obi. Didn't you say you had to work to pay your college fees? But if you die, you can wear a Satsuma weave with Hakata obi. How pompous. Father, it's all right if I show him what it's like to be with a woman, isn't it?"
"You're obscene," scolded the old man, but the woman paid him no heed.
"But I'm *dead*!" The student shrank away from her.
"I don't mind, I'm telling you." Her hand reached for the knot of his obi.
"But it's the middle of the day…"
"Since when did the time of day make any difference to a dead person?"
"But *he's* here."
"Don't bother about him. Father sometimes gets the urge during the day, too, but he never lets it stop him. Isn't that right, Father?"
The old man scowled and busied himself filling his pipe.

"It's because you're such a wimp that an evil spirit took advantage of you, you know."

"I *can't* let you get away with that!" The inner door slid open to reveal a young woman standing there. Oh, but her black hair was cut short!

"Tamae…" murmured the student. It had been three years.

"I've been quietly listening for some time, but you've just been going on and on about evil spirits this and evil spirits that."

"So you're the demon called Tamae, are you?" demanded the middle-aged woman. "Such impudence. You go around Nakasu acting as if you own the place, barging into people's houses without so much as a by-your-leave. When did you come in?"

"You're not the only ones in Nakasu, you know. I've been living here longer than you have," retorted Tamae. "As for this young man, I've had my eye on him from the start. Hmm, I don't suppose you even know him, let alone his name. He's called Tokio,* you know." He snuggled his cheek against the student. "I was waiting for you, Toki. I kept sending you tidings of my hair, but you didn't understand. I wasn't annoyed, though. After all, you're in the realm of the dead. Even my hair can't get to the bottom of that realm."

"Don't demons and ghosts get along?" sneered the woman, still hugging her cat.

Tamae picked up the pillow and opened a little drawer in the wooden box support.

Black water spilled out.

"I put my hair in the drawer to stop it from making trouble. And I even gave you my finger, Toki, but you're just so heartless."

Nestled in the melting black hair was a single white finger.

"Is that a demon's version of a love suicide? But even cutting off your finger, you don't bleed."

"And what about you? Let's find out!" Tamae took a hairpin from the breast of his kimono. Its tip was sharp.

---

* Written with the characters for "time" and "man."

"Tamae, stop it, please!"

"You're dead, so stay out of it."

"What a way to speak to your lover! No wonder Toki gave you the cold shoulder."

"You only just learned his name from me a few moments ago, so don't be using it so familiarly now. How imposing of you. Toki, if you're of a mind to loosen your obi, come and do it with me."

"But that thing dangling between your legs will just get in the way of doing it with a man!"

"It's a lot better than an old hag's ugly mug when it comes to servicing customers in bed. Eh, Toki?"

Tamae leaned against the student, fending the woman off with the hairpin clutched in his hand.

"Damn you!" exclaimed the woman. She kicked open the door and went inside then reappeared clutching a big kitchen knife.

"Oh, please stop it," begged the student.

"I've been in love with Toki for three years, but you've only just met him!"

"A demon spurned for three years has no business barging in now. Get out!"

"Toki, you believed that it was because you were sick that you could see my hair and my aunt, didn't you? It's not that you hated me. Now that you're no longer human yourself, there's no need to keep on being so stubborn, is there?"

"Go on, get lost!" The woman thrust her knife at Tamae, who nimbly dodged it.

"If I go, it'll be together with Toki. You can't leave this world—just try it."

"In that case, I'll be a ghost too," said the woman, pointing the knife at her own throat. Instantly the old man leaped nimbly up and plucked the knife from the woman's hand and then wrested the hairpin from Tamae's grip.

"You randy old goat. You're jealous, aren't you?" cried the woman.

"You fool!"

"I have my pride too, don't I? Father, think about it. Some demon comes to Nakasu to steal my customers, and I'm to sit back and let him get away with it, am I?"

"Um, it's not that I'm your customer, or anything. I'm only a ghost," said the student nervously.

"Enough! Don't disparage yourself like that," the old man reproved him. "Young man, which of them are you in love with?"

"Neither in particular…"

"You're not in love? Right, as you wish." The old man strode into the inner room, opened the lid of the armour chest, and took out the suit of armour. Setting it down beside the chest, he reached up and took the spear from its place on the beam and unsheathed it. The vermilion-lacquered hilt glinted brightly in the darkened room.

Tokio, Tamae, and the woman all had their eyes glued on the old man, scarcely able to breathe.

The old man came back out and pointed the spear at Tamae. "Get in there!" he told him, chasing him into the room.

"That'll show you!" crowed the woman happily.

"You too!" The spear was turned unflinchingly on her.

"In there," the old man told the pair cowering before the spear, indicating the armour chest.

They tried to refuse, but the old man showed himself quite prepared to skewer the pair of them. Left with no choice, they stepped over the edge of the chest and crouched side-by-side inside.

The old man closed the lid and plumped himself down on top of it. "That's better!" He smiled faintly at the boy. "Those women don't half yak on."

"But one of them isn't a woman."

"Something of the sort, though."

"How long are you going to keep them locked up?"

"Nakasu's going to be filled in before long."

"I heard a rumour to that effect."

"And my time is nearly up. What little that's left to me, I want to enjoy in peace and quiet. There's some sake in the kitchen. Could I possibly trouble you to bring it to me, along with a cup?" Only a samurai descendant could use such a courteous turn of phrase.

Tokio brought the large bottle and a pair of cups.

"Oh, you'll have a drink too?"

"I'll keep you company."

The cat meowed.

"I forgot about that one," said the old man wryly. "So do you intend to stay here drinking with me until they come to fill the place in?"

"I'm afraid I'll have to be getting back."

"To the realm of the dead? No need to rush back to such a gloomy place."

"There's something I have to do. I'll be coming back to Nakasu soon for Yumimura."

"Is that the role you'll be playing from now on?"

"Yes. It's not one that everyone can get used to, but it suits me. I'll come for you too, when your turn comes."

"I'd be most grateful. Please do. But first, a drink."

"Let me pour you a cup."

He tilted the bottle and poured some sake into the cup in the old man's hand.

"You've certainly helped to alleviate the tedium."

Everything was quiet in the chest. Perhaps Tamae and the woman, both spurned, had hit it off.

"If you're ever bored, do come and visit. I just have to open this lid to start off some more boisterous merrymaking."

Indeed. The student smiled. The cycle of rowdy then quiet, rowdy then quiet, would carry on repeating itself. Time would stand still; nothing would change.

HEAVEN ON EARTH
Jenn Ashworth

First published as "Midsummer Eve" in Midsummer Eve, *edited by Steve Shaw (Black Shuck Books, 2020)*

Jenn Ashworth (b. 1982) is a British author who studied at Newnham College, Cambridge, and the Centre for New Writing at the University of Manchester. Before becoming a writer, she worked as a librarian in a prison. Her first novel, *A Kind of Intimacy*, was published in 2009 and won a Betty Trask Award. On the publication of her second, *Cold Light* (Sceptre, 2011), she was featured on the BBC's *The Culture Show* as one of the UK's twelve best new writers. Her third novel, *The Friday Gospels* (2013), and her fourth, *Fell* (2016), are also published by Sceptre. Her work has been compared to both Ruth Rendell and Patricia Highsmith; all her novels to date have been set in the North-West of England. In 2019 she published a memoir-in-essays about reading, writing and sickness called *Notes Made While Falling* which was a *New Statesman* Book of the Year and shortlisted for the Gordon Burn Prize. Her latest novel is *Ghosted: A Love Story*. She lives in Lancashire, is a Fellow of the Royal Society of Literature and is a Professor of Writing at Lancaster University.

"Heaven on Earth" (Jenn's original title for the piece) is a Covid-set story, and my jaw dropped the first time I read it. It is a story about entitlement, emasculation and being closed away from everything familiar. And the sun, it just keeps shining, hotter and hotter.

"Nothing yet from the embassy, John?" Terry asked. He was the type of man that called any male who served him "John", and was so absorbed in his own business that he hadn't noticed the reception desk was empty until he'd already spoken. He leaned against the polished counter.

"John?"

Funny that. John was there just a second ago, his neat clean smile signalling he was ready to assist. But Terry could have been thinking of this morning, actually, and another John entirely. If Terry was going to tell the truth, he had to admit he couldn't confidently tell the Johns apart. Not in a racist way: they all, despite the heat, wore the same white shirts and silk waistcoats. It was the uniform that made each John hard to tell from the next—not their skin colour. And relying on context didn't help—he could no longer think of this one as *the reception John* and that one as *the bar John* and the other as *the turndown service John* because the diminished team were all doing double duty now, *the shoe shine John* turning up with the morning newspaper, and *the mango sorbet by the pool John* sometimes appearing in the suite to get his evening bath started.

"Nobody there?"

Alone in the massive, sparkling lobby, he shook his head with careful regret. This was no way to treat a client. He'd see about this. Make a complaint. Client was the wrong word. He was a guest: he and Tilly both. They were guests of this hotel. The best hotel on the island, it was, standing alone on the southern edge, overlooking the lagoon. You could even say, given the hotel's position on the island and the island's position relative to the mainland (beyond the lagoon, on the island's southern aspect there lay nothing but thousands of miles of clear blue ocean), this was the best hotel in a three thousand mile radius. Give or take. Terry should give them that one for the brochure. He looked over his shoulder. No Johns to be seen anywhere.

"Hello? Service?"

He should not, given what he had paid and was probably still paying, through no fault of his own, be treated as just any guest. One in a line of guests. He expected, despite everything, standards to be maintained. The highest standards of hospitality. The island in general, its people, and this hotel in particular, was famous for it. Hadn't they advertised that very thing in the brochure? Impeccable service? Every need anticipated and fulfilled? Well what Terry needed now was the embassy or the travel insurance company or any one of a number of people Tilly had been phoning in the last few weeks to step in and handle this situation.

"John?"

A fly buzzed around his ear and he waved it away. It was no good, that. No good at all. The lobby was silent—other than the regular swish-sweep of the overhead fan and the bubble of the somewhat murky aquarium. Standards were dropping, just slightly—you saw it in these tiny details—others wouldn't notice but a man like Terry—a man used to the finer things and who had learned to expect them (given the price he had paid and was almost certainly still paying) noticed that the inside of the aquarium was growing a skin of algae and the fish inside, bubble mouthed and candy-coloured, were starting to look unhappy. Nobody in this hotel should have anything other than a blissed-out smile on their faces at all times, not at these prices.

"I'm going to the pool," he called, on the off-chance John was lying stretched out behind the counter recovering from a fainting fit and on the brink of returning to his post. "If the embassy send a message…"

There was no answer. Terry waved his hand around his head. These insects. Inside the hotel. His skin burned and, despite the smooth expensive swish of the fan overhead (which was just for the show of it—this was the type of hotel that had hot and cold air laid on invisibly in every room and you could—if you could work it out—control it from your smartphone), it was too hot. He'd never meant to be here until full summer.

"Never mind, John," he called cheerfully, guessing that he was probably on a security camera somewhere, and not wanting to look a fool. "I'll just go for a swim. Tell my wife where I am if you see her, will you?"

Terry turned and walked through the wide spotless glass doors. It could only be a matter of days now. Hadn't the hotel manager himself, on a rare personal visit to the establishment and during an unprecedented gathering of the guests—a small crowd, they were, back then, in the main entertainment suite—bowed deeply, many times, and promised that they would be—each of them, all of them—taken great care of. Hadn't he said—hadn't he *promised*—that the embassies of their respective nations would almost certainly sort something out? The international picture was unresolved and fast moving, he said, in perfect English, then again in perfect French, Italian, Swiss. But most governments of rich countries were chartering planes, sending vouchers, making some sort of arrangement—it would just take time, that's all. And in the meantime, they all remained—would remain—honoured guests. Over the following days—Terry had lost count of how many—the hotel had slowly emptied, the staff thinned out, and standards—Terry regretted to note—had steadily declined.

He hesitated. Should he perhaps pop upstairs and get Tilly himself? She'd be having a lie-down, or putting something on her face, or getting a hair treatment. Was almost certainly lying in bed with her face in a book, or hunched in front of her tablet trying to read the news, or soaking her feet in bowls of iced rosewater and complaining—*complaining*—about the heat. She should, Terry had advised, make the most of this. Extended honeymoon. Holiday of a lifetime and, more than likely, the tab picked up by Her Majesty's government.

She couldn't say they hadn't been looked after. Every night, every single night without fail, the two of them were served their full five courses out on the terrace, their lonely table crowned with flowers, candles, the works. Four serving waiter Johns all to themselves, and a violinist John between courses, making music a respectful distance away. A rose for the lady. Every night. What had she to complain about? They couldn't provide every single choice on the menu, not on a reduced staff, but still, it was pretty good. Apart from the insects that is, which of course outdoors and in the evening were to be expected—one of the natural hazards of the tropical environment, he supposed, though the agent had not mentioned them and neither had the brochure, and he had already made a note of that. No, Terry thought, decisively leaving the hotel and walking briskly along crazy paved paths so carefully swept there was no real need for shoes—he'd go to the pool on his own and leave Tilly upstairs.

Terry reached his preferred lounger. It was set up as he liked it, the rolled towel at the end for his feet, the table set out ready with his paper, his water, his iced fruit platter. They had a knack, these Johns, for coming and going invisibly. It was high quality, that.

The pool was kidney bean shaped, the water cool and still and bright. He admired the colour of it, the bright flowers in the shrubbery, the discreet towel bins. It was the sort of life a man could get used to. Though it had been a while now. Three months of the lounger, and cocktails on the terrace, and paperbacks on the beach, and five-star meals on silver service, and a steady stream of news from home and the rest of the world coming through on Tilly's phone. And now it was Midsummer's Eve and the heat was becoming difficult, the insects unbearable, and Tilly was in all probability still sulking in the room because she was too hot and she wanted to go home. He arranged himself on his preferred lounger then called into the empty air.

"Will you take a message up to my Tilly? Tell her I'll wait down here for her?"

He didn't wait for an answer.

"She's up in the room. Headache. Leg ache. Face ache!"

He laughed. You could say what you liked to these people. English perfect—every single one of them. It was part of the training, he supposed. More languages between them than Soft Mick but they had discretion too, and knew when to turn a blind ear. The service was unobtrusive to a fault. He was, as he unbuttoned his shirt and kicked off his beach shoes, about to launch into what Tilly would have called "one of his diatribes" (he wasn't totally confident she knew what the word meant, or where she'd have picked it up) about her wandering off out of the resort, off in search of shops, or souvenirs, and yes, he knew a place like this—catering to the clientele it did—was probably safer than the high-street back home at pub kicking out time (and he wouldn't let her wander alone and unsupervised at night in Didcot either, not a woman like her—with her looks, he meant), but with the taxi drivers gone, downed tools, and all the shops shut, the resort generally and the hotel particularly was really the best place for her. He was about to say all this. Then, suddenly tired, he lay on his preferred lounger and closed his eyes.

The sun tightened the skin on his face. Three whole months of heaven on earth with the angelic Johns and the pool was about as far as he got, these days. At the start of their honeymoon, he'd taken Tilly to the beach every day. That was the main attraction of a place like this: the white, unspoiled sand. That's what had been advertised in the brochure and that's what they'd got. They made full use of it, despite the crowds.

Some days, early on, you could hardly see the sand between the spread-out beach towels and white, slowly burning flesh. Topless women too, though Terry hadn't expected it to be that sort of place, nobody was going to catch him complaining. He just didn't let Tilly catch him looking. This was their honeymoon after all. As the situation with travel and curfews and quarantines progressed the resort gradually emptied and he'd insisted on taking advantage of it by going to the beach more often, and staring for longer. Tilly had got as brown as he'd ever seen her and Terry himself enjoyed it more now that there was no competition for the sun loungers, no sellers and hawkers disturbing their peace.

He stood on the hot sand sometimes looking past the bent palm trees and the surf and the sea—light blue darkening to navy—little fishes twitching in the shallows like a real life nature documentary—something by Attenborough—and felt like he owned the place. In the absence of any other non-John humans to lay a claim (the resort really did empty out that fast—down to the fuss the press made, no doubt) in some sense, now he did.

But eventually, with just the two of them, and the weeks progressing into full summer, it was too strange and too hot and they stayed by the pool and worked through the pile of tattered paperbacks left in the bar by the tourists who'd managed to get themselves home. John would come out every hour or so to offer them drinks and nibbles, and Terry, after checking whether they were on the house, part of the all-inclusive deal, or to be paid for (he was no fool) accepted them. They slept a lot while the rest of the world—a world that existed very far away—fell into chaos. Tilly cried a lot and spent a lot of time on her phone. The sun gave them both migraines and sometimes they lost whole days to their headaches.

Terry sat up. The little fruit platter by his elbow had been replenished. He helped himself, feeling a cold wet slice of some strange tropical thing on his tongue. He should go easy on Tilly. None of this was her fault. Maybe she wasn't sulking, but sleeping off her poorly head. He still felt a bit dodgy himself. He'd spent most of the previous day—or was it days?—in the hotel room, turning and turning in damp cotton sheets and having bad daytime sleeps where he woke sweating, into a nightmare, then woke again, sweating, from that nightmare—the dreams boxed up one inside the other like those tricky foreign dolls you could buy in toyshops. The beach wasn't far away: maybe tomorrow. Today the pool was enough.

Because even though (he put an arm over his eyes) he probably should be in bed himself, he wasn't going to waste the day. He'd told Tilly to make the best of it and had done his best to show her a good time and a positive example. It was no wonder they had argued: her attitude left a lot to be desired. Tilly had spent a lot of what was prime man and wife alone time, in one of the most exclusive resorts in the world, now enjoyed entirely by them only (the thought that they were the most waited-on honeymooning couple in the entire world occurred to him regularly, and the thrill did not dissipate by dint of repetition) glued to her phone, eating up news of home. She watched video clips of the roadblocks and the riots. The police patrolling the public places. The pictures of ambulances queuing outside hospitals, and doctors and nurses sleeping sitting up in hospital corridors or sprawled out like dead bodies on spattered operating theatre floors.

"Just tell me if the embassy emails and keep the rest of that nonsense to yourself," he'd said, lain back on his lounger and twitched his hat over his face. But Tilly inhaled the articles and insisted on giving him little titbits from the headlines. Daily counts of the infected, the sick, the hospitalized, the dead. There were graphs, though he didn't hold with that sort of thing. Anybody with a computer could make numbers mean anything they liked, after all.

"They've run out of body bags," she said. And once, "they're digging mass graves. Outside Luton."

"Terrible airport, Luton," Terry had replied. "Make sure they don't fly us back there. I want Heathrow or nothing. When they get in touch."

He will admit now, in retrospect, he was trying to annoy her.

"Do you think they'll fly us back first class?" he asked. "We paid for first class." Tilly didn't answer.

The army sprayed the ports and airports with disinfectant, then they closed them. They'd missed their original flight home, of course. Or it had been cancelled. It was hard to keep hold of the details. The Johns brought parasols and chilled towels and little cucumber water sprays and apologized, bowing deeply, for current events and the climate, but none of those things were any help at all.

It wasn't that Terry lacked sympathy. Terrible shame for those who were sick, both here and at home. Unprecedented, obviously, though no need for the press—he'd seen the headlines of the English language newspapers while they were still being delivered and fanned out on one of the shiny tables in the breakfast room—and the fuss they were all making. The drama. Fomenting was a word he'd been keeping in store for a time like this.

"Don't bring me the papers anymore, John," he'd decided one morning, over his full English (they provided a good enough version of the traditional classic). "They're fomenting unrest!" He jerked his head at Tilly, who was weeping over her fruit salad. The Johns had made a special effort over that fruit salad—everything she brought to her mouth was in the shape of a flower. She left most of it untouched, and it was down to the newspapers, so Terry made his executive decision and they stopped appearing.

There was just no need for it. The things they'd been printing. Hadn't they all had coughs? Some of the Johns. Housemaids, sneezing and red-faced in the hallways. On the last night they'd had proper entertainments one of the dancers had keeled right over, her feathery headdress coming undone and falling off the front of the stage. The compere John could not apologize enough. But if you got some rest and fluids inside you and didn't play silly beggars, no worse than a bad cold, after all. He'd suffered himself and not made such a song and dance about it.

He and Tilly had both had sore throats, tight chests, and on the second or third day, a fever that had brought both of them to their beds. Mango sorbet by the pool John had intuitively, silently diversified and brought hot black tea and fresh towels and jugs of ice. By this time the hotel had closed its doors and the housemaids had been at a loose end so they'd also had their bed sheets changed and bathroom scrubbed twice daily. "Treated like royalty," he'd said to Tilly, who was burning up, her eyes dark and glassy.

One day—a week or two days or a month or six weeks back, it was impossible to tell the days apart from each other now—Terry had been swimming in the pool when one of the Johns had come and motioned him towards the edge. He'd made his way over, half wading, half breast-and-belly-stroking along, until the water slopped over the lip of the pool and lapped at John's feet. It wasn't like them to interrupt your relaxation in that way. The waiters had not relaxed their standards—not where it counted—and he was still wearing the shiny black lace-up shoes that came with the hotel uniform.

"A call, Sir," John said. He was holding a tray—one of the little round black plastic trays from the bar. But instead of a brightly coloured cocktail with fruit in it (Tilly) or a bottle of beer, condensation beaded down the glass (him) there was a cordless phone and he tried to reach for it—tried to reach for the phone, with the impression that if he could just get that phone into his hand, and get one of the Johns to come—to get some help for he and Tilly both—well then things would be fine. But he was so hot, and so tired, and every muscle in his body ached (the sunburn, and the swimming—which he was unused to—he supposed) and the bed sheet caught around his elbow, and it felt easier just to lie back, and let the phone lie in its cradle, and after a while the urge had gone away and he had slept. The water sloshed against his ears and no matter how he arranged the pillows he couldn't get comfortable. Tilly was crying—he could hear her, but he had no time to deal with her today.

Terry got up from his preferred lounger, feeling the heat in his skin. He'd pay for that later. But right now, a dip in the water would be just the ticket. It was silent now: you'd imagine there'd be monkeys in the trees or fancy birds talking or squawking or flying about, but there was nothing like that. The water was cool and soothing and he lowered himself in gently. Sometimes, on days like this as he dozed in the hot sun or swam endless laps around the small pool, he wondered about the bill he was racking up. Was he eating every meal in the hotel bar now? Were they still setting up the table for them on the terrace? They should still be getting room service, shouldn't they?

Things between he and Tilly would be fine. Two people crammed in close to each other, in these circumstances, with no other company—well, they were bound to get on each other's nerves a bit. He'd tried to get her out—gave her the credit cards and told her to visit the salon or get someone to the room to do her hair and her feet—but she was still getting over her cough and wasn't in the mood, then when she seemed to be feeling a bit better she'd gone quiet on him—and whether this was the way she was when she was very relaxed, or the prelude to an argument, he could not tell. All the extra amenities in the resort—the ones he was paying an arm and a leg for—closed down. He managed to wangle them some complementary room service—some bottles of champagne and breakfasts on the hotel—in respect of the diminished services, less than the brochure had promised— but she was still upset. No evening entertainments. No masseuse. No cooking demonstrations or scuba driving trips. It wasn't what he'd promised her. He did know that. Still, she needed to show a bit of Blitz spirit. Show these people how the English did things. He swam another lap, the backs of his toes scraping the bottom of the pool uncomfortably as he reached the shallow end, paused, then turned. The water slopped at his ears and he lifted his chin proud of the water and continued.

He missed her. His Tilly. Strange to say that, given they were on their honeymoon. He was—it had come to him late in life, unexpectedly, and now he was like a big soft lad and he'd have to watch himself or she'd have the upper hand for the rest of their lives together—besotted with her. He thought about her all the time. He needed her. It had not been the best honeymoon. He'd admit that. They'd both taken to sleeping during the day—there was hardly anything else to do other than eat the things the invisible Johns brought on the trays, and lie by the pool—no newspapers now, and the internet not working properly, at first not enough, and then not at all—so of course they dozed, and yesterday or the day before—perhaps last week— woke unexpectedly in the hot sun and felt sick and dehydrated. They had to traipse, sunburn itching, through the hotel and up in the lift and back to their room. At the door Tilly had said, "let's not go in there" and for the first time in what seemed like a long time, had touched his arm. He'd forgotten she was with him, in the lift, right beside him—but where else would she be but by his side, the two of them here together in this five star place, on their honeymoon, heaven on earth, starting off in luxury as man and wife—the luxury she should get used to, he liked to joke. He looked at her reflection in the mirror.

They were still in the lift, or they'd got out of it and were in the hotel lobby, with the big clean gold-edged mirrors everywhere (was it gilt? Was that the right word?) or they'd got out of the lift on the wrong floor, or they were still in bed, looking at themselves in the mirrored wardrobes—he can't remember now—but he looked at her in the mirror, wan and pale beside him, her eyes all black, and she touched his arm and her hand was cold and her touch made him shiver all over and he thought *get a handle on that, Terry, or she'll have you under her thumb forever*. He was going to shrug her off but because in his heart of hearts he didn't want to, he couldn't make himself, and anyway her hand felt deliciously cold against his skin and it made him remember his sunburn, and he made a note to himself to ask John to get him some more sun-cream. Some of that aloe vera stuff. The good stuff, the stuff the locals use. But that won't be right. They must make it for the tourists. The locals won't have sun cream will they, they'll be used to it. He hasn't seen any locals. Only the Johns, and a maid or two, and not even a maid for a couple of days. Maybe longer. His thinking wasn't working properly. He was dreaming, or inside a dream of a dream again, and Tilly was always there—at the edge of his vision, or walking away, or vanishing as the lift doors closed and swept him away from her—and he felt the water against his chest and arms and submerged himself, letting the water fill his ears, then pushed upwards, making splashing noises.

"Not there," Tilly had said, he was sure of that, and she'd clutched at his arm and he let himself be guided back to the lift or was it to bed and yes, it hadn't been the honeymoon he'd promised her but it wasn't like they'd got the flu on purpose, was it? There was a buzzing noise, the insects terrible, and so early in the day, and he shook his head then ducked it under the water again. It was the only proper escape from them. He should ask John for a breathing tube. A little scuba mask and pipe. A decent John would have thought of that already. Standards had declined slightly: he wasn't going to pretend he hadn't noticed. But that special skill the waiters and maids and so on had—of being both at your elbow and anticipating your every need and entirely invisible—like fairies, Tilly said, delighted by the rose petals that appeared on the bed while she was bathing on the second night—was nearly magical. And they were (he recalled the tray on the edge of the pool, the jug of iced water, the little silver dish of mango sorbet they'd worked out—as if by occult means—was his favourite) doing their best to keep it up: the illusion it was business as usual. The water closed in around him, cool, but not unpleasantly so. They got that right, this hotel—the water temperature. He couldn't fault it. Cooled you without chilling you. Neither of them were that good with the heat. That's why they'd booked early—middle of March, which would be a nice spring. Plenty hot enough for English people, the agent had said. And then the flu, and now it was coming into full summer. Midsummer's Eve, was it? It must have been months.

He should go and find her. He waded across to the ladder and emerged, water streaming from his mouth and nostrils, running down his legs and evaporating the moment it hit the tiles, so he didn't even leave a footprint.

"Tilly?"

He saw his Tilly sometimes, as he emerged from the water, his eyes cloudy with chlorine. She was sitting at a table with her sunhat and glasses on, a paperback novel in her hand. Or she was leaning against the closed bar, sipping at a cocktail, a flower in her hair. Once—thrillingly—he saw her in one of the poolside showers, as naked as a baby, the water running down her back as she washed her hair. He was about to shout at her—tell her to get some clothes on—she was for his eyes only, after all, then laughed at himself. Who was there to see? Only the Johns, and they wouldn't dare—not at this sort of hotel. She was a walking fantasy, was his Tilly. His princess. How had he got hold of someone like her? For the life of him he could not remember. He called to her a few times but she kept her back to him, soaping her hair for a long time, and when he wiped his eyes, she was gone.

Where was she now? There wasn't anywhere to go. The main restaurant had closed, and the tennis courts shut up and the instructor gone home, and all the evening entertainments cancelled and if he was paying this extra bill—which he wasn't, Her Majesty's Government could see to that—he'd expect the lack of evening entertainments to be reflected in the price.

The tray was there, next to his preferred lounger. A fresh fruit platter, and a phone. The Johns were always leaving phones out for him. He didn't like it. Didn't like the thought of the strange black object in his hand. He stared at it. It was a reminder of home, of the business, of all the work left undone. But that wasn't it. Something else? Something Tilly wanted him to do. Or wished he'd done. He reached for his shirt, ignoring the tray, and when he turned back to retrieve his beach shoes it was gone, the discreet John having received the message loud and clear. No phones.

Terry found himself still lying on his preferred lounger. He made himself get up—stand up properly before he fell asleep again—and saw it was evening. It got dark suddenly here; the lamps around the pool gently dimmed then switched off by unseen hands. Beyond the pool was the terrace, where he and Tilly had been taking their evening meals—simpler and simpler as the days passed, the romantic quartet dwindling to a single violinist, who himself faded into the surf and the dark until Terry could hardly remember him being there at all. And beyond the terrace's lamp-lit crazy paving, dark now, a low-whitewashed wall it would be easy to climb over, and beyond that, the beach, palm trees, the sea.

There was a faint pink glow at the horizon—like the dregs of a sunset, and not—and when that flickered out, the sea and the beach disappeared. Terry rubbed the back of his head with the towel, still staring out at what he could not see. He could sense it—the vastness of the expanse of water, black as treacle now, and softly lapping at the sand the brochure had promised would be white and unspoilt. He took a step or two towards the terrace, towards the wall, towards the sand and the sea, remembering the remoteness of this island, the way that on its southward aspect, there was nothing at all between the sea-view windows of the hotel and the southern edge of the entire world but water. A few weeks ago—give or take—he'd seen a cruise ship out there. It was after the trouble had started and the ports were turning the ships back, so they had nowhere to go.

"He's out of his way, John," Terry had remarked. The John had silently agreed. The boat—a big white liner—had gone back and forth a couple of times, making some kind of distress call with its horn and ruining the atmosphere—and then it had gone back to wherever it had come from. John hadn't thought about it since, not up until now. There were no horns sounding tonight. The black water out there was invisible to him, but he could hear it sloshing back and forth. He could go down there now, he supposed. A night swim. He couldn't remember if the brochure had said anything about sharks. Stinging floating things in the surf. But no. Tilly would be upstairs, waiting. Wanting him to get showered and get a jacket on so they were decent for their dinners. He would do what she wanted. It was her honeymoon and he wanted to make sure she had nothing to complain about. He turned away and walked around the pool, back towards the hotel.

He and Tilly had not seen eye-to-eye about everything on their honeymoon. He had perhaps, Terry reflected, been a little harsh at times. She couldn't be blamed, in the circumstances. As the time wore on, each day a few minutes longer than the last, and nothing to mark the changes except the rotation in meals (simpler as the days went on, but still served on the terrace, impeccable service from the waiter Johns, he must note that) tempers were bound to fray. She'd been on the phone to the embassy. To the travel insurance people. Both offices overwhelmed, of course. Engaged tone more often than not, and no messages returned as yet. There'd been calls to his son—at international rates, no less—back in Didcot, who was running the business. Things needed to be taken care of. Tilly did most of it—he wasn't really a phone person. But there were nice facilities for wives: the evening entertainments, a spa, two saunas and a beautician and hairdresser who'd come to the room. There was a shop. Perfumes and scarves and earrings and so on. Plenty for her to be getting on with. She, on balance, had no grounds for being disappointed.

Tonight he'd put on his jacket and tell her to get her nice dress on and get John to provide some music. Some proper English tunes. Things she'd recognize. The Johns would be able to do that. And it would cheer her up. They'd get what they were paying for. Still paying for, until the insurance or the embassy intervened. He'd have to ask for an itemized receipt. He made a note of it. As he reached the hotel he saw that the main lights in the reception were out, the wide atrium lit by some fluorescent strips above the doors. Emergency generator. It gave the place an unwelcoming appearance.

"Power cut, Tilly," he said. "Can't be helped. Tropical storm, or something along those lines."

Still in his towel, which was slightly against the hotel's rules, he wandered through the reception area towards the lifts. Nobody called out. Nobody greeted him or humbly, tactfully reminded him about the buttoned shirt and shoes policy. Still, as the last remaining guests, they'd felt comfortable taking a certain amount of leeway, and expecting a certain latitude given.

"John? Where are you? John?"

His voice did not echo. He hardly heard it at all. Must be something to do with the carpet—which was as thick and spotless and soft as you'd expect for an establishment like this—and the walls, which were of some pale, veined marble-like material—probably a plastic veneer of some kind (he made a note of this—would check properly the next time he came through) and absorbed all sound. He made his way towards the lift, the doors of which stood open.

The thing is (even in the lift, the insects were intolerable, buzzing around his face with their high-pitched, machine-like whine) Tilly needed to be more understanding. They'd both taken this cough thing pretty hard, and it wasn't his fault that the airports and so on had closed. They'd made the best of it. He turned to explain this to her, before remembering she was in their room. He emerged from the lift, feeling or remembering feeling or dreaming her hand on his arm, pulling him back.

"Not here, Terry. Not in there."

Her voice came gently but he could tell she was irritated. Had been irritated. She'd told him this before.

"Not here."

He went on along the corridor regardless. One room was as good as another in a hotel like this. She'd been so excited about choosing when he'd shown her the brochure. The remoteness—the isolation and unspoilt nature of the island—had been its main selling point. Reflected in the price. She didn't care about the rooms at all. It was the island she wanted—the loneliness of it. He was flattered by it—she wanted to be alone with him. Have him entirely to herself. It was not often you found yourself wanted like that and he'd given her what she wanted. This place, and himself. She wanted him to herself, and she could have him. An insect flew past his ear. Landed on his arm. They never bit you. He'd noticed that, of late. They started off biting you, and you needed the cream and the repellent and what have you, but after a while they got used to you or you got used to them, and they stopped biting. The midges or mosquitoes, or whatever the local word for them was, tended to leave them alone now. They'd fly around, gather in clouds, and he could hear them—hear them more or less all the time, these days ("Can you hear that, Tilly? Driving me mental," he'd said in bed one night, and she'd hardly raised her head from the pillow, she was so hot and tired, but only blinked at him and smiled, her eyes sticky.) The fly—it was a fly—just an old-fashioned blue bottle, the same as they had at home—they were unclean, those sorts of flies. They landed on shit and rubbed their legs about in it and picked it up on their feet and then landed on your food or cutlery and the hotel was very good about hygiene, all the dishes on the breakfast buffet covered in silver cloches the morning John would lift up to display the food, when you asked him—even when he and Tilly were the only ones going down; that was a nice touch, that, and he'd note it—anyway, the point was, mosquitoes were a natural feature of the tropical environment and as such, couldn't be reflected in the tip, or otherwise noted, but bluebottles—blue-arsed flies, as his dad called them, like the ones at home on Didcot tip—and in such a quantity as this, well, that was certainly unacceptable and he would make a note of it. One of the buggers landed on his arm. He swept it away with a hand as he padded along the endless corridor. Or was that her hand now, cool on his sunburn?

"Tilly? You there?"

She wasn't talking to him. Hadn't been, really, for a while now. She should have nothing to complain about. This wasn't the sort of place where girls like her ended up—not outside of fairy tales and the more sentimental kind of film. Every morning, the clean towels folded up into bears or pigs or swans or what have you, and roses in the bedroom, endless minibar (included) and a cigar on a napkin on the table on the balcony, just for him. The brochure didn't call the place heaven on earth for nothing—and no, they hadn't expected to be here so long, not until full summer, but he couldn't be blamed for that. They weren't the only couple to have faced quarantine together, and if she was upset she could always ring down for John—get him to fetch her something. One of those pink drinks, or a little cake, or a fruit salad or something, if she was getting worried about her waistline. Better not mention her waistline. He laughed.

"You're looking lovely, Tilly. Never better. Give me a twirl."

He looked at his hand—pale and wrinkled from the water. He had been in the pool a long time. It seemed all he did these days was walk around the hotel waiting out Tilly's sulk, swim endless laps in the pool, and wait for John to set them up with their little candlelit meal on the terrace. Same every day, menu getting a bit simpler now. John arriving, with the tray, or just the tray, or just the phone, appearing there, and John, impeccably discreet and nowhere to be seen. He'd reached out for the phone, but it had been dark and his hand was wet, and they were both too hot, the sheet tangled around his arm. Was that her problem? The phone? It wasn't a breakages must be paid for sort of place. He should spell that out to her. He'd dropped the phone and it had fallen to the floor and it felt, in the end, like too much to bother with. No need to fuss with the details, he'd decided. This was supposed to be a time of rest and relaxation. The phone handset rolled somewhere under the bed and Tilly didn't ask for the doctor again.

He felt someone touch his arm.

"No, not in there."

He touched his bare chest. His skin was warm. Hot, even. Burning up. And he had been assiduous with the sun cream. A fair man like him couldn't be too careful. But standing there in the dark, the lights up here not working either (the lift on a different circuit, it must have been) he started to wonder if maybe she had not, after all, had a point. A point, perhaps, about the doctor, and getting hold of room service on the hotel phone. He remembered the noise she made—half whimpering, half coughing, the phlegm bubbling in her throat—and remembered that last thought, about how she wasn't pretty any more, not his wife, not the one he'd guided down the steps of the sea-plane with a proud hand in the small of her back, or the one who'd rolled her eyes and blushed when he'd picked a flower from one of the big bushes outside the hotel and tucked it into her hair, or the one who had whispered, furiously, about him making too much of a fuss when he'd sent her entire five courses back and ordered again because she'd took one look at his and changed her mind.

"I'll ring now," he said, looking at his empty hands. "Fear not. I'll do it now."

She must have everything, must his Tilly. The whole world, he must take it and buy it and drop it at her feet, every single shining trinket—for how else would he ever be able to repay her for the miracle of wanting him all to herself? That wife—his own lovely wife—well, she wasn't pretty any more. She was, he would admit it now, remembering her sticky eyes, her swollen neck, the weeping cracks in those lips of hers, pretty unwell; and he himself, he felt how hot his own skin was and understood he had a touch of the flu too (stands to reason, the two of them shared everything—every coin and scrap that belonged to him was hers now—and the virus too, had passed between them as though they really were one flesh) though he (he reached for the phone, or had a thought about reaching the phone, or remembered a thought about reaching for the phone—one or the other of these) was still a believer in mind over matter. They could put that on his gravestone, he joked or had thought about joking or had decided after the fact would have been a good sort of joke to make at the time—to cheer her up in her dark times, as he had promised to do—but either way, whichever one of these it was, she had not laughed. His new lovely wife was not pretty any more, and still, he loved her with his entire squalid and craven little heart. He made a note—he must tell her that in the morning, when they were feeling better. He dropped the phone and it rolled away under the bed or somewhere else out of reach, and it didn't matter because sooner or later a John would come anyway, and as he waited he heard the horn of the passing cruise ship: the low dull blast of it, felt the vibration of it in his chest—this calling for help, a crying out—it felt like love.

Terry wiped his eyes. Sentimental old sod. Sunstroke. And three or four too many of those nice little cocktails that kept appearing at his elbow. He couldn't be blamed. He was tired, that was all. And in a place like this, there was no need to explain yourself. Self indulgence was expected. He thought of the Johns out there in the dark on the terrace, waiting silently for him and Tilly to turn up to their table. They'd wait all night, if needed, invisible in the shadows, the infinite black bowl of the sea and sky lurking behind them, the horn of the pacing cruise ship. No need to feel guilty. What else where they there for? Reduced only to their training, they were fulfilling the function required of them, these Johns, whether they were actually required, or not. As he himself was, remaining faithfully as exacting a guest as he was capable of, in the present circumstances. No need to report in. To explain that he and Tilly were under the weather and probably would not be requiring their table, their meal, their music tonight. The Johns would understand. He pushed open the door of the room and as the bluebottles billowed out at him in a great black wave, he saw the two still and sticky shapes in the bed, the great big honeymoon bed it was, the best in the place for the hotel's last guests, he'd been told, and he understood.

ACKNOWLEDGEMENTS

To Family Mains, who were with me through a serious heart procedure that didn't *entirely* go to plan late last year and helped me through the strange weeks after it—even on the darkest days you are the brightest lights.

To the magnificent Jonny Davidson and Cerys Savinkina for helping put this book together. These volumes are serious immersive projects, we're like the literary *A-Team*. I am, of course, H. M. "Howling Mad" Murdock.

To Mike Ashley and Jim Sangster for research help.

To Jon Fawcett and Elf Lyons for their work putting together one of my highlights of 2024, the British Library event *Tales of the Weird: An Autumnal Festival*. I'd like to thank Jon especially for his help working with me on the line-up of "The Panel of Doom", in which I interviewed A. K. Benedict, Peter Strickland and Reece Shearsmith. As part of the opening panel with myself, Jonny Davidson, Elizabeth Dearnley and Travis Elborough, I performed Revi's remarkable horror-tastic prose poem "Hallowe'en: Or, A Tale of Terror" from 1807, and that is a memory I'll never forget.

It was brilliant meeting everyone, some people who I've only known online, and thanks for everyone who also streamed the live event, but I must make special mention of Hannah and Anni who flew over from Germany just to attend the day. That's dedication to the weird!!

To *you*, the reader of this fine tome and any of my other books in the Gilded Nightmares series. I am having the time of my life putting together these volumes, and if the feedback that I've been getting online or in person is anything to go by, you are too with your collecting and cherishing of them. I don't take you for granted and I promise to continue to be eclectic to a fault!

JM

ACKNOWLEDGEMENTS

JOHNNY MAINS is an eminent horror anthologist renowned for recovering lost stories from the archives. His books edited for the British Library include *Celtic Weird* (2022), *Scotland the Strange* (2023) and *Halloweird* (2024). His latest books are *Bound in Blood* (Titan, 2024), *The Anthologist's Folly* (Ramble House, 2024) and *His Beautiful Hands: The Short Fiction of Oscar Cook* (Ramble House, 2025).